CW01511786

LET'S

2   4

LOREN LEIGH

Copyright © 2022 by Loren Leigh

All rights reserved.

No part of this book may be reproduced in any form or by any electronic or mechanical means, including information storage and retrieval systems, without written permission from the author, except for the use of brief quotations in a book review.

This is a work of fiction. Any resemblance to actual persons, living or dead, or actual events is purely coincidental.

Editing by Cassie's Book Services

Proofreading by Forbidden Worlds

Beta Reading by Jen Sharon and LesCourt Author Services

Cover by LL Designs

LET'S DO THIS

A NOTE ABOUT LET'S DO THIS

Let's Do This is a work of fiction, and as such, has taken liberties with both NHL and NCAA hockey. Any views expressed in no way reflect the policies or opinions of the actual organizations.

Content warnings: homophobia and emotional abuse by a parent

Words that I will forever remember:

1. "I think you should trust yourself, Burkie."

CHAPTER ONE

Shaw

"*Pffft.*" I flatten a hand over my eyes, stifling a groan as the doorbell chimes.

It's way too early. And I was up far too late.

The bell rings again, and I squeeze my eyes shut under my palm. My side smarts from where I took that puck right between the goalie pads during yesterday's game, my mouth is dry, my thoughts are as sluggish as a legless turtle, but my bare ass is snuggly warm under the sheets, and it does not want to move.

Unfortunately, of the five bedrooms in the house, mine is the closest to the front door, which means I've officially been tagged as the roommate who gets his ass up to answer.

I sigh and roll as far as I can toward the edge of the bed, right into soft flesh.

Honestly, it's not like I was sleeping all that well anyway. Too many people are crowded in my bed.

Violet murmurs as I disentangle myself from the sheets and then try to smoothly crawl over Sandra, although I'm pretty sure I knee her in the thigh. Arms and legs are jumbled everywhere, and I can't tell what belongs to who. Which was sometimes the case last night too.

It was . . . fun. I guess.

I mean, that's what it's supposed to be, right? They definitely had fun. And I—

The doorbell hollers for a third freaking time, and I stumble off the bed and tug on a pair of shorts before adjusting my morning chub and snagging a ballcap to cover my messy hair.

"Coming," I call out on the way down the hall. Jeez, my voice sounds like a pound of gravel hitting concrete. I'm gonna choke back a gallon of water as soon as I deal with whatever this apparent emergency is. I round the corner and have to toe aside an empty beer bottle to pull open the door, a wall of winter cold air slamming into me as a guy retreats down the steps.

Older guy, brown uniform. Delivery.

Not an emergency.

"Are you Eden Burkehammer?" He holds up a brown envelope. "I need a signature."

"Yep, I'm Burkehammer." I'm definitely not Burkie. He's probably sound asleep in his comfy bed with that monster-size fluffy pillow he owns while I'm fetching his packages.

But tagging myself with Burkie's last name makes me smile. It's a cooler name than Keenan. At least across the back of a hockey jersey, which is what counts the most.

The delivery guy keeps staring at me. His eyes seesaw down to my chest and linger.

I scan myself, trying to suss out why a middle-aged, paunchy dude is looking at me like that.

I clearly just rolled out of bed, but nothing else is amiss. Other than my morning wood, which is shriveling from the cold. And I guess there's some bright pink lipstick around my right nipple. And down by my navel too.

Okay, maybe there are a few things for him to snicker at.

"So . . . do I need to sign?" I ask, itching over my ribs.

He holds out the electronic pad, and I take the stylus and scribble *Burkie owes me* in the signature spot. The guy extends a large envelope to me and winks. "Have fun."

"Uh, yeah, thanks." I snag the cold envelope and step back into the house. Closing the door, I take in the disaster that used to be our living room. Cups, beer bottles, and various discarded clothing cluster in every corner. A lime green tutu spins lazily on the ceiling fan, which is no small feat considering the height of the ceiling.

Last night's party must have gotten even more OTT after I snuck away with the girls. Usually we don't party that hard on a Thursday night with classes and stuff the next day. But it's not surprising after the win we pulled out against DU. It was a total barn burner—high scoring with Vain snagging a game-winning goal late in the third to clinch it. We were hopped up, to say the least.

I climb the stairs, stepping over a pile of popcorn that we'll have to vacuum up later, and head down the hallway, past Vain and Leslie's closed doors to Burkie's room at the far end. I raise a fist to knock on the IFU Wolfpack sticker plastered in the center of his door and then glance down at the envelope.

Anal.

Butt.

I blink. Wait . . . what?

I'm frozen in front of Burkie's door, fist still raised to knock, squinting to read in the low light. Sure enough, it's addressed to Eden Burkehammer. I roll my thumb along the cool, smooth brown paper to the stickered address label.

But our address isn't what I'm staring wide-eyed at.

There's a customs declaration in the upper left corner, noting where the package came from: China. The date of shipment: three weeks ago. The category: gift. And, here's the kicker, the detailed description of the contents . . . *Anal sex toy for men, gay, butt.*

Holy hell. I choke out a surprised laugh-snort. Burkie ordered a sex toy from China?

That's freaking *awesome.*

I tip the envelope, and a rectangular box slides around inside.

What is it?

I shake it. A dildo? Anal beads? A prostate massager? A monster anal cone?

Does he use things like this a lot? I look back up at the big D-man's door and that perfectly aligned Wolfpack sticker. Never in my life would I have guessed he'd be an ass toy guy.

Is this his thing? I get it. I mean, I've lubed up my finger and explored up there a time or twenty while jacking off—who hasn't? But this . . .

I drag a thumb along the rectangular box, following the straight edge, my heart kicking up a couple of beats.

It's kinda hot that Burkie ordered this. I'm not really sure if I'm supposed to think that about the guy I live with, hit the gym with, study with, the guy I pretty much consider my best friend.

But I guess . . . I am.

I lick my lips. This intrigues me. Like a whole freaking lot.

I raise my fist again. My side still stings from that puck smack, but now there's something else too. A little tendril of heat flares through my abdomen when I think about knocking on Burkie's door with his ass toy in my hand. How he'll look up at me, with his longish hair that brushes his shoulders and his thick morning scruff. The way his brown eyes always settle on me, like he's taking me in, listening, paying attention, right there with me. Although he usually turns away kinda suddenly.

Not sure why.

But, regardless, it's just Burkie. I knock on his door pretty frequently. Honestly, I probably spend more time in his room than my own. I've even crashed in there on some nights when we're up late studying or talking or whatever. So, I shake off my apprehension and rap my knuckles against the wood.

Silence.

I knock again.

"It's Shaw." I clear my throat, my voice still rough, then reach down to adjust the morning chub that's not going away. "You've got a . . . package."

Shit, I'm smiling.

He's going to bust a nut laughing when he sees this.

I'm about to knock again when Burkie grumbles something unintelligible through the door, then his low voice comes clearer, edged with the faint hint of his drawl. "Can you drop it outside?"

"Hmm." I tap my thumb on the envelope, my smile expanding. "I don't think I can leave it. It's a *special* delivery."

His bed creaks under his weight. "Door's unlocked."

I stifle my grin and turn the knob.

Burkie squints up at me from where he's sitting on the edge of his bed. His feet are parked on the floor, and he quickly tugs a dark green sheet over his lap, covering his crotch as sharp winter sunlight streams in from a crack between his curtains and highlights the curve of his shoulder, then darts across the mattress, illuminating a path right down the center of his room.

"Morning." I smile.

"I guess." He itches at the side of his hair, and it tangles around his fingers, messy from sleep in a way that's kinda . . .

Shit. Am I checking him out?

Wow. So that's new.

Wait . . . is it?

His heavy brow furrows. "Shaw?"

"Yeah, sorry. Package." I hold up the envelope, waggling it back and forth and stepping farther into the comfortable

5

little universe that's Burkie's room. It's always so serene and orderly, deep greens and soft grays, everything in its place.

Burkie frowns, still combing his fingers through his hair, his big ol' muscular biceps flexing, a smattering of dark hair under his arm. The hockey tattoo inked along his triceps shifts as he tenses. And jeez . . . I have to physically tear my gaze away from him.

What the heck is going on in my head? I mean, I'm definitely not opposed to a little dude-on-dude attraction. In fact, it's something I've been thinking about lately. I even thought I might hook up with this one guy from the baseball team a couple of weeks ago—but this is *Burkie*. Roommate, teammate, best friend.

His package clearly messed me up.

I just need to slide back into how I usually am around him.

So I hold out his ass toy and wink. "You got the best delivery *ever*."

"Uh, thanks?" He stops futzing with his hair and reaches out to grab it. "Obviously you needed to knock on my door at the ass-crack of dawn for whatever this is."

"Obviously." I take a step closer so I can hand it to him, inhaling. It always smells nice in here, like warmed vanilla. Kinda relaxing. "Although technically it's like eight. No longer ass-crack hour."

I bite on the inside of my cheek as he takes the package from me, trying to contain myself. I'm so curious. I mean, seriously. What's *in* there?

The box inside slides around as he takes the envelope and flips it over, and I bounce on my toes, about to jump out of my skin. Does he know it's a sex toy?

Has he been waiting for it? Will he tear the envelope open as soon as I leave?

He's got a serious poker face right now.

"Uh, Shaw?" he says, not looking down at the envelope. "What's going on with you?"

"Oh, I'm fantastic." The floor creaks as I shift my weight, my toes splaying against the carpet.

Look at the envelope, Burkie. Look.

His eyes rove over me quickly and then down to my crotch. His chest expands with a deep breath. I stop bouncing, realizing that it's bouncing my half chub too.

Not that he cares.

"You're fuckin' odd today." He licks his lips, and it almost looks like he's about to say something else when he glances down at the envelope. And stills.

I click my tongue against the roof of my mouth. "*Bow chicka wow wow.*"

"Fuck." He shakes his head, a smile slowly spreading across his face as he stares down at it. "Seriously, *fuck*. Is this real? Discreet packaging, my ass."

I waggle my brows. "Pretty sure your ass is what it's all about."

He groans, falling back on the mattress and tossing the envelope aside. He pinches the bridge of his nose, that tattoo of two crossed hockey sticks moving when he flexes. "You're going to give me endless shit about this."

"That's the plan." My smile is so wide it must take up my entire face. And, hell, he looks so brutally *huge* laid out on his bed like that. Flat on his back, the sheet settled two inches under his navel, his thick abs tensing with his fading laughter. A shadowed space lingers between his thighs, the sheet tented generously over his dick. He's really . . . hot.

I pivot toward the window. What would he think if he looked up and saw me ogling him?

Would he be flattered? Maybe.

Would he be uncomfortable? I don't know. We're together a lot, and I don't want that to change. I don't want to make things weird or strained or anything like that.

7

Just the thought of things changing between Burkie and me sends a shot of ice down my back.

"So . . ." I start, focusing back on why I came up here. Whatever's going on in my head, I can sort it out later. "I've got questions."

He laughs. "Of course you do."

He props himself up on his elbows, his thighs widening an inch, his eyes lit with so much humor right now. Burkie has these super soft brown eyes, like cashmere brown, and I never realized how darn cute he is.

But then the light in his eyes fades.

He sits up, spine straight, kinda stiff. "Actually, uh, maybe we could keep this one just between us."

"Sure." I shrug a shoulder. "Not a word. Promise."

His teeth scrape over his bottom lip. "Thanks."

A beat of silence passes.

Another.

He clenches the sheet over his thigh, his knuckles popping out.

I'm not sure the air's ever felt so thick between us before.

"Why not?" I finally ask. "Is it because it's about your ass?"

He groans out a laugh, but his shoulders ease a bit. "I *knew* you were going to ask that."

"Well, I'm curious." I snag the wooden, library-like chair from his desk and flip it so I can straddle the seatback, giving him a tentative smile. "Are you feeling weird about it? There's no reason to be. Asses are cool."

He stiffens. "It's not that exactly."

"Then what?" My hands slide down to grip the sides of the seatback. It still feels like there's a lot of dense air between us. I don't like that. I want to know what he's thinking.

"It's just . . ." He opens his mouth.

Closes it.

Looks like he *really* has something to say.

Then he frowns. "Maybe you don't want to know."

"Except, I totally do want to know." I press my chest against the cool wood, intent on him. I know I'm pushing him, but he keeps opening his mouth like whatever's on his mind is right there, lingering on the tip of his tongue. And I can't think of anything that he could ever tell me that would turn me away. "Hit me with it."

He glances past me into the hallway, unease spiking out in all directions. I stand up to close the door then settle back down.

Should I say something more?

Or maybe I should back off?

"Burkie?" I ask.

He swallows hard before he drags his attention back up to my face, but only for a moment before he's looking past me again.

"It's nothing," he says gruffly.

"Okay," I say, even though it definitely doesn't look like nothing. But I don't want to be a dick if he doesn't want to talk. I push up to my feet.

"I ordered it weeks ago," he blurts.

I freeze, legs spread over the chair.

He works his jaw a little, then sighs. "Not sure why I'm telling you this."

"Why not? We talk about sex. And girls." I shrug. "Why not your ass? Seems like a hell of a good conversation topic to me."

That gets a small smile from him. "No. *You* talk about girls. And sex." His forehead creases. "A lot actually."

"You're saying you don't talk about girls," I clarify, sliding back down to a seat.

His shoulders are tensing, muscles jumping a little. I've only seen him wound this tight before a big game when he's impatient to get out on the ice.

"That's what I'm saying." His words are quiet. And a

whole boatload of anxiety lingers in them. Unspoken meaning, and . . . did he just come out to me?

I think maybe he did.

I scooch the chair forward another inch. "Are you telling me that you're gay?"

He rubs at the back of his neck.

I've never once thought that Burkie might be into dudes. If I did . . . Well, I don't know. But that's not important right now.

"Totally cool if you are," I continue when he doesn't talk. "Or maybe bi? Pan?" I study him, considering. "Or maybe ace? Regardless, it's all good."

He shakes his head. "Fuck, I don't know, man."

"Okay." I try to sort out what to ask him next. "Are you out to anyone? I mean, have you talked about it?"

"No. Just now. Just you. But I haven't . . . *Fuck*." He squeezes his eyes shut, and it's so vulnerable that it makes my lungs crush. I rarely see him like this, and it makes me want to jump out of the chair, smother him with a hug, and tell him it's all going to be okay.

Everything is going to be okay.

Can I promise him that?

I don't know. But I want to.

He peeks through one eye. "What are you thinking?"

"That I'm glad you told me," I say.

"You sure? Especially considering that you've been crashing in here some—"

"Heck, *yes*." I scoot the chair closer. "Of course. No question. We're absolutely one-hundred percent cool."

He drags in a deep inhale, puffing out his chest before letting it slowly go like he does right before a big lifting session. He still seems uneasy, but his shoulders relax a little.

"It's been hard for you," I say. I can see it all over his face.

His scruff-covered jaw tics. "It's just . . . fuck, I don't know. It's been confusing, I guess."

10

"Confusing how?" I ask.

He sighs. "You sure you want to know?"

"Yep."

He shakes his head, looking up at the ceiling for a moment. "It's just that I didn't grow up in a house where it's okay to do . . . any of that. And when I moved here, it was easy enough to hook up with girls even if I always left feeling fuck-ass awkward. Like my dick could get off, but the rest of me was watching from above. An out-of-body experience, you know?"

"Not sure I personally know what you mean," I say, but then I pause.

Is that true?

I think about last night.

I mean, I'm attracted to women. Absolutely. But there are times lately when it feels like something is missing. Where I'm not fully dialed into the moment. I don't think it's exactly what he's describing, but maybe it's something similar. This pit-of-my-stomach feeling like there's more.

I've wondered if everyone feels like that. If it's something that comes along with growing up, getting older, realizing there's more to life than hockey, guzzling some beers, and getting sweaty between the sheets.

He smiles faintly. "Just pretend like you know what I mean."

"Okay." I nod. "Keep talking."

He flattens his palms on his thighs. "There are women I've gotten along well with, of course. Like Kelsey. She's cool as shit. But it's never sexual. And with a guy, it's still not . . ." He shakes his head, his jaw clenching harder. "There aren't a lot of out hockey players. None at IFU."

I frown. "Are you worried about what the team would say?"

His fingers tighten. "Do you think they would care?"

"Our roommates? No."

Vain's very vocal about respecting everyone. Dare would likely go all in and probably try to hook Burkie up with every guy he knows who might be interested. I can't see it bothering Leslie.

But the larger team . . . I'm not sure. There's been some homophobic bullshit going on over at SCU recently, which isn't all that far from here, and the SCU Blue Devils are our biggest rival to re-clinch the Western Division. As captain, Vain keeps a pretty tight lock on any shit like that happening at IFU, but that doesn't mean it isn't going on when we're not around.

"I'm not that worried about our roommates," he says. "They've never said anything hateful that I've heard, and believe me, I would've noticed." He pauses. "You've never said anything hateful either."

"No," I say. "I haven't."

"Although the team . . ." He presses his lips. "Who fuckin' knows? It's not just them though."

I connect his thoughts pretty damn fast. "You're worried about your family."

"How'd you guess?"

"It wasn't entirely a guess. Your dad's a dickhole."

He rubs at his neck. "Sometimes you have no filter."

"Especially around you," I agree.

Burkie's parents show up for one weekend a year—always the match with SCU—and it's never a good visit. His dad rides him hard about not doing enough, not being enough. About not being scouted yet. About anything and everything, and I fucking hate it.

I despise what his father does to him. Constantly tearing him down. Burkie's always grumpy for a solid week after his parents leave. Just closed in his room, fighting through all the demons his dickhole dad leaves in his wake.

"It's not just him," Burkie continues. "The family I grew

up in, being anything other than straight and cis wasn't okay."

"That's really fucking stupid." And so far away from my life experience that it's almost hard to grasp. I grew up on the north side of Chicago where my parents took me and my brother to Pride every year. And even though we had some outside struggles growing up, there was always a steady stream of unquestionable acceptance from both of my parents. I get the feeling my life growing up wasn't just different from Burkie's, but polar opposite.

He sighs. "Anyway, my family won't stop me from coming out eventually, but it's just . . . it's hard to say it. Like the words don't come. Maybe it's how I grew up. I don't fuckin' know."

A hard knot clumps in my throat. "I think you should trust yourself, Burkie."

"I'm really tryin'." His fingers squeeze his thighs. "Someday."

"And until then . . ." I nod toward the envelope.

"Uh, yeah." He follows my gaze, then his eyes waver to the window, then head to the door, before coming back to where I'm sitting, legs spread around the back of the chair. "I figured I'd, um, ease myself in."

"Ease yourself in," I repeat. "With an anal butt vibrator gift for men. Sounds like a good plan to me."

He huffs out a low laugh. "Guess so. Should be entertaining, at least."

And, holy hell, my brain gets this immediate picture. Of Burkie. Opening that envelope, looking down at it with his hair falling across his forehead, the tendrils tangling in his dark eyelashes. Maybe he'd be sitting right where he is now as he takes it out and lubes it, his hands shaking with anticipation. His breath catching as he thinks about what he's gonna do. His dick tenting under that sheet. Thighs spreading wider, balls pulling up.

And that whispering tightness of heat flicks and curls as I stare at him, trying to reconcile the image in my head with the man sitting across from me.

I slide my hands up to the apex of the seatback, resting them there, suddenly much more conscious of how I'm sitting. Of how little we're both wearing. And also of how my dick just responded to that visual as well. It's not just morning chub anymore.

"So . . ." I feel like I need to tell him something. I worry that if I don't say it now, it'll be weird later. "Can I ask you something?"

"Sure."

"Okay, so, for you . . . and I'm not meaning to disrespect *anything*, I'm genuinely asking this question . . . Do you think hooking up with a guy would be that different from hooking up with a girl?"

His forehead lines. "I think it would be different for me."

The chair is hard against my ass as I sit with my legs spread, the carpet soft against my bare toes. My heart rate picks up, pounding against my ribcage. "I don't know if it would be different for me."

He stares at me for a long moment. "You're serious?"

I nod. "In my mind, parts are parts. And all those parts aren't really what makes sex good anyway."

"I wouldn't know about good sex." The sunlight cuts across his Adam's apple as he swallows again.

He wouldn't know.

Does he want to know?

"I hear what you're saying," he says. "But for me, good sex would probably require a dick. Or a guy. Maybe not a dick, but something masculine. You don't think it would be different for you?"

"Not sure." My hat's suddenly warm on my head, pinpricks of sweat dotting across the back of my shoulders. "But I almost hooked up with a dude the other night."

He stills.

I shrug a shoulder, attempting to look casual. "Didn't go through with it. I guess I was worried what would happen if I suddenly backed out. Like if I got in there and realized that sucking on a dick isn't for me, what then? Just ask him to dry it off and tuck it back in and continue on with my night?"

Burkie stiffens, head to toe. "Shaw, you have every right to back out of any situation. Change your mind at *any* fuckin' time you want. If someone *ever* made you do *anything* you didn't want—"

"I know." I smile a little. On the ice, it's part of his job to protect me. D-men look out for their goalie. But sometimes, Burkie gets that protective vibe off the ice too. And I get it. I feel that way about him. I don't like bad things happening to him. He's such a good person, right down to his core. "I wouldn't do anything I don't want to do. But that doesn't stem off the potential awkwardness. And it felt like there was something missing anyway. So, I figured it was smarter to back out before dicks were on display."

Burkie eyes me. No sound except for the steady hum of the heat vent and my thumb as it taps on the top of the seat-back. My dick's still half hard. And that sheen of sweat across the back of my shoulders? Not going away either.

"But this guy . . ." Burkie's lips part, and his tongue glints in the darkness between them. Should I not be noticing that? I don't know. "You were into him?"

"There was something I liked."

His size. I liked his size. Big hands and a broad arc to his shoulders, thick biceps and enough scruff along his jaw that it hints there'd be some on his chest.

Like Burkie.

A lot like Burkie, as I look at him now.

Eden.

Burkie's name is Eden. It's odd in my thoughts, and it might be even stranger to say out loud, but he's not always

Burkie or Burk or Burkdog or The Hammer. Maybe sometimes he's just *Eden*.

"When was this?" he asks.

"Remember when we went to that kegger at the Sigma house?" My thumb keeps tapping, my stomach muscles coiling like a spring.

"I do." He nods. "We left early and came back here, watched some NHL SportsCenter recaps, and then we crashed."

"Yep," I say, popping the *p*. That's the situation. I almost hooked up with a guy, backed out, and then came home and crashed in Burkie's bed until I woke up at three in the morning. Then I stumbled downstairs to my room, where I'm pretty sure I jacked off good and hard, then crashed again until he woke me up for morning practice by knocking on my door.

It wasn't the first time I've fallen asleep in Burkie's bed. Neither of us has an easy schedule at IFU. Compound that with practice and games and travel and everything else we've got going on, and it can be pretty exhausting. So I end up closing my eyes sometimes.

But, if I'm being super honest with myself, I could walk down the stairs to my room. And I never fall asleep in any of the other guys' beds. The thought of crashing next to Vain or Leslie or Dare—it's not a bad thought necessarily, but it's not something I'd do. And I definitely wouldn't think about how nice and comfy their pillow is. Or how I kinda like waking up to the smell of them next to me.

So . . . there's that.

Burkie licks his lips. "What about a different guy?"

My thumb stills. It feels like there's a whole lot of subtext going on in this room right now.

Unless I'm reading it wrong.

Shit, am I reading it wrong?

"Yeah, I would." A bead of sweat grows at my temple, under the band of my hat. "What about you?"

"Depends on the guy." That hint of a drawl lingers in his words.

"Good point." I slide my palms down the chair rungs, feeling every little bump and scratch in the wood. My nerves are jumping like microwave popcorn. "You'd have to be attracted to him."

"I was more thinking that I'd have to trust him." He squeezes his fist. "That he wouldn't spread it around. And that he'd be honest with me."

"Hell." I toss him a wink, my voice lilting into a tease, and then I just say it. "What about me?"

CHAPTER TWO

Shaw

Burkie stills, nothing besides a tic of his jaw and the slight flaring of his nostrils, and I can't fully believe what I just said.

Was I teasing?

Maybe? Yeah. *No.*

No, I wasn't teasing. Not at all.

My palms are clammy, my heart is hammering. I've got no clue what he's thinking.

Maybe it was too soon after him coming out for me to say that? But I guess I just came out to him too. Although, he's still just *looking* at me, brown eyes unreadable, poker face fully intact.

Shit.

"I mean . . ." I say, my stomach twisting around like a Rubik's Cube. "It makes logical sense."

"Does it?" His lips hardly move as he speaks.

"Sure. You can trust me to keep it between us. And it'd be a lot easier to back out if we got in there and one of us realized it wasn't . . . working out."

His brow lines, but he doesn't say anything.

Did I just mess up? I mean, he's my teammate, my room-mate, the closest friend I have. We don't go around calling each other BFFs and wearing matching bracelets, but that's *exactly* what Burkie is to me.

And I'd totally wear a Burkie-bracelet.

So what happens if you ask your best friend in the entire freaking world—the guy you see every single day, grab a burrito with after practice, hit the gym with, drop in on *Dying Light* with, and sometimes crash next to while watching SportsCenter on his big, fluffy pillow—what happens if you ask him to hook up and he says *no*?

Would it make things uncomfortable? Would he avoid me? Would I lose him?

A cold bolt of fear rises up and dries my mouth.

Life has taught me that the things you least expect can disappear in the blink of an eye and there's nothing that you can do to fix it.

And now he's not responding. He's not saying anything. And I . . . *fuck*.

"Shit, I'm sorry." I stand. I need to get out of here before I make this worse. Before I completely torpedo our friendship. I take a lot of things lightly in life, but my friendship with Burkie isn't one of those things. "I was just blurting stuff. No clue what's going on in my head. I'm gonna—"

"Alright." He looks up at me, his hair brushing the top of his shoulders.

I freeze. "Wait . . . *alright*? Like you'd want to . . ."

And then I do a jack-off hand movement. Of all the freaking things to do. As soon as I realize what I'm doing, I drop my fist next to my side.

He tracks my hand as it falls, and then his eyes stay there —lingering. Not moving, not snapping to my face, they just . . . stay. And it's making me intently aware of how thin the fabric of my shorts is. And how, even though the rest of me is top-shelf nervous, my dick is thickening where it's trapped along my right thigh, held there by my shorts, the hair on my leg tickling the head. And I'm pretty sure it's Burkie's attention on me that's making all that happen.

"Are you sure?" I ask him.

His eyes meet mine. "I'm in."

My heart stops.

"You're in," I repeat.

"Yes." He inhales sharply. "As long as *you're* sure that—"

"I'm sure."

He stares at me. "Alright. How, uh. How do we go about this?"

I slide down to a seat. My heart resumes smattering, my ass cheeks clench against the hard wood. "I guess . . . we pick something to do. Something to start with."

"Something to start with," he repeats. "How do you usually get started?"

I hitch a brow at him. "You really wanna talk about that?"

He smiles slightly. "Why not?"

"Okay." I take a breath. "Well, I guess a conversation." I dig my toes into the carpet. "I usually offer a few compliments. Maybe I'd whisper something a little flirty in your ear, and if you gave me the go-ahead look, I'd kiss you."

His tongue smooths across his bottom lip. "Do you always start with a kiss?"

"Mostly because it's expected," I admit. "But kissing isn't really my thing."

He frowns. "You don't like kissing?"

"I pretty much avoid it when I can." I've never told anyone that. Although no one's ever cared enough to ask either. But kissing is personal. All up in someone's face. I'm fine with being up in their junk, but faces? That's another matter. "Kissing can make things complicated. Maybe we should . . . keep it simple."

His brows go up, and I'm sure he's thinking about Coach yelling those words at us at practice. *Keep it simple, puckheads.*

It's odd bringing Coach into this moment, but it reminds me exactly how much Burkie and I have between us. He's the guy who's defending for me during every game. Right there, all his power and determination on my right. I rely on him.

Not just on the ice.

"Simple," he says.

"Yeah." I wipe at the side of my neck. I swear the temperature keeps rising in here, like that beam of sunlight across his chest is heating the whole house. "So, I guess, if the goal is to get off? There are a few ways we could do that."

His eyes darken into a deep, vivid brown. And holy hell, I've never seen that look on him before. I doubt he even realizes that it happened, but it's so . . . potent. Like ball-squeezing *intensity*.

"Sure," he says. "Hand job. Blow job. Frotting. Fucking. Uh, toys."

Wow. Hearing him say all those words was really hot. My heel starts bouncing, but I force it to stop.

"Which of those are simple?" he asks.

"Maybe we could jack ourselves?" I suggest.

"That's good. That seems simple. And I mean, it's not like I haven't heard you rub one out in the shower before." He flinches back, like he didn't just mean to say that.

My brows rise. "No shit?"

"Uh." He looks away, but a small smile tugs up his lips. "You're not quiet."

"No, I guess I'm not." Holy hell, he's heard me? I guess that's not entirely surprising. We do live in the same house, and he's right that I'm not quiet. "Did you stop and listen?"

His teeth scrape over his bottom lip. "I don't want to—"

"Nah, let's . . ." I pause, blowing out a puff of air. "Let's focus on the problem at hand."

21

He groans, rolling his eyes. "For real? Did you really go there?"

I smirk at him. "I thought that one was a stroke of genius."

He laughs, his shoulders easing as he tips his head back. His Adam's apple moving under the light scruff on his neck.

"What?" I wink at him. "You didn't see that one coming?"

"Shot right past me." His smile widens, and it's familiar and crooked and so damn reassuring.

"Nice." I'm grinning back at him, trying to think of another stupid pun because it feels like it dropped the tension down to something manageable.

But his laughter fades, and mine does too. I'm still feeling that curl of heat low in my gut. And I'm starting to really, *really* notice the generous ridgeline of the sheet over his lap. I've seen his dick before in the locker room, of course. Maybe caught a little peek in the showers. You know, just curious. But I've never seen him hard.

"So . . ." My hands drop from the back of the chair to my shorts, palms resting on my knees. "You're in for the jacking ourselves plan?"

He exhales slowly. "I'm down."

"Cool." I tap my fingers. "Let's do this."

We both sit there.

"Who's starting it off?" I ask.

He fists the sheet. "You? Or we could do a countdown and go together if that—"

"Nah, I'll go first." That makes sense. I'm the one who brought it up. "Then you'll join in?"

He nods. "Alright."

"Okay, good."

I stand, nerves tightening my stomach, and flip the chair, settling it in front of him and then sitting back down, my legs spreading slightly, my palms damp.

I reach up to turn my hat around, the brim backward,

because that's always what I do. I'm not fully sure why. Not sure why I'm questioning it now.

"We're just wanking one out?" I ask, my voice a bit rocky. "Nothing else?"

He sets his hands on his knees, mirroring mine. "Yeah, I guess. Nothing else."

"Sounds like a plan." Both my index fingers start tapping. "And you'll join in?"

Those soft brown eyes fix on mine. "I'll join in."

"Okay." I emit a tight laugh. "It's no big deal." It's not like I haven't jacked off with another guy in the room before. Freshman year in the dorms, rubbing one out while my room-mate was around was pretty common. Except he was never looking at me. I was always on my top bunk, silent like a ninja. Or maybe I wasn't silent and he heard me, but we never felt the need to discuss it, much less watch each other.

This feels like a completely different situation. Burkie's right here in front of me, and he seems as anxious as I am, his teeth scraping across his bottom lip and leaving a little sheen of saliva there.

We're just gonna get more nervous if we don't get started.

So . . . I need to get us started.

I slowly slide my hands halfway up my thighs.

Burkie sucks in a breath, and I still.

"I've gotta admit," I tell him, "I'm kinda uneasy about whipping myself out."

"Then don't," he says evenly. "Do it in your shorts, if you want."

"Thanks." That's an option, I guess. But it sounds highly disappointing. "I don't like being all cramped though. I like to be able to cup my sack and—"

Holy crap, am I really telling him this? I press my lips. I've got no clue where the boundaries are.

He's staring across at me, eyes wide, throat moving as he swallows.

"Sorry, probably too much information." I drag in a long inhale, running my clammy palms the rest of the way up the slick fabric of my shorts and stopping close to where my dick is smashed against my thigh. Okay, I'm gonna do this. "Do people call you Eden?"

He frowns. "Not usually around here."

"Gotcha. Here goes." I nod, both to myself and to him. "I think I'm going for the Band-Aid method. Rip it off all at once."

I head straight in. I just go for it, flexing up my hips and tugging down my shorts in one fast motion. My dick springs free, and with it, a gigantic shot of worry.

I glance up, expecting to see him taking in my exposed dick—and hopefully not looking panicked—but his eyes are on my face. *Fixed* on my face.

Why isn't he looking? Is he uncomfortable?

I'm really freaking hard, but I flag a little at the thought. If he isn't into this, then I don't want to do it.

I shift on the hard seat. "So . . . do you wanna look?"

"Uh." His brows go up. "Yeah. But I, uh, didn't want to make you uncomfortable."

I emit a relieved laugh. "I thought maybe *you* were uncomfortable. You don't have to look."

"Alright."

"But if you want to, then you should. I mean, I'm cool with it."

"Then I will." He nods resolutely, pulling in a slow inhale through his nose and holding it.

His gaze sweeps downward, his eyes moving over me.

Holy shit. A twitch *rocks* my dick. Not just a little twitch, but a full on dick-convulsion.

He lets out the rush of air he'd been holding, and a blush flushes across his chest and then moves upward, light pink rising up his neck.

Damn. Burkie looks cute when he blushes.

Eden.

I don't know why, but it feels better to call him that when my dick's out. Maybe separating him from my teammate. My roommate. The guy I've become used to seeing one way over the last few years.

And . . . I guess it's time for the next step now. It's awkward just sitting here with my dick out.

So I fist myself and, stomach tightening, take a slow stroke from root to tip and back down again.

I stifle a moan. Shit, that feels good.

The elastic of my shorts cuts against my balls, and I recline back so that I can get a better hold of myself. I take a second stroke, and a bead of pre-cum wells out, glistening in all its glory. Like it knows someone is watching.

And wow. He's *really* watching me.

Every one of his muscles is so tight that I can see all the ridges of his biceps and delts and pecs, all that hockey-honed brawn on display. He's hardly breathing—if at all. And he's cupping himself. His hand is curved over his dick and squeezing softly. Absent-mindedly. Like he doesn't realize he's doing it.

I stroke a little faster, mesmerized by how he's touching himself, his fingers rolling rhythmically. Holy hell, that's . . . *hot*.

"Pull yourself out," I whisper on an upstroke then bite my tongue. Am I pushing him too hard?

But he nods again—in that resolute way—and then he pulls the sheet aside.

My hand freezes.

"Crap, dude," I mumble. Like I said, I've seen his dick before, but I was resolutely unprepared for *this*. "You're freaking thick when you're hard."

And continuing to grow right in front of me.

25

My eyes track a vein that's appearing, running the full length of his shaft down toward his sack. He's sitting like I am, legs spread, slightly reclined. We're mirroring each other, our kneecaps inches away.

But I keep staring at that . . . *dick*.

Honestly, it's not just a dick he's sporting. It's a *cock*. And everything that word implies.

I lick my lips. "Are you nervous?"

"No." He's still clutching the sheet. "Maybe."

I nod. "Me too after seeing that cobra. I'd like to—"

I bite the inside of my cheek. Whatever I was going to say probably wouldn't be within the limits of jacking off with a friend-teammate-roommate.

I've got no clue what the rules are here, but if I don't give my dick more attention soon, I'll combust. And that's what we planned to do, after all. So I take a few more strokes, then take my hand off to spit into my palm and re-fist myself.

"*Fuuuck*," he breathes. He's pressing lightly against the base of his shaft in that same absent-minded way, and then his fingers trail up, following the vein. Up, up. Until he grips himself.

My teeth grit. I have to stop a moan from spilling out as he caresses down, then up again, his cockhead darkening with another blush.

Even his dick blushes.

I can't tear my eyes away. I don't know when I started stroking myself again, but I'm definitely going for it now. He starts working himself across from me, his abs and thighs tensing. Mine do too, both of us reclining more.

Our kneecaps brush, just the lightest of touches, but a fire laces up from my balls. What if *his* hand was working me? His gravelly drawl close to my ear. His stubble rasping against my jaw.

Would he be rough with me? He's always rough on the ice, a big brawler who doesn't hesitate to get physical.

Would I like that?

I think . . . I might.

"Eden," I mumble. Or maybe it's a moan. A plea for more? For him to reach out and drag me on top of him, fisting us together, our legs threading, our cocks grinding against each other, our pre-cum slicking his fingers.

Yes. I bite hard on the inside of my cheek, and I get this sudden flash of images in my head. Of him punching my shoulder in the kitchen. Then of his determined gaze meeting mine through his face shield as we dig in to protect our goal. Lying back with him on his bed, and how I sometimes lay my head against his shoulder and drag in a big whiff, just because his smell calms me. Musky and vanilla, in this really good way.

I want to smell him now. I want to keep pressing my hips forward, closer to him, the hair on his knees tickling me.

A deep growl rattles out of his throat, and then his hand matches mine, adjusting his speed so we're stroking together, up and down in perfect timing. Completely in sync. His lips part, like he's going to say something, and then his cheeks blush a soft pink, and—

"Gonna come," I blurt. My hips kick up as my ass lifts off the seat, my thighs and forearm flexing, my back bowing. I all-out detonate, releasing so hard over my stomach that I have to grit my teeth to hold back a yell.

He tenses across from me, the entire powerful, muscular arc of him. I'm reminded of how he is on the ice—that unstoppable, brutal force—as he comes with so much intensity that the air sucks out of the room.

"*Fuck.*" He curses through his teeth as he spurts across his chest and neck, up to the bottom curve of his stubbled jaw.

Holy hell, that's a lot of freaking cum.

The sight of it glistening in his chest hair makes my pelvis ache, the very last of my orgasm spilling out. It's almost painful, like getting the air knocked out of me, and I'm not sure I have ever—*ever*—come that hard.

My ass settles back in the chair.

We stare at each other.

Our breath is ragged, my heart thuds. His cheeks are still dusted pink, his shoulders shivering a little as he releases his dick.

His eyes are dark and unreadable.

"You're bleeding." I nod at a trace of blood on his lower lip.

He brushes his thumb along his lip and then licks the faint trace of blood away. "Bit my tongue."

I spot tissues on his orderly desk and tip the chair to grab them, snagging a few out for myself before tossing the box to him.

He catches it.

We clean up silently.

But I want to talk. Our silence feels like this big, heavy thing.

I want to tell him that what we just did was intense. How hard I came. I want to ask if it was the same for him. If he's cool sitting here afterward for a bit, just kinda being together, smelling the mixture of our cum and the tinge of our sweat.

If it answered any of those questions in his head.

If we'll ever do it again?

But I don't know if all that talk would make him uncomfortable. I mean, we didn't talk during it—zero dirty talk—and there's probably a reason for that.

And what if he shrugs it off? That would hurt, actually. A hell of a lot.

Even just thinking about it makes my throat close.

Shit. This is awkward.

I toss my cum-laden tissues into the trashcan by his desk then stand to pull up my shorts. They've got jizz on them,

which I wipe in before I hear the bed creak. His feet sett
the floor as he stands next to me.

I'm nearly the same height as Burkie, but damn . . . he
looks like a beast in the buff. He's built like a hockey D-man,
cut shoulders and sturdy thighs and calves. Solid-as-hell, like
there's not a thing on this earth that could topple him.

And jeez, his *navel*. It's shallow, outlined by the deep chan-
nels of his abs. Just underneath, a faint trail of hair glints
golden in the sunlight and then tracks down to his relaxed
cock, darkening to brown and thickening along the way.

He sets the tissue box on his nightstand and then twists to
grab the sheet off his bed and wraps it around his hips. Does
he not want me to look?

Shit.

"So . . ." I run a hand across my stomach, feeling some
remnants of sticky cum. "Mission accomplished?"

His shoulders stiffen. "Uh, sure. You?"

"Definitely." I nod. "Was it—"

A shot of female laughter echoes through the house. Loud
and sudden, like a freaking gunshot. A deeper male voice
follows.

Both of our eyes whip to the door.

I flinch. I'd forgotten about the girls back in my room. Like
entirely. And I suddenly feel really weird about it.

"I should probably go," I say.

"Guess so." A cleft appears between his brows.

He's only a few feet away, and I want to reach out. But I'm
not sure what I'd do. Hug him? That might be awkward. Fist
bump him or punch him on the shoulder? That doesn't feel
like enough.

I step back, itching at the side of my hat. "Okay, later
then?"

He nods. "Alright."

I pad to the door and pull it open. I don't know what he's
thinking right now, but panic is popping in little bubbles in

my chest, and I need to know that we're still cool. That I didn't mess something up. I just *really* need to know that we'll be okay.

"Gym later?" My heel bounces on the floor. More laughter darts up the stairs, and I want to block it all out and drop down in his chair, or his bed with his big, fluffy pillow, and talk about hockey or classes or what-the-fuck-ever. "After tonight's practice?"

I don't know why I want him to say yes so desperately. We both have stuff to do, responsibilities and life to take care of. I get that.

"I'll, uh, have to check in with you," he says. "I've got an Econ test Monday that I need to study for."

I nod, trying to be easy, but I'm not easy. I'm . . . I don't know. It's Friday, and he's got all weekend to study.

My mouth feels chalky.

Did I mess things up?

I shrug, forcing a smile that hopefully doesn't look fake, and toss him a wink. "Okay, see ya."

I step into the hallway, and the door snicks closed behind me. I stand there. A brush of cool air raises goosebumps across my sweat-damp shoulders. The house creaks to life, footsteps and a conversation downstairs. A thump and a curse come from Leslie's room across the hall. I should be moving. Grab a super quick shower and make an appearance. But I don't want to walk away from his room.

I want to go back in.

I lift a hand and smooth my fingertips over the Wolfpack sticker on his door then reach down to grasp the doorknob. Maybe I could talk to him again. Figure out what happened at the end there. My fingers tense when a loud giggle echoes downstairs. Plates clank in the kitchen. All these clamorous, demanding noises, and I should probably go. I guess.

Give him space?

It all feels off.

I let out a breath, my hand hovering over his doorknob. That was it, I suppose. A hidden little moment between Burkie and me. A secret, tucked away from everyone and everything else.

And I don't want to mess it up more.

Don't want to risk making anything worse.

So I turn, my hand falling from his doorknob, and take the stairs down.

Words that I will forever remember:

1. "I think you should trust yourself, Burkie."
2. "I kinda don't want it to stop."

CHAPTER THREE

Burk

I rake a hand through my hair and stare wide-eyed at the door like it'll explain to me what *exactly* just happened. Because I'm at a complete fuckin' loss.

The faint smell of Shaw lingers, catching in my nose, making me clench the sheet tighter around my hips. Honestly, it mostly smells like sweat and spunk right now, but there's the faintest trace of his lemongrass shampoo and *holymotherfuck*—did that just happen?

My desk chair sits a few feet from the bed. Shaw's bare ass was on it not two minutes ago. His cum-wadded Kleenex is piled in my trash.

And afterward . . . he stood just inside the door—his red athletic shorts askew on his hips, hair sticking out from under his pink ballcap, and this flicker of worry in his green-brown gaze—before he put on a smile that didn't come close to reaching his eyes and winked at me.

And I didn't really say *anything*. I said some bullshit about my Econ exam, which I do have, but I stood there, silent as a post. Just trying to process what the hell happened.

Damn it, Burk.

I toss the sheet on the bed then cross to snatch a pair of joggers out of my dresser. I need to catch him before he leaves for class. Tell him . . . something.

I pull up my joggers, my muscles still quivering. My tongue smarts from where I bit it.

I have never—in my life—experienced anything like that before.

That's not an exaggeration.

But now, my hands are shaking, everything is hypersensitive and fluttery. And the memory of Shaw's fist around his dick is so crystal clear in my mind that I can't avoid seeing it replay—over and over. *His* hand. Him. Shaw.

So that makes me—

The word gets trapped on the back of my tongue. I don't know why I can't fuckin' say it. Why it feels like this mountain I'm not sure how to climb, like I keep losing my footing over and over, scrambling up a river of gravel that keeps pushing me back down.

I *want* to be who I am. But it's like I can't make that leap.

I groan. I don't have time to fester in my confused fuckin' head right now. I can't leave the situation between Shaw and me like this.

So I scrape my hair back into a low ponytail before taking the stairs down, the smell of coffee biting at my nose as soon as I get to the bottom. I turn away from the kitchen and head through the living room, past the front door, and then down the hallway that leads to Shaw's room.

I tuck a tendril of loose hair behind my ear, my hands still shaking, before rapping on his door.

No answer.

If he's still got company, I don't hear them. Which makes me expel a relieved breath.

I knock again.

Silence.

I head farther down the hallway and stop outside his bathroom just as the shower water flips on.

I raise my hand, about to knock.

I . . . fuck. What am I going to do here? Bust in on him while he's in the shower?

What if you did?

And for a second, this tiny blip of time, I picture what it would be like to step in. Water coursing over his shoulders and threading down his spine. That smile he always has, eyes lighting when he twists and sees me.

No, Burk.

Shut it down. Turn it off. Fade it black.

It's what I do when it comes to Shaw.

I close my eyes when he passes naked behind me in the locker room, snapping a towel at my ass as he calls my name. I focus on the road when he leans across the console in my truck, his eyes brightening with a sudden thought. I refuse to think about the way my whole body electrifies when he tips his head against my shoulder, reclined back on my bed, our legs stretched out in front of us, his bare toes curling as he laughs about something.

I tell myself so many things. That it's just a normal friendship with someone who uses touch as his language. That my brain's not muddled up and twisted around what I was taught growing up about how boys are with other boys.

That it's nothing. That buying some fuckin' toy off the internet had nothing to do with Shaw.

I swallow hard, stepping back from that door. Feeling like the whole world is shifting off-kilter. Like I'm climbing up that mountain, and I can't get a foothold.

He asked if I wanted to look.

And I did.

I just need to get back to normal. Take a shower. Help clean up the house. Get to class on time. Pretend like I'm not confused as fuck by everything that's going on in my head.

I sigh as I head back to the kitchen to grab a fruit cup or something quick, and then plow to a stop.

"Burk," Vain says in a deep voice as he glances up from the toaster, looking like he just got back from the gym in a pair of sweat shorts and a cutoff muscle tee. "Hungry, bro? We probably need to soak up a few carbs after last night." His brows rise as I stand motionless in the doorway, his hazel gaze questioning, square jaw set easily. He looks like the perfect picture of the hockey jock standing there—big, muscled, and cocky. Although I've learned over the years that when it comes to Vain, things aren't always what they seem.

It's not Vain who has me frozen though. Two girls stand on either side of him, both munching on bagels.

I recognize them.

They were with Shaw last night.

I grunt some kind of caveman greeting.

"Rough morning, Burk?" Kelsey's on the far side of the kitchen, sitting on the countertop with her legs swinging back and forth, her heels hitting the dark gray cabinet doors in a steady *pop pop pop*. She doesn't usually crash over after parties, especially on weekdays. But after Shaw disappeared last night, Kels and I had more than a few shots, playing cards and arguing about fantasy hockey leagues, until she crashed on the pullout sofa downstairs in Dare's basement room.

The toaster pops, and Vain snags a bagel out with his fingertips and drops it on a plate. He shoves it out toward me. "Sustenance?"

I glower at it. It's not the first time I've run into Shaw's company the morning after.

And I've dealt with it before. It's not a big deal.

Vain waves the plate, the bagel sliding around. "Getting cold. Now or never."

I scrub a hand over my face and then reach out and take the plate.

"Thanks." I cross the kitchen and lean my ass against the cabinet next to Kelsey, then rip off an edge of the bagel, chew, and swallow the bulk of it dry.

Everyone's gone silent. Kelsey's stopped popping her heels. The two other girls are shifting on their feet and looking uncomfortable as hell. Probably because of my grumpy-as-fuck expression and the way I apparently just sucked all the life out of the room.

Guess I should say something polite.

"Hey." I tear off another bite. My tongue stings, the faint taste of blood mingling with over-toasted bagel. The scent of Shaw is still in my nose, stronger than the coffee and the waft of burnt crumbs from the toaster.

One of the girls, with thick curly hair, gives me a small wave. The other, a brunette with a *summa cum laude* patch on her hoodie, murmurs, "Hi."

They're both cute. And small. At least compared to my oafish size.

Did Shaw enjoy himself last night?

Did he fist his dick for them?

Did they watch him?

Fuck.

I rip off another bite. I need to put a muzzle on my thoughts.

"Christ, Burk, you're in rare form today." Kelsey tosses her black braid over her shoulder. She's not put off by me for a second. In some ways, she reminds me of Shaw. He never seems to mind my grumpiness much either.

I force a smile. "I'm in rare fuckin' form every day."

She laughs.

My smile might be thin, but the truth is that I like having her around. She smooths things out around the house. She's solid on the ice too, a fast-as-fuck offensive player for the women's team.

Vain steps closer to us, grabbing the carafe out of the coffee maker.

"Have you seen Shaw?" he asks as he snags a mug out of the cabinet and fills it.

I swallow my bite. "Nope. Why?"

"Thought I heard him knocking on your door earlier." He nods over his shoulder toward where the girls are talking in quiet voices. "They were asking for him. Said I didn't know where he was."

I stand there, bagel drying in my mouth.

Vain keeps eyeing me. And fuck. Did he hear Shaw and me?

No. No way. My door was closed.

We weren't loud.

There's no way.

"Haven't seen him," I say.

Vain clicks the carafe back into its spot. "Alright."

He crosses back to the other side of the kitchen, opens a cabinet, and fishes out some protein powder. He dumps some in his coffee as he picks up a conversation with the girls, telling them some story about a snowball fight last night.

I stare down at my half-eaten bagel.

Shaw and I are usually together. Of course Vain would ask me.

He's probably asked me a hundred times before, and I've never once noticed.

"Burk?" Kelsey asks softly.

The curly-haired girl laughs at whatever Vain's saying, throwing a few words back that make him nod and smile. The other joins in.

My insides grate.

I can't do this.

I turn and dump my dish in the sink, mumbling a "later" to Kelsey.

I need to get over my shit. *Now.*

I can't get all mixed up because Shaw has a girl—or girls —over.

I'm acting like what happened in my room was a big deal. It wasn't.

Shaw just doesn't take these things seriously.

He's like this force who lives in the moment. That's one of the things I *like* about him. He gets me out of my head, makes me see what's right in front of me instead of grousing about the future or the past.

It's who he is. And I'd never—never in my life—ask him to change.

I need to clear my head. I pinch the bridge of my nose as I barrel out of the kitchen doorway. I should go lift some weights. Or go for a run. Maybe even—

One step out the door, and I crash right into a firm chest.

Lemongrass shampoo. Shower-warmed skin. A flicker of a smile.

Shaw rocks back on his heels, balancing himself with goalie-quick grace.

"Burkie." His fingers trap above my elbow, gripping firmly.

"Sorry," I say, my breath catching hard. "Wasn't looking."

We're inches apart, so close that I can see the brown that edges his green eyes and the small scar cutting through his brow. That little spot of dry skin on his jaw he sometimes gets from the chin strap of his goalie mask.

He's fully dressed now, in a white t-shirt that hugs his pecs and his favorite pair of running pants. The black ones with pink stripes down the sides. Beads of water cling to his hair. I rarely see him without that backward ballcap, and I miss it.

Doesn't matter, Burk.

The corner of his mouth tips up. "I'm not complaining."

"Maybe you should." I clear my throat. "I about plowed right over you."

His lips kick higher. "Did ya?"

"I, uh." What's happening here? He's always been playful with his words, but now I'm suddenly wondering if that actually means something. *Don't think about it*. "I wanted to talk to you."

"Yeah, I wanted to talk too." He tilts his head. The slant of his jaw is so smooth. I don't know how to describe it, but the arc from his cheek to his chin—it drags my attention, like sliding down this graceful slope of snow.

I plant my feet. "About what?"

"Not sure exactly," he says honestly. "Just wanted to make sure we're good."

I nod firmly. "We're good."

At least, I'll do my best to be good. And not fuck everything up by being . . . whatever I was being back there in the kitchen.

"Okay, then, good." He squeezes my arm, each one of his fingers this soft pressure point against my skin. Little coils of heat race up into my shoulder, shivering across the nape of my neck.

And, fuck*me*, I feel it.

My whole life I've struggled with what's going on in my head. The first time I felt any kind of attraction, it was to this guy I played hockey with back in high school, but it never felt solid. It never felt like something I could wrap my thoughts around. Never felt like something I'd have in my life.

But here. Now. It's all so deeply *different*. It's tangible. Standing right in front of me. It's the scratch in his whispered voice. His height and breadth, his shoulders arcing down into his hips, the easy plant of his feet. It's *who* he is, that tease of his smile and lilt in his tone when he says my name.

He's so fuckin' beautiful that it makes my chest ache. And it all tangles with the memory of his hand on his dick. More than that—the look in his eyes when he was kicked back in that chair.

Like I was something to look at.

Jesus.

I've had so many questions flying around in my head, weaving in and out, confusing me, dragging me to different places. But looking across at Shaw, it all settles. And I don't need some ass-tickling vibrator to answer anything. It only takes one glance at him. One moment of standing this close, of saying *fuck it all* and really letting myself *look*.

I'm never going to recover. Never going to be the same.

Behind me, from the kitchen, Vain breaks out with a boisterous "No shit?" and Shaw's eyes dart over my shoulder.

The girls laugh.

I bristle, my arm tensing hard under his fingers.

"They were asking about you," I push out.

He presses his lips. "I figured they might."

"Are you going to—" I bite my tongue. It's not my fuckin' business.

"Burkie?"

I shake my head. "It's nothing." And, fuck, I can't keep the tightness out of my voice. I hope for a moment that maybe he won't hear it.

But *of course* he squints at me.

"Are you jealous?" he asks.

Fuck.

"No," I say.

He nods once, some kind of thought passing through his eyes. And I get this catch, like I should rewind and answer his question differently. Just tell him the truth.

But what would happen if I did?

"Whether you are or aren't," he says, "you don't need to be. You know how it is. They're probably already setting their sights on the next puckhead on their list."

"Is that how it is?" My teeth grind.

"Yep." He tips up on his toes, shifting forward with all that grace and balance, his chest brushing mine, the edge of

42

his jaw grazing against my cheek, his voice quiet. "They don't even know me."

I pull in his smell before I can stop myself, dragging it in through my nose and trapping it in my lungs like I can keep it.

"I know you," I say.

He leans back, and there's a touch of surprise in his green-brown eyes. "You do."

The world spins. I mean, really fuckin' literally—it spins. And it's all I can do to focus on his face, still so close to mine. His mouth, right there. A beat passes.

He keeps looking at me. Not glancing over my shoulder toward the kitchen.

Just right at me, like I'm what he wants to look at.

I try to decipher every shift in his faint smile, every pause of breath, every twitch of his jaw.

"What's, uh." My voice is rough, cracking with uncertainty. "What are we doing?"

"I don't know." His smile evaporates, his heels coming back down on the floor. "But whatever it is, I kinda don't want it to stop."

I swallow. And then the truth is there. Right on my tongue.

"Me neither," I say.

His thumb rolls down the inside curve of my biceps, so lightly it tickles. His caress is like an ambush on my entire fuckin' body. Blood pounds in my temples. My joggers restrict me, my hands inch toward his hips.

"*Eşti drăguț,*" he whispers.

Fuck, the way he just said that, the words coming from deep in his throat. I know he speaks a few different languages at home, but he rarely does around here. "What's that mean?"

His lips pull up. "It means you're cute."

"I'm cute?" I'm staring at him, slightly open-mouthed.

"Hell, yeah." He winks at me. "I would have rather stayed

in your room." And then he's gone, stepping around me and into the kitchen, and I'm left standing there, pummeled. The world is still spinning. My heart's a lump up in my throat.

Vain's voice reaches me first. "Hey, speak of the devil."

The girls talk over each other.

Shaw laughs, and it's a tight sound, not like he has with me. "I see Vain and Kelsey have taken care of breakfast."

I scrub a hand over my face and pull myself away, taking the stairs up before dropping my joggers and heading to my shower.

I stand there, stock still on the gray tiles, and let the blistering water pound against my neck and shoulders until they're burning. I can't stop thinking. Can't stop replaying the way he tipped up on his toes to press his chest against mine, the rasp of his voice close in my ear.

I kinda don't want it to stop.

I fist my dick before I fully realize what I'm doing, my hands shaking as I shut my eyes and come in two seconds flat. I don't even need a buildup. And, honestly, that scares the ever lovin' shit out of me.

I've never jacked off like that.

What the fuck am I doing? Where does this go from here?

Nowhere.

I lean my forehead against the warm shower wall, breathing hard and staring down at where I released in heavy spurts across the tile.

I'm in over my head.

Completely fuckin' *in*.

CHAPTER FOUR

Burk

My father's texts are always the same.

You messed up with McKinney. Two minutes and sixteen seconds in, you were technically past the blue line, goal would have been reviewed.

My jaw clenches as my thumb jerks over the screen. I step onto campus, shivering in my pullover, and trying not to look like I'm about to pulverize my phone. It feels about a million miles away from my quiet bedroom, Shaw's heel bouncing as he sat on that backward chair.

I reluctantly read the next text.

You call that a check? Graves made you look like a fool.

Fuck him.

Not all the games are televised, but when they are, I always wake up to this. Doesn't matter if we win or lose. Doesn't matter that I dig in with everything I have—every practice, every game—with my whole motherfuckin' heart.

Missed the rebound. What did I tell you about being ready? Could have been a goal.

I blow out a stressed exhale as I pass under the clock

tower off the main quad, a cold Colorado wind whipping through the holes in my knit beanie.

The thing that sucks the most? He's right. I did miss a rebound a few minutes into the second last night. And maybe another D-man would have gotten it? Maybe if I worked harder. If I was a little faster.

Missed pass, clutched by their rightwing. Idiot play.

Good rebound in the third, but you missed Henley on the outside left.

The texts just keep coming like puck slaps to the head, reverberating over and over. It's always a constant onslaught with my father about how everyone around him has failed. He digs into my mom and sis too. When I was back home, I'd dig back, but I'm not there anymore.

Although I don't like digging back. I don't want to be like him.

I worry a lot about my mom and younger sis. I know what it's like to live in that house, under a constant barrage of negativity. Lacey, my sister, is in her last year of high school, and she'll be off to college soon. Probably at Ole Miss.

But for my mom? He's a life sentence.

I finish scrolling and then shove my phone in my pocket as I fold into the mass of bodies following the sidewalk around the Quad.

Shaw hasn't texted me back either.

I try not to let it bother me.

He's busy, just like the rest of the team. Practices and classes can be a lot. And we're all focused on the NHL—every practice, every game. We need to be in it if we have any hope of getting there. Besides, Shaw has a study group on Fridays that usually runs over into lunch.

Yesterday, I wouldn't have thought twice about him having shit to do.

I nod toward a couple of the rookies as I cut behind the

Physics and Astronomy building. I need to get it out of my head.

But, of course I'm still thinking about it when I pay for my sandwich and then head to our usual table in the jam-packed area just outside the café.

Vain upnods at me as I set my lunch on the table.

"Sup?" I hook my backpack over the chair, take a seat, and strip off my beanie.

"Hey, Burk." Vain's chomping on the biggest green apple I've ever seen. So huge that I actually laugh.

He gestures it toward the café when he sees me staring. "They've got more."

"Nah, I'm good." I poke at the turkey sandwich I bought, not hungry, but I need protein for practice later. "Just impressed with that thing."

He snorts a deep laugh and pumps his pecs under his Wolfpack tee. "Big pleasures, bro."

The chair next to me screeches obnoxiously, and Leslie drops into it before ripping open the end of a granola bar, his tattooed fingers crinkling the foil. He's got a pair of aviators tucked on his head, frosty from being outside, brown hair sticking out of the nose bridge.

"Have you heard the nonsense Cassidy's been going on about?" His silvery eyes flash as he looks us both over.

"Nope." I snag another pinch of turkey from the corner of my sandwich. "What's he going on about now?"

"He's gunning for your position, Burk." Leslie tears off some granola bar and tosses it up, catching it in his mouth. His bite makes a lump in his cheek as he talks. "Rumor has it he asked Coach to put him at left D with Shaw for practice today."

I frown. "Cassidy's a first-year D-man."

And there's no fuckin' way he's getting my starting position.

I've been the left D starter for two years. Ever since Shaw

took the starting goalie position. Shaw's goalie, and I'm left D. That's what we *do*. We're seamless together. We can read each other like no other. I've never played so fluidly with anyone else in my life.

I glance over at Shaw's empty chair, unease tightening my chest.

Leslie tips his chin toward the café where Cassidy himself is peering into the refrigerated sandwich cabinet like he's making the decision of a lifetime, his blond hair perfectly combed. His button-down shirt tucked deep into his slacks. I've tried to like the guy. I really have. He's always rubbing me the wrong way.

Leslie swallows his bite. "Watch yourself, Burk. He's a maneuvering little first-year dick-shrivel."

"Hey," Vain cuts in sharply, pointing his half-eaten apple at Leslie. "We're all on the same team."

Leslie smirks at him. "Are we, Cap'n?"

Vain's eyes narrow on him. "We are."

Leslie holds up his hands. "All I'm doing is voicing an opinion. He's always looking at people weird. No one likes that guy."

"I'm serious, Les." Vain straightens, broad shoulders spreading. "We shouldn't be talking shit about teammates like that. We've got to be better."

"I tried to be better." Leslie shrugs, his grin never fading. "But I got bored."

A small smile curls up Vain's lips before he shakes his head and crunches a big bite of his apple.

This is the usual between them.

Leslie's a wild card. Says whatever he wants. He's the guy who comes out of nowhere on lightning-fast skates and makes the surprise goal when you need it.

Vain's hockey through and through. All in for the team. Always there if you need him. Focused on the endgame. Big and strong and deeply talented. He's absolutely the guy you vote for as captain.

But you need both of them if you want to have a solid team.

"Anyway." Leslie tears off another chunk. "I wanted to warn you, Burk. I know we're all on the same *team*." He gives Vain a pointed look. "And apparently our illustrious leader says we can't call Cassidy a dick-shrivel. But the guy is capable of some pretty dick-shriveling things. And there's no reason to let the situation go unchecked."

I run my knuckles along my jaw as I think more about it.

Does it piss me off that Cassidy might be gunning for my starter position?

Yeah.

But is this how the game's played?

Yeah, it is.

"Cassidy's just advocating for himself." I push away what's left of my sandwich, frowning. Cassidy's an over-eager kid. He makes everyone uneasy because he has these weird scrutinizing stares, but I don't think he's a bad guy. He works hard. He's even asked me to help him and O'Hern with a few defensive drills after practice, which I've been more than happy to do. He's just odd, and that's not a crime. "Hell, that was me two years ago. I asked Coach to give me a chance in Redgie's spot. Redgie probably thought I was a dick at the time too. But no one wants to be on the bench."

"Very true," Vain says with a nod.

"If he wants to come at me, then let him." I tip my phone to check the time. Vain and I have a business ethics class right after this. "But I'm not giving up my spot next to Shaw."

Still no text from Shaw. I pull up Instagram. Shaw usually posts something every day, and sure enough, there's a new upload. It's a picture of both him and Dare trying to balance together on a slackline. They're somewhere on campus, both grinning widely, their hands on each other's shoulders, and the picture is so vibrantly colored that I can see the green in his eyes and the shadow under his jawline.

My thumb pauses over the screen, a slip of heat welling up between my shoulder blades. Shaw's lips are quirked in that flirty smile he has. Snow is peppered on his Pumas and backward ballcap. The comments are already rolling in. *Hot AF!!! You're so sexy.* And then a whole forest fire of flame emojis.

There are a lot of comments, which doesn't surprise me. Shaw gets attention wherever he goes. And his Instagram has been exploding the last few months. Scrolling through his last posts, ones where he's not as bundled up for the cold, I guess it's pretty fuckin' obvious why.

I rub a hand along the back of my neck, trying to look casual as I click on my DMs.

Jesus, he messaged me an hour ago. This whole time I've been feeling like a fool for wondering, and a message was here. Waiting for me.

Had to go home and grab my notes over lunch, catch you at practice? He tagged on a winky face at the end.

I must not have notifications turned on for Instagram. I click around to turn them on before messaging him back.

Yep, I type. I debate adding an emoji like he did, but honestly, I'm not a winky face kind of guy. So I hit send and start to tuck my phone away when another message dings through. Another emoji.

An eggplant.

I huff out a surprised laugh then glance up to see Vain and Les both blinking at me. But Kelsey rescues me from any awkward questions as she drags over a seat and sets down a five-course spread, heading right into some issue that she's having with her physics TA.

I half listen, tapping my thumb against my phone, debating what to send back.

But another DM from Shaw comes through a moment later: *Always wanted to send the big ol' eggplant to a dude.*

Mission accomplished, I type. *Again.*

Oh, hell yeah. Send me one.

An eggplant?

Yeah, I want a Burkie aubergine.

My breath expels in one surprised gust, nerves prickling over my shoulders. He's text-flirting with me.

I struggle with what to type. I mean, I'm not exactly an expert at flirting.

Or have any experience at all.

Flirting with girls has never felt natural to me. And there's no way I would have flirted with guys growing up.

I just . . . fuck . . . what do I say?

My throat closes as I stare down at the blank message line, my thumb hovering over the phone. Shaw flirts all the time. He's always making people laugh.

Too much time is passing, I have to respond.

I finally punch something out, settling on: *Sure that's what you want?*

I hover over the send button. Is that too serious? Probably. But it's feeling like I'm out of time, so I hit send.

I stare down, waiting for his reply, my heart jumping higher with each passing millisecond.

His message comes through a second later. *Yep. I wanna be reminded of the gargantuan cobra that's swinging between your legs right now.*

Holy fuck. A smile ticks at the corner of my lips.

I'm sitting, I type and send.

Then I grumble. That was a lame response. I should have thought of something better. I'm a fuckin' fool if I think I can keep up with—

Even freaking hotter, he sends back. *Is it down one thigh of those dark gray joggers?*

I glance down, surprised he noticed what I'm wearing. *I hardly noticed what I'm wearing.*

Kinda, I type before reaching down to adjust myself, since I'm thinking about it now.

He responds fast. *Left or right?*

A rush of warmth simmers across my cheeks. Damn, I'm blushing. I lean forward so that my hair falls across my face, hunkering over my phone.

Left. I type. *Does it matter?*

Nah. Just picturing. Come on, send me the purple monster, Burkie. Plant it on me. Don't make me egg you on.

My lips rise at his puns.

Little hearts light up next to my sent messages, and fuck, I get this balloon building in my chest. Like he's somehow lifting me up, even though he's not physically here. I've never flirted with anyone like this.

Never thought that I would. That something like this could happen for me. And the fact that it's Shaw makes it even more un-fuckin'-believable.

I click on the emojis and type *egg* in the search bar then bite my bottom lip as I send him a picture of an egg timer and wait a beat.

DUDE. There's a pause, and I can practically feel his thumbs flying over his cracked phone screen. *Uncalled for. I want a dick. A big humongous D I C K.*

I fight to hold in my laugh, a blush still heavy on my neck, and then I search for the infamous eggplant and send it over.

Not three seconds pass before he responds. *Getting a dick from a dude is hotter than I thought it would be. Next time, I want the real thing.*

Shit. I'm grinning so widely that a tendril of hair gets caught in my mouth. I blow it out.

Don't tempt me, I send back.

Do you want me to?

I stare down at his question.

Yes, I type. *For sure*. Then pause before sending.

Fuck.

Too much?

I take a breath. Then I send it, feeling like I'm sitting on a pile of thumbtacks while I wait for his response.

Then I'm totally planning on it. I'm gonna go jack off now fantasizing about your big ol' eggplant down the left leg of your joggers.

I groan, trapping the noise behind my lips when Vain, Les, and Kelsey look over again, all of them raising their eyebrows this time.

I shake my head, hoping like hell they don't see how much I'm blushing, my hair still over my face.

You're not, I type.

Oh, I am. Imma bust a nut right over your fluffy pillow.

Fuckme, Shaw.

Well, you gave me permission to unload in your room this morning, so I figure that's a freedom I get from now on.

No argument from me.

Good. Think about it at practice.

I stare down at the string of messages on my phone. There's no way a little DM exchange means the same thing to Shaw as it does it to me, but damn, this feels—

"Chatting someone up, Burk?"

I glance up to see Vain standing over me. His eyes move down to my phone for a brief second before I click out of Instagram.

Did he see?

Would it matter if he did?

I'm not sure.

"Uh, nope." I stand and grab my backpack, shoving my beanie in my back pocket with my other hand. "We ready?"

"Let's head," he says, turning and cutting between the tables. Leslie and Kelsey still chat at the table as I take one last second to DM Shaw back.

Have to go, I type quickly. *Don't jizz on my pillow.*

No promises. And he throws on another winky face.

I can't stop smiling. Little hearts pop up next to my messages as I weave between the café tables. I don't know how Shaw brings this lightness out of me. I don't know how he makes things feel so fuckin' easy. Like I'm sliding and scrambling to get up that hill, and he's suddenly there, pulling me over to a rock I can stand on.

I don't know if he even has to try. He just does it.

CHAPTER FIVE

Burk

I'm still feeling lighter than I have in a long time when I step through IFU's ice arena doors. My hockey duffle swings against my thigh as the crisp air blows against my face, and I drag in a huge-ass greedy inhale. There's nothing on earth that smells like a hockey rink. Anywhere else, I'd probably wrinkle my nose at the ammonia, artificial ice, and Zamboni fuel, but here, it's perfect.

I love hockey. It's a gut-deep love. Possibly an obsession.

I've played it for my entire life. As soon as I could tie skates on my feet. I'm on the ice every day, without fail. And that's the plan for the foreseeable future. Regardless of what my father thinks. As long as I'm steady on skates, I will play this game.

"Buuuurk." Dare jogs up behind me, holding out his fist for a bump. A couple of faded purple Sharpie-drawn stars decorate the back of his hand. Leather jacket open, his dark red hair is pulled into a messy knot on the top of his head, and it bounces around as he falls into step next to me. "We're gonna pound some puck today."

I follow along with his heavy boot steps, nodding to O'Hern and Leslie who tuck in behind us. It's always pretty jovial coming into practice, even if I've got reservations about Cassidy scrambling for my position. This is what most of us live for.

And we'd better be jovial now because, since we're not back here until Monday, Coach will drill us until we're hardly able to skate later.

We step into the monochrome locker room, dividing ourselves into the four different locker bays according to ritual. Shaw and I both change in the farthest one, by the huge stark-white wall at one end that makes your eyes hurt because it's so bright.

His stuff is here, duffle tucked under the bench, pink ballcap resting on top, but he must already be out on the ice. He usually comes a bit early to get fully limbered up.

There's chatter all around the locker bays as I quickly shed my joggers and pullover, eager to get out there too, then tug on my compression shorts and adjust my cup. Next are shin guards and socks before tying on my hockey pants. Shoulder pads, skates, jersey. I toss some tape to Vain when he asks, listening to Dare talk about some work he's doing on his motorcycle.

When I'm padded up, I tuck my duffle under the bench next to Shaw's and head out. Clicking the strap on my helmet, I push off as soon as I hit the ice.

And sure enough, Shaw's here.

He's *stretching*.

I've seen Shaw stretch lots of times. I don't know how many. Hundreds. But as I slide across the ice now, tugging on my chin strap, I take him in through the scraped and dinged-up visor of my practice helmet, and it's an entirely new experience.

He's in the crease, in full goalie pads, and down in a deep lunge. One knee bent, the other leg stretched out. He bounces, his groin inches from the ice. Then his hips shift back, his ass bending out toward the net behind him.

Fuck*me*. Flickers of heat simmer low in my gut as I skate in a slow circle, the visor of my helmet fogging, saliva thickening around my mouthguard, everything and everyone else fading into the background.

Honestly, he's got so many damn pads and guards that I can hardly see him, but that doesn't matter to the tightening in my cup as he holds the position, doing a few more bounces to loosen his hip flexor before he switches to his other side.

I skate another slow circle, pulling on my gloves. Ice hisses under my blades as I carve back toward Shaw's net. He finishes with his other side and then—so fuckin' effortlessly that it makes my breath catch—slides down into the middle splits. His legs are splayed out to either side, his elbows coming down on the ice to brace himself as he pumps his ass in the air with a few of those stretches.

Jesus.

I swallow hard, a boulder stuck in my throat. My palms sweat in my gloves, my cock throbs under my cup.

It's not uncommon to pop a little half wood here or there during resting times at practices, after blood draws away from the major muscle groups. It's natural.

But this is not a little wood.

This is a fuck-ready hard-on that remembers *exactly* how Shaw's ass lifted off my chair when he came. And it's not struggling with confusion.

It's not asking questions.

It knows what it sees, and it's looking straight at it.

I clench and release my fist, swathed in my glove, when Shaw's helmet pivots toward me, and suddenly, I'm hardly even aware I'm standing on ice. His faceplate is more solid than mine, covering his mouth with a cage from his nose to forehead.

But his eyes are bright green against the white backdrop of

the ice. He tracks the slow circle I'm skating, his gaze flicking down to my skates. Then up. Slowly. Sparking with pure fuckin' electricity when he finally comes all the way up to my face.

He winks.

Holyfuckingshit.

I am alive.

My pulse is pounding. My mouth dries.

"Burkehammer." Coach's voice cracks across the ice, and I stiffen.

Fuck, Shaw and I were staring—*blatantly*—at each other.

We shouldn't be doing that.

"Yes, Coach." I push off, avoiding another glance at Shaw's net, skating as fast as I can to the bench. Coach rarely calls me over before practice.

I assume this is about Cassidy.

And it's uncomfortable as fuck to skate, everything shifting and grinding underneath my cup.

I slide up to the players' bench where Coach is scanning his spreadsheets, his purple IFU jacket zipped tightly to his neck under his salt-and-pepper beard.

"You're with Richards today after drills." He keeps reviewing his spreadsheets, but he nods toward Richards' net, opposite from Shaw's. "I'm giving Cassidy a shot at left D today with Keenan."

"No." The word shoots out before I can take it back.

His head snaps up, his piercing blues nailing me. The rink lights glint in his full head of white hair.

"Are you arguing?" His voice lifts at the end like it's a question.

It's not a question.

And there's no good way to respond. I'm clearly arguing. So either I tuck tail and lose respect. Or I admit it and take Coach's reaming.

I tap the blade of my stick on the ice, glancing back at

Shaw. He's up on his skates now, scraping up the ice in front of his net in a steady rhythm. Even that sparks a flare of heat in my gut.

It's like once I allowed myself to really look at him, all bets were off.

"I'm not arguing, Coach." I turn back and slip my mouth-guard out so I can speak more clearly. "But I won't be complacent either."

He grunts. "You've got ten seconds to tell me what the issue is, Burkehammer."

"I want my starter position," I say. "Simple as that."

"It's practice." Annoyance clips his words. "And part of practice is moving things around and seeing what works." He jabs a finger at me. "I remember not too long ago when a punk-ass kid from Mississippi skated up and asked to be put in left D with the starter goaltender. You think someone wasn't there before you?"

I sigh. "No, Coach."

"And that guy didn't raise any shit because he listened to what I'm always telling you kids. It's about what happens on the ice." He scowls at me to let that sink in. "If Cassidy works better at left D, then he'll get the start. And if you work better, then you'll get it. Got it?"

My shoulders tighten. "Yes, Coach."

"What else?" he barks when I don't skate away.

"I'll fight for it."

"I expect nothing less." A flash of a smile crosses his face before he buries it. "Now get your ass over there on the drill line before you piss me the hell off."

I nod and skate off, sliding my mouthguard in as I go, hazarding another glance over my shoulder toward Shaw. He grabs his water bottle off the top of the net and squeezes a stream of blue Powerade into his mouth. His mask is tipped up on the top of his head now, and he's nodding to something

Cassidy says. The kid's over there probably trying to butter Shaw up.

I grouse to myself like the jealous asshole I am, then get in line when Coach yells for us to get our asses moving, tagging on a "keep it simple, puckheads" that makes me break my glower to smile a little.

Shaw snaps his bottle closed and then tosses it onto the top of the net before pulling his face mask down.

Cassidy skates over and falls in directly behind me.

I'm not annoyed with Cassidy, I remind myself.

Alright, I'm a little annoyed.

So when Coach lays out the factory drill he has us running, I hit it hard.

We go one at a time, crossing toward Shaw from the blue line, then rounding some cones before trying to net a shot past him. When I'm up, I'm fast on the ice, crossing straight toward him. Skates, stick, and puck all in control as I veer around the cones, fake right, and then slap the puck to the far lower left of the net.

Shaw drops to the half splits, and the puck bounces off his skate.

"Damn," I mumble.

He laughs, his eyes lit with so much warm humor I can practically taste it. "You're gonna have to slap it a lot harder if you want to get into me, Burkie."

My dick twitches—*hard*. My shoulders stretch under my pads. My brain is yanked in two different directions.

Before I can fully register what's happening, skates chop the ice behind me, and I duck out of the way as Cassidy comes ripping through. He slaps the puck to the upper left corner of the net, right past Shaw, who was still looking at me.

Also, it's a fuckin' *high* shot, which isn't something we do in practice. It's dangerous for the goalie—more likely they'd take a slapper to the helmet—especially when fielding shot after shot in a drill like this.

I grumble, wanting to snap at Cassidy to fuckin' watch himself, but Shaw just fishes the puck out of the net and tosses it out. He always takes everything so easy. With a wink and a smile.

I wish I had the capability. I feel like I grind through life. Like it's never easy.

"Hey," Shaw says to me, skating closer, his voice softening. "Get me on the fake. Alter your speed more. You've got those big-ass thighs, use 'em."

I frown a little. "The forwards can do that sure, but—"

"You've got this." He turns, skating back to his place at the net.

I follow Cassidy back to the line, bouncing my puck off my stick as I go. I'm not Vain or Leslie.

I'm the enforcer. The big guy who shoves his weight around.

But I contemplate Shaw's words as I watch him negotiate shot after shot.

He's so limber. The way he moves—fluid and effortless. Lithe and strong. Flexible as hell. He's this mix of power, agility, and speed that's almost mind-boggling. He'll be one of those NHL goalies people talk about for years. Like Hasek or Brodeur or Roy.

I don't doubt that he'll get the chance to play in the NHL, if he wants it. He'll be long gone from IFU.

He probably won't even remember our little jack-off session this morning. Probably won't even think about—

Cassidy punches a gloved fist into my shoulder pad. "Fucker's on his game today."

I pivot to find him staring across at Shaw, with that *look* he has.

My jaw hardens. "Don't call him that."

Cassidy raises his gloved hands. "Whoa, Burk. I didn't mean anything." He nods past me. "Um, it's your turn to go."

Fuck, I missed my mark. I take off, slower this time, trying to get past my annoyance with Cassidy. I usually hit things with full force, like a wrecking ball, but I dig deep and find some finesse, pacing my skates, slowing my breath, easing my shoulders. Listening to what Shaw told me.

He tracks my movements, his sharp, green eyes on me through his face mask, shifting right as I swerve, leaning left as I crossover. He telegraphs me down the ice, every little change in direction, every little alteration in speed. I jockey the puck with my stick, a slip of a smile crossing my face. We're in perfect synchronization. His blocker on his left hand and trapper on his right, his skates mirroring my every movement.

I forget everything. Except for the sound of my skates, carving the ice, and the slide of his to counter. In perfect fuckin' rhythm.

Halfway there, and I barely remember to stop and switch direction for the drill. When I come out of it, I put the hammer down, digging in with all my strength, ratcheting up the speed.

I'm moving full force, barreling toward him. A fake left, a twist to the right, and then a hook at the bottom of the net. I'm still following through the slap as Shaw drops into the splits.

The puck slips under him, not a centimeter away from his thigh. It slams into the back, making the net wave, and I'm grinning at him—a big shit-eating grin that splits my face.

"Holy hell . . ." Shaw twists to toe the puck out from the back of the net as I skate around the back of it. When I come around the other side, he tosses it at me, then winks. ". . . fucked me right between my legs."

A heavy breath catches deep in my throat.

I should say something.

Something smart.

Something quick.

A return flirt that I can't get out of my tongue-tied mouth.

But Cassidy is already bearing down on us. And the only thing in my head is something more real than any banter I could toss at Shaw in the half-second that I have.

You make things better.

It's something I don't know if I'll ever say out loud. And especially not at a Friday hockey practice between drills. But that doesn't stop it from being true.

He makes life better.

He makes *me* better.

He pushes me in ways that I need to be pushed.

He did it just now.

He did it this morning while his hand was fisted around his dick. He did it on Instagram, sending silly emojis.

He's done it a thousand times in a thousand different ways over the last two years.

You make me better, Shaw. And I am so fuckin' grateful.

Skates chop the ice to my right, and I shift out of the way for Cassidy.

Shaw flips his attention, his right skate jerking back, past the goal line. It's an unusual movement that I've only seen him do a handful of times before. It's a move he makes when he's bracing himself for a hit.

Motherfucker. I push off, trying to throw myself in front of the inevitable. But I'm too late, and the mass of Cassidy slams right into Shaw.

It's a full-force, reckless hit that throws Shaw back, knocking off the net, his head flying backward. The hard crack of his goalie helmet resonates across the rink.

Shaw doesn't move. He's laid out.

Time stops, hung like a counterweight between breaths.

A panic deeper than any I've ever known barrels up.

Real fear. Sharp and consuming.

I push off toward him, my hands sweating.

Shaw sits up, mumbling something. He adjusts his mask, shaking his head. My relief is short-lived, swallowed by something else.

I turn my glare on Cassidy. My skates dig into the ice, and I'm barreling in one fuckin' direction. I don't even choose to do it.

I'm just moving.

So pissed that I'm shaking. Burning like an inferno. My gloves hit the ice as my shoulder slams straight into Cassidy's gut, knocking the wind from him. I grab his jersey and uppercut one solid punch—right under his face shield, where the strap of his helmet crosses his jaw.

There's yelling. Coach is the loudest, my name booming across the rink as I throw a second punch. Skates dig in. A fist clenches my jersey. Cassidy throws a return punch that I don't bother to block, clocking my lower jaw with his gloved hand. I'm yanked back.

"Stop, Burk," Vain says in my ear.

I shove him back and then turn, dipping to snag my gloves before I skate away.

Fuck.

Coach is over the boards. There's blood on my knuckles.

Double*fuck.*

I messed up. Like a huge fuckin' mess up.

"Off my ice, Burkehammer," Coach yells so loud that my ears ache, and I don't blame him. The echo rings through the stadium as I skate off, only looking back long enough to make sure Shaw gets to his feet. Then I don't pause until I'm walking into the last bay of lockers. I thump down on the bench and tear off my helmet, whipping it on top of my duffle.

Fuck.

I slam my fist into the bench. I just risked my ice time. I fucked with the whole meaning of the word *team.*

But as the image of Shaw laid out on that ice comes back to me—splayed out because Cassidy can't control his goddamn motherfuckin' skates—I don't know that I fully regret it.

For Shaw?

I would do it again. I would fuck myself over and over.

Every time.

CHAPTER SIX

Burk

I don't know what to tell Coach.

I'm standing outside his door when practice ends, still in my pads and skates, because there's no way I'm going to change into joggers and look like I'm giving up. My father's voice rings in my head, telling me how I fucked up. How I'm not good enough to cut it. Calling me an idiot.

And I'm preparing to hear something similar from Coach as he rounds the corner and limps past me. He's got an old hockey injury that flares up occasionally, and I'm praying that leaping over the wall to yell at my ass didn't set it off.

He unlocks his door then hobbles around his desk and settles in his chair. It's a tiny office with two old metal filing cabinets, a small window with the mini blinds always open, and Coach's desk, which takes up most of the space.

"Is Shaw okay?" I sit stiffly in the single wooden chair across from his desk, far forward on the seat because my pads don't fit between the armrests.

Coach frowns. "Cassidy too, in case you were wondering."

I nod, pinching my lips together hard. I keep hearing the crack of Shaw's helmet against the ice. Visualizing it over and over.

Coach's chair creaks as he leans forward. "I'll deal with Cassidy. Right now, we're talking about you." His voice is clipped. I expected him to yell at me, but somehow this is worse. "What happened out there?"

I rake a hand through my tangled and still sweaty hair, pushing it behind my ears. "I saw the goalie down and reacted."

His eyes narrow on me. "You're a good kid, Burkehammer. But you can't punch a teammate when you're out on the ice." He jabs a finger at me. "You already know that though."

He's right. Although I don't know if that changes my mind.

Shaw was down. That's all I could see.

"I know, Coach," I end up saying. "I should have thought more."

"Yes, you should have." Coach leans back, steepling his fingers in front of his chin. "What does it mean to be on this team?"

I blink at him. "I, uh . . . a lot."

He frowns. "That's all you got?"

I attempt to shift my ass in the too-small seat. "Means everything. The guys. The camaraderie. The game itself."

And Shaw.

I honestly can't think of what the Wolfpack means to me without thinking about Shaw.

Coach nods. "It's also a means to an end. You're looking to play professionally."

I stiffen. "Yes."

Coach pulls open his desk drawer, grabs a white pad of paper, then flops it on the desk. "I want you to write down everything you love about hockey."

I stare at the paper. "Sir?"

"Just do it, Burkehammer."

I catch the pen he tosses me, rest the pad awkwardly on my knee, and get to work.

Coach types on his laptop as I write, his office quiet except for the hum of the overhead light and the click of his keyboard. He works on his spreadsheets as I jot down everything that comes to mind.

It's a lot. It's the intricacies of the game itself. How I feel so steady and sure on my skates. It's the coolness of the ice and the thunderclap of the fans. It's how proud my mom and sis are of me. It's my teammates and what we can do when we put our full weight together. And it's Shaw. His name sits alone, on its own line.

After I'm done, I tear off the sheet and hold it out to him. "I'm finished."

Coach closes his laptop. "Crumple it up."

I frown, but I do it.

"Now drop it in the trash."

I do, staring at that crumpled ball nestled in between to-go coffee cups.

It hurts to see it there. It's a reminder of exactly how much this game means to me. How I never want to live without it.

Coach nods to the lump of paper that contains everything in life that I care about.

"I don't give one half of a shit how you feel about Cassidy off the ice," he starts, his voice controlled. "Don't care if you're sharing jockstraps or pissing in each other's Powerades. But when you step on that ice, you have a common goal. *That's* what I care about." He pauses. "There's not a single NHL or minor league franchise that's going to want to deal with shit like you pulled today. Not when they've got a thousand other quality players lined up who are working their asses off for a spot."

I nod, still staring at that crumpled ball of paper.

"I'm disappointed in you." He leans forward in his chair again, those blue eyes of his sharp. "You're one of my favorite damn kids out there. You work hard, you take direction. You're always staying after to run drills with the first year D-men. So get your shit together and remember that how you feel about this game is a thousand times bigger than how you might feel in any given second. Understood?"

I look him straight in the eye. "Yes, sir."

"Good. Now get out of here. Robin's waiting for me."

I push up to my skates. "Practice Monday?"

"Don't be late," he barks gruffly. "You're skating next game. We need you against WU."

Relief floods me. "Thank you, Coach."

"And Burkehammer?" He considers me for a long moment, swiveling in his chair. "Before all that bullshit with Cassidy, you were skating like a forward out there today. I'd like to try you out for leftwing with Henley and Reyes the next time we're scrimmaging at practice."

I itch at the chest guard that connects my shoulder pads. "I prefer defense."

"Give it a try." His eyes narrow on me. "You might be surprised."

He goes back to typing. The conversation's over.

I step into the hallway, blowing out a breath and scrubbing a hand through my hair. I can't keep up with today. From Shaw waking me up this morning to punching Cassidy at practice. I want to go home, warm my muscles in a hot-as-fuck shower, and then drop onto my bed and watch a game. Preferably with Shaw next to me, his shoulder pressed against mine.

My chest tightens with longing. Shaw usually scrolls through his Instagram while we watch, showing me this or that, nudging my elbow when he gets excited about something.

I can't express how much I look forward to shit like that.

Just hanging out with him. Doing nothing. I need that right now.

The hallway is quiet as I walk to the locker room. Everyone's already gone, and I'm almost thankful that it took me so long to write that damn list because there will be four very loud opinions about what I did when I get home. But I mostly want to make sure that Shaw's okay.

I strip off my jersey as I step into the locker room, eager to get changed. A faint haze of steam lingers over the not-so-pleasant scent of hockey gear and ammonia.

I turn into the first locker bay then stop.

Shaw.

A flutter launches up from my stomach. He's sitting on the bench with his feet planted on either side of my duffle, staring down at the phone in his hand.

He glances up, pink ballcap backward on his head, his forehead wrinkling as he takes me in—head to toe. His chest expands under a tight white tee.

"Are you okay?" he asks. His heel bounces on the rubber flooring, the pink athletic slides he always wears after practice make a faint double-flapping sound.

"I'm fine." I sweep him, looking for any evidence of that hit. "Are *you* okay?"

He nods. His usual smile is absent, his eyes a vibrant green in the monochrome locker room as he tucks his phone into his pocket.

"I was worried," I say as I toss my jersey on the bench, not taking my eyes off him. He doesn't stand, and I feel like I'm towering over him in my skates.

He's still not smiling.

Everything feels off.

"I was worried too," he says so quietly that I almost can't hear him. He sits up taller, his shoulders rolling back. "What happened, Burk?"

"With Coach?" I run a hand over the back of my neck. It's been a long time since he's called me just "Burk." Is he angry?

I don't think so. But he doesn't look happy either.

"Yeah, with Coach." His jaw tightens. "But also on the ice."

I frown. I'm not sure I've ever seen Shaw this stiff before. His thumb rubs at the inside of his opposite wrist. Unease rumbles off him in waves that make me edgy.

I *hate* seeing him like this.

"Coach gave me a talking to," I say, beginning with the easier answer.

"Not surprising." He stands, sinking his hands in the pockets of his dark green running pants. "He could have taken your start in the next game. Maybe more than that. Remember when he benched Leslie for two games last season after he got into it with Richards?" He presses his lips. "You can't do something like that again."

I inhale deeply, my pads constricting me. "You were hit hard."

His eyes pin me. "I've been knocked a hell of a lot harder."

"I know."

He shakes his head. "No. If I get hit, knocked down, I want you to hold your position."

"That's not a clear line." My voice picks up a tightness. "When we're out there, if a guy is heading straight at you, I'm going to step in his path. No fuckin' question. No hesitation. That's my job as a D-man."

"I'm not talking about in a game. That's entirely differ-ent." His hands fist in his pockets. "If a situation like the one with Cassidy comes up again, at practice or anywhere else outside of a game, you hold your ground."

I swallow. "No."

He stills. "What?"

"*No.*" I'm pretty sure he won't like my answer, but I won't bullshit him. I won't lie. "I won't promise that. If some asshole goes after you—how Cassidy did—I won't let it go."

"But you risked your *start*." His voice rises, his words echoing in the empty locker room. All his usual easiness is absent. He's staring across at me now with all the burning seriousness in the world.

He shakes his head like he's annoyed with me. "It's everything you've worked for."

"It is," I say. There's no getting around that point. I've put in every moment hoping it might, someday, bring me to the NHL. That's always been my goal, from the start.

Shaw knows that. He *gets* it.

The NHL is his goal too.

He scrubs his hand over his face then stares up at the lights for a long moment. He's still tense, breathing tightly, his snug t-shirt showing every curve of his pecs and biceps, the hint of his nipples.

I want him to keep talking. I want to get to the other side of whatever we're sorting out. And that means going through it.

"Shaw?" I ask.

"I want to tell you something," he says.

"Then I want to hear it."

He pulls in a slow breath, like he's trying to steady himself. "Sometimes I think your dickhole dad has you so twisted up that you can't see what's right in front of you."

I stiffen at the mention of my father. "I can believe that. What's right in front of me?"

"You have more skill than *any* defenseman I've ever played with." His hands ball and release. "But for the NHL to come knocking, you have to be out there, on the ice during the games, making the plays that only you can make. And you risked that for an accidental knockdown in practice."

I tug at the clasp of my shoulder pads. "Are you sure it was an accidental knockdown?"

"Does it matter?" He shakes his head, his eyes dipping to my pads and then darting back up. "I don't know why you did it. Why you would risk that."

The answer is so fuckin' *obvious* to me.

I risked it for him.

It wasn't just Cassidy I wanted to go after. It's *all* of them. Every single time he's been knocked down on the ice. At practice. At games. Just fuckin' around. It doesn't matter.

And it's not just because he's the goaltender.

It's because he's Shaw. And seeing him hit, hurt, pushed —anything—puts every part of me on high alert. It makes me want to respond.

And this time, I couldn't hold myself back. Not after this morning. Not after seeing him grip his cock and come for me.

I inwardly groan. *He came for me.* Maybe that's not the way he sees it. Maybe that's not the reality. But that's how it's settled into my head, especially after those flirty DMs. Especially after he said that he didn't want things to stop.

Things have changed for me. And I honestly don't know if I can separate how I feel about him from how I should feel about a teammate. About a best friend.

Don't know if I even want to try.

I just want to *feel* it. I've spent my whole life wanting to feel it.

"You need to explain it to me." He steps closer, his gaze flicking to my pads again. "Would you have gone after Cassidy if he knocked down Dare or Leslie or Vain?"

"No."

It's quiet in the locker room, except for a steady drip of water from the showers and a fan that's running somewhere far-off. Just the two of us, alone, in a place that means a hell of a lot to both of us.

"Tell me," he says. "The truth. I think I need to hear it."

"Shaw—"

"Fucking *tell* me."

"I did it because it's *you*." My words reverberate around us. "Because when I saw you knocked down, it's like the whole fuckin' world came to a stop. And you're right, I shouldn't have risked the next game. But I did it anyway."

His lips part as he sucks in a sharp breath, his toes curling in his slides.

Fuck, maybe I shouldn't have said that.

"Maybe I would have done it too." He slips a hand out of his pocket and raises it up, his fingers slowly uncurling toward me.

He reaches out.

I don't understand what he's doing. I just know that my heart is pounding. Every part of me is *still* on high alert, even though I'm standing here, stock-still and hardly breathing. He takes another step closer, only an arm's length away, and his fingertips brush my skin, an inch underneath my pads. I can't see where he's touching me because of the thick curve of my chest guard.

But I can sure as fuck feel it.

I hiss between gritted teeth as he feathers a slow, light stroke down the center rivulet between my abs, his callouses scraping faintly. His caress slides down toward my navel and stops an inch above it.

Electricity whispers across my skin, tingling, spidering out. His touch is *soft*. No one's ever touched me like this. I get firm slaps on the shoulder and brisk handshakes or fist bumps. I get checked and Kronwalled and plastered into the boards.

But never this.

"You show up for me," he says quietly, almost to himself, my skin prickling under his touch. "Every single time."

Yes, I do.

Without question.

Without exception.

"Every practice." He sweeps a slow circle around my

74

navel. "Every game. Every time I'm hit. Probably times I don't even realize it."

He tracks lower, and I grit my teeth to hold back a groan. I'm strung taut, muscles quivering, skates wobbling. I don't know what's happening. Don't know what his touch means.

He stops a few inches above my pant strings, fingertips nearly tickling. "But I don't want you to risk yourself because of me."

"I did it willingly," I choke out. "And I'd do it again. I'd make the same choice."

His eyes ping up, and there's a kind of recognition in them. Of my choice. Of *why* I did it. That we can disagree about what I should have done.

But we're still standing here together.

"Thank you," he says.

"For what?"

"For being there." His fingertip slides up to my navel again and circles around it. Once. Twice. Three times.

Then he dips his finger inside the well.

I am finished. Right here, broken down, ready to slam to my knees. His touch feels *deep*. Like a fissure cracking open.

I let out a shaky breath, the lights too bright, my thoughts fishtailing.

He flicks his finger out, circles again, then slides back in, and I only halfway stop the husky groan that wells out. Heat coils out across my stomach. The roughness of his finger pad, the seriousness in his eyes, the way it feels like he's *fucking* me with just the touch of his fingertip. Just *him*—gorgeous as sin in his pink ballcap, so fuckin' sexy that I can hardly think.

I exhale a heavy breath as his finger slides in. And out. Deepening that fissure with every slip and glide and flick.

My tendons and muscles stretch tight, my shoulders arch back, my cock throbs.

His lips catch in a half smirk that's teasing and sexy and playful. And all Shaw.

"You like that," he whispers.

The masculine scratch of his voice rushes more blood down to my dick, and it's all I can do to push out a single, "*Yes.*"

"And it's just a finger." He pinches the bottom of my navel, and a shock ricochets down, from navel to thighs.

"*Fuuuck,*" I breathe, struggling to keep my head from rolling back. My pads restrict me. A flush crawls across my chest and up my neck.

"You're hot, Eden," he says, and like I'm on a switch, all of my attention zaps to his words. To the fact that he said them.

"Shaw?" I say, but it's only a scratch at the question I really want to ask: *what is this for you?*

Is this still just an experiment?

My tongue hovers in my mouth.

I want to taste him. I want to slam him against the lockers, know what it's like to have his lips on mine, feel the vibration of his moans in my mouth. I want to drop to my knees, feel his fingers tangle in my hair.

I dip forward an inch, my eyes fixed on his fading smile.

He tenses. Swallows.

We stand there. The only contact between us is still his finger, not moving now, just settled on the bottom rim of my navel, right where he pinched earlier. A faint twinge lingers on my skin.

We share a silent conversation.

One that echoes all those moments when we've looked at each other across the ice. Telegraphing each other's moves. Inferring each other's thoughts.

His jaw tightens as he looks down at my lips. But he doesn't move. Doesn't lean into me.

He doesn't take the invitation that I'm very clearly giving him.

Clarity rolls over me.

A kiss isn't a step he's willing to take.

The lights flicker.

"*Burkehammer*," Coach booms into the locker room from outside the open doorway. "Hurry up. Don't have all night."

Shit. Fuck.

Shaw's finger falls, swiping a line down to my pants. He steps back and jams his hands into his pockets.

"Almost done, Coach," I call, my voice undeniably rough. "Just packing up."

What if Coach had walked in here? Instead of yelling from the door.

I turn toward my duffle and tear off the rest of my gear. I'm really damn conscious that Shaw's standing behind me as I peel down my compression shorts and then pull on some joggers.

When I'm dressed, I glance back to find him laden down with his duffle, skates, and gear.

"I get it," I say, lowering my voice to a whisper. "No kissing."

He frowns slightly.

I hook my duffle over my shoulder. "You're weirdly quiet, and it's fuckin' odd, and I'm worried that—"

"I'm quiet," he says, brows pulling together under the backstrap of his ballcap, "because I wanted to."

Words that I will forever remember:

1. *"I think you should trust yourself, Burkie."*
2. *"I kinda don't want it to stop."*
3. *"I'm quiet, because I wanted to."*

CHAPTER SEVEN

Shaw

I *wanted* to kiss him. I can still feel the heat of his skin against my fingertip, how his touch sent goosebumps smattering across the back of my shoulders and up my neck.

But what happens after you kiss your best friend?

Do you just go back to casually fist bumping or spotting each other at the gym or whatever else?

"Burkehammer," Coach yells through the open doorway, pounding a fist against the first set of lockers. "Get your ass moving. Don't piss me off twice today."

"Coming, Coach." Burkie's husky voice relights those goosebumps. His Carolina Hurricanes tee is pulled tight under an open, black wool coat. His jaw is rough with stubble, his heavy duffle making his right shoulder hitch up, skates dangling from the strap of his bag by their laces.

He looks like hockey.

He breathes and emotes and exudes hockey.

He shows up for me.

I don't agree with what he did. I didn't like that he'd open himself up to being benched for a game.

But it still feels like it means something.

And I've known that for a long time. But I didn't feel it in the way I'm feeling it now. Standing here across from him, watching him closer than I've ever watched anyone. And it's like there's this whole new swamp of emotions hitting me. Except . . . these emotions aren't fully new either.

I can't explain it. It's just *Burkie*. He's always made me feel like this.

Always makes it feel like he'll be right there next to me, on my right, ready to face down anything that comes at me.

Isn't that someone I should want to kiss?

Coach steps past the edge of the locker bay and frowns when he sees me. "Didn't know you were still here, Keenan. Your head good?"

"Yep." I grab my stick and slide it through the straps on my duffle. "All good here, Coach."

Coach turns, canvas briefcase in his hand. "Then let's go, puckheads. Don't have all night."

Burkie pulls on his beanie, and then we fall in line behind Coach, walking down the shadowy hallway and out the double doors into a sharply cold evening. It feels so natural to be walking next to him. Maybe even step a few inches closer, my duffle knocking against his, our skates almost tangling.

I'm just not gonna worry about the kissing. Not yet. Not right now. I'm putting it out of my mind.

As soon as we get outside, Coach waves a hand over his shoulder and limps toward the faculty parking lot.

Burkie and I head to his truck, walking silently, our breath puffing white under the streetlights. We toss our gear in the back and then step up into the cab.

It's too quiet. But as soon as we're strapped in, my stomach lets out an obnoxious grumble that turns into a high-pitched whine, and we both laugh. And, shit, it feels good to laugh with him.

"I'm starving too." He jabs on the heat, the blue dash

lights highlighting the profile of his face as the cab slowly warms, his hair sticking cutely out from under his beanie.

"I never had a chance to eat lunch today." I shift against the leather seat, setting my elbow on the center console. "Time got away from me."

And holy hell, the way he smells is setting off fireworks in my stomach. He's straight from practice, sweaty and unshowered, and I probably shouldn't like it so much, but I really do. Musky and manly, and as he reverses out of the parking spot, I settle back against the seat, breathing through my mouth to stop from dragging in the smell of him.

He puts the truck in drive. "You shouldn't skip lunch. I can always pack you a sandwich or something."

Jeez, he would do that?

"You're such a nice person," I tell him. Honestly, you wouldn't always think so if you saw him on the ice. He's savage out there—no hesitation before he plows directly into a six-foot-something O-man, throwing a quick elbow as they crash full force into the boards, and then skating away with a glare that could wither the strongest bravado. But off the ice, he really is a fantastically nice person.

"Nah." He squints ahead, focused on the road and the swirls of snow kicked up by the car in front of us. "Just don't want to see you starve. Let's pick something up."

"I'm good," I say. "But stop anywhere you want."

He pulls out onto 5th Avenue, the back tires of the truck sliding out a little. "Your stomach's about to set off an avalanche. Let's grab something. Maybe Mexicali's?" He inhales and wrinkles his nose. "And let's take it home because I need a fuckin' shower."

I smile. "You're not smelling so bad."

He clearly doesn't have a clue that I'm imagining what it would be like to crawl over that center console and dig my nose into his neck. Maybe even get a good whiff of his armpit. Or his . . . nutsack? Wow. Never thought about burying my

82

nose in a guy's nutsack before. But I'm *in*. No question, I wanna do it.

My stomach crashes into the conversation with a kind of warble this time. Seriously, it's out of control.

And I am hungry. I'm always hungry after practice.

"You sure?" he asks. "I think you might wither on the way home."

"Yeah, it's just . . ." I hedge a little. I don't like talking about this. "Things are kinda tight money-wise right now. My sports therapy professor tossed on another textbook we need to get, and that shit's expensive."

Right now isn't accurate. Things are always tight. There's never been a time in my life when they haven't been, but I don't want to get into it.

"Don't worry about it." He takes a sharp right into Mexicali's parking lot. "I got you."

He's out and heading toward the door in a flash. I flip the brim of my hat around and follow.

But I'm uneasy.

Burkie pays for more stuff than I do. I know it. I'm sure he knows it. But we've never talked about it, and even though I wish it were different, it's never created this lump in my throat that I have now.

He holds the door open for me, and we step into the scrunched line. It's always busy at Mexicali's. Burnt orange tiles on the floors and walls, typical Colorado Tex-Mex, but they've got a sweet habanero burrito that's worth dying for. I take a whiff of freshly grilled tortillas and roasted jalapeños, and my stomach about rips itself out to get to the counter. But . . . I'm still uneasy.

"You don't have to get this." I tip my head closer so he can hear me over everyone chattering.

"It's not a big deal." He shrugs, sizing up the line.

There's an inch of space between us, and his after-practice scent pummels me. I have to drag my eyes off the hollow of his collarbone, moving as he talks, under his Adam's apple.

"I don't need anything," I say. "Seriously."

He pivots to look at me dead-on. "What's going on?"

"Honestly? Not sure," I admit, feeling the weight of about a thousand things. I don't want him paying for shit. He doesn't need to. Especially because I know he works damn hard for the money. When he goes home each summer, he works from sunrise to sundown at a soybean farm down the road from his parents' house. That's gotta be backbreaking. "I don't want you to feel like you have to pay for my ass."

"I don't feel like I have to pay." His forehead lines. "I *want* to fuckin' pay, so let me."

I hesitate. We're in line because that's the only place to stand, people crowded all around us, and I can't stop feeling uneasy.

Things are changing between Burkie and me. I mean, obviously watching him jack himself this morning was new. And amazing. But what just happened in the locker room feels different beyond that. And now I'm here, aching to smell him, and that's different too.

"It's no big deal." He leans closer, his thigh brushing mine. "Just let me."

Let him.

What if I do? What if I go with it?

I kinda . . . want to. Just jump over whatever uneasiness I have. Just let it go.

"I'll get you back," I say, easing my shoulders. "And thanks. I appreciate it."

"All good." He smiles faintly. "You do lots of things for me. It seems only fair."

A teasing grin unwittingly whips across my face, and I tip even closer to speak into his ear. "Things like belly button finger-fucking in the locker room?"

He looks so cute as a blush crawls up his neck, darkening

the skin under his scruff. And I freaking love that I can turn this big, brutal D-man's cheeks a shade of pink. It sets me even more at ease even more too.

"Actually, I was thinking more about laundry," he says. "Or shit around the house. When things break, you always know how to fix them. We all stand around looking like dumbasses while you tighten the leaky faucet and patch drywall. But I'll definitely throw in belly button finger-fucking as a bonus activity."

I bounce up onto my toes, and my junk brushes lightly against his thigh. "So . . . you're saying you take either house-work or sexual favors for burritos?"

His laugh is deep and warm. "*Dude.*"

"I'm just trying to sort out the situation here." I inhale that after-practice smell, trying not to be too obvious about it, but damn, my whole body is yearning to press firmly against him. Dry hump him right here in Mexicali's. It could get excit-ing. "I want to know what a sweet habanero burrito is worth to you, *coaie.*"

His brows rise. "I'm open to suggestions. And did you just call me 'balls' again?"

"I told you before, it's a term of bro-dearment."

Which is true, but there's something I really like about calling Burkie "*coaie*". It's not a word I've called anyone else, but it fits with him for some reason. Both as a term of bro-dearment and also something that gets me a little hot now that I've seen what's swinging between his legs.

"And," I continue, "I can think of a few suggestions for what a burrito might be worth. Pretty sure you can come up with a few options too."

"You first." His eyes drill into me, a light in them that I rarely see off the ice. "What would it be worth to you?"

I smirk at him, my gaze flashing down to where the buttons of his coat are open, his tee flush against his abs, his navel hidden underneath. I press my chest against his arm and pitch my voice low. "How much can I get for another belly button finger-fuck?"

He frowns, tilting his head like he's debating, but a smile tugs at his lips.

"Possibly a side of chips and salsa," he says.

"A *side*? That's all?" We shuffle forward with the line, moving together. "And salsa? Not even guac? I should get more for that experience. At least . . ." I debate, "half a burrito. Maybe two-thirds."

"And what am I going to do with the other third?" He laughs, and then his fingers flick against my thigh. Just this little brush, but damn, I'm getting hard, dick pressing against his leg. I'm sure he's noticing too.

"Your choice," I say.

"What if . . ." His thigh shifts, increasing the pressure, so faintly that it's hardly anything at all. Is he doing that intentionally? "What if I buy you a full burrito? *Including* a side of chips and guac."

"Holy shit." I mock gasp, eyes widening. "That'll get you to the motherfucking promised land."

He laughs. "You know I'll buy you a burrito, no exchange required. Chips too, if you want. Even a damn soda."

My smile falls. "Well, now I'm disappointed. I'm digging the food, but I kinda wanted to figure out what we're gonna do next."

Assuming there is a next? I mean, we're seriously getting close to dry humping here in line. I lick my lips, about to offer a suggestion, when I realize a girl behind Burkie is watching us curiously. And, shit, I *recognize* her.

She's been over at hockey house for some of the after parties.

I take a solid step back. I mean, my package was pressed up against his leg—no space between us—his fingers stroking my thigh. And he was pretty clear earlier about not being out, but here I am, squashed against him.

Burkie follows my line of sight toward her and then stiffens.

"Don't let me get in your way." His tone changes—distant and tight. His weight transfers to his right foot, shifting him farther away from me.

I blink. "What?"

"With the girl," he clarifies.

Wait. . . . he thought I was checking her out?

"I'm not interested in her," I say flatly, tipping closer so there's no chance she can overhear us. I mean, I don't want to be a dick to her. But I *really* don't want Burkie to have the wrong idea. "Not at all."

"Alright." He looks over at the menu hanging on the wall. His teeth clench, and we've been here enough times that there's no way he's wondering what he's going to order. He always gets a sweet habanero burrito with chicken and a side salad.

I debate what to say. I want to get back to our conversation. I want to make sure he knows that I've got zero interest in her.

Like I seriously could not give a shit about anyone else in line.

But I also don't want to out him in the middle of Mexicali's.

I pull out my phone and open Insta, typing quickly. *I promise you I've got zero interest in her.*

I press send. I can't hear his phone over the din of this place, but he digs it out and thumbs the screen open.

His forehead creases as he messages back. *Alright.*

I start to type more, then hesitate because he's writing something else.

He inhales and types quickly then pauses, that crease deepening between his brows. He taps quickly with his thumb, which I think means he's deleting something. And then he resumes typing again.

My phone vibrates, and I tear my eyes off him to read what he wrote.

It's fine if you are interested, though. You can be honest with me.

I am being honest, I send quickly.

Then I hurry through a follow-up message. *Can I be really, super, balls-out honest?*

I glance up, and he nods.

What I want . . . I type *. . . like full-on want . . . is to go home and hang with you. And your big ol' coaie, but mostly just you.*

He smiles a little, his thumbs moving quickly over his phone. No hesitation this time. *I'll never say no to that.*

I'm grinning as I send another message back. *That's pretty much all I ever want.*

You sure?

Hell, yeah.

I'm also thinking, I write as we shift forward with the line, *as long as it's habanero and not that tomatillo nonsense—that it's worth . . .* I pause, nerves clumping in the pit of my stomach *. . . a blow job.*

I throw in a couple of eggplants and squirts for good measure. Just because I'm hoping it'll make him laugh. I stare at my message. Shit, I'm nervous. I delete two squirts but leave the eggplants.

I still don't press send.

What if he says *no*?

Shit, that *scares* me.

I tap the side of my phone. I could back out. Delete my message and tuck my phone in my pocket.

But I don't want to back out. I want to go home, eat burritos, and get freaky with Burkie.

So I send it, then raise my brows at him, my heart pumping so hard I feel it in my temples.

He stares down at his phone for a long, arduous moment, his Adam's apple moving with a hard swallow.

He finally—*finally*—looks up at me, those thick lips of his parting slowly.

"That's my offer," I say.

The line down his forehead deepens. "You don't need to—"

"Take it or leave it." Anxiety is pounding in my chest like a damn bongo drum. I'm never this anxious with girls, but he set it off in me. I guess because it feels like it matters more. Like a rejection from him would really hurt.

"Either way." I shrug, trying to make it easier for both of us if he doesn't want to. "I mean. No pressure, just—"

"I'll take it." His teeth graze over his bottom lip. "But not because you owe me."

———

We don't mention the burrito deal. Not after we order and wait in line. Not after Burkie pays and we jump in his truck. We chat about our next game against SCU, which will be a brutal first of two match ups over the season. And then we talk about Burkie's Econ class, and then how there are never any parking spots in the driveway as we snag a space along the street. We also don't talk about it as we lug our duffles and gear up the porch to the door, Burkie clutching the burrito bags along with his skates.

And not talking about it? Somehow that makes it hotter.

Because I'd bet anything we're both thinking about it. The whole time we're talking about Coach putting him in at left-wing next practice, we're both wondering about what is going to happen later tonight.

Will he go down on me? Or will I go down on him?

Will it be as hot as watching him jack himself this morning? Will I bury my nose in that big nutsack of his? Will he smell as good as he does right now?

The questions don't stop as we step inside, dropping our

duffles in the entryway. What will his thick cock feel like in my mouth? Will I be able to feel the ridge of that vein with the tip of my tongue?

Will I like it?

What if I don't?

I swallow back some nerves as Burkie tugs off his beanie, his hair tangling around his ears. What if we get in there—dicks out and ready—and it doesn't work out?

What then?

I glance toward the living room and find Leslie and Dare zeroed in on the TV with controllers in hand. *Dying Light*—this zombie game with a shit-ton of blood—is splashed across the screen. Leslie shouts something at Dare, who laughs obnoxiously and shoves him in the shoulder before they both focus intently on the screen. Vain's sitting on the edge of the couch, hulking over his phone and texting someone.

Kelsey is the only one who looks over at us. "Sup, boys?"

"Nada," I say as Burkie and I get to work sorting our gear. He separates our pads and skates while I haul the laundry downstairs. After I get the washer going, I come back up to help him with wiping everything down. There's a lot of shit to do, especially because he can be pretty meticulous with his gear. But I'm used to it, and we've got a system we always follow.

After we get it all done, he nods to the stairs. "I'm going to grab a shower before I eat." He looks past me toward the guys. "And I'm not in the right headspace to hear everyone's opinions about Cassidy yet."

"I get that." I eye the burrito bag sitting on the entryway table. "Mind if I go ahead? I'd wait but . . ."

"Course not." He pulls out my burrito and hands it to me.

I glance over at where Dare and Leslie are razzing each other, both still focused on the TV. Vain is focused on his phone. Kelsey's not looking anymore. No one's paying attention to us.

I grab my foil-wrapped burrito, bouncing it in my hand.

His gaze flips from the heavy bounce of my burrito up to my face. "Uh . . . later?"

"Definitely." I fist it a touch harder and toss him a wink.

He laughs, shaking his head at me, but a cute smile spreads across his face before he heads upstairs.

I watch him go, ogling at how his muscular ass fills out his joggers as he takes the stairs two at a time.

We're really doing this? And if we don't like it . . . then we'll figure it out.

When he's gone, I head in toward the TV and then flop into the recliner across from the couch, flipping the brim of my hat forward so it doesn't smack the seat.

Vain upnods at me but keeps his eyes on his phone. He's *seriously* texting someone, all hunched over.

"Mail for you," he says, still not looking up.

"Thanks." I reach for the stack of envelopes on the table and flip through. I come across an official-looking letter from IFU and set my burrito on the coffee table before ripping the letter open and unfolding a single sheet of paper. I scan it.

The letter's from the scholarship committee, notifying me that there's been a drop in funding for next year and my need-based scholarship is being reconsidered.

Shit.

I chew on the inside of my cheek, not exactly sure what that means.

I got the same letter last year. Nothing came of it, but what if something does this year?

I don't have much to fall back on. Over the summers, I work helping my dad at his maintenance job back home in Chicago. That brings in a small amount of cash, but with hockey and classes during the year, there's not much time to get a job here. The couple of times I've tried to swing it, my boss always ended up getting pissed about all the travel for games and the occasional extra practices that Coach throws our way last minute.

If I could find and hold a job, I would.

I refold the letter and shove it in my back pocket, feeling anxious. I'm covered for the rest of this year, but if that scholarship evaporates, I'll have to figure out a different solution for next year.

"You gonna eat that?" Vain asks.

I glance over to see him eyeing my burrito. Leslie jumps over the back of the couch and heads into the kitchen. Dare yells after him, gloating about something from their game.

"Don't even think about it, Vainie." I frown at him then snatch my burrito. There's no way in hell he's stealing my BJ burrito. "Eyes on your own *schwanz*."

Both he and Kelsey laugh.

"Smells good." Vain goes back to his phone. "Mexicali's? What I wouldn't give for some of that right now."

I waggle my brows. "You wouldn't believe what I'm going to pay Burkie for it."

CHAPTER EIGHT

Shaw

The house is empty.

Vain took off to hit the gym. Leslie headed out to meet someone—didn't say who. Dare and Kelsey went over to the library.

What that all means is that it's just Burkie and me here. Alone.

I'm sure that's happened a hundred times before, but I've never thought about it until now.

We're *alone*.

And I've been standing outside his door for almost five minutes, fidgeting in the dark hallway. My stomach is one giant knot.

I scratch at my hat, take it off, reform the brim, and then resettle it on my head. Maybe I should have tugged on a shirt. I don't usually bother with one around the house, but I'm second guessing now.

This feels weird.

I mean, it *is* weird. Right? Yesterday, I was relishing our hard-fought win, drinking cheap beer, and chatting up some girls.

Now twenty-four hours later, I'm thinking about Burkie so hard that I'm sweating, a sheen of warmth across the back of my shoulders. And I don't fully know what changed.

It doesn't feel like I've changed.

And it doesn't seem like he's changed.

But something has definitely changed between us.

I stare at the circular Wolfpack logo centered on his door. I'm going to do this.

I'm going to knock.

Go in.

And suck his monster-sized cock.

Assuming he wants me to, of course.

And I'm not going to worry about what's changed. I'm not going to worry about kissing. I'm just going to hang out with Burkie because I like doing that, and it doesn't need to be any more complicated than that.

I bounce on my toes, trying to loosen my shins and calves like I would before a game. The floor creaks under my weight. I stop halfway up.

Footsteps approach. The door opens, and then he's there. "Shaw?"

"Yep." I settle my heels on the carpet, trying not to let my eyes sweep all over him, but it's really freaking difficult. He's not wearing a shirt or shoes either. Just a pair of dark blue joggers, a dusting of chest hair, and an entire mapwork of thick abs. His hair is loose, brushing and curling over the top of his shoulders. His jaw is clean shaven now, but that never lasts long. I swear he can sprout scruff in ten seconds flat.

Why does that turn me on so much? Guess I like a dude with some hair. Because I'm also noticing the dark hair in his pits as he reaches up to rub the back of his neck.

"You coming in?" He steps back into his room, leaving the door open.

I follow him inside, inhaling the warmed vanilla, which is doing nothing to calm my nerves right now. He crosses to his desk and leans his ass back against it. "Sorry, I was studying. I didn't know when you were coming by or . . . if maybe not."

"Nah, I definitely wanted to come by." I slip my hands into my pockets, nodding at the textbook. "But I don't want to interrupt you."

"You're not." He crosses one leg over the other, which makes a poofy area of fabric around his crotch. And I'm looking. Not only that, but a warm heat pools low in my abdomen. *His dick's under there.*

Which is obviously not new information. It's always been there.

It feels like new information though.

"I was, uh." He twists to flip his textbook closed. "Having a hard time paying attention."

"Yeah," I say. "Me too. I tried to finish a paper for my Nutritional Science class, but honestly, I couldn't focus on any of it."

"Sounds familiar."

I glance around his room, not sure what to say next. Maybe we should dive right in? Get past this weird, awkward part.

"So . . ." I bounce on my toes. "Are you still up for a little action? If so, I guess we should figure out who's blowing who? Or if you just want to jack off again, that's cool too. I'm down for either."

He blinks. Then laughs. "You are seriously not one for any build up."

I squish my toes into the carpet. "You mean the boring stuff?"

He itches at the side of his jaw. "I'm not sure it would be boring."

I'm not either.

"Besides, uh." His eyes flick down to my crotch before

darting back up quickly, like he's worried he'll be caught looking. "I've never blown a guy."

"Me neither." I shrug a shoulder. "I mean, I can reach my own dick, but only the very tip. And it hurts like hell."

His hands come down to cup the edge of the desk. "You're serious?"

"You haven't tried?"

"Of course I've *tried*. But there's no fuckin' way. Not without some serious injury." His bare chest rises. "I knew you were flexible, but fuck*me*, Shaw."

"I just said I can't do it." I cross over to his dresser and pick up an unlit candle. I give it a whiff. Definitely vanilla. I set it down then let my fingers trail over the dark wood box on top of his dresser.

"You know"—he says as I twist to look at him—"you don't owe me anything. I, uh." He shrugs a stiff shoulder.

Is he uncomfortable?

Did I freak him out with the burrito deal?

"Shit, I'm sorry." I pivot to face him fully. "If you're uncomfortable—"

"No." He shakes his head sharply. "It's not that. I just worry . . . that maybe I'm not so good at it."

"At what? Blow jobs?"

"That too. But I was talking about flirting. I guess." He clamps his hands tighter around the edge of the desk. "That's kinda new for me too."

"Well, shit." I wink at him, trying to set him at ease. "We're all about the new stuff lately. And you're perfect at flirting. Like all-out, dig-everything-you-say *perfect*. Don't worry about it. Just say whatever comes to mind. It's all good. We're just having fun."

His soft brown eyes fix to mine. "Just having fun."

"Yeah." My lips tip down a little. I mean, that *is* what we're doing. Right? "Let's not worry about it."

There's absolutely nothing wrong with fun.

And I always have fun around him.

"Okay," he says.

Okay.

Fun, yeah. Not worrying. Good.

I bounce once on my toes and turn back to that little box on his dresser, focusing back on what I was wondering a few minutes earlier. "What's in here?"

Nicks and scratches run along the top of the box, like he's had it for a while. I've wondered what's in it before, but it always felt too invasive to ask.

Not sure why it feels okay now. I guess once you've seen a guy fist his cock and spurt into his chest hair, it's cool to ask about his memento box.

"Open it," he says.

I reach out, but pause with my hand over the lid. "You sure? I mean, I'm wondering if there's another ass toy in here? Maybe you've got them hidden all over the room?"

He laughs and sweeps a couple of tendrils of hair behind his ear. "Trust me, there's no ass toy in there."

I skim my fingers along the wood lid. "Have you used it, by the way?"

His brows go up. "It's been *one* day. I haven't exactly had time."

"I'd make time for that."

He shakes his head. "Yeah, I guess you would."

I click my tongue against the roof of my mouth. "I think I'm supposed to be offended by that, but I'm really not."

He traps his bottom lip in his teeth, but a smile tugs at his mouth. It's so damn cute that I want to forget all about his box and maul him with a hug.

He pushes off the desk and walks over, stopping next to me.

"You can look at anything in here." He flips the lid open, his forearm brushing mine, the heat of his skin prickling over me.

Just him standing here—this close—is sending goose-bumps over my shoulders. I'm sure he's been this close to me lots of times before, but like thinking about his dick under his poofy crotch area, this feels entirely new. I shift my foot an inch closer to his, enough for my little toe to brush against his.

Then I focus on the box because I'm really curious. All sorts of stuff is crammed inside. It's very un-Burkie like, with his need to have everything orderly. It's so jam-packed that a folded piece of paper sitting on top pops out. It exposes a moonstone that must be the one his sister gave him when he left for IFU. Golden hockey pins are tucked around the stone.

"High school letterman pins?" I fish one out.

"Yep." His jaw ticks.

It sucks he has such a conflicted relationship with his hockey past.

It makes me want to punch his dad. Kinda how he punched Cassidy today.

I wouldn't do it. The only place I ever feel any aggression is on the ice. But I want to somehow make that dickhole of a man realize that treating a person like he does Burkie has repercussions. I see it sometimes in Burkie. The doubt, the feeling like he's not good enough, like he's somehow not equal. Burkie's harsh with himself sometimes.

I wish he'd had a dad like mine, who has never *once* made me question if I'm capable of doing whatever I set my mind to. Who ran Kickstarter campaigns so I could get goalie gear. Who always got me to practice, even when things were tough.

"I wish you'd had a family like mine," I say, dropping the pin inside. "We would have been there for you in a heartbeat."

His lips part, and then he presses them closed. I don't know if what I said bothered him, so I go back to sorting through the box. "So were you Mr. Popular in high school? Big, athletic, super hockey jock?"

98

He laughs. "No. Not at all."

I raise my brows at him. "Really? Even looking like you do? And with your skill on the ice?"

A crease forms between his brows. "I mostly wanted to get out of the Delta. Somewhere I didn't have to worry so much."

Jeez, I want to hug him. I swallow and grab the opaque moonstone, bouncing it in my palm. I set it back and snatch out a pack of ticket stubs. "Exactly how many NHL games have you been to?"

He shrugs. "You could count them. Have you ever been?"

"Three times," I flip through his ticket stubs, realizing that even though we've been friends for a couple of years now, there's still a lot we probably don't know about each other. "I told my parents I wanted to play in the NHL when I was a sophomore in high school, and they scrounged up for my birthday every year after that. Then I came here and haven't made it since."

"We should drive down to Denver and catch an Avs game." He crosses to his bed and then flops down to a seat, the mattress bouncing under his weight. "We could rent a room or something. Stay the night."

I roll my thumb over the pack of ticket stubs. "That sounds really cool, actually."

Like *really* cool. All that time just with Burkie. I'd like that. I mean, I could never afford it. But I won't let reality crash into a dream like that.

I dig out a worn piece of paper on the bottom of the box then unfold it carefully. "Aww, I remember this. How did you get it?"

It's one of Coach's spreadsheets—the lineup roster from my first Wolfpack game. My freshman year and Burkie's sophomore. Both our names are on the starting list, and I'd drawn a smiley face next to his column.

Coach yelled at me for writing on his clipboard, but I

didn't care. It was our first time on the starting lineup together. Even back then, there was something about us being on the ice together. Of all the guys I've skated with, I've never felt so in sync with someone as I do with Burkie. It's like he can read my mind out there.

"I stole it," Burkie says. "Although I think all Coach's papers get tossed anyway. But I snuck into his office after the game and stole it."

I smile down at it. "Feels like so long ago."

"It does."

"Can't believe it's coming to an end after this season."

His lips press. "Me neither."

I've still got another year, but Burkie will be off and graduated. In the NHL, most likely. I'm so happy for him. But I also can't picture playing without him.

Or this house without him?

Tension sparks across the back of my shoulders. We all know this is how it goes after graduating. The closest NHL team is Denver, which is a two-hour drive, and there's absolutely no guarantee that any of us will end up there. The choice isn't up to us. If we get scouted, we go. Rookies rarely get a choice of teams.

Vain's likely going to the Montreal Canadiens.

But me, Les, Dare and Kelsey still have another year before graduation. Although if I were scouted now, I'd go. It would also solve my scholarship problems. But the odds of Burkie and me ending up in the same place? It's not just unlikely, it's solidly impossible.

I refold the paper and tuck all his items carefully into his memento box, keeping things in the same order since I know that's important to him.

"That's a cool little box. I like it." I close the lid before heading over to drop down next to him. "I don't keep mementos."

"Your Instagram works for that." He's sitting like he was

this morning, feet on the floor, knees slightly spread, his palms on his muscular thighs.

"Guess so," I say. "But that's all in the past few years. Nothing before that. Kinda wish I had some stuff, but I guess I don't keep much in general."

He eyes me curiously. "Why not?"

I shrug. "Not sure. I wish I had a picture with my parents and brother though. Like in a frame or something."

His forehead lines. "Is your family going to come down to a game this season?"

"Don't know if they can," I say. "When I texted my mom after the game yesterday, she wasn't sure."

He itches at the side of his neck, that tattoo on his triceps catching my eye. Along with the hair under his arm. It looks kinda . . . snuggly. "They don't get to visit much."

"Nope, Dad works a lot. It's hard for him to get away." I shrug a shoulder. "They live in an apartment on the first floor of one of the buildings my dad does maintenance for, so it's cool when I go back because I just crash in an empty apartment. Bring a sleeping bag and drop. And then I help my dad out with stuff around the buildings or my mom with the *sarmale* or play video games with my brother."

He blinks. "What's *sarmale*?"

I laugh, lighting up at the thought of family holidays.

"It's like a cabbage roll." I make a gesture with my hands, but then let it fall when I realize he's got no clue what I'm talking about. "We don't do a lot of traditional stuff anymore, but Christmas day *sarmale* cannot be missed. Or, shit, *cozonac*." I grin, thinking of snowy, crowded holidays with everyone talking over each other, hockey too loud on the television, and all my family crammed together in the apartment. "You'd love it. Too much food. Although we take an eating break to help dish out Christmas brunch over at SHC."

He tips his chin, eyes curious. "SHC?"

"I, well . . ." Fuck, that just slipped out. "Samaritan House Chicago."

He keeps looking at me steadily.

Shit.

Okay.

I guess I could tell him this. "I think I've mentioned that my brother Raleigh has a heart condition? Congenital." I pick carefully through the words. Most people don't know this about me—definitely no one at IFU. "Well, he had a few surgeries before he turned two, and the bills added up, and my mom lost her job because she had to keep missing work to take care of him, and there was a lot of stuff that we couldn't keep up with."

He searches my face, the curiosity in his eyes turning more focused. "That must have been hard."

"Yeah. So, we had this house in Lincolnwood." My shoulders tighten as I think about what I'm going to tell him. Will he look at me differently? Does he even want to know? But he nods, urging me on.

"Anyway," I continue, "we lost the house for a while. Or, well, for good. It was a couple of years later that my dad got the job for the apartments, but there wasn't anywhere to stay for a while. And some nights we slept in the car or wherever. And there was SHC." I shake my head, my lungs feeling like they're tightening down hard.

Homeless.

We were homeless. Or "a family temporarily without a home" as the counselor at SHC taught me to say. But it's all the same for a kid whose life got suddenly upturned.

It's not about the four walls and a roof. It's about *home*. Knowing that you have somewhere to go. That you have somewhere to fall back on.

And back then, it was twice as scary since Raleigh always needed care. There were times we all slept at the hospital, curled up in uncomfortable plastic chairs, worried that he wasn't going to make it through.

"It wasn't my parents' fault," I add quickly. "There's always these assumptions that Mom and Dad were lazy or didn't care, and that couldn't be further from the truth. But people always think they know better. That it would never happen to them."

Most people don't realize how easily things can just be *gone*. How quickly shit can collapse. And sometimes you can't do a single fucking thing to get it back.

I scrub my hat off my head. Tucking the brim between my palms, I lean my elbows on my knees.

"I didn't assume anything about your parents," he says.

"Yeah, I know." I focus on shaping the brim of my hat. I sound pissed. He didn't need to hear about that, especially when I came in here with the promise of cocks and blow jobs and kickass things like that. Instead, I'm going off on a tangent about shit that happened in the past.

I keep reforming the brim, not wanting him to see how my eyes are heating. How scared I am that him knowing changes things somehow.

"I don't want to talk about it anymore," I say. "It's all just the past anyway."

"Shaw?" His voice is so close, and I choke back all this stupid fear and nod, waiting for whatever he's going to say.

I expect him to say he's sorry. Or that shit happens. Or anything that people say to end a conversation.

But when I finally drag my eyes up, I find him looking across at me with that steady gaze, which always makes things feel better. He's not filling up the space with words that wouldn't matter anyway.

Instead, he nods at me, exactly like he does before a game, like he's saying, "We fuckin' got this." Strong on his skates, big and determined, and a force to be reckoned with. Standing on my right, ready to be a barrier to anything that comes at me. To take down any fucker who dares to slam into me.

He's the guy who always shows up. Steadfast and strong.

He never vanishes. He's never just *gone*.

He's here. Like he is now, only a few inches between us, his shoulder almost touching mine. He nods again, then moves his knee closer until it presses against mine. He still doesn't say anything. Doesn't crowd me with his thoughts.

We sit like that for a long few minutes, knees bucked up together, the thicker fabric of his joggers warm against the slick of my pants.

I press my knee harder against his. "I made it awkward."

"No." He shakes his head. "You didn't."

Another beat of silence.

He clears his throat. "Do you want to watch some SportsCenter or something?"

"Nah," I say. "Not really."

Not at all.

"Alright." The hollow above his clavicle tenses as he swallows, his knee pressing firmly back against mine. "What do you want to do?"

I drag in a slow breath. "You know, earlier, in the locker room when we were about to maybe . . ."

He stills. "I remember."

My eyes settle on his lips. "What if we pick up where we left off?"

CHAPTER NINE

Shaw

Burkie stares at me.

"You don't have to," he finally says, in not more than a whisper, and my throat tightens as I blink at him.

He's giving me an out.

I don't want an out. I want to do this with him. I want to kiss him.

I *like* Burkie.

I mean, of course I do. I've liked him since the moment I met him.

But I really *like* him.

That's what it means when you want to be around someone all the time. When hanging out with anyone else could never be better than hanging out with him. When just looking at him makes goosebumps rise up the nape of my neck. Makes my palms clammy. Makes me want to keep shifting closer and closer. A little contact between knees feeling strangely significant.

My hat is still cupped in my hands. I hook it backward on my head then set my palms on my thighs, my fingers tapping.

I lick my lips. "I want to, *coaie*."

He inhales, his chest expanding, pecs and sternum and abs all pressing out. "You sure?"

The barest hint of his drawl sneaks into his words, and that makes this little shiver flick out across my shoulders. I stare down at the mouth that drawl came from.

Adrenaline zips down my spine.

"Yep," I say. "I'm sure."

The beat of his pulse echoes just underneath his jaw.

Okay, so we're gonna do this.

I concentrate on shifting forward.

One inch.

Two.

I move slowly, right until I'm a half breath away from his lips, his musky scent surrounding me, my own heartbeat spiking and balls clenching.

His lips are *right* there.

I'm so damn nervous.

I'm never this nervous.

Something's stopping me. I'm not sure what it is. That bit of tension sparks across the back of my shoulders.

I swallow. My mouth is *really* wet. "Can you go first on this one?"

"Alright." A half-smile crosses his face, and I jump when he slowly closes the distance, a fraction at a time. When he's centimeters away, his eyes hold mine, and I suck in a sharp breath.

Our mouths meet.

His lips are so *soft*. I sink, lost in a millisecond as I open my mouth to his. I clutch the nape of his neck and pull him closer, my grip rough in contrast with the silky, velvety ache of our kiss.

It's unlike anything.

I mean, really, seriously unlike *anything*. Any kiss I've ever had.

He kisses me like he's being careful with me, like he cares, and the urge to be closer wells up so strongly that I'm moving before I realize it, crawling over him, our lips gliding and searching as I settle over his lap. My balls skim over the thick ridge of his cock, and a surprised moan slips out of me. I dig my fingers into his hair, my hips canting. His tongue curls against mine before he pulls back, dark eyes searching my face.

"Fuck, Shaw," he says in a voice so gravelly and low that it *fists* my dick. It's physical, in a gut-check way. So much that I almost expect to look down and find him stroking me. My ass clenches, my dick thickening, the desire to ask him to do exactly that hovering on my tongue.

He tips up and takes my lips again. His softness is over-whelming, completely mind-consuming. I break the kiss to suck across the bottom edge of his jaw, my hat knocking askew. His rougher skin chafes at my lips as I lick to his ear.

Holy hell, Burkie is razor-sharp sexy. Every sound, every touch highlighted as I work my mouth down the slope of his neck and across the breadth of his shoulder, tonguing against his light trace of hair.

He groans, his fingers digging into my hips.

I tongue the ridge of his collarbone, and then my teeth close over his skin, a sharp little nip that makes him cut out a breath.

I *bit* Burkie.

And it was *hot*.

"Do that again," he grits.

I smooth a kiss over his reddened skin, then drag my teeth down toward his pec, licking along the way. I give him another little nip, and his hands slide around to palm my ass. He tugs me against him.

Jeez, he's hard. Not just his cock pressing up against my balls, but his shoulders and arms, thighs and chest. He's tightly coiled underneath me. Heat drums off of him as I kiss up to his mouth. His tongue laves across my bottom lip before sliding against mine.

I mumble something unintelligible into his mouth, and he groans, the low sound rumbling, and then he squeezes my ass.

All my muscles flex. The bolt of desire that wrecks through me is close to painful, and I'm grinding along the full length of his cock. I just need to freaking feel him. His shocked inhale resonates in my ear.

I don't think. I shove him back onto the bed. My knees are spread on either side of his, digging into the mattress, and I roll my hips and gasp, rutting my dick along the full, hard length of his.

I squeeze my eyes shut, breathing through my nose. One more grind like that and I could seriously lose my nut without a single bit of other contact. "I can't wait. Dicks out?"

"Yes. *Fuck*." His eyes are so dark that it heats my veins, and I hate that I have to roll off of him to shove my pants down. He pushes his joggers off, his dick springing free, so thick and full that my ass clenches as I crawl back over the top of him.

This time, nothing is between us. Our bare dicks are inches away, his muscular thighs trapped between mine.

Holy shit, *we're really doing this*.

My tongue is heavy and wet in my mouth as I stare down at him spread out below me.

I want to lick him.

I want to taste. Suck. Savor. Swallow.

Tease.

I bend to take his mouth, nipping at him lightly, our tongues flirting as I brace one hand by his shoulder, and with the other I reach down to my dick, taking one stroke. He rasps out a guttural curse as my knuckles scrape along his shaft.

It's so damn sexy that I shiver, breaking the kiss and looking down to where I'm hovering over the top of him.

"I like how we look together," I mumble.

Defined pecs and abs, hard cocks, strong thighs.

I want to tell him more. To verbally make sense of how desperately my heart's thumping. Of how good that kiss was. Of how I want to drift my nose all over him and see if I like the taste of his cock in my mouth. But I bite down on the inside of my cheek.

I don't want to make him uncomfortable. I don't know where the lines are.

I know that we're way past jacking off, but otherwise, I'm lost.

I just . . . "I want to touch you."

He drags in a breath. "Anywhere."

Okay, here goes.

I shift my hips back, still fisting myself, before meeting his eyes and lightly brushing the head of my cock against the base of his shaft.

Holy hell, sensations rush through me. That was . . . wow. I do it again, whimpering at the feeling of his smooth shaft against the sensitive head of my dick. My hands pick up a shake.

He hisses, his abs flexing.

"*Fuck*." He bows underneath me as I slowly draw my dick up his full length, leaving a faint sheen of pre-cum along that strong vein.

We're both hardly breathing. Both staring, eyes wide, as I drag my dick back down, my ass canting in the air. His cock twitches with every touch, his muscles all tightly bound, and I go lower. I get to the base of his shaft, and I roll my cockhead down to his sack, mesmerized as his balls pull up.

It's so freaking hot. His *sack* gets me hot. Of all the things I would have guessed, I never would have thought that

Burkie's sack would turn me on so much. I give him the faintest slap with the head of my dick.

He squeezes his eyes shut. "*Shaw*."

Need rattles in his voice. I settle lower on my knees, loosening my fingers wide enough to capture his cock alongside mine, watching him carefully so I can stop if he looks uncomfortable.

His eyes flash open as I fist us, and I smile at the way his mouth drops halfway open.

My grip is easy since both our dicks are fairly dry. The flare of his cockhead is both soft and firm against mine, and the weight of him, the heat of him, it's all so potent as I stroke us, careful not to chafe. A mangled groan comes from deep in his throat as our pre-cum slicks my palm.

I want to tell him how hot it is. How our dicks fit so perfectly together. But I don't know if . . .

I look up to find him biting down on his bottom lip.

Is he trying to hold back too? He hasn't said anything except for a few words.

"Do you wanna talk?" I push out roughly, still stroking us and hoping like hell that I'm not making him uncomfortable. "I kinda like to talk. The dirtier the better. Or not. Anything. Say anything. Only if you want."

Shit, that was awkward. I keep stroking, not wanting to lose the moment. Am I messing things up?

His lips part, and my rhythm falters. Shit, what if I've misread him? What if this is—

"I want you to fuck my mouth." He licks his lips, his chest pitching with a shaky breath. "Until I fuckin' *gag* on you, and I don't want you to stop until I've sucked every drop of your cum deep down my throat."

My hand stills. "*Dude*." Holy hell . . . "Were you thinking that the whole time?"

"Pretty much." His abs tighten, dick jumping in my hand. "Guess I'm worried about chasing you off."

"Don't be," I reassure him. "I want to hear it." *All of it.* "Every dirty thought in your head. Stack 'em all up and throw them at me. Hell, I've kinda wanted to say things too."

"Like what?"

"Your sack is *hot*. I want to nuzzle it." My brows rise. "Can I nuzzle it?"

"Fuck, *yes*." He laughs, this deep humor warming his eyes, and he's all Burkie for a moment. Just my best friend who *gets* me. Who I love to be around more than anyone else. Who apparently is cool with me nuzzling his sack.

He's still smiling, and he's looking up at me, and I'm looking down at him as I slowly resume jacking us. We're silent for a moment, a good silence, and it feels like things have suddenly slipped into place.

"You're hot," I say. "I want to lick all over you. Every bit of sexy skin."

His head falls back, a husky groan winding out of him that's louder than any sound we've made before. It's a deeply genuine noise. Like he's letting himself go.

"Make that sound again." I take my hand off to spit in it and then grip us, stroking a touch faster, heat throbbing deep in my balls.

He arcs up closer to me, and my knuckles run along the ridges of his abs as his warm breath brushes my jaw. "I'll make that sound around your dick if you fuck my mouth."

I half-laugh and half-moan. "Holy hell, I *love* this side of you." I take his mouth again, then nip at his bottom lip before I lean back. "And I absolutely want to bury my cock in that sexy-hot mouth of yours, but you're going first. I want to taste you."

He groans again, falling back. "Not going to make it much longer. Just you above me is about to set shit off."

I smirk down at him. "Well, you should try to hang on for at least the first suck. Give me the full experience."

"I'll try." He huffs out another low laugh, but it catches as

111

I lean down to lick over that bite mark on his shoulder. Nerves hit me again as I crawl down him, but they're different now. Tinged with excitement as I flick my tongue around his tight nipple, sucking and playing a little.

I taste him, moving lower, tonguing along those deep abs that would be so damn sexy full of my cum. Or his. Both? I whimper and suck on his navel before shifting down until my knees are on the floor.

I take a breath, my anticipation roiling, and then I close my eyes and drift my nose around his sack.

Yes.

I make some sort of choked noise and grind my nose in deeper, relishing the way he feels, the hair tickling, the *smell* of him—so headily masculine. I could bathe in this smell. I could spend the rest of the night, right here, nuzzled in his sack.

Longer.

But I'm pretty sure he's eager for something else.

I tip up to look at him. He's watching me, his eyes hooding as he takes me in.

Okay, here goes. It kinda feels like a big moment.

I don't break eye contact as I turn my head to take a tentative lick at the base of his cock.

"*Fuck.*" He squeezes his eyes, a shock bolting through him, and my smile widens. I lick again, loving the instant way he responds. I trail my tongue up his length, adjusting to the new sensations, the musky, salty taste and the feel of his skin moving over his firm shaft. His breath fractures as I reach his cockhead, his shoulders arching back.

I flick the tip of my tongue against the wetness at his slit.

"Jeez," I mumble. "You've gotta try this."

He grits his teeth. "Hoping to."

I close my lips to suck on his slit, then open to slide my tongue around his smooth cockhead.

His knuckles turn white as he clenches the sheet. "Fuck,

Shaw. *Fuck.* Are you sure you've never given a guy head before?"

I laugh, my breath making him shiver. "Think I would have noticed a dick in my mouth."

"It's not quite in your mouth."

I'm grinning so big my cheeks hurt. "Is that a challenge?"

He shakes his head. "No, it's—"

I take him into my mouth. Just suck him right down without giving him time to adapt, and fuck . . . he's *big*. He flares against the roof of my mouth, and I sputter and choke, saliva pooling at the corner of my lips as I pull off.

"Holy hell." I take him again, more prepared this time.

He groans, his head rolling to the side and eyelids fluttering as I suck him down. His hips start to work with me, his low, gravelly sounds getting louder. His eyes intermittently squeeze shut and flash open, like he's trying to watch every single second.

It's so fucking hot. And this is Burkie. *Burkie.*

Eden.

I take him as far as I can and swallow around his cockhead, my own dick throbbing at the way his cock *fills* my mouth.

"Shaw," he grits. He lets go of the sheet and grabs my shoulder, his chest and neck flushing a deep red. "I don't want to come yet. I can't . . . *fuck*."

I drag my mouth off him, taking one more greedy lick at his tip when a bead of pre-cum wells out.

He stares up at the ceiling.

"I need to, uh." His Adam's apple rolls as he keeps looking up. "Give me a second."

I laugh while getting to my feet. He's wound so tight, skin reddened and cock twitching, and even though he's a mass of muscle and brawn, there's something so cute about him that I want to dogpile on him, hug him, and bury my nose in his neck.

"Alright, better now." He scrubs a hand over his face and sits up. "Think I can look at you again."

"Like what you see?" I waggle my hips, my dick bobbing.

He exhales a laugh as he takes me in. "You have no fuckin' clue how much."

I reach back and palm the brim of my hat to toss it off, but he shakes his head.

"Leave it," he says in a deep, gravelly voice that's got this touch of command.

Shit, I like that.

"Yeah?" I drop my hand, smiling as he tracks my every movement. I grip myself and take a slow stroke, then give him a wink. "You wanna try?"

"Fuck, *yes*." His eyes widen. "*Please*."

He looks so eager.

I step forward, between his spread knees, my eagerness shallowing my breath. His hands warm the outside of my thighs, tugging me closer, but I keep a little distance, still stroking myself, inches from his parted lips.

I can't stop *smiling*. My pelvis is tightening with anticipation, and I'm feeling all the usual heart-thumping, ball-clenching need too, but it's even better with Burkie. It's so *honest*. Maybe that's not the right word. Open. Genuine.

He knows me.

"I like doing this with you," I say, and he blinks, focusing up on me instead of on my dick. What I just said feels like an understatement. Like just a fraction of what's going on in my head, but I don't know how else to say it yet. "Are you ready?"

"Beyond ready." His eyes are all over me, like he can't figure out where to look.

"Here goes." I step forward, and I brush my cockhead over those thick, reddened lips of his. We both groan. My anticipation ratchets higher than it's ever been. I *want* this. So freaking deeply that it scares me a little.

What if he doesn't like it?

Anxiety pinches at me, but then his hands glide up the outside of my thighs, and he pulls me in. I let out a long, relieved exhale as my dick slides into the wet heat of his mouth. I hesitate halfway in, wanting to give him time, but he grabs my ass, palming and squeezing with both hands, and pulls me deep.

It's ridiculously sexy. His lips glisten as I pull out and then push back in. He watches me as he tongues around my shaft.

My fingers thread through his hair, and I'm practically whimpering as I watch my dick, slick with his spit and so achingly hard, slide between his lips. He keeps kneading my ass, his fingers slipping toward my crease. My abs harden, my balls draw up.

I want to shove deep. I want to fuck him, but I stiffen my stance, tension welling up my spine as I try to control myself.

He pulls off. "Don't hold back."

My knees go weak with relief as he sucks me back down, his groans vibrating all the way to my balls. His tongue strokes along the underside of my shaft, and heat localizes deep in my pelvis, blistering up from my balls. I start to fuck his mouth *hard*. His eyes meet mine, and that's all it takes.

I know I'm coming fast, but I don't fucking care.

"Gonna detonate." I'm hardly able to get the words out before I do. I strain tight, my head tipping back as I shudder through my release then meet his eyes again as he finishes swallowing me down.

I don't pause afterward, just thunk to my knees. He grunts in surprise, but in half a second, he's fucking up into my mouth so hard that he hits the back of my throat. I gag, and he pulls back, but that gag only gets me hotter. I take him as far as I can, working him with my tongue, tightening my lips, aching for the sound of each ragged breath as he gets closer.

He gives me a gritted-out, gravelly warning and then fills me so full that I can barely suck him down. I'm still pulling on him and swallowing, his release dribbling out, when he whispers, "Too much, Shaw. Too fuckin' much."

He flops back on the bed, breathing hard, trembling. I wipe at my mouth as I crawl up next to him and collapse, every muscle spent.

"*Holyfuck*," he mumbles, scraping a hand over his face and twisting his head toward me. "I'm *gone*. Entirely fuckin' gone, never comin' back again. Don't want to."

I inch closer to him until our shoulders are touching. "That was hot. Like holy levels of hell hot. We're doing it again tomorrow. Or maybe in five? How's your recovery?"

He laughs, then coughs. His shoulder is hot and slick with sweat as it presses against mine. "Alright, I'm in. Give me like twenty minutes though. Maybe a short nap first. Move up by the pillow?"

He gets up to click off the light, then we worm up to the top of the bed before collapsing again. My legs are like jelly, my muscles sore from flexing. My dick is fully spent and stupidly happy. My cheeks hurt from smiling.

I'm just so damn *good*.

I snag off my hat and toss it somewhere on the bed and then roll onto my side to face him, only to find he's done the same. We're a foot from each other, naked, half shadowed in the dark, only lit by the moonlight streaming through the open curtains.

"You're staying for a bit, right?" he asks, hope lingering in his voice.

"If that's cool."

"Yep." He inches closer. "Do you want to catch the recap?"

"Actually, yeah." I forgot I had news about one of our past IFU teammates. "Did you hear Redgie got traded in a two-for-one deal with the Sharks?"

"No shit?" He twists away to grab the remote and flips the TV on, pale light filling the room. "Good for him."

We keep inching closer—little by little—until there's

hardly any space between us, and I drape my leg over his, nestled against him. We snuggle into his fluffy pillow.

In the background, SportsCenter runs, and we lazily chat about stats and today's NHL games. Players and trades, injuries and how the playoffs might look this year.

I clear my throat during a lull in the conversation. "Cup my ass."

"Yeah?" His tone lilts up. Like he's curious. He reaches over and cups one of my ass cheeks, his big hand warm and firm and a touch sweaty. I sigh, eyes closing, shoulders relaxing.

"That good?" he asks.

"So damn good. Don't let go." I sync my breath to the steady rise and fall of his, listening to the recap beyond that. His arm is firm around me, the cup of his hand on my ass is so comforting, even better when he lightly massages, and just like his kiss, I sink in. I just . . . let go.

I don't know what happens after that.

Guess we fall asleep.

Words that I will forever remember:

1. "I think you should trust yourself, Burkie."
2. "I kinda don't want it to stop."
3. "I'm quiet, because I wanted to."
4. "We would have been there for you in a heartbeat."

CHAPTER TEN

Burk

I wake with my hand on Shaw's ass. Softly gripping him, my index finger grazing the top of his crease. He's rolled against me, sharing the big-ass pillow I bought when he started crashing over some nights.

I *agonized* over that pillow. Standing there in Bed Bath & Beyond, in front of a wall of pillows, for like twenty fuckin' minutes debating what the protocol was for when your room-mate crashes in your single-pillow bed. Do you buy him his own pillow? Would that weird him out? Or get the double-long one, hoping he doesn't question it too much?

And now he's sound asleep on the double-long, lips parted as he snores lightly, our skin hot and sticky because we're mashed together.

A swell of heat pangs low in my abdomen as I turn to stare at the ceiling.

I have never, in my life, been more turned on when waking up.

Actually, I'm not sure if I've been this turned on ever.

It's painful how hard I am. I came so hard my balls ached

last night, and yet with Shaw here and his ass in my hand, I'm ready to do it again. I'm not used to having this kind of sex drive. I usually don't.

I let out a restrained groan as I let my finger shift to the top of his crease, just a little, not enough to—

"Are you exploring?" Shaw's rough morning voice floods warmth across the nape of my neck.

"I might be wandering a bit." My voice is rough, cracking as I push the words out. "Is that a problem?"

"Depends." His palm settles on my hip, his thumb rolling over my obliques. "Are you just gonna tease? Or are you gonna go full pioneer on my ass?"

I laugh. "Are you going to give me a map and a compass?"

"I've got no clue what you could possibly need a compass for, *coaie*, but I'm *in*." He's got lines from the pillowcase across his cheek, his short hair sticking out, but that smirk already spans his face, and fuck*me*, it's not just down low that's thumping in response. It's my chest, my throat, behind my eyes.

He wiggles closer, his breath heating my lips, which I admit has a bit of morning-after going on, but I couldn't give one single fuck.

I've woken next to him before, but I've always rolled away. Tried to put whatever I was thinking out of my head.

Now I erase the distance between us, tugging him fully on top of me. We kiss, slowly tasting each other, his weight on me so perfect that I want to trap him here forever.

This. This is what I fuckin' want. Yes, the other stuff too. For sure. But his kiss. His closeness.

Just because I haven't really felt this kind of attraction before doesn't mean I haven't ached for someone to lie on top of me. To be close. To kiss.

I enjoy every second of it. The satisfied smile not leaving my lips, even when he reaches out to grab his phone off the bedside table and then wrinkles his nose. "It's seven. I don't remember sleeping."

"Me neither." I stretch my hand down to fully palm his bare ass, still shocked that I'm allowed to. That he even gives a guy like me a second look. "Vain will be here soon. Promised him a jog this morning. I'd ask you to go, but there's something he wants to talk about, and he's being cagey about it."

"Cassidy?"

"Not sure." I frown. "Probably, I guess."

"Then we better get going." He sets his phone back on the table, his cock digging into me as he shifts. My fingers tighten on his ass, and I groan as he wiggles his hips.

He winks at me. "Wanna come first?"

"Fuck, *yes*."

His laughter makes me smile, and then his tongue licks the full length of my jaw—broadly across with zero hesitation —before he sucks on my earlobe.

"Don't stop wandering," he whispers. His teeth graze my neck, giving me another little nip that calls up a deep, rough yearning. I flex my fingers into his ass, spreading his cheeks a little. I let my index finger slide over, pressing at the top of his crease before dipping slightly lower, down the beautiful line of him.

Touching a man like this is something that felt forbidden for so long. But for the life of me, I can't understand *why* right now. It feels natural. It feels exactly fuckin' right.

I rub up and down the top of his crease, feeling the thinness of his skin there, the way it makes him harden against me. I can't fully reach his hole from this angle, but his breath becomes heavier in my ear.

"Feels good," he mumbles.

"Want me to get some lube?" I whisper, turning my head to better read his expression. "Or is this enough?"

He clenches his ass cheeks. "Not enough."

I reach over, trying not to move us, and pull open the bedside drawer then dig around blindly. I finally find the lube and flip open the cap as Shaw licks along my neck, his hips working slowly and steadily now, rolling our dicks between us in a way that sends me straight to heaven.

I want to explore this. I want this first with him.

My door rattles with a pound. "*Burk*. Get your ass up."

Fuck. Vain. My head falls back on the pillow, and Shaw smirks, his hips still rolling.

"Hold on, man," I call out, my voice scratchy and pained. "Be out in a second."

I'm still holding the lube, cap off. I'm not even close to ready to get out of bed.

"Hurry up," Vain calls. "We need to be over at the rink at nine, and I want to shower before then."

"The rink?" I ask.

"We've got a meeting with Coach. And I need to talk to you first. So get your ass moving." Vain's heavy footsteps retreat down the hallway.

"Motherfucker," I bite out. But there's no way I'm leaving Shaw. It's Saturday for fuck's sake.

"You should probably go." Shaw's forehead lines. "Something's up."

"I, uh." I feel like shit about leaving him.

"*Go*." He tosses me a flirty smile. "It's cool. You can finger my ass later."

I laugh. He's so easy about stuff. "You promise?"

"Yep." His grin widens as he rolls off me. "All ass, no waiting. A big all-you-can-eat buffet." He waggles his brows. "With a compass."

I chuckle again, then groan and scrub a hand over my face. "How do you make me laugh and get me going so hard at the same time?" I drag myself to sitting, dick ramrod hard and my balls throbbing as they settle against my thighs.

I stand and grouse at the angsty weight between my legs

as I cross to my dresser to locate some tight boxer briefs for jogging because I'm definitely going to need extra support. I bend to pull them on before snagging out a pair of joggers.

When I turn around, Shaw's kicked back on my pillow, hands clasped behind his head, all the sleek lines of his muscles pointing down to where he's so gorgeously hard that my mouth waters. I want him in my mouth again. A million fuckin' times over.

He nods toward my dick. "Are you gonna be able to run like that?"

"No clue." I sigh and step one foot into the leg of my joggers.

His eyes light with curiosity. "Would you pound one out if I weren't here?"

I pause, one leg in, one leg out. "I guess."

Although there's no way I'd be this hard if he wasn't here.

He clicks his tongue. "Then do it in my mouth."

I'm motionless. Joggers partway up my thighs. "Now?"

"Yep."

I glance at the door.

"I bet we can do both of us in three minutes flat." He sits up, feet falling on the floor. "You and me? I'm pretty sure we can do anything." His hand moves to his dick, and then he drags his index finger slowly up the side of his shaft, from root to tip.

Fuck.

Me.

My heart launches up, my eyes permanently affixed as he makes a slow, rolling track back down. He side-walks his feet a few inches apart, his balls tight between his thighs.

"Three minutes?" I rasp. There's so much damn gravel in my voice that the words are almost garbled. My lungs feel like they're pulsing. Hope flares through me like a jackhammer.

Is this how we are now?

Shaw and me? Snuggling and waking up together and laughing and *being*.

I can't fuckin' hope. It's too big.

Too much to hope for.

"If you want." His grin is wicked. Fiercely heated and downright devilish. He waggles his brows at me again, teasing—playful—so fuckin' gorgeous that it feels like my chest is going to collapse.

His finger tracks up again and slides around his cockhead, taking a lazy circle. "Vain can wait three minutes. But the time's already counting down, so get your cute, muscular ass over here or get moving out the door, so I can rub myself out on your pillow."

I drag my teeth over my bottom lip. "You wouldn't."

He fists his cock and takes a languorous stroke. "Oh, I will. If you don't do it for me."

I shove my joggers down and cross to him like the floor is lava. I'm not sure exactly what I'm going to do, but I bend to kiss him.

He kisses me hard. Then in one goalie-fast motion, plants a palm on my sternum and shoves me up, dipping forward and licking the front of my boxer briefs, right over the top of my cock, moistening the fabric.

"Fuuuucck," I mumble as he sneaks one hand under the leg of my boxer briefs, pulling the fabric tight as he works his way up to grip me from below. He strokes the lower half of my shaft, and it's all going so fast that my head swims.

He bends forward and lightly nips at the head of my cock through the fabric. I grit my teeth, heat already brewing low in my abdomen. Not sure I'll need close to half of our three minutes.

"Wanna see that thick cock," he says, and with his free hand, he yanks down on the elastic waistband of my boxer briefs and sucks just the head of my dick into his mouth. I groan loudly, not able to hold it back.

I'm twisted up, my boxers being yanked from both sides and squeezing my balls. He looks up at me, licking at my slit, and my release sparks deep in my pelvis. It's always hovering right there with Shaw, never far away. It's hard to hold it back, and this time I let it wreck through me, not staving it off.

He laps at my head as I release, green eyes sparking, some of my release dripping onto his chin.

"Holyfuckyouregorgeous," I choke. I can't make out what I'm saying.

But it's a reverence.

An ode.

An end-of-my-life offering because there will never, *ever* be a time that I'm not thinking about him.

I'm never going to recover. Never going to return to the man I was five minutes before he flipped that chair around, fisted his dick, and came for me.

It's a heady wealth of feelings that rip into me as I tremble through the last of my release. I know it's too much. I know my feelings are too deep.

But how can I turn them off?

I *want* to feel everything I'm feeling.

"You okay?" He looks up at me, wiping a hand over his mouth and chin. I blink as I realize I'm hogging our three minutes.

"Sorry," I say, my eyes sailing down him from reddened lips to the dusky, eager head of his cock. "I'm taking up too much time."

He must read something on my face because his expression shifts to concern. "It's okay, we can just—"

"No fuckin' way." I grab his jaw, angling his face up, and I kiss him. I fuse our mouths. I dig my fingers into his skin, keeping him right where I want him.

He shivers, and when I pull back, his eyes are wide. His swollen lips parted.

I drop to my knees, pausing only to plant a single kiss close to his ear and then another on the upside of his pec, and then on his obliques because I can't help myself.

"Eden," he mumbles, and I have to close my eyes for a split second, relishing in the fact that it's his voice saying my name.

He widens his legs, trembling as my breath rushes over him, and I cup his balls, enjoying their soft weight in my palm, the wrinkle of his sack, the firmer roundness of his nuts, and the way he twitches as I roll my fingers. I didn't get to do this last night, so I stretch our time out another minute —probably longer than I should—before I take his cock into my mouth.

His fingers grasp my hair as his hips kick up. His breath fractures as I suck him down, deeply and eagerly.

The door rattles with a bang.

"*Burk*," Vain hollers. "What's taking so long, bro?"

"Almost there," Shaw hisses between clenched teeth.

"What?" Vain yells.

Fuck. I start to pull off, but Shaw's fingers tighten in my hair.

"Keep your fuckin' pants on," he yells, deepening his voice. He sounds a hell of a lot like me, but he lets out a husky moan at the end.

Vain grumbles. He probably thinks I'm jerking off. Which is completely fine with me. I don't give a shit.

"Hurry up," Vain yells as his footsteps echo down the hallway. "Stream some porn or something."

Shaw laughs, then moans, clutching onto me, pumping harder into my mouth. He goes all out—not holding back. His knees squeeze on either side of my chest, his dick ramming into my throat, flexing so hard that he's shaking.

I adore every fuckin' second of it.

"Gonna come." He shallows his strokes, then grits out a half-muffled shout, flooding my mouth in an instant.

Pure heaven.

"*Eden.*" He flops back on the bed. "Jeez, you're good at that. And I'm going back to sleep. You wore me out, *coaie*. I want to snuggle on your pillow."

I rise to my feet, adjusting my twisted boxer briefs. They're still slightly damp, and that might make running outside cold, but I have zero desire to change out of them. "Alright."

"Yeah?" He peeks through one eye at me before squirming onto the pillow. "You don't mind if I stay? It smells good. All Burkie-like."

I drag a hand over my mouth, aching to crawl back into bed with him as he rolls onto his stomach, his bare ass up, his spine bending as he relaxes into the mattress.

"Then stay," I whisper.

It's scary how deeply I mean that.

CHAPTER ELEVEN

Burk

Vain eyes me when I jog downstairs. "Better mood than yesterday?"

"You could say that." *Understatement of the decade*. We step out into the cold, gray morning. I tug on my IFU beanie then pause on the porch to stretch out my hamstrings, struggling to adjust from the quick transition between the warm bed with Shaw and the nut-shrinking cold out here with Vain.

After a short stretch, we head out, passing by a few of the nicer sorority houses before the path we typically take that winds between the trees.

Vain nods toward the last house before we turn. "Party at Alpha Kappa Friday. You in?"

"Not sure." I steady my stride, trying to fall into a rhythm. "Depends if I feel like I need to take it easy before Saturday's game."

"I hear that." Vain matches my pace. "Not sure I'll stay long, but Les and Shaw will want to drop by. Even Dare said he might."

"Yep." He's not wrong about Shaw. He rarely misses a party.

Although Shaw usually hooks up at parties like these.

Which . . . *fuck*.

My feet pound hard on the cement path. There's no way I can watch Shaw turn that flirty smile on someone else. Would he hook up with a girl?

Or with a guy?

My shoulders tighten, my steps becoming stiff.

"Burk," Vain snaps, and I sidestep right before smashing into a trash can.

"Fuck," I grumble.

I force my mind back to the jogging path, lengthening my strides and forcing Vain to pick up his pace.

Whatever Shaw does, it's not my decision. It's his. And I won't get in the way of what he wants. So I'll figure out how to deal with it.

The remaining houses give way to rolling hills covered in skinny evergreens. A few picnic spots dot the side of the pathway here and there. It's not very busy on the west side of town, far from the river and the falls. It's peaceful. Especially at seven in the morning.

We usually take a short rest by a specific cluster of picnic tables, and sure enough, Vain side-glances at me before he comes to a stop there.

"So . . ." He rolls a thick shoulder. "You put me in a shitty position, bro."

I nod, glad that we're hitting the issue straight on. "Is this about Cassidy?"

"Kinda." He squints at me, his hazel eyes grayish in the wan morning light. "The day before you went off on him, I told Coach that I wanted you to co-captain with me for the rest of the year."

"Me?" The shock reads loud and clear in my voice.

"Yep." He pulls his right arm across his chest, stretching it out. "I've had a lot less time lately and could use the help. You've got a good rapport with the guys, Cassidy aside. You put in the work. You're consistent. You stay after practice to take shots with O'Hern and some of the other first years. They like you." He lowers his arm, shaking it out. "It's good for the guys to have someone they're comfortable with."

"Comfortable?" I laugh a little. "You sure about that?"

"I am." He stretches his other arm. "I think it'll be a good move for the whole team. And you and I work well together. We're usually straight with each other, and I appreciate that."

"Yeah, me too." I puff my cheeks, thinking about it. "But I don't know, man. Captaining requires the guys to listen to me, and—"

"They do."

I itch at my scruff. "Feels sudden."

"I guess it is." He looks across at me. "I've been debating about a lot lately. And there's something else that's been on my mind. I need to take a bit of time to deal with it."

I frown, thinking about all that extra time Vain's been on his phone lately. "You want to talk about it?"

He shakes his head. "Nah, bro. Not yet."

"Alright."

"But the problem is," he continues, back on topic, "you can't exactly co-captain if you're punching guys at practice."

"I can see where that would be an issue."

He drops his arm stretch and slaps me on the shoulder. "We can figure out this stuff with Cassidy. Smooth things over somehow, but I've got to ask you a question first. Do you *want* to captain? It's cool if the answer is no. Zero expectations. All good either way."

"I don't know." I'm just a D-man. I'm not Vain. Not the guy everyone looks to.

But I've always liked the comradery, the support, the team. The fuckin' *Wolfpack*. It was never something I had growing up, even though I've played hockey since forever.

There is nothing like the kind of brotherhood that comes along with this team.

"Think about it," Vain says. "We're supposed to head over to talk to Coach about it after this, but I can give you a couple of days if—"

"I'm in." It feels right. Like a step forward.

"Hells yeah, Burk." He tosses me a smile. "This is good. Just don't punch anyone else for a little while."

"I'll try." I huff out a laugh then scrub at the back of my neck. "Sorry if I fucked things up with Cassidy. Maybe I should apologize to him."

Do I owe him an apology? Maybe I do. If I'm being fully honest, it's hard for me to look around Shaw sometimes. He takes up so damn much of my view.

"Up to you." He shrugs. "You need to figure out how to work with the guy, but it's your own business if you want to apologize." He pauses, tilting his head. "I've got you. Whatever you decide to do."

I reach out a fist that he bumps. "Same."

"I know." He pulls up a leg to stretch his hamstring. "There's something else. You know Khalid Kazi, right?"

"Kazi? Yeah. SCU rightwing." I thumb my side, remembering getting tagged by him last time we faced off against the Devils. "Don't know him all that well, but I do know he's got a hundred-mile-an-hour slap shot that hurts like a motherfucker when it hits between the pads."

Of all the SCU players, Kazi's pretty much the only one I can stand. Most of them are cocky as shit. Not cocky in the way that Vain is—which is more overly self-assured while still being able to laugh at himself—but cocky in the way that they feel like they have a right to treat anyone however the fuck they want, without any care or respect.

Like my father.

Kazi's not like that though. He's a good guy. He just plays for a shitty team.

He's friends with Dare too. They went to high school together or something.

Vain nods. "He got kicked off SCU."

"Seriously?" I blink at him. "What for?"

Vain leans his ass back against the picnic table. "It's all rumor right now, but it looks like he was hooking up with someone else on the Blue Devils' roster." He crosses his arms over his chest. "Someone else on the starting lineup. No one knows who the other guy is, but shit hit the fan and the coaching staff kicked him."

I'm staring across at him, taking a long minute to digest what he's saying. "They kicked him off the team for hooking up with a teammate?"

"They did. And it's sparked some kind of pushback. I don't know what's going on, but it's fucked up."

I stiffen. "Not a suspension. Just . . . gone?"

Vain's lips press. "Apparently."

I struggle to wrap my head around that.

Kazi isn't the kind of guy who went to college and then decided to try out some hockey. He's in it for the NHL. He no doubt went to SCU because he thought it would be his path to get there.

And now that's gone?

For hooking up with a teammate.

Jesus.

I itch at the scruff on my jaw, sorting through what Vain said. "Was Kazi kicked off because he was hooking up with a teammate? Or because he was hooking up with a guy?"

Vain stares across at me steadily. "I don't know."

I shake my head, a rock growing in my stomach. I'm well aware there are intolerant assholes in the world. I grew up in a family of them. I've encountered them in hockey before. And you never know who is going to be a dick.

Coach could be, and we don't know it yet.

Vain kicks a toe into the dirt. "But we've all heard shit

about SCU. If I had to guess, I'd say that Kazi's sexuality was a factor."

My stomach churns. "Do you think that could happen on the Wolfpack?"

Vain shakes his head. "We wouldn't let something like that happen."

"Are you sure?" My frown deepens. "I mean, yeah, I've heard the SCU coaches are assholes, but Coach can be pretty rough too. And it's not like we get to decide these things."

"We're *not* them." Vain's forehead lines as he looks across at me, and shit . . . my brain's going a thousand miles an hour. He sounds pretty confident, but does he really know? As far as I know, there's never been an out player at IFU. We're playing into the dark here.

"Hope so," I mutter.

Vain pushes off the table. "Maybe we need to make it more clear to all the guys that we're not SCU. Say something in the group chat."

I nod. "That would be good."

But somehow that doesn't feel like enough.

Vain rolls his shoulders, glancing down the path toward home.

I think about saying somethin' else, but the words get stuck. I still haven't fuckin' said them yet. And besides, I'm thinking that when I do, it's someone else I want to say it to first.

"We can't be like that, Burk," he says. "Hockey house—the five of us—we'd never go down without a fight if something like what happened to Kazi happened on the Wolfpack."

I'm not sure what else to say. I just hope like hell he's right.

———

Shaw's still asleep when I get back, stretched out on his stomach and hugging the pillow underneath him without a shred of clothing on. My eyes track across the smooth spread of his shoulders, down the small ridges of his spine to the arc of his ass, and I stand there for a hushed moment, *looking* at him. My throat closes halfway.

Fuck*me*, he's gorgeous.

I scrub a hand through my hair. I can't believe he's naked in my bed.

I want to talk to him about this Kazi stuff at SCU. I assume he hasn't heard yet, or else he would have said something. But he's sleeping so damn soundly that I don't want to wake him.

I steal my clothes out of the dresser and then pick up Shaw's—folding his shorts over the back of my desk chair and setting his ballcap on top. His phone's on the bedside table, and I know we've got the same hookup, so I snag my charger out of the drawer and plug it in.

Fuck, I want to stay. But we both have shit to do. So I take one last look before padding quietly out of the room.

———

Coach seems genuinely happy to have me on board as co-captain, but he doesn't say anything about SCU, and that unsettles me. I guess he's waiting to talk to the whole team, but there's still a big-ass rock in my stomach when I cross onto campus an hour later, thinking about it as I pass under the dome of the old stone clock tower. I upnod to a couple of the rookie guys as I nab a seat outside where I have my Econ lecture.

My phone vibrates, and I dig it out of my back pocket. It's the team group chat. Vain dropped a message about inclusivity, and I read over it, then give it a thumbs up emoji. A lot of the other guys do too, and that makes my shoulders relax, but it still doesn't feel like enough.

I'm frowning down at my phone when a notification for Instagram comes up.

Shaw.

My heart jumps as I pull it up to see a post from him. It's a picture of him lying on the pillow—*my* pillow—the camera cutting so it's mostly just his face, and he's wearing that sexy smirk—playful and relaxed and exactly like the one he gave me last night. The one that answers every fuckin' question I've ever asked.

I scrub a hand over my mouth, staring at those flirty greenish-brown eyes of his. It's absolutely #FacePorn, and my pulse jumps. I don't want to stop looking at him. And it does something to me that I don't expect. In only a few beats, it washes away all the other concerns in my head.

I don't know how he does that. I just . . . smile. I'm sittin' all by myself and grinning down at my phone.

It's a public post, captioned only "Morning", and comments are loading in already.

But fuck if it feels like his post is just for me. Like it's reaching across the distance between us, stretching out to me. I slide my thumb over my screen, like I can touch him. But of course I can't, so I scroll to the bottom of the comments.

I want to say that even though I saw him an hour ago, I already miss him. That I can't wait to see him on the ice later today, doing what we do best.

I can't say any of that.

I have to say something though. So I click on the little comment box, and I type, *Morning* and send it. Then I feel lame about it.

Especially since most of the other comments are strings of hearts or fire emojis, with the occasional *Handsome* or *Woof* or *Sexy AF* or *On my knees*.

They're all true.

I blow out a long breath.

They're all true. And it makes it even harder to wrap my head around the fact that he's in my bed. That I get to see him every single day. That I get to practice with him, laugh with him over a burrito, just have him in my fuckin' orbit. That he bothers to take a second look at me.

A heart appears on my reply.

He didn't heart anyone else's comment, but he hearted mine.

And for a guy who doesn't smile much at all, I can't seem to stop lately.

CHAPTER TWELVE

Burk

The week flies by. It's an all-out race to keep up with practices, our weekly workout requirements, classes, and a Thursday night game where we trounce WU. Not to mention that Vain and I have been working on a few offensive plays after practice. So when Shaw and I drop in bed at night, we're mostly so exhausted that we go for some three-minute blow jobs, and then I draw him against me, and we sleep like the dead. In the morning he pads out, heading back down to his room to get his shower stuff and clean clothes.

I hate that I can't mention the co-captaining to him until Vain clears it. I don't like keeping things from him.

We also don't talk about Kazi. And I guess we probably should. I know he's heard about it, but if I bring it up, we'll have to talk about if we should be doing what we're doing. And I'm not ready for that conversation.

Mostly because I don't want to risk anything changing. I can't keep a lid on how much I love every single second. His whip-quick smile as soon as he wakes up. Or the way his eyes pin on mine through his goalie mask. The playful towel snap he gives my ass in the locker room.

It's all so damn perfect.

I'm even smiling to myself as I step into practice on Friday, knowing that I'll get a few hours with him tonight— no late workout, no classes or game tomorrow since we played on Thursday. Hopefully, we'll have a hell of a lot longer than three minutes.

"Hiya there, *coaie*." Shaw grabs his gloves from the bench in front of his locker, gives me a wink, then passes so close that his leg pads brush against the outside of my thigh.

He's already decked out in all his pads with his goalie mask propped on top of his head. I don't know how he can be so fuckin' sexy with all those pads covering him, but an eager heat is already fisting in my stomach, making me think of how he looks when his hand grips our cocks, his muscles all taut as he whispers dirty words while he strokes us.

Fuck*me*.

I pull on my pants and tie my pads. I can't wait to get out there with him.

It's the third practice that Coach has had me on offense. There were a few hiccups as I adjusted to the new position, but now I'm on the fuckin' ball. In part because every time I look over at Shaw, I get this shot of electricity zapping me. It's not just attraction—it's something else. Bigger.

He fuckin' believes in me. And that's chasing away some of the other voices in my head.

Vain bumps my shoulder halfway through practice. "You're killing it, bro."

Even Coach comes over the boards to clap me on the shoulder. "Good job, Burkehammer. Solid practice."

"Thanks, Coach." I head toward the locker room, but then I notice Cassidy and O'Hern staying after to work on some drills. I need to talk to Cassidy. I've given us both a few practices to cool off, but now it feels like we need to deal with shit.

I take a breath and skate over to him.

"Hey, man." I nod at Cassidy. "Can I talk with you for a minute?"

He skates toward me and comes to a slow, measured stop. We're over by the blue line, and I'm aware there are eyes on us. Coach and Vain have paused their conversation. Shaw's watching as I glance back at his net.

He nods, and I turn my focus to Cassidy.

I've debated what to say to him. But standing across from him now, I'm reminded how *young* he is. He's just starting at IFU and along comes this fuckin' senior knocking him on his ass.

I don't want to be the kind of man who can't admit that he crossed a line. I don't want to be my father.

So I straighten up and do what needs to be done.

"I'm sorry," I say. "I should have addressed you with my words instead of my fists."

Cassidy studies me warily as he slips his mouthguard out. "I wasn't surprised. I know that you and Shaw . . ." He shrugs a padded shoulder. "That you're friends."

I frown at him. Should I be reading something into that shrug? I'm not sure. "I'm glad you're on the team, Cassidy."

He blows out a disbelieving laugh.

"I'm serious," I say. Maybe he messed up with that hit on Shaw, but he did it because he's eager to prove himself. That counts for something. Most of this game isn't physical—it's mental. "You've got a lot of fuckin' heart."

He blinks at me. "Thanks. I, er . . . Thanks."

"Don't thank me." I turn toward the locker room. "You're the one putting in the hard work."

———

"Give me a ride, Burk?" Leslie asks fifteen minutes later as he passes behind me, dragging a towel over his damp hair.

"Vain's got something to do with a new mural for our big white wall."

I'm packing the last of my duffle, trying my damnedest not to stare past Les to where Shaw's pulling on a Wolfpack tee. He snaps his pink ballcap on his head, glances over his shoulder at me, and then winks.

And, fuck, it's like I can't breathe. Like I'm shoved up against the boards. Completely flattened. No thought except for whatever just rammed into me.

He pivots on his heel and thumbs at his nipple as he takes in my reaction, his toes curling in his pink slides.

"Burk?" Leslie tosses his towel in the laundry bin and fishes some jeans out of his bag. "You in there?"

"Uh, yeah. A ride." I school my features and tear my eyes off Shaw. "Of course."

Leslie pulls his jeans on and zips them with quick fingers. "And I hear you'll be helping Vain out too. That's cool."

Shaw hauls his duffle over his shoulder and steps closer to us. "With what?"

I grab all my gear, and we head toward the hallway.

"Vain asked if I wanted to co-captain with him," I say quietly. I'm not sure when the announcement will be, but if Vain told Leslie, then I'm sure I'm good to tell Shaw. Finally.

Shaw stops. Right in the middle of the locker room. "Burkie, that's *awesome*."

A grin whips across his face that's all lightness. Just this kind of sudden unreserved *joy*. This big-ass smile that makes his eyes crinkle, and I feel so fuckin' good. Kinda proud. Happy for myself, I guess.

It's a new feeling.

"Hell, *coaie*." Shaw swings his duffle so it bumps into mine. "We gotta celebrate."

Leslie jogs to catch up with us. "Pretty sure that's already the plan at Alpha Kappa tonight."

Fuck. I'd forgotten. Why was I thinking it would just be Shaw and me for a few hours?

"Yep." Shaw grins at me. "Ready to get down and dirty?"

My teeth graze my bottom lip. "Sure you want that?"

"Hmm . . ." His eyes flick down as we stroll toward the front doors. "My ass is up for anything."

Jesus. I clear my throat, at a complete loss for words.

"Les and I agreed to help with some of the set up," Shaw continues. "You wanna go, Burkie? The Kappas want sparkly, crêpe paper covered tables and streamers and stuff. Dangly gold stars and shit."

"Uh. Think I'll pass on sparkles and streamers."

"But you're going, right?" Shaw asks, brows rising. So much *hope* lingers in his voice.

"Yeah, sure," I say before I can stop myself.

I have no fuckin' clue how I'm going to handle this party tonight. But I've done it before. And what else am I going to do? Ask him to only be with me after a couple of blow jobs?

Leslie slaps me on the shoulder. "You can always count on Burk."

"Hope so," I mumble. I pause, glancing down at Shaw's feet.

"Your shoe's untied." I nod towards the shoelace dragging alongside him.

He just laughs and steps out the side doors. "Think I'll survive."

My truck's parked at the end of a row. We toss our gear in the bed, and Leslie slides into the backseat as soon as I unlock it. Shaw gets in the front, and I have this little pause before I turn over the ignition.

"Do you always sit in the back?" I ask Leslie as I reverse out of the parking spot.

He laughs and pulls out a baggie of grapes. "Nah. But Shaw always sits in front."

"He does?" I blink at Shaw, who flips his hat around and

settles into the seat, his legs spreading, his eyes lighting under the brim of his hat as I look across at him.

"Yep." Leslie tosses a grape into his mouth, sliding it over to poof out his cheek. "Not always with Vain. But with you, he does."

"I hadn't noticed." I frown as I pull out onto Fifth Street.

Shaw grins at me, looking completely unfazed.

"Oh, come on, man." Leslie scoffs at me through the rearview mirror. "You and Shaw have a thousand rituals. Who will start the laundry when we get home?"

"Shaw." I palm the top of the steering wheel, staring out at traffic backed up at a stop sign.

Leslie chews and swallows his grape. "And who will hang up the skates and pads?"

"Me." I flip on a turn signal and make a left. The arena's not far from home, but our gear's heavy, so it's easier to drive.

"Yep," Leslie says as I pull in front of the house, glad to find a parking spot for once. "And then you'll reorganize your duffle because Shaw never does it in the exact way you want. And then afterward, you'll remind him to put shit in the dryer. And then you'll ask if he's hungry, and he'll waggle his brows and say 'for what?' And it's like you two never realize you're having the same conversation every single time." He shakes his head, chewing again. "Fucking old married couple."

He crinkles up the baggie as he gets out and then grabs his shit from the bed before he hops up the steps to the house.

I turn to Shaw. "Are we an old married couple?"

"Would it really be that bad?" Shaw winks at me before he slips out, grabs his gear, and follows Leslie, yelling something after him.

I don't move.

They head inside, leaving the door open since I'm usually just behind.

143

But *fuck*. I'm stuck in my seat, thoughts multiplying like dandelions.

Did Shaw mean what he just said?

I get this image in the quietest, most honest, most hidden corner of my mind. Of Shaw and me. Five years from now.

Ten.

Twenty?

A shiver stretches across my shoulders. I could want that if I let myself. If I'm being honest, if I'm listening to those thoughts in the deepest recesses of my brain, I could want five years, ten years, twenty years.

I could want . . . more. I could want to reach across when he's in the passenger seat, his wrist propped on his side of the console, and take his hand. I could want to take him on a date, somewhere that would surprise him and make him smile. I could want to tell people about us. To come out. Even knowing that it could be hard to be out in the NHL. I could risk that.

I could want to know that he's going to show up at my door every night. Except, what if it's not *my* door?

What if it's *ours*? Even right now, it doesn't feel like my room. I don't want it to be. I'd buy him a dresser and help him move his stuff in. Not even a question.

Would he ever consider that?

My chest tightens as I finally slide out of the seat. I grab my duffle out of the back before locking the truck and heading up the stairs. I'm moving a hell of a lot slower than normal because I can't stop thinking.

Even though I'm pretty sure I know the answer.

He's *Shaw*. He hooks up; he has fun. He feels so free. Like he could do anything. I've wanted to feel like that my entire fuckin' life, and the only time I ever do is when I'm with him.

When I step in the front door, Shaw's standing over his duffle, but his attention is fixed on his phone. His fingers scroll quickly, and he's ramrod straight.

"Hey, you good?" I ask.

The brim of his hat blocks my view of his expression. "My mom texted about my brother." He shoves his phone in his pocket and goes back to digging around in his bag.

"Everything alright?"

Bumps and thumps come from the basement, probably Dare making a loud entrance after practice. Leslie heads toward the kitchen.

"Shaw?" I ask, stepping closer.

He glances up. "Just an upcoming surgery. It was planned, nothing unexpected. Just replacement of his stent. Hopefully the last time, but it depends how much he grows."

"Are you worried?"

"No more than usual." He nods at my duffle. "Give me your stinky stuff. I need to get it in the washer. You know, old married couple ritual." He tosses me a smile that doesn't reach his eyes.

I want to press him with another question, but what he asked me for was really fuckin' clear, so I set down my duffle and zip it open. I gather what he needs and hand it out to him. He takes it, his fingertips brushing against mine.

I swallow hard, still struggling through all the things I want to say to him. Want to ask him.

"Thanks." The green in his eyes is muted, all the color and life in him dulled.

"Anything," I say. And I fuckin' mean that.

He nods then turns and heads to the basement.

I stare after him, a growing knot of worry fisting in my thoughts.

CHAPTER THIRTEEN

Burk

Unsurprisingly, I'm still thinking about Shaw a few hours later when Dare leans against my door frame and kicks one boot over the other.

"You heading over to Alpha Kappa anytime soon?" He tilts his head against the frame, dark red hair falling to cover one eye.

"Uh, yeah." I'm crouched down, reorganizing all the shit in my nightstand drawer. Earlier when I tugged it open—when Shaw was flat on top of me this morning—I'd rifled through it to find the lube and messed everything up. I didn't have time to fix it before, but it's been in the back of my mind all day.

This kind of stuff can get to me sometimes. When I was younger, it was about the only thing I felt like I had control over.

Dare pushes off the doorframe and takes a couple of steps into my room, his thick boots surprisingly soft on the carpet. "It's almost ten."

I still, my hand above the drawer. "No shit?"

He reaches out a hand, two fingernails painted dark green, and taps the edge of the drawer. "Good quality lube, dude. Nice."

I laugh. "Thanks."

"Don't mention it." He kicks one toe against the floor. A couple of Sharpie designs are drawn on his jeans above his left knee, his asymmetrical leather coat hanging open. Honestly, Dare drives my brain a bit crazy. I love the dude, but the way he's always off-center throws me.

He eyes the drawer. "How long have you been organizing this?"

"About an hour, I guess." Has it been that long? I frown, looking down and trying to see it from his perspective. Everything is neatly tucked away. Lined up carefully, no dust or trash, and yet I'm still messing with it. I'd been mostly lost in my head—about SCU. And about Shaw and what's bothering him.

Shaw stopped by a few hours ago to say he was leaving. He *seemed* good. He'd talked to his mom, and everything was cool with his brother. But I just kept getting this idea that something was still off. Like I should have said something else to him.

I re-tuck a pack of tissues into the corner of the drawer, even though they were already straight, then look up to find Dare still eyeing me.

"Do you need some help with this?" He crouches down next to me. "I don't mind."

"Nah, man. I'm just . . ." I take a breath and sort through my head. "Thinking about stuff."

He nods, still watching me.

I slide the drawer closed. "But thanks."

"No problem." He stands up and backsteps away.

"Ready to walk over?" I stand too, then pass by him to grab a coat from the closet.

"For sure." Dare follows me down the stairs and out into

the quiet street. It's normally not so empty on this part of campus, but the whole sorority row is having parties tonight, so most everywhere else is dead.

A few snowflakes swirl in the streetlights overhead as we walk, but it's too warm for them to reach the ground, and they melt on my eyelashes and nose almost as soon as they touch.

"Have you talked to Kazi at all?" I zip up my coat.

"Yep." Dare jams his hands in his pockets. "We talked for a while."

He doesn't elaborate, so I decide not to press him.

I frown as we trudge ahead. "Have you noticed that Coach hasn't said anything?"

"Yep, I noticed that too."

I nod. "It feels like something needs to be said."

He snorts. "Then maybe we need to be the ones to say it."

"You and me?"

"All of us," he says. "Maybe hockey house needs to be louder."

"Be louder," I repeat. We turn onto the block where the Alpha Kappa house is located.

"I told Kazi he should come to IFU," Dare says. "But I don't think he's got a lot of trust for anywhere right now. Although he said he might show up tonight—have a drink with us. But he's pissed. And he should be. He could sue those SCU motherfuckers."

"He should." I scrub a hand over the back of my neck, my stomach tightening. "I can't even imagine. To work so hard for something and it's gone."

"Right?" He shakes his head. "And you know all this shit is about him being bi. If he was hooking up with some cute blonde female team manager, he'd have gotten a slap on the ass and a high-fucking-five."

My forehead lines as I track the cracks along the sidewalk passing under our feet. He's absolutely right. In fact . . .

148

"Jamison Graves had a thing with a female team manager last year, right?"

I remember because it got ugly at one of the games.

Dare grunts. "I think so. It's all complete shit. Which is what Shaw said too."

I frown. "You talked to Shaw about it?"

"Yeah, he was there earlier when Vain and I had a conversation."

"What'd he say?"

"He was quiet." He shrugs a shoulder. "But Shaw's not one to grab a picket sign and get on the front line. He mostly just wants everyone to get along. If the world were ending, he'd be the one making us laugh at the afterparty."

"He would." A knot builds in my chest as the white Alpha Kappa house comes into view, glowing in the moonlight. As excited as I am to see Shaw—because I'm always excited—I'm really fuckin' uneasy too.

Dare stops by the front steps to talk with some guys from the baseball team, chatting about our record this season, contemplating their upcoming one. They all talk, but I'm hardly saying anything. I've still got way too much bouncing around in my head.

My thoughts go to shit when we step into the house a few minutes later.

I see him immediately.

Shaw's in the back rec room area, which is all decorated up, playing beer pong with some Kappas and telling a story that requires him to swing his hands in a pull-up motion. Gold stars glint above his head as the girls around him laugh at his story—*genuinely* laugh. Not that flirtatious, restrained laugh, but real, eye-watering laughs. He's laughing too. All evidence of what was bothering him earlier today has completely vanished.

That's good. Really good.

He's also wearing a tight-as-shit, baby blue Alpha Kappa

t-shirt—so small it fits like a crop shirt and shows off a few inches of skin above his athletic pants, including his abs and tight navel. And *fuck*me.

I scrape my teeth over my bottom lip, trying not to stare at how the shirt pinches under his arms and against the firm lines of his delts as he reaches up and flips his hat backward before he bends over to concentrate on a beer pong shot. I'm sure he got the shirt from one of the Kappas. He was wearing a Blackhawks t-shirt earlier when he stopped by my room.

So I guess he left it somewhere?

I itch at the back of my neck, hating that the question of where he left his shirt bothers me so much.

Should I go over there? I really fuckin' want to.

"Hey, Burk." Vain slaps me on the shoulder. "Beer?"

"Uh, sure." I scrub a hand through my hair as I force myself to follow Vain to the downstairs bar and then out to the back porch. It's probably for the best. Let Shaw do his own thing.

Vain fist bumps some guys as we step outside, and I pivot toward them, trying to get out of my fuckin' head. So Shaw's wearing one of the girls' shirts. That doesn't mean anything. Am I going to over-question everything? Because if so, then it's going to be a long night.

"Hey, man," Vain's saying behind me. "Good to see you here."

"Yeah, thanks."

I turn just as Jae Jin upnods me. He's a cool guy, lots of solar system tattoos, thick, black hair that always seems to have a mind of its own. He's been tutoring Vain in a bunch of his classes this semester. I don't know him all that well, but I glance around for the guy who is usually with him that I know a hell of a lot better.

"Sup, Dex." I hold out a hand, which Dex takes, tossing me a dimpled grin. Dex and Jae Jin are pretty much always together at these parties. We call them the twins because, well . . . I have no idea. They look nothing alike.

But Dex and I were in a few study groups together freshman year, and we always have a lot to talk about.

"We were at that last game," Dex says, leaning back against the railing. "That goal you got against WU was *intense.* I was hoarse the next day from screaming so loud."

I tip my cup and take a small drink. "I felt it the next day too. WU is brutal with the board checks."

We fall into easy conversation. Dex brightens as we chat about his student-teaching this semester. And, honestly, it feels good to be talking about something other than hockey.

Not that I don't love hockey, but sometimes it feels like that's all I breathe, sleep, and eat. And it's worse now that thoughts about SCU are in my head. So I listen contentedly as Dex tells me about this fundraiser he's been planning.

"I was hoping maybe some of the team could go?" he asks. "Kinda worried no one will show. But I know if the hockey house goes, then a few others will follow."

"Fuck, yeah." I nod. "Of course we'll go."

It's important to all of us that we support other stuff around campus. We're all in it together at IFU.

"Thanks, man. Appreciate it." Dex takes a sip from his cup. "Feels weird to ask but . . ."

"Not weird at all," I say. "What exactly is it for?"

"Art supplies for the kids I'm student-teaching for."

"Nice." I frown slightly. "So you put the whole fundraiser together?"

"Mostly me and London." Dex nudges his elbow toward Jae Jin. "And J here too, when he shows."

"London?" Vain's low question catches me, digging into our conversation from out of nowhere. "Is he here?" There's an edge to his voice—one that I don't hear from him often.

Dex's eyes move from Vain to me and then over to Jae Jin

before coming back. "Ah, no. Said he was doing something with his roommate."

I glance around. "Who's London?"

Vain shakes his head, itching at his chest.

"Um." Dex straightens. "He's a friend of ours. Cool guy. He's in the art program. You've probably seen him around with us before."

"Probably," I say, although it doesn't ring a bell.

We're all looking at Vain like we expect him to say something else, but he takes a drink from his beer and then stares down at it.

"So, um, yeah," Jae Jin says, breaking the awkward moment. "Dex is the one who's running everything. The man with the plan. And the huge-ass to-do binder."

"And you just decided to do it?" I ask Dex. "Saw a need and then came up with a plan?"

"Well, I had help," Dex hedges.

"But you decided," I press on. Even I can hear the low urgency in my voice. I mean, the situation is completely different. But if a guy like Dex can just decide that something needs to be done and do it—why can't I?

"Yeah, he did," Jae Jin says. "Which is pretty incredible, if you ask me."

I glance over at Vain, but he's sweltering in his thoughts still. I don't fully know what I'm thinking, but Dare's words keep ringing in my head.

Maybe we need to be louder.

"It's nothing," Dex says with a dismissive shake of his head.

"No," I say. "It's something."

I take a drink, then look back toward the house. Shaw's over by a homemade horseshoe pit. He must have just thrown a horseshoe because he's walking half-backward toward the far pit, chatting with Leslie, when he stumbles over a clump of grass.

I shift my weight to my toes, the urge to dart across to him pounding through me fast as wildfire, but Shaw catches himself with a hand on a girl standing along the edge of the court. He turns and says something, quick and easy, and she laughs, pivoting toward him and away from her friends.

Two seconds later, he's shaking her hand and then waving Les over into the conversation.

Ten seconds later and she's smiling coyly up at him.

And, *fuck*.

It's just a conversation. A backward stumble into someone he didn't know.

I need to ignore it. Just let Shaw be Shaw. Like Dare said, he'd be making us laugh at the world-ending afterparty, and he does that with *everyone*. It's part of what I admire about him.

But even so, it's hard to rip my eyes away. Harder to remember what I was saying to Dex.

I take a long swig of beer and try to get back into the conversation. Vain is acting normally now, chatting like nothing happened.

I try to pick up what they're saying, but who the fuck am I kidding? I glower over my shoulder again.

The girl is tipped in toward Shaw. Her fingers brush against his forearm as he says something.

"Fuck," I grumble to myself. That was fast.

But I've seen him do it before. Shaw has this ridiculous kind of magic, and clearly, I'm not the only one who it works on. Leslie teases him about it sometimes, how Shaw can go from meeting a girl to full-on hookup in less than five minutes.

And I *get* it. It's not just how gorgeous he is with those greenish eyes and that effortless smile. It's the way he moves, the way he draws you in, the lightness in his voice. The interest he takes in you. Just the easy, effortless way that he's *Shaw*.

He nods at whatever she's saying, then tips his drink and empties it, the brim of his hat brushing between his shoulder blades. His forearm flexes as he crushes the empty cup.

I try to turn back to the conversation, but I can't.

I keep watching him.

And . . . fuck. I can't watch this.

I need to go. I don't know if I'm strong enough to handle this.

I can't watch it happen.

I lean back from Dex. "I'm need to—"

I don't even finish. I just step around him, nod at Jae Jin and Vain, and take the far steps down the porch, out toward the side of the yard. I toss my half-drunk beer in a trash can and turn down the strip of grass between houses. A small picket fence runs the length of the house, and I trudge to a stop at the gate.

The faint beat of music echoes—bass only from out here. A car door slams out on the street, and a couple of guys laugh as they walk down the sidewalk. One shouts something, but they don't see me in the dark.

I should flip up the gate latch and go.

But I *miss* Shaw.

That's the biggest, most ridiculous mind fuck of all. It would tear my guts out to watch him go off with someone else. But as soon as he's out of my sight, I *miss* him. How am I supposed to deal with that?

I have zero illusions. Shaw is who he is, and he has never once pretended to be someone else around me. I wouldn't want him to.

But watching him—*knowing* what he's doing, *seeing* it—it's going to rip me to shreds one motherfuckin' hookup at a time. And then what? Afterward, is he going to come up to my room?

And if he does, will I let him in?

I groan.

Of *course* I will.

There's not even a question. I'll welcome him into my room. Into my bed.

I won't turn him away.

A chalky taste fills my mouth as I stare blindly out at the street.

I need to find a way—for both of us, for my own fuckin' sanity—to deal with it.

What if . . . I did the same?

I swallow hard. I could head over to that anything-goes bar on Clement. Taverns, I think it's called, and . . . I have no idea. But I can go, and whatever happens can happen.

Even if it's just to get my mind off that pink backward ballcap and the way he *smiles* at me. All humor and hockey and sex wrapped up in the half quirk of his lips and the soft click of his tongue.

Fuck.

No.

I can't go be with someone else.

I don't *want* to. There's not a single shred of desire in me. Not when it comes to anyone else.

I stand there on the grass, shrouded in the dark, the only light coming from the basement window wells and a fat-ass moon that makes everything a murky silver. The snow's mostly stopped, but it's still cold enough to see my breath.

The thought of being with someone else, it gnaws a raw spot in my stomach.

I'm so fuckin' *fucked*.

I glare down at the gate latch. I need to go. Maybe somewhere I can have a few shots and try to forget what's happening back here. Just . . . do something.

I flip the latch, about to step out, when a voice stops me cold.

"Where are you going?"

CHAPTER FOURTEEN

Burk

I don't have to turn around to know who's behind me. I'd know his voice anywhere. I'd know it in my sleep, a thousand miles under water. I'd know it twenty years from now, even if I never saw him again after this moment.

I pivot to find Shaw standing there, sexy as ever in his ridiculously tight baby blue Kappa shirt, hands in his pockets and shoulders hitched up like he's cold.

My stomach twists into a thousand shards.

I want to step forward and grab him. I want to warm him up. Want to fit him against me.

And I want to turn the fuck away so that I won't have to feel the pain of what's going to happen when he decides that he'd rather have someone else.

I'm so fuckin' torn.

But I tuck it all away, strapped down in a tight little box he can't see, because I *need* to if I have any hope of keeping our friendship.

"I figured I should go," I say and force a shrug that he can probably see straight through. That's the other problem

—he knows me too fuckin' well. "Let you have a good time."

His shoulders hunch closer to his ears. "And what part of that means you have to leave?"

"Honestly . . ." I press my lips. What am I going to say here? "I'm not really feeling it, and it seems like you're getting along pretty well. I'll catch up with you later."

He puffs out a cloud of white breath. "Are you going home?"

"I guess. Or . . ." I shake my head. I can't lie to him. "Maybe a bar."

His lips quirk. "Maybe I'll tag along."

I stare at him. Completely confused.

"Unless you don't want me along?" His smile fades.

"I always want you," I say quietly then drag a hand over my mouth. Was that too honest? "But that girl, she seems pretty into you."

Fuck, I sound jealous.

Probably because I am jealous. I'm a hulking, green ball of jealousy.

He frowns slightly. "She was."

Fuck.

I can't hear this.

I try to harden myself. Try to push away the hurt. "I, uh, would have thought you'd want to—"

"I don't." He bounces on his toes, shivering. "I'm kinda drunk, actually. A lot of shit today, and it caught up with me."

"Fuck. I'm sorry." I step closer to him. "Are you thinking about your brother?"

His jaw tightens. "It's messed up because I've been trying to swing a flight home, but then I got some news about my scholarships for next year, and I've got no clue what I should do."

I frown. "What does that mean about your scholarships?"

"Not fully sure yet." He shivers harder, and I start to take off my coat for him, but he shakes his head. "Maybe I'm done at IFU after this year? My advisor gave me a bunch of other options, but I apparently had like eight tequila shots instead of dealing with reality."

Fuck, my heart squeezes. "We'll figure it out."

He needs to be here next year. It'll be his senior year as starting goalie—there's no question he'd be scouted. And his brother. If he needs to go home, then I need to help him get there.

"There's got to be other ways," I say. "We'll sit down and—"

"I was pretending," he says.

I blink. "Pretending?"

"Tonight, I mean." His biceps tighten under that tiny shirt. "I was putting on a fucking Shaw-show. Then I saw you on the porch and . . ."

"You saw me?"

"You were talking with Dex, and I know he—" He shakes his head. "Don't know what I'm saying. Not saying that."

"Alright," I say, trying to follow along. He takes a step closer, and I get a drift of lemongrass shampoo. A bit of beer and sharp liquor and sweat too, but somehow that only makes me want to grab him more. "What are you saying?"

"I guess . . ." He wobbles back, and I reach out a hand to catch him. "I just want to go somewhere where shit's okay. Where I don't have to pretend to be anything. And that's kinda turning out to be your bed. But if that's not where you're headed, then I'll go where you are." His green eyes come up to meet mine. "Because I don't think it's actually about the bed."

All the air between us evaporates. My mouth opens, but nothing comes out.

The only thing moving is my pulse, beating in my throat, and the tips of my hair as they pick up in the cold breeze.

Shaw is too much to hope for. If I let myself—truly let

myself—then there's no going back. There's no U-turn on this road. It's right off the fuckin' cliff.

Can I do that? Just drive off knowing there's nothing to catch me?

I think I already have.

He tilts his chin up to look at the sky, his tee hugging his pecs and rising two inches above his navel. His hands are sunk in his pockets, his shoulders still hunched. He's tall and hockey-built. He's heat and sex. But more than that, he's energy and brightness and everything that makes the world better.

He's *Shaw*.

And he stumbles as he takes another step forward. "I don't care where we go. Even if we just stand here, on the side of this house, shivering in the dark."

"You're cold." I step close enough to set my hand on his arm. He tips forward, and we shift together, like on the ice, an invisible give and take. One that only we can feel, that only we understand.

His eyes drop to my lips, and then he's suddenly there, his mouth on mine. His hand tears out of his pocket to seize the nape of my neck, and he yanks me to him.

I should stop us. He's been drinking, and we're standing on the side of a house where anyone could walk by. But I just . . . don't.

I *kiss* him. Like my life depends on it. Like I've wanted to for so much longer than I've even realized. Not just since that first morning he came to my room.

But before that. Every time he glanced over at me from the passenger seat of my truck. Every time he flipped his chair around in the café. Every time he clicked his tongue or made me laugh. Every time I looked away.

I don't know exactly when it started, but it's been a long time now.

I plant my feet to hold his weight, one hand grasping his

arm to hold him steadier, the other smoothing down to palm his tight ass. A moan resonates on his tongue, and fuck, I could bury myself in him. Shove him against the side of this house, kick his legs apart, and—

We're in public.

I rip my lips away from his. "Fuck."

I inhale a breath that's supposed to calm me, but all I smell is *him,* and it makes me want him more.

But if there's one thing that I know, it's that I'll always look out for Shaw. And with everything around what happened with Kazi . . . there's no fuckin' way we should be kissing out here.

"Want you," he says, leaning in to nip at my jaw. "Bury your cock in me. Don't care where."

"Fuck," I mumble again. "No." My forehead falls against his shoulder, and then I force myself to step back, feeling like I'm tearing myself off him. I clasp just above his elbows and guide him backward. "That kiss was un-fuckin'-believable, but I'm not solid about this right now."

Those are not words I want to say.

"Okay." He lets me guide him a half step back, still shivering.

"Not here, at least." I groan and look down at the six inches I've managed to put between us, although his dick is definitely tenting into the neutral zone.

My mouth waters. My hand isn't connected to my brain.

I brush my thumb down the tent of his pants, his bulge achingly noticeable. He moans at the one small touch, and I keep stroking, sliding my palm up and down, feeling him harden, watching as his abs strain under the hem of his half shirt. The breeze chills us. Laughter and music well up from the basement.

Would we be noticed?

"*Eden.*" His hips kick forward, grinding himself into my hand. I'm two seconds from letting go. Falling onto my knees right here. Or turning him around, seeing what it would be like to lave my tongue over his ass while he grinds back on my face, his hands gripping the picket fence, his moans rolling out.

Fuck*me*.

"You're sending me mixed signals," he breathes, looking down at where I'm stroking him. "You said no, but then . . . I kinda need a firm answer here."

"Fuck, I know." He's drunk. We're in public. I step back. "Not here."

"Then can you take me home?" He reaches out and balances against my chest drunkenly before letting his fingers swipe down. He grabs my hand, threading our fingers. "Take me home, put me in your bed. Maybe let me suck a nut out of you. That's all. Or not. Shit, I don't know. We can stream a game and do whatever. I just . . ." He tips forward, trying to get closer. "I want to be around you. Wanna be in your bed. With you. Like a whole lot. Just you."

And like that, my whole heart buckles.

I *hope*.

Words that I will forever remember:

1. "I think you should trust yourself, Burkie."
2. "I kinda don't want it to stop."
3. "I'm quiet, because I wanted to."
4. "We would have been there for you in a heartbeat."
5. "I don't think it's actually about the bed."

CHAPTER FIFTEEN

Shaw

I'm stumbling.

Burkie guides us home, his hand coming up to brace my back when I trip over a sidewalk crack.

"I've got you," he says in that sexy, gruff voice of his, and I freaking melt. A drunk-ass puddle on the snow-dusted sidewalk.

I didn't mean to drink so much. I just kept throwing them back. Thinking about not getting home for Raleigh.

And shit. Next year.

IFU is my home. It's been my home for two and a half years. Right here, with Burkie. And Vain and Dare and Leslie and the whole team. It scares me thinking about Burkie not being here next year. I don't know if I can—

He stops suddenly and kneels down on the sidewalk.

I blink down at him. "Burkie?"

"Your motherfuckin' shoelace." He grabs my laces and ties them, his big fingers working quickly.

I laugh, swaying forward and balancing a hand on his shoulder. "It's not my fault."

He finishes the knot and looks up, squinting against a few lazy snowflakes. "No?"

I shake my head. "That shoelace hates me."

He stands up. "The shoelace does?"

"Yeah, I'm telling you, *coaie*. It's an asshole."

He laughs. "It's just woven nylon."

"Yeah, you'd think. But I swear that little bastard's out to get me."

I'm not lying.

He shakes his head, still laughing, and looking so damn cute with the way he's smiling.

He turns towards home, and I follow, stepping closer. Feeling him so big and solid next to me. Right there on my right. I brush the back of my hand against his. When he doesn't move away, I thread my knuckles between his like I did earlier on the side of the house. He squeezes his fingers, locking me there. We walk home, both shivering, not letting go until we step inside the empty house, the warmth swamping us and the creak of the boards under our feet louder than normal. Especially when I look over at Burkie and he swims.

Shit, I'm drunker than I thought. And my nose is freezing. It's probably bright red.

But I'm so glad he's here with me. That it's only the two of us.

He cups my shoulder. "Let's get you some water."

I reach up to pull off my hat and miss the brim completely. I laugh at myself.

He smiles then takes my hat off and tucks it brim down in his back pocket. "Follow me."

"Eden Burkehammer," I mumble as he heads toward the kitchen. "You put that cute ass in front of me, and yeah, I'm gonna follow it. Lemming style. Wherever you're going."

"Works for me." His brows hitch as he looks over his shoulder. "Feeling okay?"

"Feeling drunk and horny. And I like your ass. Wanna grab it. Wanna lick it. Snuggle my nose between your muscular butt cheeks and warm it up." My smile fades, and I sniffle from the cold. "I want to rim you." I pause. Apparently, I'm honest-drunk. "Eden. I like calling you that. Sometimes. Like getting to know you again. Still you. Just the you inside of you. Shit, I'm not making sense."

He half turns, eyes flicking around my face. He's quiet long enough that it worries me, and I reverse over everything I said. Was it the rimming part that stopped him up?

"I'm sorry." I shake my head. "I don't know what I'm saying. I don't have to rim you. I'm—"

"Shaw." His voice is deep as he pivots to face me. He snags the bottom of my t-shirt and tugs me closer. I stumble, but I grin when his hands go around me and sink down to cup my ass, keeping me steady. I expect him to haul us together, grind our dicks or something because we're clearly both eager for that, but instead he moves around behind me, his chest hard against my back. His arms wrap around my waist, his chin resting on my shoulder. His scruff rasps against my jaw.

"Call me whatever you want," he says. "And, fuck yeah, I want you to rim me."

I smile. "Hell, yeah. Right now. Don't tempt me."

He draws his nose down the slope of my neck, breathing in. "Fuckin' amazing that I can tempt you."

I whimper at the tip of his nose nuzzling in under my ear. I like that his nose is cold too. "But we're waiting until I'm a bit more sober, aren't we?"

"Probably a good idea." He guides me toward the kitchen, walking behind me, holding me firmly with those powerful arms of his. The ridge of his cock nestles between my ass cheeks like it belongs there, like it's cuddling, and half of me wants to stop, bend over, and beg him to plow me right here against the couch. My ass clenches at the thought of what his thick cock would feel like, slick with lube as it presses in.

Would I like it?

Yep, pretty sure I would. Pretty sure I'd be begging him for more.

His breath warms my ear. "Let's get some aspirin and water for you."

"Okay, but you're getting pretty friendly back there," I say as we step through the doorway into the kitchen. "You keep this up, and I might get the idea you want more. That maybe I could seduce you a little."

He huffs a laugh against my ear, his thighs pressing against the back of mine with each step. "Trust me, the thought crossed my mind."

"Yeah? How do you seduce a Burkie?"

His voice is quiet. "You be Shaw."

I'm grinning so widely my face hurts. "Shit, that's all it takes?"

"For you, yeah."

"Jeez, you're cute."

"Cute," he says. His entire body fits flush against the back of mine, warming me from behind.

I wiggle my ass a little against his cock. "I've called you cute before."

"You were teasing." There's a catch in his voice. "Flirting."

"Of course I was flirting." I lick my dry lips. "I freaking love flirting with you. But it's also the truth. I think all of you is cute. Head to toe. And all the parts between. Cute as hell."

"You don't have to say that." He reaches out to the side to grab a glass from the cabinet, then walks us around the countertop island, leaving the lights off, still flush behind me as we stop before the sink. The kitchen is dark, his breath warming my cold ear.

"I know I don't have to say that." I lean my head back against his shoulder, closing my eyes. All his strength at my back, holding me up. "You're not allowed to argue with me, *coaie*. You're hot. Can't stop thinking about you. It's been like that ever since I saw you grab your huge cock and come with your huger load. It's like a dam broke, and now things are different."

I bumble the words out. Not sure what I'm gonna say until I say it.

He swallows. "What do you mean by different?"

"I don't know. Words are muddled right now." He feels so big wrapped around me like this. He's not that much broader or taller than me, an inch or two here or there, but it feels like it really counts right now. He's just so safe and big and warm. So Burkie. "Just different. Like I want to snuggle you. But I also want to wiggle my dick all over you. Both. At the same time."

He chuckles as he reaches around me to flip on the faucet to fill the glass with water. "I could go for some snuggles and dick wiggles."

"Oh, I am so in." I drink from the glass when he brings it to my lips and then sink back on him, feeling the shift as he widens his stance to balance my weight. "Water's good."

"Want more?"

"Nah."

"Alright. Let me know." He reaches around me to set the glass on the counter, his lips brushing against the nape of my neck. I shiver. His mouth opens, more of a taste than a kiss, sending a smattering of goosebumps rising across my shoulders and down into my forearms. His hips pitch forward, his cock thickening between my ass cheeks.

I let out a groan, grinding back. The world is still spinning, but Burkie's holding onto me, in the dark, empty kitchen, and that makes everything okay.

"Let's get you some aspirin," he says.

I laugh. "Jeez. Keep getting a dude hot and ready and then dropping him."

"Only you." He pushes off from behind me and steps into the walk-in pantry. "And you're still pretty drunk."

"Yeah, I know," I grumble and follow after him.

"Don't worry." He digs around in the bin where we've got aspirin and pain relievers and a whole basket of shit for rough games and practices. "Giving you a blow job is first on the agenda when we get upstairs."

"Can I give you one too?" I ask, stepping in behind him and using the pull-string to turn on the light so he can see better. "Wanna taste you."

My hat sticks out of his back pocket. I'd forgotten he'd taken it from me. I cross to him and dip my fingers into the other pocket—the empty one—and pull his ass back a few inches.

He half twists so that his lips can reach mine, then we're kissing, open-mouthed, under the bare, overhead bulb. I'm pretty sure we'll be doing this all night. That we're not going to be able to stop. We'll be tangled up when we climb the stairs to his room and sink into his bed. We'll be balls deep in each other's mou—

A door slams. Burkie pulls back from me. I don't think. I reach out and yank the door shut.

Voices come from the other room. Male voices. One is Leslie, telling someone that he's hungry. The other I don't recognize, maybe because he's talking in a low hush, but there's a bit of muffled noise.

Something screeches across the tile kitchen floor.

And then a low moan.

Holy shit. I raise my brows at Burkie. Is that what I think it is?

We're both staring at the door, mouths ajar. I list a little to the side, and Burkie steps closer, his chest firm against my arm.

"Uh, what should we do?" he whispers.

"Probably shouldn't interrupt," I whisper back, shifting my weight more against him.

Laughter echoes on the other side of the door. Another moan followed by a hushed curse. That is absolutely what we think it is.

And, wow, listening to two guys is *hot*. It's getting me all worked up—mostly thinking about how Burkie sounds when I fist him. I twist to take his lips, flicking my tongue against his as his hands slide down to my ass.

The door flies open.

I jump back. We both gawk at Leslie. He stares back at us, his palms raised defensively in the air.

"Holy maloney," he gasps. "You scared the fucking life out of me."

"Uh, sorry," Burkie says, wiping at his mouth with the back of his hand.

In a few sweeping glances, the three of us take each other in. Burkie's reddened lips, my ridiculous boner, Leslie's finger-tousled hair.

"Les?" The hushed voice calls from the kitchen.

Who is that?

"Just a sec," Leslie says over his shoulder, his eyes staying fixed on us. "So . . . I'm thinking this is one of those moments that we don't mention again."

"Alright." Burkie's brow furrows.

I shrug. "I'm in."

Leslie scans us a second time, a grin crossing his face. "Damn, you guys are adorable. Don't jizz on the food."

He reaches in, grabs a jumbo bag of M&M's, then laughs as he closes the door.

I stare after him. "Holy shit."

Burkie's lips press. "Guess it's not a secret anymore."

CHAPTER SIXTEEN

Shaw

"*Eden*." I dig my head back into his fluffy pillow, my dick deep in his mouth. I'm oscillating between watching him as he sucks me down and arching back helplessly, my eyes squeezing shut, attempting to hang on to some sense of reality. "Fuck, you're too good. Are you sure you haven't been practicing on a bunch of other dudes?" I tease him.

He pulls off my dick to tongue one of my nuts, and I moan. My hips shift up, chasing the heat of his mouth.

This is the definition of bliss. Perfection. Heaven.

He's been edging me—with his mouth, his hands, his breath, and his words—for over an hour. Slowly sucking me down until I'm close and then drawing off to flick his tongue around my nipples and nibble along my jaw before taking me again while I whimper and fist his hair.

And trust me, there's been some whimpering.

"Only dick I've ever had is yours," he says quietly before he engulfs me again. I tangle his hair around my fingers, my hips moving, matching his languid rhythm.

"So hot," I mumble, squeezing my eyes shut as he picks

up the pace. I *like* it just being me. "Best moment ever. Not even a contest."

He takes me to the very back of his tongue and swallows, his throat constricting around the head of my cock. Never in my life has someone done this for me—for a solid hour—just *caressed* me in this way that pushes every other thought, every worry, out of my mind.

I blow out a soft breath as he pulls off my dick and languishes open kisses over my sack. His fingertips slip up along my abs, following the indentations, his biceps flexing with the stretch, that crease between his delts and traps deepening as he reaches higher.

My balls quiver in his warm mouth, muscles aching from how tight they've been for the last hour. I've staved off an orgasm, but it's getting more difficult, and I have to grit my teeth when he tweaks my nipple.

"Need to come," I push out. I'm writhing, my spine bowing, my hips moving. "Jack me or suck me, I don't care, but I'm there."

He nods and fists my cock. When I hiss, he seems to understand it's from lack of lube, and he replaces his hand with his mouth, pressing up onto his knees so that he's fully over me. His hands slide underneath my ass to cup me, and he pulls me up, deeper into his mouth. His fingers slide toward my crease and . . . *holy hell*.

"Too good," I mumble.

Yes, yes, yes.

Heat trembles in my balls and squeezes low in my pelvis. I can't stop writhing, my ass trying to get closer to his fingers. The last hour of pent-up need balloons so hard and fast that I'm drowning in it. He grips my ass cheeks, spreading them as his thick fingers slide deeper into my crease. He brushes lightly against my hole.

"Oh, fuck, gonna come." I squeeze my eyes shut and let loose, flooding out, making sounds I didn't know I could make. I hover in some kind of cloudy space—only half aware of the world—until my muscles release, and I feel him climbing up next to me.

"Kiss me?" My voice cracks as I ask the question. A whole bunch of emotions I don't know how to name swirl around in my chest. Pinch behind my eyes.

He settles next to me, and his lips find mine. His weight presses me into the mattress as we make out until we're fighting to breathe. Then he rolls back so I can snuggle in next to him, shivering as my sensitive dick nestles against his sack.

The room is a dark, deep red. Only the bedside lamp is on, which Burkie threw a Hurricanes t-shirt over.

"Feel better?" he asks. There's only an inch of pillow between us, the world coming slowly back into focus.

"Fucking amazing." My shoulders relax into his mattress. "I'm never getting out of your bed again. Although my ass is lonely. It could use a Burkie-shaped cock in there."

He groans. "You don't know what you're getting yourself into."

"Nope. I completely don't." I reach down to grip him, slowly stroking. He fucked my mouth hard when we first got up here, but I wonder if he needs to go again. "But a little ass play's not exactly foreign to me either. Can I see the infamous ass toy?"

He laughs, then stretches over to his bedside table and pulls out a sleek, black box. He sets it on my stomach. "Here it is."

I release his dick, sit up, and flip the box over in my hands to discover the tape is still intact. "You haven't opened it?"

"I haven't needed it."

I grin. "Because I'm so wickedly good at getting you off?"

"Yep."

He tucks his hair behind his ears and then folds his hands behind his head. It bends his elbow, flexing his biceps, that hockey tattoo shifting as he moves, the soft hair in his pit calling to me. Wanna nuzzle it.

"You can open it." He nods toward the box.

"Oh, hell yeah." I tug at the tape. I pop the end of the box open and slide out the formed plastic to reveal a vibrator.

"It's black," I mumble, finally answering a question that's been lingering in my head.

It's fairly small—probably good for a first time—and has different power settings. With a silicone exterior, it's almost slick in my hands.

I waggle it, and it jiggles on the moveable base. "We've gotta use this."

His voice gravels. "You're into it?"

I laugh. "Dude, when it comes to you, I'm into everything."

I press the power switch.

Nothing.

Whelp, that's disappointing.

I swing my feet to the floor and unwind the cord as I cross the room on a mission to hook it to the charging station on Burkie's desk.

I plug it in then turn around and stop. Burkie's watching me from his place on the bed, eyes thoughtful as he takes me in from head to toe. "Thought you weren't ever getting out of bed again."

"Priorities, *coaie*." I grin as his eyes flash up and down me again, his hands still crooked behind his head, completely naked with all those thick abs and D-man thighs on display. I palm my sack and tug on it a little, waggling my brows at him, then groan because I'm still so sensitive. But at least I'm standing fairly steadily. The world's no longer swimming. "You checking me out?"

"Constantly." His eyes darken as he sweeps me again, a kind of sedate contentment on his face. "You're so fuckin' gorgeous."

Shit, I feel that. Not gonna lie—I get complimented a lot. But him saying it? So much better.

I crawl back onto the bed and nestle back into my spot. His hand glides over my hip and then around, his fingers tightening into a soft cup, massaging my ass cheek. My eyelids flutter. I don't know why it feels so good. It's not just about sex. It's about something else—intimate and tender. Something I didn't know I ached for.

His smile is so cute as I worm closer to him. A blush crawls up his cheeks as he hauls me halfway over the top of him, one of my legs settling between his.

"That felt good with Les earlier," he says. "Him knowing, I mean. Not necessarily about us, but about . . ." He swallows thickly. "I think I want to come out."

I arch up so I can get a good read on his face. "You're ready?"

He bites out a low laugh. "Fuck, no."

"But you want to anyway?"

"It's becoming important to me that I can just . . . be me. Especially around here. With you and Les and Vain and Dare." He drags in a slow inhale, his stomach moving against mine. "Just getting to hang out with you and not having to think about what I'm saying. I didn't realize how *good* that would feel. I wish I felt this way all the time." His eyes shift around my face. "Does that make a bit of sense?"

"Hell yeah, it does."

His fingers flex into my ass cheek. "But this shit with SCU, I'm not sure what to think about it."

"Me either." Like I really don't know what to think.

"And what are we supposed to do?" Burkie stares up at the ceiling. "Pretend like it's not bullshit? Pretend like it's fair? I don't fully know what happened, but it doesn't seem like it's in the ballpark of fair to me. And what happens if we get louder?"

I study him, the clench in his jaw, lines along his forehead. He's been thinking about this.

"I don't know," I admit. "But if getting louder is something we need to do, then we'll do it."

"Even if it's a risk?" He drags his teeth over his bottom lip as he looks back at me. "You got pissed at me about Cassidy."

"That was an entirely different situation," I point out. "This is speaking up for something you believe in. Something we both do."

His lips press. "What if I step out there?"

"Then I'm going with you." No freaking question. Right there on his left. Just like he always is for me. "Eden, if we need to do something, then let's do it."

He wraps both arms around me, hugging me hard. "I have no clue what I'm thinking. And how am I going to do anything if I can't come out? If I can't fuckin' *say* it." He squeezes his eyes shut, like the first time we talked about it. Like it's hard for him to actually say that he's gay.

Shit. Is it? I think back and realize that he hasn't said it once. Which, maybe he hasn't felt the need with me, but maybe it's more than that.

I press a kiss against his jaw. "Come out to me right now."

He laughs. "Pretty sure you already know."

"Yeah, but I could hear it."

He leans his head back to see me. "You'd want to?"

"I'd *love* to hear it." I smile down at him. "Hit me with it, *coaie*. I'm ready."

"Alright." He stares at me for a long moment, his jaw twitching, but I'm pretty sure it's not at me. "I'm, uh, gay."

He expels a breath that huffs into a half laugh.

"Say it again."

"I'm gay." He mirrors my smile. "And maybe demi. But definitely gay. Fuck, that feels good."

"Oh yeah?" I prop myself over the top of him, planting my hands on either side of his shoulders and tamping his legs down with mine. I've got him locked down—at least as much as he'll let me because I know he could probably throw me off. I bend down to give him a huge, wet, slobbery kiss on the cheek. "Say it again."

He laughs, twisting away from my lips. "Shaw, you motherfucker."

"Say it again." I hold him with all my weight and lick him this time, but I'm smiling so big that I can't get my tongue out that far, and I end up nibbling on his cheek. "Or say you like to suck my cock."

"Oh, is that what you think?" He grips my hips, his bulk solid underneath mine. "You think I like sucking *your* cock?"

"You love it." I click my tongue playfully, grinding my half-hard chub against him. "Hot and heavy and eager in your mouth."

"Maybe," he says, but he's grinning so big that it makes my throat tighten.

"Maybe?" I lean down to slobber another kiss on him, but this time he tips up, turning it from a hot mess of a slobber into a kiss.

He sighs when his head drops back against the pillow. "You always make things feel okay. Not sure how you fuckin' do it. But you always make me feel like shit's going to be okay."

"You have no idea how much you do the same for me." I slowly release my weight down onto him, relaxed this time, chest to chest, and I breathe out, splayed over the top of him, completely pliant. "Wanna come again? I feel like I might have left you hanging. All chubbed and blue-balled."

He slides a warm palm up my spine. "I'm good for now." He massages between my shoulders in a way that makes the very last of any tension drain away. "I'm liking this."

"Me too." I close my eyes. My brain's still a bit fuzzy, but I don't want to fall asleep yet. I want more time with him. All the time I can get.

I've never wanted time like this with someone before. Just *time*. To talk. To snuggle in closer. To do this.

I nuzzle into his neck. "What do you think Leslie's doing with those M&M's?"

He laughs, deep and happy. "I have no idea. I wondered that too. It was a big-ass bag. Although it's probably less exciting than we think."

"Nah, I'm gonna keep thinking it's exciting." I drag my nose along the rough scruff on his jaw. "Tell me something else."

"Like what?"

"What were holidays like in the Burkehammer household growing up?"

"You really want to know?"

"Yep," I say, settling my cheek on his shoulder. "Holidays are my favorite. Tell me all the Burkie stuff. Wanna know."

He tells me, his voice soft and gravelly in the dark as his hands knead me from ass to shoulders, and I sink into the warm vanilla scent of his room, listening to him talk about his family—mostly his mom and sister and cousins. He hardly mentions his father.

There's nowhere else I'd rather be. There haven't been that many places in my life that feel like home. But Burkie's room? I'm not sure I have another word to describe it.

CHAPTER SEVENTEEN

Shaw

Leslie drops into the chair next to me, a bright blue sucker popping out his cheek.

"Have a good night?" He arches a brow, smiling around the sucker stick.

I wink at him. "Could say the same to you. Finish off the M&M's?"

He shrugs. "Had a few."

Shit, I'm so curious.

Past him, in the food court, Vain's sorting through a basket of bananas and chatting with Dare. I haven't seen Burkie yet, but his DM read, *Had to pick something up. Running late.*

I set my forearms on the chair, flipped backward and butted against the table, my feet flat on the floor on either side. "So, are we still agreeing to the not-mentioning-it plan?"

Although I *really* want to mention it. Not just because of lingering questions about M&M's. My brain's been working overtime sorting out who that hushed voice belonged to. I won't press Les to out anyone, but a few candidates have sprung to mind. There's the guy I almost hooked up with

—Asher—who I saw hanging with the baseball team. Dex was around too, although he was mostly talking to Burkie. Kazi, I guess? I mean, not out of the realm of possibilities. Someone else on the Wolfpack? That would explain his silence on it. Or someone I don't know?

The sucker clicks against Leslie's teeth as he studies me back. "Probably for the best that we stick with the plan right now."

"Fair enough," I say.

His lips turn up. "How long has it been going on between you two?"

I laugh. "Is this your way of not mentioning it? Because it's a complete fail."

His gray eyes brighten. "Humor me before everyone else sits down. A few months, maybe?"

I blink at him. "Not even close."

His brows rise. "A year?"

A year?

I stare at him, open-mouthed. "It strikes me as odd that you assumed I meant longer. It pretty much just started like a week ago."

He pinches the stick end of the sucker and pulls it from his mouth with those inked fingers of his. "You're serious?"

"Why wouldn't I be?"

"I've been listening to you sneak out of his room in the morning for *months*." He points the sucker toward Vain. "And my guess is I'm not the only one who's noticed. But we're all feeling twitchy right now. So no one's saying anything."

My heel bounces in my slide, the chair cutting a line across the bottom of my thigh. "Wasn't really sneaking. I just crash in there sometimes."

"Uh huh." He tosses me a wide Leslie-style smile—laugh lines on his cheeks, a whole bunch of teeth.

"Nothing happened," I say. "We just crashed."

"Frequently."

"Well, yeah, I guess."

"And that didn't make you pause and think?"

"No."

It didn't.

Like at all. I just like being around Burkie. I've never questioned that.

Should I have?

I mean, shit. Am I doing something wrong here? I don't think Leslie intended to make my brain go in that direction, but suddenly, I'm really thinking about it. I like Burkie. I like spending time with him. I like it even more now that we're sucking each other off.

So I want to keep doing it. As much as possible.

Does it need to be more complicated than that?

Is it more complicated for him?

I tap the back of the chair. "I haven't exactly been celibate these last months . . ."

Les shrugs. "You're both adults. I don't know what kind of agreement you have. But I haven't seen you with anyone all that much lately."

Is that true? I frown as I roll back over the last few months. I mean, there were the girls the other night, but I didn't actually have sex with them. We'd had some fun for sure, but I'd stopped things pretty early. And they were more than happy to be with each other, so it was all good. Like I told Burkie before, they weren't all that interested in *me* anyway.

I guess I haven't really hooked up with anyone in a while. At least, I haven't had sex with anyone since I started crashing in Burkie's room a few months back.

What does that mean? *Does* it mean something?

Would it mean something to Burkie if he knew?

Maybe I'm starting to think about sex a little differently. I've enjoyed the hell out of it in the past, but I've been feeling like something is missing. I felt it the other morning with those girls, which is why I stopped before getting there.

I've felt it before then too.

Leslie tilts his head, studying me. "You're thinking pretty damn hard over there."

Yeah, I am.

I mean, what *is* friendship? At its core, it's just a relationship with someone you like being around and who likes being around you.

Whatever's going on between Burkie and me, it still feels like friendship.

Leslie kicks back on his chair. I like being around him too. And with those silvery eyes and all that well-placed ink, he's a decent-looking guy. But Les doesn't give me that same rise of goosebumps up the back of my neck like Burkie does. I don't get that same lightness in my chest, that urge to bounce on my toes. The all-body, gut-deep, smile-inducing *reaction* I get when Burkie steps into the room.

What I feel toward Les is definitely friendship.

With Burkie? Maybe like *extra*-friendship. With a side of all those heart-pumping emotions.

But that doesn't fully quantify it either.

I press my lips. "I like being around him, Les. I honestly don't know anything more than that."

His expression softens as he slips the sucker back into his mouth. "I hope like hell I'm that lucky someday."

His eyes jump behind me, and I follow his line of sight to the café. The biggest smile zooms across my face when I see Burkie hunting through the chip bags. I want to get up, run over there, and crash into him. Bear hug him as he glowers down at the chips like they've pissed him off somehow.

Goosebumps, lightness, eagerness. I get it *all*.

Vain's next to him, Dare on the other side. The three of them are talking about something pretty serious as Burkie grabs whatever he was searching for and they head over to the line, still talking just as intently.

My smile gets even bigger as Burkie pays and then

heads toward us, weaving around the tables, food basket in one hand, backpack on his shoulder, beanie on his head, still talking seriously with Vain and Dare, but he perks up when he sees me. That glower vanishes in an instant.

Maybe he feels it too.

He tosses a bag of chips down in front of me as he pulls out a seat. "No clue how you eat that shit."

I grin at the bag. "You didn't have to."

"But figured I would." He crinkles the cellophane around his turkey sandwich, and I'm suddenly staring at his hands and his clean fingernails, wide and blunt, as he slowly opens it. Those hands were fisted around my dick last night.

I tear my eyes away, remembering where we are.

"Thanks." I reach for the chips, clearing my throat. "I'm touched."

I *really* am. He's been doing little things for me. Charging my phone. Replacing the frayed laces on my skates. Buying those bubbly watermelon waters I like and stocking them in his mini fridge. Maybe even things I haven't noticed?

Shit. I hope I'm noticing them all.

They mean a lot.

"It's no big deal." He wipes his mouth with a napkin, dismissing his kindness like always. "Besides, we got you something better."

I blink in mock confusion. "What the hell is better than jalapeño chips?"

A chair screeches next to me as Dare sits down. I give him an elbow nudge and he upnods me. Vain plonks his books down. Kelsey's cutting through from the other side of the café.

Shit, we're all here. That never happens.

And they're all looking at me. No one's eating as Kels sets her spread down. I tap my thumb against my chip bag. "What's going on?"

Vain pulls an orange out of his pocket and starts to peel it. "Burk told us about you needing to get home to Chicago."

"What?" I straighten.

Burkie pulls an envelope out of his bag. "I wasn't trying to spill a secret or—"

"Wasn't a secret," I say. They're all still looking at me. It's freaking weird. "Is this an intervention? I feel like I'm about to get dogpiled. And not the good way."

Burkie sets the envelope flat on the table. "We took up a collection. From us and the team. Kels organized it over at the women's team, too. Everyone pitched in a couple of bucks. And I'm pretty sure it's enough to get you to Chicago and back."

I stare at him, my heart beating hard. "*What*?"

He pushes the envelope toward me. "There's a flight out late tonight. You can go and be back before we play against SCU next week."

"Wait." I look around, taking them all in. "This is for real?"

Vain nods. "Heck, yeah, bro."

Leslie pushes his sucker to his other cheek. "Should be enough."

Dare nudges me. Kelsey grins.

Heat builds behind my eyes. "You guys seriously did this?"

"We're teammates," Burkie says.

They all keep looking at me. And . . . hell . . .

The envelope blurs, my vision fuzzing. "This is phenomenal, but I can't take it. It's not your—"

"Take it," Vain says.

Burkie nudges the envelope closer. "If you don't, we'll leave it on the fuckin' table and someone else will grab it." He looks across at me, dark brown eyes telling me it's the truth. They did this for me. "Take it, Shaw. It's for you. From all of us. Go see your brother."

I rest my elbows on my knees, trying to get comfortable on the plastic chair, and wipe my fingers underneath my eyes. I'm exhausted. Late flight into O'Hare. Barely made it in time to hug Raleigh before he was wheeled back. His doctor said the surgery will only take a little over an hour, although the seconds always crawl when we're in the hospital. One hour feels like four days.

But I'm here.

I still can't believe the guys and Kelsey did this for me.

My mom steps around the corner with a paper coffee cup in each hand. Yellow Styrofoam cups I recognize from all the time we've spent here at Northwestern Memorial. Her curly hair flies everywhere as she plops down next to me and hands me one of the cups.

"Your dad ran across the street to get a newspaper." She takes off her lid and blows on the coffee. "Raleigh was so relieved that you made it. It means a lot to him."

"I needed to be here." I glance around at the drafty little sitting area. The gray Chicago winter sky outside the windows makes it feel chillier than it is. "I know I'll be home in a few weeks for Christmas, but you know . . ."

I've never missed one of my brother's surgeries. I actually got benched once last year for missing a game, but fuck it. Some things are more important.

Mom replaces her lid and then reaches over to pat my knee. "You look good. Your hair's gotten longer."

"Has it?" I run my thumb over the steam coming out of the little drink hole on top of the cup. "I've been feeling pretty good lately."

She smiles. "So, things are going well?"

"You could say that." I've already DMed Burkie like fifty times. Sent four pictures. Flirted with him about all the dirty, dirty things we're gonna do over FaceTime later.

But being here . . . it's making me think a whole lot about next year.

Burkie will be gone. And I guess that means all this fun we've been having will be over?

I press my thumb over the drink hole.

His room will be empty. He won't be there when I climb the stairs. Or in the locker room. Or on campus. My throat tightens, a stark coldness lingering there.

Mom takes a sip of her coffee and then wrinkles her nose. "Did I ask the wrong question?"

"No." I straighten and take my finger off the hole then hold the paper cup with both hands, warming my palms. "Of course not. I've just been thinking a lot the last few days. About stuff in the future, I guess."

"Like what?" Mom waits for me to answer, blinking expectantly.

When I still don't talk, she just keeps staring, dark brows raised, brown eyes alert. She doesn't say anything more, just waits.

And it *always* works. I swear, I can't hold shit in around her if I tried. Voodoo Mom magic.

I carefully swirl the liquid in my cup. "Nothing to worry about right now. We've got a lot on our minds with Raleigh."

Mom gives me an admonishing look. "I can multitask."

I nod. "Okay, well . . . I'd always thought I'd graduate and then try to get picked up by a team. If I'm really lucky, somewhere near Chicago. Be close to all of you. Maybe play for the franchise that started this whole dream."

I saw my first Blackhawks game on TV when I was four or five years old, but it wasn't until later when I played that I got hooked. The sound of skates on ice. The way a goalie could knock a slapshot out of the air. A defenseman's bone-crushing hit into the boards.

I smile. Like Burkie, hammering someone into the board

with zero reservation. Apparently, I've been enamored with hard-hitting D-men before I knew exactly what that meant.

I bounce my knee, smiling at my untied shoelace. Then I try to get back on track. "What if it doesn't look like that?"

"What do you mean?" she asks.

I look over at her, sitting next to me, untamable hair and keen eyes.

"What if I surprise you?" I ask.

She laughs. "You better."

I blink at her. "What?"

"You better surprise me." She nudges my elbow with hers. "Maybe it'll be about whatever's on your mind right now. Or maybe it'll be about something else. But the surprises are my favorite part."

"I've surprised you before?"

She rolls her eyes. "Constantly. I had no idea you were going to pick IFU. Or some of your Instagram posts?"

I groan. "Not all of those are for my mother's eyes."

In fact, over the last few days, they've pretty much been for someone else.

"Well . . ." She takes another sip and wrinkles her nose again. There are still lines under her eyes, but they've eased a touch. "All I'm saying is that if you don't surprise people sometimes, then I'm not sure you're doing it right."

I think of signing for that ass toy package and then standing outside Burkie's door.

"I think you might be onto something, Mom." I take a sip of coffee.

Wait . . . not coffee.

Something so much better.

I smile. "You got me hot chocolate."

"That's what you like." She reaches over to pat my knee again. "And don't you dare hold back, Shaw. Not ever."

I stare at her for a long minute. "Sometimes I think you know what's in my head better than I do."

She laughs, about to say something else, but then her eyes fix past me. Her face pales, like it always does when the doctor comes out. She rises, and I stand with her.

Raleigh's doctor smiles warmly as she makes her way toward us, and we blow out twin breaths of relief. I still get so fucking *scared* sometimes. It makes me feel small.

Makes me feel out of control. Like the things I really care about can be tugged away in an instant.

But looking at his doctor's face, I know my brother is okay. I can feel it in my bones.

And maybe, just *maybe*, everything will be okay.

Words that I will forever remember:

1. "I think you should trust yourself, Burkie."
2. "I kinda don't want it to stop."
3. "I'm quiet, because I wanted to."
4. "We would have been there for you in a heartbeat."
5. "I don't think it's actually about the bed."
6. "I'm with Burkie. All the way."

CHAPTER EIGHTEEN

Burk

I stare down at the pride patch in my hand. Not just any pride patch. It's a pair of crossed hockey sticks, the blades wrapped in rainbow. An IFU hockey pride patch. One that will fit on the shoulder of our jerseys, right under the Wolfpack logo. I roll my thumb over the neat stitching.

They were delivered five minutes ago. A rush order barely in time for our game with SCU tonight. *If* we decide to wear them. I've called hockey house over here to talk about it and sort out how we want to present them to the full team.

If we do.

I really fuckin' hope we do.

A car passes, and I glance at the door. I've been listening for the airport van for the last twenty minutes.

I'd wanted to pick Shaw up, but he argued that we shouldn't both risk being late for the game since a storm is due in. I grudgingly admitted he was right, but now I'm thinking—*fuck it*—I should have driven down to get him.

I missed him these last three days. Even more than I

expected. It felt like I was out of step with myself. My bed was a hollow cavern; my big-ass pillow was huge and empty. I'm well aware three days isn't that long, but there's something about having him around that sets me at ease. Makes me feel like everything is in the right place. Like *I'm* in the right place.

We FaceTimed and DMed every chance we got. I swear I've never spent so much time on Instagram in my life. Thankfully, his brother's surgery went smoothly, and Shaw sent me some pics afterward. His whole family was gathered around the hospital bed and smiling, and Shaw was right there with them, that smirk I know so damn well lighting his face, one arm around his brother, the other around his dad. His mom was ruffling Raleigh's hair.

His family looked so happy together.

It makes me think about my mom and sis. Will they talk to me after I come out? Will they want to see me?

I have no clue.

It scares the shit out of me.

The door handle moves, and my head whips over, my free hand raking through my hair, my stomach jittery. I'm suddenly worried that things will be different.

He'll walk through that door, and it'll go back to the way it was before.

And then he's there, stepping in the front door, a small duffle hanging over his shoulder, a worn Wolfpack hoodie under his jacket. His ballcap is tilted on his head, and his eyes light when he sees me standing there. He doesn't stop moving, just crashes full force into me, his bag and hat tumbling to the floor as he all out bearhugs me. I brace my feet to hold his weight, my eyes closing and arms wrapping around him, under his jacket, the soft cotton of his hoodie against my forearms, and the strong lines of his back underneath that. The pressure releases in my chest.

We're still here. Still doing this.

His lips move against my jaw, cold welling off him. I hug him tighter. I can't let go.

"Fuck," I mumble. He smells so damn much like Shaw. I kiss along his jaw, sucking on his cold neck. Then bury my nose against him.

"You aren't worried about anyone walking in on us?" He squeezes the back of my neck.

"No one's home," I say, my voice gravelly. "But we've only got a few minutes."

As soon as I get the words out, he's kissing me. His fingers tangle in my hair, his mouth opening against mine. He slides a hand down and cups where I'm thickening against my zipper.

Fuck*me*. I close my eyes, breaking the kiss and settling my forehead against his. I shiver as he strokes over my jeans.

I feel like I need to talk to him. After that party—and these few days apart—I don't know if I can hold back anymore. If I can keep back everything that I'm starting to feel.

"I missed you," I grit out.

"Did ya?" His voice is all playful tease. I smile, dropping my head to nuzzle against his neck, breathing him in.

He strokes me faster.

"*Shaw*," I groan, my hips rocking forward.

He squeezes my dick hard enough for my eyes to roll. "Want to get on my knees right here."

I shudder, my heart thumping so hard and urgently it's like he has a direct line in. One word, one touch, and I'm his.

The door opens partway, stopping when it smashes into Shaw's bag on the floor.

Fuck.

We bolt away from each other. Shaw swoops to grab his hat and bag. I scrub a hand over my face and take a blood-pressure reducing breath before Vain and Leslie walk in, talking loudly. Les takes one glance at us, laughs and shakes his head, then heads over and drops on the couch. He kicks his feet onto the coffee table.

Vain moves a little slower, his eyes pinging between us.

"Everything good with your brother?" he asks Shaw.

"Yeah, great." Shaw bounces on his toes. "It'll still be a few weeks before he's fully recovered, but all is going well."

"That's good." Vain claps him on the shoulder, looking over at me. "Dare's behind us."

Vain takes a seat on the couch next to Les, and I let out the breath I'd been holding, turning to adjust myself as Shaw smirks at me, eyes flicking down to my obvious bulge.

He only looks away when Dare blusters in and sets his motorcycle helmet on the table.

"Hey, how's Raleigh?" Dare asks Shaw as they head toward the couch. I grab the box of patches and follow after, a nervous knot fisting in my stomach.

"Good, yeah." Shaw snags a seat on the arm of the couch, finishing up his conversation with Dare, but I keep standing.

When the conversation falls silent, everyone looks at me.

"What's all this about, Burk?" Vain leans back against the couch, spreading his knees wide and resting his hands on his thighs. "We're all here now."

I take a few of the patches out of the box and set the rest aside. "We're all here for this first part, yeah."

"Alright," Vain says. I nod at him, but then my eyes flit to Shaw. He smiles. It's not teasing this time. It's encouraging. He's the only one who knows what I'm about to suggest. We came up with this idea together.

Or, well, it was seeing a photo of him and his brother together in matching Wolfpack t-shirts. It got me thinking about where hockey players are heard the loudest.

It's on the ice.

If we want to say something loudly, that's where we need to say it.

"I've wanted to do something about SCU," I start. I hadn't

planned exactly what to say. And maybe I should have because anxiety is kicking me hard right now. If they ask why this means so much to me, I'm not sure what I'll tell them.

That I'm gay?

I guess . . . I could.

Although I'd rather the focus be on the patch and who we are as a team.

"I, uh." I look around at them. "I've got an idea." I hold up a patch, and everyone leans forward.

Dare's over to me in three fast boot strides.

"Fuck, *yes*, my man." A smile extends across his face as he takes a couple of the patches and tosses them out to everyone. "Where'd you get these?"

"It was Shaw," I say. "He knows someone on Instagram who makes them."

"Burkie's idea," Shaw says.

Dare palms my shoulder. "We're wearing them."

I glance over at Vain and Leslie, my brows rising. "What do you think?"

Leslie grins. "I think it's perfect."

Vain nods. "They're good, Burk. How many do you have?"

Fuck, that was easy.

"Enough for the entire team. But . . ." I frown at the box. "I'm not sure how to go about asking."

Dare stiffens. "We just tell them—this is what we're doing."

I rub a hand over the back of my neck. "What if they argue?"

Dare shakes his head, holding the patch to his arm where it would fit on his jersey. "As far as I'm concerned, anyone who argues can get tossed out on their ass."

"It's not that simple," Vain says.

Dare spins on his heel, looking down at him. "The fuck it isn't."

Vain holds up a palm. "I don't disagree with you. Not at all. But Burk is right. There are complexities here in how this comes together."

Dare shakes his head at Vain. "I don't see any fucking complexities. We get the team over here and tell them we're wearing the patches."

"Before tonight's game?" Vain asks. "That's not a lot of time to pull it all together."

"Fucking *yes*." Dare takes a boot step toward him. "If there's any team that needs to see this, it's SCU. It needs to be loud and clear that we're not like them. I'm ready for a fight. I think we all should be."

"I'm with Dare," Leslie says. "We need to say we're different. And we have to do it now, before too much time passes. This is just like in a game. If a guy checks you, you check him back. If you don't respond, he's going to run all over you."

Vain taps his palms against his thighs. I know he's in. He's just thinking about how it's going to get done.

"We can sew them on," I say. "Everyone will pitch in. Like we always do. I'd bet the women's team would be more than happy to help too. We're all hockey."

Vain raises his brows at Shaw. "Shaw?"

"Is there any doubt what I'm gonna say?" Shaw winks at me. "I'm with Burkie. All the way."

I close my eyes for a split second and then open them, trying to look like I'm not about to propel myself across the room toward him.

Vain nods. "I'm in too, Burk. A thousand percent. This is good."

There's an expansion in my lungs, a warmth that I *know* simmers up to my eyes. I don't try to hide it.

There are moments in life when you have to stop and look around. Just take it in because you know those few minutes might be fleeting, but they'll be the ones you remember for the rest of your fuckin' life.

I'm there now.

Looking at the guys around me.

Friends. Teammates. Roommates. Guys who I depend on. Who I try to always be there for.

It feels a lot like family. Not the one with my father at the helm, but the one that could exist. When people care about each other. When they listen to each other. When they fuckin' *value* each other.

And we can be that. We can show that. We're not just a bunch of fuckin' hockey jocks.

We're people who care. Who fight to make things better.

Vain pushes up off the couch. "Let's get it done. I'll message the team chat and tell them we've got a meeting."

———

An hour later, the room is silent. I just finished showing the entire team the patches and explaining my thoughts. Shaw's on the arm of the couch again, nodding as I speak the last words. Vain's standing a few feet to my right. Les is reclined against the kitchen door frame, and Dare paces in the back, looking like he wants to say something as I lay it all out to the team, but for now he's biting his tongue.

Cassidy purses his lips. He's been leaning against the back wall, a sour look on his face from the second I began speaking.

"I agree with everything Burk said." Vain stands behind me. "We're a team who welcomes everyone, and we're prepared to show it. The conversation about SCU is going to go on—in locker rooms and coaches' offices and the stands— and we need to be part of it." He pauses, brow furrowing. "Inclusion isn't optional on this team. Anyone who has an issue with that can go elsewhere."

Cassidy pushes off the wall, and every muscle in my body tenses as his eyes settle on me.

"I've been thinking a lot about this," he says. "I'm glad we're doing something."

I wait for something else. Wait for the other shoe to fall, but he just steps back, nodding like he's said his part.

O'Hern scoffs, then leans closer to Cassidy and whispers something in his ear.

Cassidy turns his shoulder.

"Anyone else want to speak?" I ask. "Or is it time to vote?"

O'Hern presses his lips and shakes his head before glaring off toward the kitchen.

"I'm a *yes*," Les pipes from the doorway. "We need to show that anyone is welcome in the Wolfpack. Kazi too, if he decides that way."

"Absolutely," Dare says.

"For sure." A voice comes from across the room, another rookie that's in Cassidy's circle.

"I'm in." Shaw winks at me. Like he knows what's coming.

And then it starts. Assents from every corner of the room, one after the other, calmly and steadily, a resounding, heart-thumping *yes*.

CHAPTER NINETEEN

Burk

I shift my weight between skates and glance over at Shaw. We're standing in the hallway, waiting for the announcers to call our names. He rolls his neck, his goalie mask propped on his head, hair sticking out through the hole in the face mask, all padded up.

We're ready. Intensity vibrates around us, the whole team clustered together while we wait. My heartbeat is deep but steady as my hand wraps around my stick, turning back to focus on the far end of the hallway and the strip of ice beyond. I itch to move, so I tap each of my pads, checking that my gear's all tight and set.

There's a hell of a lot riding on this game.

There are likely scouts in the stands. There's the path toward the division finals—the midpoint of our season. There's a school rivalry that goes back years.

And as I glance down at the pride patch sewn on my jersey, I get a kick in the chest. We have to win today. Stand out there with SCU and make it clear that we're a different kind of team.

To top it off, my family's here. They're going to see this patch on my arm.

The announcer calls the names of the guys ahead of us, booming over the bass of the music and the cheers, the noise rising higher as our timber wolf mascot gets everyone to their feet. One after the other the guys skate out, and we shuffle forward. I'm back on defense today to keep the line strong— back with Shaw—and I'll get called before the offensive starters. As goalie, Shaw is always announced last.

He looks over at me, goalie mask still propped on his head, hair sticking out around it. His pride patch is sewn on his shoulder, and I reach up to flick my thumb over it.

Coach gave an approving nod when he saw us—something that we rarely see from him. Maybe he thought the conversation had to come from us. Honestly, it feels better this way. If he'd just stood in front of us and said the words, I don't know if we would have believed him.

Instead, we're believing in ourselves.

"You ready?" I ask Shaw. He's beyond gorgeous—the way he always looks in his pads. I burn to tell him that. To tell him how perfect this is. How he checks every box that I've ever wanted to check. To finally lay it all out there with him.

But we're lined up with everyone else, whoops and hollers coming from behind us, everyone close together. I double check his skate laces.

He reaches a gloved hand over and slaps my ass. "They called your name, *coaie*."

"They did?"

He grins. "You ready?"

I nod. "Sure."

"Hey." He winks at me and then pulls down his mask. "It's you and me. We can do anything."

"Fuck, yeah." Then I'm off, stepping out on the ice and skating through the swirling lights, skating toward the lineup. I hazard one last glance over my shoulder to see Shaw bouncing on his skates.

And then it's game fuckin' on.

SCU's forward slams right into Shaw within the first three minutes. Jamison fuckin' Graves is all cocky arrogance and dark blue eyes, like a blue devil himself, as he throws me a haughty grimace after the ref stops the play. I'm about to give him a little *fuck off* shove when he eyes the patch on my arm. His sneer falls, a cleft appearing in his chin.

And he looks almost . . . well, not like arrogant Jamison Graves.

He looks thoughtful, and when he looks at me, it's only for a second. Then, instead of saying something obnoxious like he usually would, he pivots and skates away.

His reaction surprises me, but I shove it out of my mind—focusing on the here and now. I lock on the puck in the ref's hand. The sounds of the stadium muffle into a low background rumble. I perch over my skates, stick held lightly while I wait, tensed for the rebound.

The puck falls and I'm off.

A few minutes later, Graves fucking *snows* Shaw, ice sprayed right in Shaw's face, and I'm fuckin' livid. My gloves are a split-second from dropping.

I grit my teeth, my blood pumping so hard that it's echoing in my temples. The ref skates over, inserting himself between me and Graves as he hands the SCU forward a two-minute penalty. I back up as directed, then skate in a circle, blocking out the hammering against the plexiglass from a crowd that's yelling for a fight.

I'd be more than happy to appease them.

Shaw catches my gaze through the cage of his mask.

Back off, Burkie. Calm down.

I hear the words as clearly as if he'd said them. I rein myself in for the powerplay, then plant myself next to Dare on the bench when my shift's over.

Dare nudges me with his elbow. "SCU is trying to piss us off."

I pop out my mouthguard. "It's working."

"Don't let Graves get in your head." He's focused on the ice too, watching Graves as he lines up for another puck drop. "He's a dick."

I frown slightly. Yeah, we all know that. But the way Dare just emphasized "*dick*" seems like there's another layer.

I'm about to ask about it when Coach yells my name, putting me in early, and I shove my mouthguard back in and jump over the wall in half a breath.

The game is brutal. Back and forth for the entire first period. They're not playing like they have a forward down. It's almost like the situation with Kazi pissed them off.

Halfway into the third, we're still at zero. There are shots on goal for both sides, but nothing in the net. I'm beaten the fuck up, bruised jaw to go with a busted eyebrow, right shoulder screaming from a hard check. We're burning on pure adrenaline, and some of the rookies are dragging, not used to this kind of intensity.

There aren't any more hits on Shaw, but we're waiting.

It's going to happen.

Not just because of our rivalry. SCU is calling us back to protect the goalie. They're playing with our heads so we're worried about that instead of getting shots on goal.

And it's working. Especially on me.

Vain skates up after a timeout, only eight minutes left— still no score. It's going to come down to the wire.

"He'll go after Shaw again soon," Vain says, gripping my shoulder pads to pull me closer.

My jaw locks. "Yep."

"You're not going to go after him."

"Yeah, but a fight would—"

"You're going to score instead." There's a spark in his hazel eyes. "They're expecting you to dig in and protect the net, like you've been doing all game. So we'll use that. Look for the pass from Dare. If you get it, I want you to break position and swing into leftwing, Cassidy will fall over more toward center ice, then you and I are going to surprise these fuckers."

I frown. "You sure Cassidy's ready for that? If they catch us, we'll be fucked. There's a lot of risk in that plan."

Vain palms the top of my helmet, shaking my head back and forth as he grins. "We've been working on this move, bro. Cassidy too, working with you after practices. Do *not* doubt yourself. None of us doubt you."

The refs motion to circle up, and I settle into my crouch for the face-off, my focus zeroing in on that puck. It drops. Vain gets the edge of it and hooks a sharp pass to Dare.

Dare glances at Graves.

There's a pause. It must only be for a fraction of a second, but it's like time thunders out on the ice. While I break position, Graves is caught staring at Dare, scowling at him, blue eyes narrowed, jaw clenched. Looking like he's ready for a fight. Except he won't get one.

Dare shoots a blind pass, trusting that I'll be where I'm supposed to be.

I am.

The puck hits dead center on the blade of my stick. And then I see it.

I fuckin' *see* it.

The path through their line.

I see how I'm going to bury this puck in the back of their net and change this whole game.

I don't hold back. Fuck finesse. I throw the hammer down and zero in on my destination—the upper left of the net. The only place the SCU goalie consistently fails to defend. I'll nail the fucker right there.

I'm already skating with every bit of power I have, a quick fake to the right, my skates automatically doing it all—exactly like Shaw's pushed me to do so many times during practice, in those drills, trying to get shot after shot past him.

I have a fraction of a second to line up a shot, and I hit a slapper toward the net. Just as I'm following through on the shot, their D-man slams like a freight train into my already injured shoulder, crooking my neck hard, but the only thing I see is that puck. To my far side, Vain rushes in, preparing for the rebound.

We're not going to need it.

I can still see the path.

The puck flies right over the goalie's outstretched hand. The net waves with the impact.

Goal.

Fuckin' *GOAL*.

The entire stadium erupts in one massive scream, Vain crashing into me on one side, Dare on the other, howling in my ears, arms wrapped around me, jumping up and down as we all fold into a big-ass happy dogpile. The wolf howl echoes through the stadium. From us. From the seats. I'm howling with them, tears streaming down my cheeks, but the first thing I do is push around Dare so that it's Shaw's eyes I catch. From all the way across the ice.

And it's his smile that means the most.

CHAPTER TWENTY

Burk

The locker room is crazy as fuck. Dare, who's our resident DJ, plugs in his phone and cranks up the music, all of us crowding in the center, helmets and gloves flying everywhere, just this *release.*

You'd think it was the fuckin' Stanley Cup. We're loud and chaotic and so damn exuberant that my face hurts from smiling and my lungs ache from howling, and when I turn and Shaw is right there, we collapse against each other, wrapping each other in a hockey-padded hug.

"You were magic," he yells over the noise, and fuck if my chest doesn't expand with pride. We won. *Barely.* We're beat up and bloody, sweat drenched and exhausted. But this is the best kind of win. The kind of win that feels like a triumph.

"You played a shutout," I yell back, gripping onto his shoulder pad so that the chaos around us doesn't pull us apart. "They didn't have a fuckin' *chance.*"

Even in the last two minutes after our goal, when they pulled the goalie and put *four* forwards on the ice, Shaw was unflappable. Focused. Fast. Never taking his eyes off the battle in front of him.

He was perfect.

His grin widens even more. His hair is plastered to his head with sweat, his eyes a bit bloodshot from the cold and his complete focus on the puck for the last two hours, but fuck, if he isn't more gorgeous than he's ever been.

"We did good," he yells. "And that goal. Hell, I wanted to rush over to you and—"

His eyes settle on my lips.

The locker room pulsates—everyone hugging and singing and howling—but with one little downward flick of Shaw's eyes, it's like I'm in a cocoon, tucked away with him in our own little moment. His gaze lingers on my mouth. I want to kiss him. So fuckin' bad.

Vain yells something into my other ear, shaking my sore shoulder, then he turns to Leslie. But I'm all out staring at Shaw as his eyes lock with mine, his nose flaring, his lips parting for a hard exhale.

Fuck it.

I grab the front of his jersey and tug him back to the far edge of the white wall. His eyes spark bright green as I drag him around the corner, out of view of the throng. His lips crash against mine almost before we're out of view. My heart lodges in my throat as he grips my pads and shoves me back against the wall, his tongue demanding its way into my mouth.

He tastes like sweat and blood and hockey. I growl into the kiss, our pads crushing, the taste of the game in our mouths as we fight to get closer.

Sound carries from around the corner, the music, the cheers, and for a split second, I don't give one single fuck that someone might catch us. I kiss him like I need to—desperate and hungry—all reservations torn away with the slide of his tongue against mine.

I fist Shaw's damp hair to keep him locked to me, opening to him as his hand pushes underneath my chest pads, over my navel, and then he's tugging at my pant strings, gripping and tearing at my gear. He shoves his hand under my pads and cup and palms me. I gasp into his mouth, my dick already thickening.

He shoves aside my cup. It's awkward and tight, but somehow he's fisting me, stroking me as the throng of noise continues. Just a few feet from us.

"Fuck, Shaw." I break the kiss, and my head smacks back against the wall. I meet his eyes, green and brilliant.

The music pounds and the cheers continue as I grip his hair and fuck into his fist with a need that goes past anything else. Past the fact that someone would just have to walk around the corner. And well past the fact that I'm falling so fuckin' hard for him that I don't know how to stop myself.

I have to tell him. I have no fuckin' clue what he's going to say.

Would it end all of this? Would it be too much?

He leans forward and presses his lips against my ear. "Come for me. Right fucking here. With everyone else just around the corner."

"Fuck," I grit out, and for once that playful smile doesn't whip across his face—he's too damn heated, too intent on me. And just that look—that fuckin' *look*—makes a pulverizing heat crush through me, my release wrecking up, almost violent in its intensity, clawing out of me.

"About to," I mumble, even though I doubt he can hear me, and then I bite back a shout as I release, a fuckin' mess in my cup, his gorgeous gaze fixed on my face as my hips push forward.

"*Burk.*"

My name echoes over the music. Shaw tears his hand out of my compression shorts as Vain steps around the corner, and fuck . . . I'm still coming, the last of it welling out. I grit my teeth, struggling to stop my hips from moving.

Fuck.

"*Hey*," Vain yells over the music. "Get out here and celebrate."

He's giddy, laughing, and probably too excited to notice our expressions as he grabs Shaw's jersey at the shoulder, then mine, and drags us both back into the fray.

My head's spinning, my brain trying to catch up as we stumble back in. Shaw laughs and winks at me. My cup is hot, sticking to my skin, my dick still twitching, my tongue thick with the taste of Shaw's mouth. I reach for his hand, clasping it as we're tugged away from each other by the throbbing, jumping mass of hockey players.

He grips my hand firmly, our palms sweaty, a bit of my cum on his, but he's grinning ear to ear as he shouts my name, and he starts a chant: "*Burk. Burk.*" It's repeated over and over, and I can hardly put into words what I feel, but it's like the whole world is vibrating, like there's nothing but here and now, like we're unstoppable, reckless, unconquerable.

We're *invincible.*

Shaw grins at me. The locker room echoes with my name. *He* did that. And I realize with stark, sure clarity that I would never—*never in my life*—want to do this without him.

––––––

"Burkehammer." Twenty minutes later, my name jolts across the locker room. Coach's voice is unmistakable even with the bedlam. I'm finishing my shower, rinsing shampoo out of my eyes. I'd had to sneak in here, a towel around my hips, washing off quickly before anyone noticed anything strange.

Although the showers are interesting today, to say the fuckin' least. There's a hell of a lot of towel slapping and laughter. Dare and Leslie toss handfuls of water at each other.

It's almost childlike in a way. Other than the fact that they're both over six feet tall and fit as fuck.

There's a small part of me—maybe a *hopeful* part of me—that wonders if that little patch we sewed on our sleeves isn't partly the cause of that. That little reminder that you can be whoever the fuck you are when you play for IFU.

Maybe we've created something pretty damn special.

It gives me so much hope. Like tossing off a blanket that's been suffocating me for so fuckin' long.

Maybe I could come out. And it would all be okay. Here at IFU at least.

"*Burkehammer*, hurry up," Coach calls.

I step out from under the spray. Shaw slaps my ass as I move past him. It's a physically painful effort to not let my eyes linger on the water coursing over his shoulders and down the subtle curve of his back.

We haven't showered together yet—other than in the locker room surrounded by seventeen other dudes—and that's a situation which needs to be rectified. Although I'm pretty sure it's something Vain and Dare would notice. Guess it doesn't matter if Leslie notices now.

"Coach?" I ask as I step around the corner into the locker bays and grab a towel off the stack. I rub it over my shoulders then drop it down to cover myself when I realize a blonde woman is standing next to him. Although she stands casually in her heels, like she's used to being around a bunch of naked hockey jocks.

"Get dressed," Coach orders. "Three minutes. In my office."

"Yes, sir." I head toward my duffle to grab my joggers and a t-shirt as Coach yells at Vain that he wants to see him after me. I slip into Shaw's pink slides, my toes hanging over the edge, figuring he won't mind, and take off after Coach and the woman, ruffling my fingers through my wet hair.

I plow to a stop outside the door.

Fuck.

I'd forgotten.

"Sir?" I blurt. My father's dark brown eyes scan me.

I knew my family was coming, but I'd been so focused on the game—and then Shaw after—that I haven't thought about it since earlier. But, really, why is he here? He's never happy. Just pissed off and annoyed.

"Congratulations," he says stiffly. His eyes fall to Shaw's slides and linger there.

"Thanks," I say.

Neither of us smiles. It's not a smiling moment.

We're standing in the middle of the hallway, a few other people moving around, but it's mostly empty here. Families and friends are supposed to wait elsewhere, but my father always feels like he has some special right to be back here.

He shakes his head at Shaw's slides. "You could have circled on the far-right side during that second powerplay."

Fuck. I don't want to do this. I don't want to hear how I could have connected a pass toward center ice during that play. I don't want to listen to how I fuckin' failed. Not right now. I just want to have this goddamn moment.

As a team, Coach will go over the tapes later. See how we could do better. But right now, I want to be proud of what we did out there.

Even if it only lasts for a little while.

But he starts in, his voice hard over the muffled chatter and laughter from the locker room.

". . . and you must've had wax in your ears during the ref call." He crosses his arms, sinking into that I-know-better stance he has, legs wide apart, frown deep. "And on that last play—"

"This isn't a great time," I cut in. "Coach needs to talk to me. We can pick this up at—"

"What does your coach want to talk to you about?" His brow furrows. "Are you failing at practice?"

"No."

"You sure?" His frown deepens. And for a second, I see so much of myself in him. That fuckin' frown. That furrow across his forehead. That voice deep in my head that's always insisting I can do better.

The one that tells me I'm not good enough. Not just on the ice. But maybe with Shaw too. That he'd never actually pick a guy like me.

You were magic. Everything my father says is such a stark contrast to Shaw. To the way Shaw tips his chin and smiles at me. The way he pushes me. Not because he believes I'm shit, but because he believes I'm *not*.

"Be honest with yourself," my father snaps. "That one time with Coach Dirby, you—"

"I was *eight.*" My annoyance rises, burning like hot coals. I don't get why we're still here. Why do we keep going with this charade?

My father shakes his head. "That's not the point, boy. You need to—"

"I've got it covered." I straighten to my full height. "Thank you for coming, but you can go now."

He stills.

And, fuck, I freeze too. I've never spoken to my father like that before, and there's this instant bolt of cold that rushes down my back. A familiar fear that I've carried around him ever since I was a kid and learned that the consequence of talking back is him getting louder and meaner until he finally drowns everything else out.

But then it fades.

Because I don't give a fuck. In fact, I'm finding it hard to remember why I cared. I'm a grown-ass adult.

I didn't ask him to come. I don't ask him for anything. And I haven't in a long time.

I care about my mom and my sis, but I'm long past giving a fuck about him. It was always my mom who held us together. *She* was the one who did all the hard work—who got me to practices and taught me how to take care of my gear. She was the one up at four in the morning on travel days, driving me to who the fuck knows where and reminding me to pack extra snacks and Powerades.

It was my mom who helped me get here. And I owe her so damn much. I need to tell her. Thank her. I want to share good moments with her and my sis. Not him.

Honestly, he's not even a father to me. He's just a person who always makes me feel worse about myself. That's not the kind of person I want to be around.

It's not the kind of person *anyone* should be around.

"Son," he starts in that tone, like he's about to tell me I'm fucking up. Or that I'm not good enough. "I know what I'm talking about."

"Do you?" I don't sound that angry anymore. It's like something has shifted, and I don't need to be angry. I can do what I want to do, and he can fuckin' deal. "How long did you play in the NHL?"

He didn't. He didn't get close.

He frowns. "Well, I—"

I shake my head. "You made your choices, and now I'll make mine."

"You don't understand the first thing about making choices."

"Really? Because it seems like I'm doing pretty damn well for myself."

"Why?" he snaps at me. "Because you impressed some college kids with a lucky shot? You're not even close to the biggest name on the roster, and this is *college* hockey. Nothing to be proud of, especially the way you missed that rebound in the first half. You're reflecting badly on me."

Jesus. Is that what he cares about?

Shaw's right. My father is a dickhole. I don't know why he wants so much power over me. Or maybe he's angry because he didn't get anywhere close to the goals he set out for himself, so it makes him feel better to hammer down on me. Or he wants to use my name to say he did something with his life.

I don't know. I don't care.

I stare across at him, cycling through what I really want from him after all these years. I cut myself off from my father in lots of ways: started paying my own way a long time ago, stopped responding to his texts, stopped asking him for anything. The only reason I'm around him is because of my mom and little sis.

I won't abandon them. But I won't put up with his shit anymore either.

"I don't think we need to do this anymore," I start. "I don't think we need to pretend. I'm stoked to see Mom and Lacey at dinner tonight, but from now on, you and I don't have anything we need to talk about. So unless it's about either of them, then I don't want to hear it."

I go to step around him, but his hand darts out, catching me just above the elbow.

"Don't walk away from me." He squeezes my arm. "You don't have the right. I need everyone to know *I* did this. That *I'm* the one who got you here."

We stare at each other. A stark tension crackles in the hall-way. We're eye level and dead-on. And I see the truth.

What he wants from me.

It's never been about me. It's about him.

"Take your hand off me." My voice hardens.

His lips press angrily as he releases me. "You're making a mistake not listening to me."

"I don't think so." I step aside, then stop again, looking back at him.

Fuck it.

Fuck it *all*.

"I'm gay." I just say it. Right there. Clear as day.

The truth is that I'm not sure I give a shit if he knows or not, but for some reason, I needed to say it. It's been building for so long that I needed to stand here, look at him, and fuckin' say it.

He flinches. "No, you're not."

I huff out a laugh. "Nice response."

His eyes narrow. "Is this a joke? Are you trying to hurt me?"

"Nope." I turn and walk down the hallway to Coach's office, not bothering to look back. Even when he shouts that we're going to rectify this "gay business" at dinner.

No, we're not.

I walk away, down the hallway and around the corner that leads to Coach's office. I feel . . . done. Free. Like I can finally move on. Get on with my life. Spend my energy focused on the people who I really care about.

I stop in front of Coach's door, taking a moment to push my father out of my head so I can concentrate on whatever the team needs from me. Even that feels easier now. His voice doesn't even echo.

I can do this.

Whatever it is.

Whatever needs to be done.

I rap my knuckles on Coach's door and wait until he calls me in.

The woman from earlier is sitting in one of the chairs across from his desk. She taps on an iPad and looks over at me as I take the seat next to her.

I give her a polite nod. "Ma'am."

"Burkehammer, this is Debra Schofield." Coach's eyes narrow, his crow's feet spreading out. It feels like he's trying to communicate something to me. "She's from the Canadiens."

"Nice to meet you," I say.

"You too." She extends a hand, which I take, and then I sit

silently while she taps her iPad awake and scans it. "Eden? Or do you prefer Burkehammer?"

"Burkehammer." I pause. "Or Burk, please."

"Call me Debra." She taps the screen a few times, but the glare from the overhead lights makes it impossible to see what she's doing. "Burk, I understand that you've been starting in left D since your sophomore year here."

"Yes, ma'am." I nod, not sure why I'm here.

"That's right," Coach cuts in. "Although Burkehammer's strong no matter where I put him. He's been running offensive drills at practices. The kid's got more dedication than half the team tied together."

Debra taps on her iPad. "How long have you been playing with Henley?"

Understanding dawns. This is about Vain.

"We've been playing together since we both came to IFU," I say. "Three and a half years now. He's a solid player. A good captain. A good teammate. Zero complaints about the guy."

She nods, still tapping on her iPad.

Holy fuck, she's really planning on signing him. There's no other reason she'd be in here asking about him. I try to tuck back the smile that's growing deep inside. He deserves it so damn much. One of us getting signed feels like a victory for all of us.

When she glances back up, her brown eyes zero in on my face. "That's good to hear. We're looking to deepen our lineup, and Henley's been on our radar for quite some time."

"He'll be a hell of an asset to the Canadiens."

"Good of you to say." She tilts her head. "I also noticed the way you two played together out there today. You earned a tough win."

"Thanks. It wouldn't have happened without Shaw shutting everything down in the third. Especially with that last swing around from Graves after—"

Coach squints at me. "I don't think Ms. Schofield is here to discuss goalkeeping."

I flash Coach a look I probably shouldn't and then catch myself. Honestly, I'm not fully sure why I'm still in this office. She's looking for information about Vain, but it feels like I've answered that question now.

Debra arches a brow at Coach, and his chair creaks as he leans back.

She turns back to me. "It might have been a different game if the entire defensive line weren't so on point. But the Canadiens are settled on goaltending at the moment."

"Toussaint's been amazing in the crease all season." I rub my hands on my thighs, trying to sort out what to say. I can talk Habs hockey all day, but she knows the team far better than I do. "If you want to talk more about Vain, then I'm happy to—"

She arches her brow. "I'm here to talk about you."

"Me?"

"Yes, you."

"Uh." I've got nothing. Other than a ringing noise in my ears.

Is she serious?

Her smile fades. "Your coach has provided me with a significant amount of statistics, and I'll look at them over the next few days. Unlike Henley, you haven't been on our radar for as long, so I'm not prepared to discuss an offer at this time. However, I want to know if you'd be interested in a trip to Montreal to join practice on a tryout basis. It would be an opportunity for us to take a look at you and determine if you might fit into the organization."

Holy fuck.

I'm frozen in my seat, not a single coherent thought in my head.

"Practice with the Habs?" My voice breaks, my lungs aching since I've forgotten to breathe for the last minute.

"On a tryout basis." She tilts her head. "Are you interested?"

"I . . ." I lick my lips.

Shaw.

He pops into my head, so clearly it's like he's right in the room with us, wearing that backward pink ballcap and smiling while he bounces on his toes, *excited* for me. I get this second weight in my chest that isn't about a lack of air.

"Of course he's interested," Coach barks. "Get your tongue out and answer, Burkehammer."

Debra turns cool eyes towards Coach. "Coach Howell, would you give us a few minutes?"

Coach tenses. "I, um . . . sure."

He stands and limps around his desk.

Shit, I've never seen him take direction like that before.

When the door closes behind him, Debra sets her tablet on her lap. "I'd rather be direct about the situation, Burk. There's no requirement that you're interested. And if that's the case, I'd prefer to know now, before we proceed any further."

"I'm interested," I say. "A bit shocked."

"I understand. Is there anything you want to discuss?"

Shaw would tell me to ask questions. He'd tell me to follow this through. He'd tell me to go for it.

"How long would I practice with the team?" I ask.

She nods. "Forty-eight hours maximum if we cover all expenses."

I nod. "When?"

"Next week would be preferred."

"That soon?"

"I understand you have commitments here," she says. "But we're on a tight schedule. I'm sorry, but that's the way it is."

I rub a hand over the back of my neck. My fingers are trembling, and my toes feel numb.

She looks at me expectantly. "So will we see you in Montreal?"

Shaw is so bright in my thoughts, leaning against Coach's desk, grinning at me in the way he does. *Believe it, Burkie.*

Playing in the NHL has been the focus of my entire existence. A dream so big that it's never felt achievable.

But what if you suddenly wake up and realize you have two dreams? The one you've carried around for all your life—that you've struggled and battled every day toward—and then the one that you just found?

A man so vibrant and present that it feels like he's here even now.

What if those two dreams might not be on the same path?

Debra crosses her legs, leaning in closer. Waiting for an answer.

I have to give her one.

"Burk?" she asks.

Words that I will forever remember:

1. "I think you should trust yourself, Burkie."
2. "I kinda don't want it to stop."
3. "I'm quiet, because I wanted to."
4. "We would have been there for you in a heartbeat."
5. "I don't think it's actually about the bed."
6. "I'm with Burkie. All the way."
7. "I'm happy."

CHAPTER TWENTY-ONE

Shaw

The moment I see Burkie, I know something's wrong.

It's not even the scowl on his face or the way he's standing stiffly next to Vain, lost in his thoughts. It's something else I can't physically pick out.

It's a feeling, a sense. A tightness. Something honed from being around him so much.

I set my cup aside and lean closer to Kelsey.

"Hey, I've got to take care of something." I nod to the half-completed beer pong game. "Step in for me?"

"Don't mind at all," Kels says with a smile. She's been eyeing one of the girls I've been playing with.

But I'm already beelining toward Burkie before she takes my place.

Something's very clearly *wrong*.

Everyone else is too pumped to notice. Cassidy and O'Hern chat nearby. Les is talking with some players from the women's team. Vain's laughing big and loud. When I head over, he slaps my shoulder and then shouts something at Dare.

I'm not listening. I'm one hundred percent focused on Burkie and that deep line down his forehead. I don't know when he got here. I'd expected him to find me. But I push that aside too, and I just step right up to him and pull him into a hug.

He grunts in surprise, his body stiffening, and then he exhales a long breath, his shoulders relaxing slightly. He's still tense though.

And holy hell, he smells good. Vanilla and that musky, masculine smell of his. I squeeze him tighter, feeling the hard strike of his heart as I lean close.

"What's wrong?" I whisper. And I know I shouldn't do it, but I press my lips under his ear. Just for a second—less than that—a fraction of a moment. My body pulls toward him, like it always does. A groan rattles in his throat, and his arms tighten around me.

We *hug*. I don't give a shit that we're standing in the middle of the living room, surrounded by our teammates.

I don't give a shit that this is probably looking less and less like a bro-hug by the second.

I fucking *hug* him. Because something's wrong.

After a few more thumps of his heart, I force myself to step back. I meet his gaze as I reach up to resettle my hat backward, and his eyes darken before his Adam's apple moves with a thick roll. Everything is loud and rambunctious around us, but I feel so *still* with him.

But he hasn't answered my question.

"How was dinner?" I ask, trying to take a different tack.

His lips press. "They didn't show."

I blink. "You were there by yourself?"

He itches at his scruff, his fingers tight. "I sat at the fuckin' table, staring at a basket of bread. And they didn't show. Didn't respond to texts. Even my little sis." He glances away from me, like he's trying to tuck away some of his emotions, but his jaw is so tight it's twitching.

I try to read every single thing I can on his face. "Did something happen?"

Jesus, like a car accident or something? I don't say it out loud. I don't want to stress him more than he already is.

He shakes his head, still not looking at me. "Sorry, but I'm not up for this tonight. I'm going to—"

"*Burk*!"

Burkie's attention flits behind me, then he forces his shoulders to relax as he reaches around to fist bump Leslie before Dare slaps him on the shoulder. They're both talking a thousand miles per hour, and Burkie shoves a breakable smile on his face.

There's talk of doing a shot. We take what Dare hands us, but I'm hardly paying attention as we do a wolf howl and throw them back. I'm watching Burkie.

As soon as we're done, I lean in close. "Let's go upstairs."

He shakes his head. "You don't have to—"

"Follow me." I turn and push between bodies to climb the stairs ahead of him, not stopping until I open his door and step inside. The door snicks closed behind us.

We're in the dark. Finally alone, and a million questions race through my mind. "Are you—"

He fists my shirt and drags me to him, then he's kissing me, lips firm as he leans into me, my shirt tugged tight under my armpits.

We just *kiss*.

For a moment. For eternity.

Time stops. It's me and him—alone in the space that's only us. No lights, no one else. Just kissing, him fisting my shirt like he needs something so desperately that the only thing he can do is grip on to me. And I hold him right back.

He finally breaks the kiss, his hands falling to my sides, his forehead settling on my shoulder. I wrap my arms around him, tightening the bulk of his body against mine, his chest expanding and contracting raggedly.

"Want to tell me what happened?" I thread my fingers through his hair, stroking the nape of his neck with my thumb. "Eden?"

He's shaking, and that scares the hell out of me.

"I came out to my father," he says into my shoulder.

Holy shit. And then they didn't show up to dinner? His family *ditched* him because he came out? Left him sitting there alone. I squeeze my eyes shut. A hard knot builds in my throat. The cold anger that settles deep in me is completely unfamiliar. I'm rarely angry, but I'm pissed as hell about this.

"*That's* why they didn't show?" I cut out. His fucking father. I don't like confrontation, but for Burkie, I'd step toe to toe with that man.

"The thing is, I only told my dad." His thick biceps flex as he hugs me so fiercely that it nearly collapses my lungs. "Not my mother or sis, but they weren't answering texts either, so I don't know. I knew he wouldn't understand, but I thought that maybe they would. That they'd at least talk to me."

His voice cracks, and it feels like my heart might too.

"I'm here." I don't know what else to say. I don't have control over his family. I can't answer for them. I can't fix things.

All I can do is widen my stance to hold his weight, stroking my fingers through his hair as he presses his forehead against my shoulder. Keep standing here next to him the same way that he always does for me.

"Shaw," he whispers as he turns his head to brush his lips against the base of my neck, kissing with an open mouth along my jaw and then across to my lips. He palms the nape of my neck, keeping me close, our kiss slow and deep. Meaningful.

Not that dirty words and the fun we've had together aren't meaningful. But this is different. Something that makes my pulse feel heavier, my feet more firmly fixed on the ground.

He's my rock. Steady and strong.

And I can be his.

Outside of my family, I don't know if I've ever been someone's rock before. But it's easy to be his.

I want to be.

He steps back and yanks off his shirt before walking us backward, tugging me with him toward the bed until he pulls me down, and I go with him. Wherever he wants to go.

We move up until he's lying back with his head sinking onto his pillow, the light just bright enough for me to see his hair curling around his ears and brushing his neck. His lips part before his teeth graze over the bottom one.

I brace myself above him, just staring down. "I like looking at you." The shadows hide part of his face, but he's so big and solid underneath me. Thick scruff and deep brown eyes and a steadiness that grounds me. Makes it feel like I'm exactly where I want to be.

My knees settle on the mattress on either side of him, my palms splayed by his shoulders. I bend to kiss him, and his hands smooth up my back, tracking lightly under my shirt, along my spine, and then across the full breadth of my shoulders.

"Let me get lost in you," he whispers, picking his head up off the pillow. "*Please*, Shaw. Use that magnificent fuckin' tongue on me."

I hesitate. I can't fully explain the weight of emotion in me right now. So I don't try. Instead, I bend my elbows and move down him, licking across that dusting of hair, flicking my tongue at his nipple, and relishing the way the little bud firms in my mouth. I'm hesitant at the bruising along his shoulder from today's game, but when I dip below to kiss his navel, he arches, powerful and firm and beautifully strong.

He groans, palming my shoulders before he slides his hands between us and unbuttons his jeans. I shift onto my knees and move his hands aside, undoing his zipper, my breath catching at the sight of him, commando in his jeans. I yank them partially off, the fabric tight around his thighs. I crawl back and take his cock into my mouth.

I don't tease. Don't play. I take him down to the back of my throat, and he lets out a long, arduous exhale as he thickens against my tongue.

We're silent. Except for the low guttural groans he makes, and the wet sounds as I suck him down. The taste of his pre-cum fills my mouth, his deep, sexy smell surrounding me. His fingers brush through the tendrils of hair that stick out from under my hat, his dark eyes fixed down on me. We move together so effortlessly. In sync. Aware. This kind of intense comfort vibrates between us. Warmth and quiet solace.

Comfort.

I've never felt anything like it before. It's like taking what we have on the ice and multiplying it times a million. Like how it feels when I snuggle into him, except it's edged with this fierce sexuality as his cockhead flares against the roof of my mouth. His pelvis pushes up.

"Too close," he mumbles, gripping my jaw gently. "Give me a second."

"Okay." I scoot back so I can shimmy his jeans the rest of the way off. I lay kisses on his thighs before I toss his jeans on the floor.

I look back at him, my heart thumping a double beat at what he went through tonight.

He stretches a hand out towards me, and I lace my fingers through his as I crawl back on the bed. He tugs me down next to him, and I snuggle in, resting my cheek on the top of his shoulder.

"What do you want?" I ask. "We could talk. Or go back to the party."

"Don't want to go anywhere," he says, pressing me closer against him. "Right now, right here, with you, everything is okay."

Shit, I *feel* that.

It's always how I feel when I'm around Burkie. Like a million other things can be swirling around, the noises from the party going on, the extra practices, or the stresses about classes, but if he's there next to me, it will all be okay.

Everyone should have a Burkie.

Someone who makes things okay. Someone who makes a place feel like home just because they're in it.

We lie together. The thump of the music resonates beyond the door, but we're tangled together on his bed, breathing the same air, thinking the same thoughts. Just me and him.

After a few long minutes, I slide off the bed, and he tips his chin down toward my junk in a silent request that I know pretty freaking well by now. I smile at him as I tug down my pants, popping out like I'm on a spring. Then I drag my shirt over my head and resettle my hat backward.

He tucks one hand behind his head, the dark, thick hair underneath his arm making my dick twitch hard. "You're pretty fuckin' sexy."

"Oh, yeah? You think so?" I wink and fist myself. "What are you planning on doing with me?"

He reaches over and flicks on the bedside light then relaxes back into the mattress, his muscular thighs spreading. He's hard as hell, his reddened cock brushing against his stomach, but I'm fixated on his face, those dark eyes jumping all over me.

"Uh." He scrapes his teeth over his bottom lip, a little flush spreading across the top of his cheeks. "Still want to rim me?"

My entire body tightens in anticipation. "*Yes*. Right now. Let's not stop to talk. Legs up, *coaie*. Let's go."

He laughs softly, but I'm not fully joking. I mean, a little. But I can't think of anything I want more right now. His laugh fades as I climb back over the top of him, bending to kiss him, my dick grazing against his in a way that makes us both groan. He palms my ribs, dragging me closer.

We kiss, drawing it out, enjoying each other until I finally pull back.

"You ready?" I ask him.

He nods. "Yeah."

Okay, good. We're doing this.

I take in an eager-nervous breath, and then I scoot down so that I'm between his thighs, a groan rolling as I lower my head to nuzzle against his sack. My eyes roll into the back of my head. I know I should probably be moving, but I stay there, my hands splaying on his thighs, his hair tickling against my nose and cheek, the heat of his palm warming my shoulder.

I *missed* this. I seriously dreamed about Burkie's sack while I was in Chicago. Dreamed that I was snuggled against him, with my head right where it is now. Not really doing anything. Just being *with* him.

He sits up partially, his abs all washboarding in a way that makes my own clench, and reaches down to clip his fingers around the brim of my hat. He slips it off my head.

I tip my chin up to look at him. "Put it on."

He holds it by the brim. "Think my head's bigger than yours."

I laugh. "Jeez, trying to make a guy feel inadequate around your big heads?"

"Trust me, you've got nothing to feel inadequate about." He smiles down at me as he flips my hat and tucks it backward on his head.

"*Ești drăguț*," I say. My hat is small on him, his hair sticking out messily, the brim tipped to the side. "So damn cute. You should wear my hat more often." I waggle my brows. "Maybe we can get some matching ones. Old-married-couple style. We can be twinsies."

227

He chuckles. "I'd be twinsies with you anytime. But I'd rather wear yours."

"Oh, hell yeah. I like that." My smile falls, and I tip my head to bury my nose by the base of his cock, smelling him again.

A rumbling groan resonates through him, and I can feel his thighs relax as he lies back and sets my hat on the bedside table.

"Kick a leg up," I say.

Anticipation does a heavy loop in my stomach as he draws one knee up, bending so that his foot rests on the bed, his sack resting on his thigh. I push his other knee up and kiss the inside.

"Think we're ready for this?" I lick my lips, my eyes flicking back to his face. "I mean, we've been talking about it a bit, but doing it feels like a new thing."

"I'm ready." He drags his teeth over his bottom lip. "Are you? We don't have to. Blow jobs are heaven as far as I'm concerned."

"Nah, I want to." I reach down to adjust my thickening chub against the mattress. I *really* want to. "So . . . I'm going in."

I wiggle down a few inches, my eyes rolling as the sensitive head of my dick nestles between the mattress and my stomach, and then I dip my head to draw one of his balls into my mouth.

He drags in a sharp breath, and I take him into my mouth, letting my tongue flick around delicately, before pulling back and sucking on his scrotum. We've done this much before. But I've never moved lower.

I scoot down another inch and turn my head to kiss the inside of his thigh.

Jeez, I love being down here. Between his legs, his junk all in my face. Is it weird to say that it makes me feel really close to him? To be able to do this. To know how he smells, how he tastes. To hear his breath catch as I press my nose underneath his sack, surrounded by him, my ass cheeks clenching as I lick down farther, along his taint, lower, closing my eyes as my tongue flicks just to the side of his hole.

His reaction is instant, his thighs flexing as his feet kick off the bed.

"*Shaw,*" he groans, guttural and needy, his thighs widening on either side of me.

I have never in my life heard my name spoken like that. I want to hear it again. A thousand times over. I drag my tongue around him, and then, nerves still popping, I lick right over the top.

His hole puckers against the tip of my tongue.

"Wanna see it," I mumble and wiggle back, positioning myself so that I can see his tight hole, puckered and catching my attention so fiercely I forget everything else. "Holy hell, that's *hot.*"

Intensely hot. I thought it might all be about the mental game—thinking about fucking, about how tight it would be around my dick. But it's more than that. His hole is hot just as it is. Just looking at it. I wet my index finger and scrunch my shoulders together to reach up and stroke over him.

"Fuck, Shaw." He hitches his knees up higher. "Fuck. *Fuck.*"

I expected him to be more reserved, but it's such a turn on that he isn't. That he's all in for me. I lower my head and take a slower lick, this time licking a circle around him. Feeling the way he puckers, the way his thighs tighten against my shoulders, the full-on *smell* of him.

I pull back. "This is so hot-edged sexy. You have no idea."

"I *want* to know," he breathes out. "Need to do you, too."

I laugh, and my breath must tickle him because he shivers, his ass flexing. The sight makes my dick throb. And my mouth feels empty. I lean in to taste him again, tapping my tongue lightly over his hole then licking around his rim and blowing soft breaths.

I can't get enough. Like seriously, *not enough*. This is absolutely going to be a staple in our nights now. And it only gets better when I carefully and slowly complete another circle of his rim, my mind jumping back to him standing in the locker room, my fingertip sliding around his navel. How sexy he was. I groan and focus on the present. *Rimming* him. I freaking love it. I push the tip of my tongue in, feeling the contraction of his first ring of muscles.

He curses, saying my name like he did earlier, pulling his legs up even more, his hands clasped around his knees. I go in deeper, feeling him tighten, another tremor racing over him.

"Fuck, Shaw. More?" His voice trembles.

And, shit, I'm *right* there with him. My balls are throbbing, my hips rolling against the mattress, my tongue aching to get deeper. He contracts around the tip of my tongue, and I lick another circle around his rim and up to his taint before going back down and pressing into his hole. I don't stop, just keep going until he's writhing. Until he can't do anything but groan.

Not sure I'll ever get my fill of this.

But I finally pause because I'm pretty sure I'll have a jaw cramp if I don't. "Gonna get some lube."

It's almost painful to move out from between his legs, but I scooch over toward his bedside drawer. Once inside, I pause, my fingers lingering over a sleek, black sleeve.

One that I'm assuming houses the ass toy. I grab it and the lube before sliding back over to him, breathing out a sigh of relief when I'm close to him again. I drop my head to kiss the inside of his thigh, nibbling, licking.

"Ready?" I pop the cap off the lube and spread some on my fingers, rubbing them together to warm it.

He nods. "Think so."

I lick my lips and slide my slicked finger over his perineum then, very carefully, press the very tip into his hole.

He exhales sharply, jaw tightening.

"You good?"

"Yeah." His hands are still tucked around his knees, and I pause to take all of him in before I push my finger in a touch further. He's so tight and hot that I groan.

"How's that?" I ask.

He drags his teeth over his bottom lip. "Different than your tongue."

"Good to keep going?"

He nods, and I press in deeper. With a crook of my finger, I *feel* it. His prostate. Firmer against my finger pad. He clearly feels it too because he grunts, staring down at me between his knees with this kind of shocked, glassy-eyed gawk.

I think that surprised him.

"Fuck," he mumbles. "It feels like . . . I'm going to come. But . . . not. *Don't stop.*"

"I won't." Not unless he asks. "You're really fucking sexy, Eden. Spread out for me like this."

His head falls back on the pillow, his eyes closing. "I'm nothing compared to you. You're on-my-knees gorgeous. So much that it *hurts*. Like this blinding ache in my gut."

I blink at him, taken aback. "That's going a bit overboard."

"It's not." He smashes his lips together. "Just trust me."

"Well, I'll trust that my finger up your ass is making you see certain things."

"It's more than—" He exhales a sudden groan when I press my finger pad just slightly firmer against his prostate. "*Fuuuck.* I'm . . ." He shakes his head, his hand going to his dick.

He takes a sexy stroke, his lips parting with another groan, and the head of his cock deepens into a blush. I inch forward to nibble along the inside of his thigh, slowly working his prostate, licking and kissing. Just enjoying. I love when my hands, tongue, mouth, dick, *anything* is on Burkie. Being next to him . . . It's not like being with anyone else.

I could stay here forever. In this bed. Watching him. A deep thrum vibrates low in my balls, and if I let myself, I could come just doing *this* with him.

Which is freaking mind-blowing. Never in my life have I come by watching someone else get off.

I could because it's him.

Whatever's changed between us these last two weeks, it resonates between us right now. Zinging through every cell as I stare at my best damn friend. A raw heat slips up my spine, and I dip to kiss along his thighs and then slip my finger from him.

"Want to push things a bit further?" I ask, twisting to grab the ass toy that rests a foot away on the mattress.

"I'm good for anything." He smiles cutely. "Seriously, fuckin' anything."

"You know I'm in." I slide the vibrator out of the silky black sleeve. "Did you wash this?"

He tracks my movements. "I did."

My grin widens. I don't know why it's so wholesomely cute picturing Burkie washing his ass toy—getting it all ready, his hair falling in his eyelashes—but hell, it is.

"You wanna?" I ask, waggling it.

"Yes. Except . . ." He scrapes his teeth over his bottom lip. "I want to use it on you."

CHAPTER TWENTY-TWO

Shaw

I freeze, ass toy waggling in the air, the music and noise of the party fading away to nothing. "Didn't you get this to answer questions about yourself?"

He tilts his head, taking a slow, measured stroke of his cock. "Already answered all those questions."

My brows go up. "Yeah?"

He takes another slow stroke. "Conclusively."

I get this lump in my throat. It's so clear from his expression that he means *us*—what we've been doing. And, shit, so many emotions all crash together. The backs of my eyes heat a little, but I'm not sure what to do with all this freaking emotion. It's all jumbled in my head.

I just know that I like being here with him. A hell of a lot.

He tips his chin down, still smiling slightly as he unfists his cock and reaches a hand down toward the toy. "Turn around."

I blink at him, swallowing back the lump. "Like sixty-nine?"

"Yep."

Oh, shit.

YES. I try to keep my excitement contained, but I slam my knee into his side, making him grunt, in my haste to crawl on top of him. I am not capable of playing it cool.

Don't wanna have to play it cool. Nerves hit me hard as I straddle his chest, sixty-nining him and exposing everything right there to his face. My stomach pinches a little. I glance toward the door but then calm myself. Door locked. Everyone else is occupied.

It's just us.

Burkie palms my ass cheeks. "Your ass bending out like this . . . fuck*me*." He sucks in a sharp breath, and blows it out, puffing against my balls. Goosebumps rise across my shoulders.

"Inch back," he says. "Can't reach."

I set my hands on either side of his hips and scoot back, my spine elongating, my jitters tightening my shoulders. His breath grows warmer against my ass as he must sit partly up behind me. I twist to see him messing with the pillow behind his head.

"I'm kinda nervous," I tell him as I twist forward again. His cock is a little way under my chin. His thighs are spread. The light just bright enough to see the hair covering them, and past them down to his shins, and beyond that, his socked feet.

My stomach does a swoop, taking him all in.

"Just relax. I'm right here." His low voice behind me makes me close my eyes, my breath expelling, my nerves abating.

He guides me back, positioning me where he wants me. "And how is this so sexy?"

"I know, right?" I smile, but it vanishes into a throat-caught moan as a wet heat suddenly tongues across one of my ass cheeks. No hesitation, he just goes in, and then, before I can get my full balance, wet warmth grazes over my hole.

I forget to be nervous.

I pant out a cluster of pleas, squeezing my eyes shut. The entire world around us fades—all completely gone. The only thing I'm fully aware of is the wet heat of his tongue as he licks again. Every nerve zaps alive, from my ass to the nape of my neck, like they're all colliding and quaking. I whimper, eking out a few confused words as the pressure mounts, his lips moving, tongue pushing inside of me.

My mouth drops open, and I dip down, sucking the head of his cock into my mouth. I can't really give him head from this angle, only suck on the flared tip, but I just hold him in my mouth, wet and slick with pre-cum.

The vibration of his responding moan ricochets against my hole, and fuck . . . I'm clinging to the edge. Trembling. My lips shivering around his head, his body underneath mine.

He's all around me. Right there. And suddenly there's nothing to be scared of. Like there's nowhere to unexpectedly fall. Nothing that can be taken away.

I'm barely cognizant enough to hear the pop of the lube cap and then the low hum of the vibrator right before it brushes against my inner thigh. I shiver harder, and it's so much damn input that I don't know what to focus on. The way he's tonguing me? The tip of the vibe dragging up and down the inside of my thigh? The flare of his head in my mouth? The deep thump of my pulse in my throat? It's overwhelming as hell.

"Fuck," he mumbles, but he keeps tonguing me, rubbing my thighs with that ass toy, and I moan, canting my hips back to get more. And then his tongue is gone, and a vibration touches against my hole, echoing deep into my pelvis.

"*Eden*." I'm shaking so hard that I can hardly hold myself, my muscles all feel spent, but it's all forgotten as the vibe presses slowly into my hole, pinching at first. I relax my muscles, my eyes rolling back in my head, my saliva slicking down his shaft.

"So fuckin' sexy," he says. "Watching this black shaft slide into you. The way you clench." He shutters, pre-cum flooding my tongue. "Your beautiful ass spread for me."

I think I whimper. I don't know. It might be a mewl. It's the only sound I can make as he presses the vibe deeper, then angles it until I'm hardly able to get a read on reality.

He groans loudly, drowning out the sound of the vibrator, the sounds of the music from downstairs, the sounds of everything else as he fills me, pressing in until the curved base settles against my taint and balls. He kisses my ass cheeks, tilting me back more, then his tongue laps at my crease. His chin must be holding in the toy, and he rocks it softly.

The heat inside me is scorching, coursing across my shoulders, making sweat rise on the back of my neck. Even my scalp feels like it's a million degrees. It's a whole-body palpitation that's far beyond where he's licking me, touching me.

And it's good. And I could come like this, no question.

But I want *him*.

"Fuck me," I mumble around his cock.

His body stills underneath mine. "Shaw?"

I pull off his cock. "Want you to fuck me."

"Are you sure?"

I nod, squeezing my eyes shut, that vibrator still pulsing deep. "Want you inside me." I didn't realize how much until now. I've imagined it, pictured him bending me over the arm of a couch or maybe right in the locker room showers, the slap of our skin echoing off the tiles, but it's a different kind of need that presses through me now. It's not because it's new, or different, or hot. It's because it's *Burkie*. "Want that big, beautiful cock of yours all up inside of me."

He's quiet, still not moving, so I open my eyes and twist to see him. I can only see part of his face, but he's staring at me, those lines on his forehead. Then it's like something releases, like what I've said finally sinks in because he palms my ass harder, his cock twitching against his abs.

"Do you want that?" I ask him, whimpering as the vibe slips a little. "Do you wanna—"

He *smiles*. "Fuck *yes*."

And then we're both moving. I whine when he slips the vibrator out and turns it off. He tosses it aside somewhere and then fumbles in the bedside drawer for a condom. We move fast, a thousand percent focused on goal. It can't happen quickly enough. It *needs* to be now, and it's only a half breath before he's on his knees behind me.

"Eden," I mumble, my hips already moving back. It's insane how much I want him.

"I'm here," he says. And then the fat head of his cock presses against my hole.

I take a ragged breath, forcing myself to relax, my shins on either side of his knees as he palms my hips, pulling me slowly back.

We both moan. Pressure binds across my pelvis as he stretches me, bigger than the vibe, and so much more potent.

"You control it." His hands stay on my hips, not moving me, letting me push back. Letting me set the pace as I fill myself with him. I don't know why that matters so much. But it's like this little proof of how much he cares. He's always taking care of me. Looking out for me.

I let out a fractured breath, willing myself to relax as I take all of him, filled so full that it seems almost impossible.

"Shaw?" His palms tighten on my ass cheeks, massaging them lightly, his heavy weight behind me dipping the mattress.

I breathe out, slowing my thoughts, realizing *exactly* what's happening. He's inside me. And just that realization is making my release start to swell.

"I could come already," I grit out. I can't stop myself from grinding back, squeezing my eyes through the pinch, but it morphs into a spreading kind of throb, making my toes curl, my calves flex.

He lets out a husky groan. But he's not moving.

"Don't hold back." I dip forward until my forehead falls against the bed, my ass in the air. I *want* him to pound into me, to feel him everywhere. My knees and thighs shake with anticipation. My fingers splay on the mattress even though he's hardly moving. "Fucking pound me, Eden."

"Patience." His fingers dig in hard. He pulls back, then he slowly thrusts back in. "You feel so good."

"You do too," I manage. "Big and thick in my ass. But want more." I'm not breathing as he does it again—that slow pull back and thrust in. Once, twice. My eyes squeeze shut, and a sudden pleasure wracks through me so hard that it about knocks me off my knees. I've had my prostate massaged before, of course, but it's nothing like what I'm feeling now. I don't know if it's because he's bigger—or hitting it at the right angle—or maybe it's the connection that *he's* inside me. Maybe it's about a hell of a lot more than just dicks and glands.

"Fuck, Shaw," he whispers, and I get the idea he's clenching his teeth, restraining himself. He pulls out the third time, and I expect the controlled thrust back in, but he hesitates.

Then he slams in.

My mouth falls open. I'm lost in that hazy world again, just me and him, alone, as he starts to fuck me—*really* fuck me. Driving deep, making moans tumble from my mouth. I struggle to brace myself against his force, the thrust of our bodies moving together.

His hand slides to my shoulder, and he braces himself, driving in harder, the slap of our flesh echoing, our grunts and curses getting louder, my dick bouncing every time he pounds into me. I linger on the edge of pure, absolute rapture. I didn't know this world existed.

"Wanna see you." I grit my teeth, struggling to stave off back the release that's starting to crest, then he's suddenly gone, pulling out and gripping my hip, pushing me to the side.

"Ride me," he says close to my ear, and I'm nodding as he rolls onto his back next to me. I crawl over him, straddling him high up on my knees, then I grip his condomed shaft and meet his eyes.

I want to say something dirty. Tell him how freaking hot he looks underneath me as I slowly sink down, his shoulders bowed forward as he reaches for my thighs, but I can't get a single word out.

It's another experience. Getting to see his expression, the flare of his nostrils as I adjust to his thick cock, the groan that vibrates his Adam's apple as I rotate my hips. It kicks everything to a new level.

I lean back, my feet coming up so that I'm squatting over him and my hands fall back by his knees to support me, and I start to fuck myself on him. Just all out, using all the strength in my thighs and stomach and arms for support.

"Fuck," he groans, taking all of me in, from my face to my tensed pecs, from my bobbing dick to my knees and my feet. There isn't a part of me that he doesn't look at. "You're so flexible."

We move. Finding that rhythm together.

It's not just sex.

It's something more. Growing between us as he focuses back on my face, his eyes catching on me like he can't see anything else.

It's a high that I've never come close to hitting before. Not in the bedroom. Not on the ice. Not a single time in my life.

I all out ride him, my release building fiercely. His jaw tightens, that blush deepening on his face, and I swear I can feel his cock swelling in me.

"Come in me," I pant. "Want to feel it."

His rough groan razors up my spine as he slams hard into me. His jaw clenches hard, breath halting, every part of him goes rigid, and he comes, the heat pulsing inside me. I can feel it—even through the condom. The spasms of his cock. The almost feral look in his eyes.

And with that, I'm gone. My release wrecks through me, and I spurt hard, covering his chest and abs. I'm still coming as I realize that there isn't a single bit of friction on my dick.

I come from watching him. From his cock in my ass. From the expression on his face. It all comes together in this perfect melody.

He calls my name as he milks out the last of his release, and then we both collapse, all the rigidity leaving my body as I flop on top of him, my cum sticky between our chests, our breath ragged.

His arms wrap around me, dragging me closer. He kisses the side of my jaw with dry lips.

"Holy fuck," I whisper. And I . . . fuck . . . I can't stop trembling. My throat's closing up. And I'm not sure what's going on.

I'm feeling *a lot*. Like way more than I usually do. It's swirling all around me and making a clusterfuck in my head, and I want to tell him, but I don't know that I can explain it coherently.

So I reach for the only emotion that's vividly bright in all the chaos.

"I'm happy," I whisper.

I start to say more—that sounded stupid, I think? But he must get me because he hugs me tighter against him. His hands slide up to my shoulders, pasting me against his damp skin so there's no space between us.

"Me too," he says, and there's a thick catch in his words.

Are we both freaking crying?

Sometimes I wonder if I'm processing everything that's happening between us. Like it's too damn much. I hope that

maybe someday, I'll understand it all more. But for now, I do the only thing that makes sense to me: I hug him so furiously that my arms ache. We stay like that for long minutes, until my chest itches from drying cum.

My ass feels empty, stretched. The rest of me feels like the complete opposite.

"Do you want to get cleaned up?" I ask after a while.

"Yeah, I do." He moves out from underneath me.

"Nah, I got it." I stand up, my legs shaky. "Let me."

He blinks. "You sure?"

"Yep." I kneel next to him and set my fingers at the base of the condom, slipping it off his softening cock. He lets out a strangled breath when it comes off.

I pinch the condom closed and laugh at the bulge in the tip. "Do you ever have a normal amount of cum?"

He settles his hand behind his head, watching me as I cross to the trash can by the desk. "What I do is normal."

I laugh and grab a box of tissues before crossing back to him. I kneel on the bed and wipe along the deep tracks of his abs. "Your big ol' bulge of cum is pretty hot."

"Well, it's your fault." A half smile spans his face. "I have something else to tell you."

"What's up?" I crumple the tissue and get another, not sure that it's necessary, but getting to tickle around his navel is getting me worked up again.

"I met with the scout from the Canadiens."

I freeze, tissue hovering above his stomach. "What?"

"Today, after the game. You were still in the shower." His eyes shift around my face. "I didn't tell you."

"You're telling me now."

He nods. "I needed to think about it for a bit. The scout— her name is Debra. She offered me a tryout."

Holy shit. "In Montreal?"

He licks his lips nervously. "I'd be gone for a week. To see if it's a good fit."

"Seriously?" I blink down at him.

"Yep."

"You got *scouted*?"

"It's just a practice—"

"Holy hell, Burkie." I crash over him. Our knees knock, and I'm bouncing up and down, the whole mattress lurching under us. I kiss him. Wet sloppy kisses all over his face, and he laughs.

I pull back. "I need the details. When? For how long are you going? And why aren't you jumping out of your skin? This is *huge*."

"I, uh, didn't answer. Told her I would respond in the morning."

"What?" My mouth falls open. "Why?"

His brow lines. "Not sure I'm going to take it."

I freeze, straddled over the top of him. "*Why?*"

"I'm not sure it's what I want to focus on right now." He runs his tongue over his bottom lip, and there's something in his eyes that I can't decipher.

I'm clearly not connecting something. This is what we've both wanted from day one. It's not something that I'd expect either of us to question.

But is he?

"Not something you want to focus on? After a lifetime of going after *exactly* this?"

"It's just . . ." He presses his lips. "The thought of leaving the team in the middle of the season—even for a week—it's shitty."

"The team," I repeat.

He nods. "I'll miss a couple of games."

"Pfft, Wyoming and NMU. We got it covered. Then it's winter break, and we're off for almost a full week. The timing couldn't be better."

"You're telling me to go," he says.

Shit.

I *am* telling him to go. A twist of cold fear tingles down my spine at the thought of not seeing him every day. That he could just be gone. All those emotions crowd up again.

But I wipe it off my face. Doesn't matter. "It's an opportunity you might not get twice. We're all leaving at some point." I scooch back until I'm sitting on his thighs. "Leaving the Wolfpack. Leaving hockey house."

That little twist of fear down my spine quivers harder.

He stares at me, eyes dark.

"This is what we do," I finally conclude—because that's the truth. This is why we're here. Why we get up in the morning. Why we push ourselves. This is it.

The dream.

Burkie's dream. And that fucking matters.

The sharp pinch in my chest doesn't change that. It shouldn't.

Shit. I swallow. I don't know how to sort through what I'm thinking. Or how to read the look that passes through his eyes. Something almost pained.

And, fuck, did I hurt him?

He catches my hand, lacing his fingers through mine. "I want to ask you—"

"*Burk.*" His door rattles with a pounded fist. We both sigh.

He groans. "For fuckin' real?"

I scrub my free hand over my face. "Is there always someone about to smash in your door?"

"Usually." He sits partway up. "But it used to be you."

"That sounds accurate."

The door rattles again. "Hey, Burk, man. You in there?"

"Sounds like Dare." I let my hand fall. "It's probably just another round of shots. We could probably miss that shit."

His fingers tighten around mine. "Are you proposing that we not let anyone know we're here?"

"Yep." I wiggle my hips. "Not done with you yet."

He laughs. "That so?"

"Figure you can fuck my ass up at least once more."

He raises a brow. "I'd be down for—"

"*Burk.*" The door rattles longer now. "Dude, I'm sorry if you've got someone in there but—"

Burkie hitches a brow, and I bend to kiss him.

"—your mom and sister are here," Dare finishes.

Well, shit.

Words that I will forever remember:

1. "I think you should trust yourself, Burkie."
2. "I kinda don't want it to stop."
3. "I'm quiet, because I wanted to."
4. "We would have been there for you in a heartbeat."
5. "I don't think it's actually about the bed."
6. "I'm with Burkie. All the way."
7. "I'm happy."
8. "I just want to be us."

CHAPTER TWENTY-THREE

Burk

I lie there for a second longer, my arms locking harder around Shaw.

They're fine. I'm smacked by relief.

When Shaw asked earlier what happened—why they didn't show for dinner—about a million things flipped through my head, because I really don't know. First I was afraid it was because I came out to my father. But there was another fear too. That something else bad had happened. I drove around town for a while, past their hotel, down the busier streets. But I hadn't found them.

"Go." Shaw slips out of my arms and reaches off the side of the bed to snag my jeans off the floor. He tosses them to me.

"Be there in a sec," I call out to Dare, pulling on my jeans and bouncing to zip them.

Shaw stands up next to me, beautifully naked. And, fuck . . . I stare at him for a half a second, all lithely muscled and the corner of his lips turning up in a familiar half smirk. I had no fuckin' clue that sex could be like that. And certainly didn't think that *I'd* ever experience it. And least of all with a man like him.

I clutch his neck and drag him in for a kiss before grabbing my shirt and stepping out the door. The urgency to find out what happened with my mom and sis is building, though I stop to wash my hands and throw some water on my face before jogging down the stairs.

The sight in the living room is one I never expected to see.

The house is in full-on party mode. Bodies crush everywhere. It's not insane, but it's not calm either. And my mom —dressed in her puffy, lime green jacket with her curly hair falling over her shoulders—is standing inside the door with my sister, both of them looking so out of place that it tugs at my heart.

I cut through the chaos toward them, a knot forming in my throat. My mom's eyes widen when she sees me. She steps into me, her arms going around my torso, her head resting on my chest as I hug her back. She always kind of folds into me, ever since I grew taller than her in middle school. I look over her head to take in my sis, also taller than my mom but still my little sis, with the big, blue glasses and the long limbs and the knobby knees.

Fuck. My throat closes even more.

"Are you okay?" I push out as my mom steps back, my hand grasping her shoulder. "I was worried about both of you."

Mom's chin wobbles, and I swear my heart crushes into a pulp. "He didn't tell us, Eden. He said that you were celebrating with the team and that you didn't have the time to eat with us."

My jaw twitches, and I lean closer to hear over the music. "He did what?"

"I didn't know." She reaches out and grabs my t-shirt, her hand fisting into a small ball. "Not until Lacey saw your messages. We went to a movie, and then she showed me your texts and we asked him, and Eden . . . I would *never* not want to see you."

I close my eyes to stem off the heat racing up behind them. When I open them again, Mom's lips press thinly.

"I told him . . ." Her chin trembles. "That he's not allowed to ever get between me and my son again."

I glance over at my sis, raising my brows in silent question. My mom's not always direct about the things my father does, but Lacey usually is.

My sister purses her lips. "Dad yelled."

Fuck.

"Was it bad?" I ask her.

Lacey's eyes are big in her glasses, magnified from being far-sighted, and they hold so many damn thoughts and feelings that are so familiar. Because I grew up with that man too.

Maybe I never should have left them.

But then I wouldn't be here. Wouldn't know Shaw. I can't give that up either.

Regardless, it's a moot point, already decided and done.

I step toward my sis and wrap her in a solid hug. Her coat is still cold from the chill night. Lacey and I have never hugged much. Growing up, we were dirt bikes and skinned knees and catching crawfish in the creek out past my parents' property, Lacey wearing her white shrimp boots with unicorns drawn in blue Sharpie all over the sides.

But never hugs.

It's stiff and awkward, but it's still a hug.

"If you ever need a place to go," I say into her hair, quieter now that the music has died down. "All you have to do is tell me, and I'll find a way to get you."

Her thin arms squeeze me. "I'm finding my own way."

"I'll be there for that too." I kiss the top of her head and then step back.

Mom's watching us, her lips in a sad smile. "He said things, Eden," she says. "I don't know if they're true."

Around us, it's not just the music that's quieted. People are probably noticing that something's going on. Conversations are fading. Eyes flit to me and then away.

Shaw's right there at the bottom of the stairs with his hands in his pockets. His pink ballcap is backward, his hair sticking out of the sides. He tilts his head. I'm not sure if it's a nod or not, but it settles in my chest. My feet feel steadier, my breath comes easier.

I'm no longer scrambling up that mountain. He pulls me onto that rock. Except, the rock feels bigger than it used to.

Dare, Vain, and Leslie are here too. Most of the team is. Some of the baseball jocks and Kelsey and half the women's team and a whole host of other people.

I turn back to my mom.

"You can say it." I keep my voice steady. It's silent enough in the room now that most everyone can hear me, but I don't care. Or maybe I do care. I care a lot. And that's why I want to say it too. "Dad told you that I'm gay, didn't he?"

"What you must have thought when we didn't come to dinner." Mom tilts her head to stare up at me. "And I know that this probably isn't the best time for your mom to show up, but I tried calling and didn't get an answer." She wrings her hands. "Lacey and I couldn't sit in that hotel room knowing what you must be thinking. We had to see you. And your roommate Darren said that he'd find you."

"You're always welcome here, Mom."

Mom reaches out to touch my arm. "You know that you're my little Eden, right? You always will be, no matter how old you get or how your life changes."

I swallow. "I know that back home—"

She shakes her head sharply. "The door will always be unlocked for you."

I hesitate. As much as I want those words, I don't know how to take them. It's pretty much the opposite of what I've been told for my entire life.

"It's different," she says, scanning my face, seeming to read me pretty fuckin' clearly. "I . . . I don't know that I've ever known someone who is gay."

"I'm sure you have. And you know me."

She pales. "I was so stupid to say that. An—"

"Mom," I cut in. "No, don't beat yourself up."

I can hear my father so clearly in her words. The same voice that I have, plaguing my thoughts.

"I know it's different for you," I say. "Just you being here means something."

She blinks hard, and I hate that she's almost crying.

"I love you so much, Eden." That little southern twang in her voice is so comforting, in a way. Even though it makes me think of home. There are still parts of that place I miss. "And I'll learn. I want to be in your life. Your *whole* life."

I draw in a deep breath through my nose. "I love you too." I get this memory of her cheering at the top of her lungs when I was not more than six years old and bumbling around on skates. She was there too—next to my father. I don't know why I always focused on the shit he would yell instead of how she tried to prop me back up. Maybe it's easier to hear the negative sometimes. "And you're not messing it up. It's different for me too."

I glance over at Lacey. "And whatever you're thinking, it's—"

"I love you too, big bro." Lacey wrinkles her nose. "Most of the time. When you're not being a doofus."

I mock gasp. "I'm never a doofus."

She rolls her eyes. "Uh huh."

Mom's fingers brush my shirt. "Can we talk outside?"

"Alright." I take one last glance at Shaw, who's moved over next to Dare. I want to ask him to come with me. I want him to meet my mom and sis—not just as my roommate. But as someone who's important to me. Would he want that?

I have no fuckin' clue.

And there's no way I'd do that unless I'm sure he'd want to.

So I just nod at him and then follow my mom and sis out into the cool night. A sharp wind whips between the trees, and they both huddle deeper in their coats. Mom looks at me in concern like she's going to tell me to put on something warmer, but I shrug it off.

"Not cold," I say as we take the steps down. "It's hot in the house."

And my blood is still pumping after being with Shaw. The cold feels good.

Mom turns to face me on the sidewalk. "I've wanted to tell you something for a while. I've already talked to Lacey about it on the way over here."

I frown. "What's going on?"

"I'm leaving your father." She digs her hands deep into her pockets. "I've thought about it for years. But after tonight, I won't stay any longer."

She's *leaving* him? I stare at her, completely clueless about what to say. But I get a hopeful flutter in my stomach. She's actually leaving him?

"I'm so sorry, Eden." She sighs. "I tried so hard to be there for you."

"You *were*." Fuck, I'm still in shock. This is real? After all these years? "Are you going to divorce him?"

"Separation first." The wind flicks her curly hair across her face, and she tucks it behind her ears. "I tried to get us into counseling years ago, but he refused. So I saw a lawyer, and I've been saving. I have a college friend, Mindy. Do you remember her? I'd always planned to stay with her for a while."

I'm dumbfounded. This isn't a sudden thought. It's a plan. A plan she's had for a long time. But she stayed because . . . I don't glance over at my sister. It's not just about her. It's about me too.

She stayed because of us.

"I'll help with whatever you need," I say. "Have you told him?"

I study her carefully as she puffs out a breath of white.

"I did," she says. "He was . . . quiet. He hasn't really said a word to me since."

I step forward, pulling her to me. The breeze tugs strands of hair into my mouth as I give her the biggest hug I've probably ever given to her.

When she steps back, she nods resolutely and reaches for Lacey's hand. "We should get back. We got a room at a different hotel—that nice one I've always wanted to stay at. But we haven't brought up all our stuff yet."

"I'll go back with you." I turn to go inside and grab my keys, but she brushes my elbow.

"We're fine." She gives me a small smile.

"Are you sure?" I frown, but she just nods again.

"I'm sure." She pulls rental car keys out of her puffy jacket pocket and pushes the remote. A black sedan flashes behind my truck.

"Alright." I'm a bit uneasy, but I trust her. "Text me when you get in?"

"Sure." She steps toward the car. I follow after them, giving Lacey another kiss on the head before she slides into the passenger seat, and then I walk around to the driver's side.

"Eden?" Mom asks, her hand on the door, just about to pull it shut. "Do you have a boyfriend?"

"Uh, not really." I look over the roof of the car toward the house. "No."

Fuck, that feels like a lie.

But it's not, I guess.

I don't fuckin' know.

She grips the inside handle. "I want to be part of everything. All of your life."

I swallow. "I'd like that."

She closes the door, and I watch their car disappear around the corner before turning and taking the steps up.

The music's going full volume again when I get inside, the house packed, heat slamming into me. I scan the living room. Shaw's standing with Les and Dare over on the far side, and the second I step inside, our eyes meet. Like he was waiting for me. Fuck, that feels good.

It's been an emotional day.

A *big* day.

I cut across to him. Vain heads over to our foursome when he sees me, motioning to Kelsey, who quickly completes our circle. I rub a hand over my jaw and try not to let my eyes roam all over Shaw as they close in around me.

Fuck, I want to haul him against me, bury my nose in his neck, maybe drag him onto the impromptu dance floor, feel his hips grind against mine.

I want to kiss him right here.

He smiles at me—eyes brightening like they always do—and I have to tear my eyes away, pivoting toward Dare.

"Thanks," I say. "Mom said you were nice."

Dare slaps me on the back. "No problem, man. If it were my dad and sister, I'd have wanted one of you to look out for them."

I smile. "Your sister would be taking care of us." Dare's twin sis is a force to be reckoned with.

Dare laughs. "Yeah, Nova could probably take us all down, if she wanted."

I glance around, lingering on Shaw for an extended moment. Well, no time like the present. "So you all probably overheard the conversation. Guess I'm out."

Shaw smiles at me.

Leslie squeezes my arm, his grin huge. "Glad you came out."

Vain nudges my elbow with his. "I'm glad too, bro. This is a good thing."

"So glad you told us, Burk." Kelsey raises her Solo cup in a small toast.

Shaw steps over and squeezes me in a hug, leaving an inch of bro-space between us.

"You know we all love you," he whispers in my ear.

Those words. Jesus, I don't know if my heart can take it right now. I know he didn't mean it like that, but they bolt right through me.

And fuck, I'm left so *uncertain* as he steps back. I want to reach for him again. Want to say something to make it clear exactly how much he means to me. I obviously would never out him though. And what I want . . . that doesn't mean he wants the same thing.

He didn't pause before telling me I should go to Montreal.

"Thanks," I say. "It means a lot."

Dare flips his dark red hair to the side, giving me an amused kind of smile—one that almost feels like he already knew. "All the love, B-man."

Maybe they knew? Maybe they were waiting for me.

I glance around at them. "I guess . . . we should probably talk about if this changes anything. With the team or house arrangements or—"

"Fuck, *no*, it doesn't." Vain drills me with a look, and it's him speaking, but the others are nodding. "We're all good here. You're in good company." He breaks into a grin. "After all, who doesn't like a bit of dick from time to time?"

Holy fuck.

I blink at him. Then laugh. "Good question."

Kelsey raises her hand. "Uh, yeah. Me? I'm not as partial."

Dare wraps her in a sideways hug. "And our circle's the better for it."

She tips her head against his shoulder. "Best hockey family ever."

"You know it." Dare releases her and then nudges my shoulder with his. "It sounded like I interrupted something fairly interesting earlier tonight. Pounding a bit of puck with someone, Burk?"

I still, my neck heating, trying my damndest not to look at Shaw out of the corner of my eye. Dare's razzing me—like we all do. I *want* them to razz me. I want shit to be normal.

"It was nothing," I blurt out.

Nothing. Did I just say that?

It was *everything*.

Dare laughs. "Kinda wondered if you've been sneaking dudes around on us."

"No." The word comes out chalky. Fuck, fuck, *fuck*. "There's no one."

Shaw takes a sharp step back, shoving his hands in his pockets and looking off to the side.

And, fuck, it feels like I've ripped out my heart. Just torn it straight out of me.

But I don't know what I should have said.

That I'm falling so fast and hard for the most incredible man I've *ever* met. That it's changing everything about my life. Changing who I thought I could be. Chasing all those negative voices away. That he makes everything better. Just by standing next to me. Just by looking at me. Just by existing.

"Yeah, I hear you." Dare's smile fades, maybe seeing something on my face.

I scrub a hand across my jaw, fighting for what to say.

Shaw stands stiffly, pushed back physically from the conversation, not looking at us.

He never does that.

He's always right in the circle. He usually *is* the circle.

He flips his hat around and tugs the brim down over his eyes. "Happy for you, Burk. Really. I'm gonna grab some fresh air."

He turns, except instead of heading out toward the clusters of people like he normally would, he heads down the darkened hallway that leads toward his room.

Fuck, I want to go after him.

Does he want me to?

"Burk." Dare's eyeing me, his smile completely gone now. "Shit, man. Did I say something?"

"No, I—" I shake my head. "You're fine."

Dare's forehead lines as he looks after Shaw. Then back at me. And I swear I see the wheels turning. Things clicking. But I don't wait for it to all come together.

I have to go after Shaw.

No fuckin' question.

I don't say anything else, I just go.

CHAPTER TWENTY-FOUR

Burk

I have no clue what I'm going to say, but I step into the hallway, my heart thumping. The need to sort this out is overwhelming.

"Shaw," I call after him.

He pauses. His hand is on the knob to his bedroom door, and he stares down at it, not looking at me. But I know he heard me.

I cross to him, step by step. I want to grab him and haul him against me. I want to tell him a thousand things that I don't know how to put into words. But I force myself to stop next to him with my hands at my side. Give him his space.

If he wants it.

His hand falls from the doorknob. "I'm so proud of you."

My eyes jump around the side of his face. "I didn't know what to say. Dare asked me, and I had no clue, I just—"

"I know." He looks up, his eyes shadowed by the brim of his hat. "Eden, I *know*."

"I don't want to hurt you." *Ever*. "It wasn't nothing."

His smile is faint, but it's there, and my mouth dries as I

take another step forward, the urge to tell him the complete truth about how I feel rising up.

"I'd tell them all," I say. "Come out. Be with you. I'd risk everything."

Everything. The Wolfpack. The NHL. No hesitation. No looking back.

His chin tips up, and I catch the green-brown of his eyes under the brim of his hat. "Can I hug you?"

"Yes."

He turns into me, his hands sliding around me, pulling me close.

"I just want to be *us*." He tightens his hand against my lower back. "All the time. Not just when we're alone."

I kiss him.

Right there in the hallway.

I push him against his door, knocking his hat to the side, my tongue sliding against his as my hand cups his jaw.

Voices echo from somewhere nearby, but he grips my waist, locking himself against me, and we kiss, holding onto each other with every bit of strength we have. I don't know how long we stay there, welded together, my whole body thudding as our tongues caress deeper, our pelvises grinding forward.

We don't break until he reaches behind him to open his door, and we fall inside, never more than an inch apart, our touches becoming frenzied as we stumble to his bed. We halt only long enough for him to sheath me with a condom before he tugs me to the bed. His eyes devour my expression as I push into him, my toes curling, my thighs already shaking, my breath faltering. We start slow because we're still feeling this out together—fucking. *Us.*

But we find it together as I drive into him—deep and strong—his groans and curses matching mine.

He *begs* me for more. His words are like fire, his muscular body moving underneath mine as he grips onto my biceps.

We don't let up until he bares down in his orgasm, his ass squeezing around my cock and bringing me to climax so urgently that I slam us hard into the mattress. A loud snap echoes through his room. The bed tilts.

We're laughing, even as I'm still barreling through my peak, choking on my breath as his thighs squeeze hard above my hips.

I tumble down on top of him, and his arms snake around me, his fingers lazily threading through my damp hair. "Don't think my bed was made for two six-foot, muscle-bound hockey jocks."

"Nope." I close my eyes, enjoying the flex of his fingers between the strands of my hair and the twitch of my cock still deep inside of him. The way that he takes my weight. All so fuckin' perfect that I never want this moment to end.

"Not sure I can afford a new one," he says. "I'll have to find another solution."

I smile against his cheek. "Are you suggesting something?"

"Would you want me to be suggesting something? 'Cause I'm thinking that I like your bed better anyway. And now that we're not hiding . . ."

Fuck, my heart fills. I tighten my arms around him. "I fuckin' love having you in there."

"Maybe I can drop some clothes and deodorant there too," he says. "You know, for convenience."

"Convenience, eh? I'll clear out a drawer."

"Yeah?" His voice lilts up. "A whole drawer?"

I'd clear my whole fuckin' world for him.

"Yep," I say, my cock softening and sliding out of him, my release leaving us slick. "Anything you want."

"Well, shit. In that case . . ." He pauses, and I pick up my head to see him. He looks . . . nervous? His jaw tightens, and he shifts, no doubt feeling the wetness silky on his thighs.

"Tell me," I say softly.

"Just thinking." He tugs on a lock of my hair. "That if we're fucking, maybe we should get tested."

"Alright." I lick my lips, the smell of both our releases heavy on the air. "I mean, of course. Sure."

Shit, does that mean something for us?

I squeeze him, debating how exactly to ask when his thumb slides over the back of my neck.

"Are you going to Montreal?" His hard body doesn't move under mine—just the expansion of his chest and the tension in his shoulder as his fingers pause.

I drag in a slow breath. "I think so."

This is what we do.

I've worked my whole life for this—and I'm not the only one. That was pretty fuckin' clear talking to my mom and sis today. They've sacrificed.

I've sacrificed.

"It's only a week," he says.

I nod, closing my eyes and trailing kisses along his neck, fitting together with him, slanted on the bed.

I want to ask him to come with me.

The question lingers on the back of my tongue. But I won't ask it. There's no way that's fair to him.

He needs to be here at IFU. Out on the ice. Playing his heart out, like he always does.

He has dreams of his own.

———

"You excited?" Shaw grabs my chair and flips it. He sits down with his forearms across the back and watches while I fold my clothes and tuck them in my dark green duffle.

The week has gone by too fast.

It's been a fuckin' whirlwind trying to get ready for this trip. We had Dex's fundraiser, which both the men's and women's teams showed up for in full supportive force. Then I took my finals early and had to get flights, a hotel, and logistics set. I also took calls from the defensive coordinators and the team travel admin since the Canadiens will be on the road for part of the time I'm there.

I scan what I've got left to pack. "Uh, yeah."

He frowns. "That didn't sound very excited."

"Nah, I am." I glance up at him, my carefully folded socks in my hand.

If I were sitting on my bed, he'd look almost exactly like he did that first morning we hooked up. Eyeing me curiously. Hat backward. Shirtless. Red athletic shorts. Knee bouncing from excitement or nerves or both.

"You're gonna kick ass." Shaw leans back in the chair, stretching out his arms, his heels settling on the floor.

He's always moving. And I fuckin' love watching him. Just the constant energy he has.

"I'll try." I cross to my dresser for a final load of clothes. "I guess I won't be around to bother you for a week."

"Two weeks, actually." He straightens. "My mom texted me this morning. She surprised me with a plane ticket home for Christmas."

"That's great, man." *Really* great. I'm sure he wants to see his brother.

But it's also another week. I try not to let whatever disappointment I feel show through. I mean, shit, this is good for Shaw. I know he misses his family. And holidays at the Keenan household sound pretty fantastic. Besides, it's only an extra week.

"So you're coming back here after Montreal?" He itches under the edge of his hat and bounces his knee some more. "All alone?"

I frown. He already knows that. Not sure why he's asking. My mom told me it might be best if we postpone the holidays until she's settled. And Lacey had a school trip to Italy.

"Dare will probably be here for part of the time," I say. "He usually is."

"Holidays with Dare?"

"Yep."

His heel bounces again. "Come home with me."

I pause, hands over my duffle. "What?"

"Chicago is on the way back to Colorado. Can you get a layover?" He scoots the chair closer to me. "You could stay with me."

"With your parents?"

"We'd snag an empty apartment. But for the holiday, yeah. Tiny plastic Christmas tree and *cozonac* and the whole deal. My dad would probably put you to work a few times, but otherwise, we'd just hang. Sleeping bags on the floor." He tilts his head. "I'm gonna miss you. So this way, I'll miss you a little less."

I scrape my teeth over my bottom lip again. "Are you sure that it would be cool? I don't want to—"

"It's cool," he says. "Trust me."

My eyes flash around his face. "Who would I be going as? Your roommate? Your team—"

"As the person I like being around more than anyone else." He shrugs, like there's nothing simpler. "Do you want to?"

"Of course I do." I'd never thought he'd ask.

A grin slides across his face. "Then I'll pick you up at the airport."

"I'll be there."

He winks. "Better be."

CHAPTER TWENTY-FIVE

Burk

It's another world in Montreal. Even just entering the locker room, passing by the wall of twenty-four miniature copies of the Stanley Cup—one to represent each year the Habs have won the title. My feet whisper across the heavy red carpet, centered with their logo, into the spotless dressing areas. There are photos and trophies and retired jerseys on the walls. There's so much history hidden in every corner that I spent an hour after the first practice just walking around, taking it all in.

It's more than I thought. It's like taking this dream I've had—that's been far off and vague—and making it rock solid and right before me.

What would it be like to walk into this place each day? To be part of something like this?

It's in another fuckin' league than IFU. Not just the dressing rooms, but the focus of the team. The determination. The way these guys are all in. There's no trying to jigsaw school and practices. There's no hesitation in these guys.

Hockey is what they *do*. Full time. No fuckin' around.

Well, there is some occasional fuckin' around, but when it gets right down to it, skates are on the ice, and the arena practically crackles with resolve.

I could fit in here. I could do this—everyday, without question. All of my determination and passion given to this.

The only thing that's missing is Shaw.

It's a huge miss. One that I feel sharply when I'm getting showered after practice and I turn, and he's not there.

I finish getting dressed and packed, then I snag out my phone and pull up Instagram on my way out.

I'm heaving my duffle across my shoulder when I see Shaw's posted already today. It's a photo of him standing in front of my bathroom mirror, lifting the bottom hem of his shirt. His tight abs are on display, gorgeous as all get out, and he's grinning into the mirror. But I come to a stop, a surprised huff of laughter eking out, when I realize what he's showing off.

A tattoo.

A *pride* tattoo.

And, of course, hockey too.

The new ink runs along his obliques, matching our IFU patch—two crossed hockey sticks with rainbows across the blades.

And he posted it on Instagram, tagged *#me*. Nothing else. The brevity is a statement all of its own.

It's his way of coming out.

My stomach tightens.

I should have been there.

I'd have gone with him to get the tattoo. I'd have been there when he uploaded and posted the pic.

When he read the comments.

Fuck. What are the comments?

I scroll through quickly, hunkered over my phone in the middle of the hallway, my damp hair falling into my eyes.

There are hundreds of likes. Comment after comment even though it's only been posted for an hour.

I'm not seeing anything except for positive responses. Support. Kindness. Excitement. A few say that Shaw inspires them.

Holy shit.

Shaw.

I can't even . . .

My fingers are shaking as I exit out of Instagram. I'm about to call him when a hand cups my shoulder.

"Burkehammer?" Toussaint says in his thick French accent as he squeezes my shoulder. A handful of the guys stop around me in a half circle, watching me. And I'm two seconds from bawling my eyes out in front of all the miniature Stanley Cup copies.

"Uh, yeah. I'm good." My voice is rough. "Just a friend's Instagram post."

Toussaint frowns. "Looks like it fucked you up, *gros.*"

Fuck, tears are gathering in my eyes. The last thing I need is to cry in front of all these guys, but I can't stop myself. "It's a good fucked up."

"*C'est bien.*" He keeps looking at me, his hand still palming my shoulder.

I take a shaky breath, attempting to get myself under control. "A friend of mine came out. And there's a lot of support."

I'm watching his reaction really fuckin' carefully. I've thought about coming out to the team. It would be weird to just fuckin' blurt it out, but I want to know what the response would be. I'd rather know before I have to make any kind of decision.

"Yeah. I, uh." I glance at the other guys lingering around us. One's on his phone, but the others are watching me curiously. Probably because it's obvious I'm about to have a fuckin' breakdown. "He's a good, uh, friend. And I came out recently too, so I guess the support he got hit me pretty strongly."

"I bet." Toussaint squeezes my shoulder. "Sounds like you're a good friend to him too."

"Try to be."

His lips break into a smile. "Hey, we're about to head to the Cloakroom for a bit. It's this bar across the road. You up for grabbing a beer with us?"

I blink at him. He hardly even *paused*. He's just one guy, of course, but he's the captain—the guy everyone looks to. And I'm getting the idea that I could . . . be me. I mean, I know it can't always be so easy to be out in the NHL. But it suddenly feels doable.

"That would be great. But I have to . . ." I raise up my phone.

"We'll be over there." He nods toward the outside doors. "Come when you're done."

There's a murmur from a few of the guys as they all go.

Someone slaps me on the back as he passes. "Burkehammer, see ya in a bit."

Fuck, that was Geoff Taylor, team enforcer and hardest hitter on the defensive line. I stare after them as they walk away, trying not to look like a little kid who just met his favorite superheroes.

Except I am.

I'm that little kid.

And I'm grinning as I walk by the miniature Cups and tuck into a little alcove.

And smiling even bigger when Shaw answers on the first ring. "Heya, Burkie."

"Hi." I fumble over what to say. That I miss him. That the way he came out is so fuckin' perfect.

"We're all here," he says. A clamber of noise and voices echoes behind him. "Vain, Dare, and I are over at Mexicali's. Les is on his way."

"Habanero burritos?"

"Hell, yeah."

A chair screeches on the floor in the background. Vain's saying something. Dare laughs loudly. My heart warms as Shaw tells them it's me, and they all give a chorus of "*Burk*"s. Then Shaw must cup his hand over the phone because the noise is muffled.

"You don't usually call me this early," he says. "Did they make an offer yet?"

"Nope. That's not why I'm calling." I can't stop grinning. "I saw your Instagram."

"Yeah? I didn't know if you'd have time to check it while you're living the big life up there in Canada."

I laugh. "I check it like thirty times a day. Every chance I get."

"Really?" The surprise in his voice hits me so fuckin' hard. "Didn't know if you'd have time."

"I make the time. And I wish I could've been there." My voice cracks, and fuck, I don't want to make this conversation difficult or weird. After all, it's not about me. It's about him coming out. "The post was perfect. Everything. The tattoo. The picture. *You*. All perfect."

"Sorry I didn't tell you before." He feels so close, in my ear. "But Les was going for some ink, so I went along and found myself asking if his artist could fit me in too. Then I posted it. It was spur of the moment."

"However it came about, it's still perfect."

And the reality is that if we're apart, then we can't always tell each other things first.

That's the fuckin' deal.

Can I live with that?

I'm not sure. The NHL season is long. Nearly ten months from training camp in September, before the preseason starts, to the Cup in June. There aren't a lot of breaks. I'd never see him.

Not unless he were close by. And the odds of that happening? Slim to none.

"Yeah, well." He blows out a breath. "There are a few assholes on Insta."

"Jesus, Shaw, I'm sorry."

"Fuck 'em."

"For sure. Delete and block?"

"You know it," he says. "Vain's been helping, running through the new comments this last time around."

"That's good. When I get back, I'll help too."

"Yeah, I know." Muffled movement comes from his side, and then his voice is quieter. "So, you like the ink?"

I groan, but I'm smiling. "That whole picture. It'll probably come in handy tonight."

"Handy?" There's a tease in his voice. "Sounds promising. Wanna get kinky over FaceTime later?"

I laugh. "Deal."

"Whatcha doing now, *coaie*?"

"Heading over to a bar with some of the guys."

"Yeah? Look at you. That's fantastic."

"They felt bad for me or something." I chew on my bottom lip. "Lonely newbie."

"Screw that. You fit there. Of course you do."

"Well, yeah, the team's been good." I clear my throat.

But I miss you. So fuckin' much.

I take a breath, trying to get up the bravery to say it.

I open my mouth, my heart squeezing.

"Foods up," Shaw says. "Gotta run. But call me later? If you have time."

"I'll have time."

"Cool. Okay." He pauses. "I miss you. Like a whole lot. There's a Burkie-shaped hole next to me in your bed."

I close my eyes. "Miss you too."

Then he's gone. I stand there, the phone in my hand, still about two seconds from breaking down, not wanting to lose the connection to him. Not wanting him to go. Not wanting to say goodbye, like I can hold on to him for a few more moments, the wavelength still connecting us.

I miss you.

It was like he read my mind. Like across all this distance, he can still telegraph the movement of my feet, the tiny shifts in my stance, the thoughts in my eyes.

This time away from each other. Maybe it's weighing on him too.

Do I hope it does? Or do I hope that he's fine without me? Just over there being Shaw, easy as ever.

I honestly don't know which to hope for.

CHAPTER TWENTY-SIX

Burk

Snow peppers the airplane window when we touch down at O'Hare, small flakes swirling against the Plexiglass. I itch at the scruff on my jaw and stand in the airplane aisle, feeling tremendously huge, and try to keep from barreling right over the line of people slowly—so fuckin' *slowly*—gathering their bags from the overhead compartments.

I've never ached to see someone as much as I ache to see Shaw in my life.

It's physical. Like a hard gut-check. Something way beyond missing a person. My feelings keep being so *big* when it comes to Shaw. So fuckin' deep.

Too deep? I don't know anymore.

The line finally moves, and I straighten, banging my head on the overhead bin.

I hurry as fast as I can through the crowded concourse, decorated for the holiday and packed with families. I grumble at the Christmas music and try to tamp down my excitement as I step on the escalator to baggage claim. I need to play it cool. Not freak him out with exactly how much I've missed him. Not make it weird.

And I still don't know exactly who he's going to introduce me as, but my plan is to go with the flow. After all, I know it's a hell of a lot more complex than whatever is between the two of us. I'm not sure if he's fully out with his family—or if he wants to be—or what his family dynamics are. So I'll follow his lead.

I'm dumped out at the top of the escalator into Christmas Eve chaos. It's packed—people everywhere—and I pivot looking for Shaw, trying to spy that pink cap and brilliant smile.

Although I guess we never agreed where we'd meet.

Maybe I'm supposed to DM him? Maybe he's out waiting in the pickup line.

I pause, stomach tightening. Why did I assume he would come inside to meet me? That's more boyfriend territory as opposed to picking up a friend territory, and I shouldn't have presumed that—

"*Eden.*" My name razors over the noise, and I spin, all my attention zeroing in on where it came from.

And, fuck, he's *there*, jogging toward me through the crowd. He grins so wide it might crack his face. He must have rushed inside because snowflakes still cling to his scarf and dust his ballcap. That shoelace flying lose as he comes to a hard stop—fifteen feet from me—and then flings a sign above his head.

He made me a fuckin' sign.

Any ability to play it cool goes right out the window. My chest crushes with this sweep of emotion that I'm not sure I can hold back.

The sign's written in black Sharpie. Block capital letters that crowd together at the end.

BEST DAY EVER

Just . . . *fuck*me. I swallow, my throat closing. I'm just standing here. I know I should be moving, but I honestly don't trust my feet.

Or my voice.

Or my *heart*.

Jesus, my fuckin' heart.

I never in my life thought that a man like Shaw would look at me the way he is right now. That I'd be worth it. Except there's this tiny voice in the back of my head that's starting to speak up, and it's saying that maybe—just *maybe*—I am worth it. It's a whisper compared to everything else, but it's there. And it doesn't sound like my father. It doesn't even sound like Shaw.

It sounds a lot like me.

Shaw's grin widens, and it knocks me awake. I start moving, crossing the white tiles between us.

And then I'm there, standing in front of him while he lets the sign drift down to his side.

I clear my throat, hardly trusting my voice. "I like your sign."

"It's the first thing I thought about picking you up." He bounces in his Pumas, the laugh lines deep around his eyes. "I've been kinda excited."

"Fuck, *me too*," I say in a frantic rush. "Longest flight of my life."

"I bet." We're standing here, in the middle of all these people, both grinning, and I might vibrate apart with excitement at seeing him. At being close enough to catch the way his eyes light. The way his laugh lines soften as he presses his lips together, still smiling, but glowing so bright that he blots out *everything*—the twenty-foot Christmas tree behind him, the pressing crowd, anything and everything else.

I want to kiss him. I want to wrap him in my arms and smell lemongrass shampoo and feel the snowflakes melting on his coat. To remember how he fits in my arms.

His smile falls. Does he want me to kiss him?

What are we here? Just two friends? Or more?

Can I hope for more?

"I guess we should get your duffle." He scans the television monitors that list out flights and carousels. "And we should get moving because it's snowing pretty hard."

"Alright." I drag in a breath and step back. My hope doesn't die. It waits. It'll be there, ready when he is. "Let's go get my shit."

"Hey, wait." He digs into his hoodie pocket, pulls out his phone, and holds it out as he raises the sign up behind our heads. "For Insta?"

"Fuck, yeah." I smile at his phone for the picture.

A split second before he snaps it, he turns his head and smacks a wet kiss on my cheek. I flinch with surprise, then laugh.

I itch my cheek right over where he kissed me. "Your lips are cold."

He pockets his phone. "Well, your dick can warm them up later. Let's go grab your stuff."

———

"Tell me every detail," Shaw says as soon as we're settled in his dad's work van. "Did you get an offer yet?"

I shake my head, peering out at the Chicago skyline, although I can't see much with the flutter of snowflakes in the headlights. But that's fine with me. I turn back to the view I'd rather be looking at.

"Haven't heard anything." I pull off my gloves. "Although I haven't heard anything bad either, so I suppose that's good?"

"Nah, that's amazing," he says, his attention fixed on the Interstate because it's getting pretty messy out there. But, fuck . . . it's the first time I've ever seen him drive. We're always in my truck, and I wasn't prepared for how damn sexy he looks over there, legs parting slightly as he presses on the brake, jaw releasing as he smiles, a quick wink when he glances over at me.

"You're gonna get an offer," he says. "I have a feeling."

I rest my shoulders back against the high seat. "The whole thing was pretty surreal."

"I bet." He flips on a turn signal and takes an exit off the Interstate. "But they've got to see how good you are. It's obvious. So, if they do, you'll take it?"

"Probably," I say, because that's what I should say.

But is it what I want?

Half of me, yes. Completely.

The other half? I shift against the stiff seat, itching at my scruff again.

I'd miss things. Like him getting that tattoo. Or knowing how his day went.

The windshield wipers beat steadily, snow melting on the glass as it falls. We pass by some warehouses before turning into a neighborhood bustling with restaurants and shops.

"I can't wait to see where you go," he finally says as we slow at a crosswalk. The shops are just closing, crowded with last-minute Christmas Eve shoppers. "I'll be watching you on the SportsCenter recaps."

"Wish you could be there." The words snap out of me so fast that I can't hold them back. "I mean, I wish you could have seen it. The stadium, the dressing room. It was out of this world."

"Would have loved to see it." He unwraps his Blackhawks scarf, pulls it off, and tosses it in the back. "I found out yesterday there might be a second-string goalie position at a new AHL team. Coach messaged me about it, and I was able to schedule a tryout next month. Brand new team."

"Shit, that's fantastic." I study the side of his face, falling into shadows as we pull down a side street. "Where at?"

He licks his lips, concentrating on the road. "California."

There's a long beat of silence. The unspoken is so damn loud that it drowns out the swish of the wipers.

"That's great." I swallow, trying to ignore the way my pulse is echoing in my temples. And the way his words cut into me.

Fuckin' selfish. I won't let myself be like that. No matter what happens, I won't be a selfish dick when it comes to the man sitting next to me.

Shaw should absolutely be playing. Not just because he's good but because it's what he loves.

But the odds of us getting signed by the same franchise are almost zero. I nudged Debra about goalie positions while I was in Montreal, but she was clear that they're not planning to add to the goalie lineup for at least five years.

This is the reality.

Shaw taps his thumb against the steering wheel. "My scholarship is most likely gone, but my advisor said I can finish the last of my credits online. I can't play for IFU if I'm online-only, but I can play for an expansion team and do that. The salary is almost nothing, but I can get by. I don't need much anyway. And then hopefully, I'll get my shot at the NHL."

"I'm sure you will."

I fuckin' know he will. He'll be one of the greats.

He shrugs one shoulder. "Guess we'll see."

"Well, your Instagram's been insane," I say, hating that I don't know all the tiny details of the last week. I miss the way he drops on my bed and rests his head on my shoulder, telling me about his day, making me laugh and snuggling in next to me.

"That's an understatement." He shakes his head, slowing for a turn. "I can't keep up with it. I've been growing followers for the last few months pretty steadily, but last week was something else entirely. It's pretty mind-boggling how many people are out there. But it's also . . ." He taps his thumb against the steering wheel. "I get a lot of comments about coming out and being an inspiration and stuff, and I guess it feels like I haven't done anything to deserve it. I mean, I didn't fully think about it. I just did it. And it's not like I grew up struggling with my sexuality." He sighs. "Maybe I shouldn't have done it."

"Shouldn't have gotten the tattoo?"

"Nah, I like the tatt. But maybe I shouldn't have posted it."

"It's genuine." I twist to look at him more fully. "It's all you, Shaw. They're finding inspiration and hope in *you*. Honestly, it doesn't surprise me at all. That's who you are."

He glances over. "You think that?"

"Fuck, yes, I do." I nod. "And you're talking like your experience is invalid or something. No fuckin' way is it invalid." My shoulders tighten against the seat at the thought of anyone treating him like it is.

"I missed you, Eden." He turns down a narrow alleyway. "Vain's been helping with all this, but he's not you."

"Well, that's the truth." I smile. "I missed you too."

Fuck, it feels so good to be able to say that.

He slows at a line of dumpsters and then pulls into a low garage door that's hidden past the dumpsters, descending out of the snow flurries. "We're here. Apartment, sweet apartment."

"Yeah?" I look around curiously. It's an unevenly-lit, underground garage, but it's Shaw's unevenly-lit—and admittedly kinda creepy—underground garage.

I want to see it all.

Where he grew up.

What he remembers.

How he became the man that he is today. Because that person is fuckin' incredible.

He parks in a narrow spot and twists toward me. "Are you ready for Christmas Eve with my family?"

"Yep." I hesitate, wondering if I should ask how he'll introduce me.

But he's already halfway out the door. "It might be a bit overwhelming."

I unclick my seatbelt. "I'm ready for anything."

CHAPTER TWENTY-SEVEN

Burk

Shaw's home is nothing like mine.

That's obvious from the second he ushers me in, introducing me as Eden, and I'm in the middle of a whole bunch of people shorter than me, shaking hands and knowing that I have no fuckin' hope of remembering all these names.

Different languages bounce around us. Romanian. German too, I think. Shaw moves effortlessly through them, flipping back into English without a pause. It's a whole new side of him that I haven't seen, and I wonder what else there is. What else I don't know.

And then all the greetings suddenly disperse, and I'm standing in the middle of the room, a flat-screen blaring a Hawks game on one side, a cramped dining table on the other, a tiny fake Christmas tree with a handful of gifts underneath right next to me, having no clue what to do with myself.

Shaw grins at me. "Wanna help with the tortellini?"

I blink at him. "Tortellini? That's what you eat for Christmas Eve?"

"Yep. *Sarmale* tomorrow because it takes half the day to make. Tortellini tonight. Hungry?"

"Fuckin' starving." I glance around. Shaw's uncle is carefully lowering himself into a seat across from the television. Shaw's dad is wiping down the table. Shit. I probably need to watch my mouth.

Shaw laughs. "No one cares about English curses. You might want to watch your Romanian and German ones though."

I laugh. "That I can do."

I follow him into the kitchen, and we squeeze in side by side at a yellow table with a bench along one side. Shaw's grandfather shows me how to pinch together the tortellini and lay them carefully on baking sheets lined with parchment paper.

It's challenging work for my big-ass fingers, especially since we're squished together at the table. I feel huge as I try to keep my elbow from digging into Raleigh. I focus hard, trying to do a good job, while everyone talks around me. My tortellini look nothing like Shaw's, and he's barely looking down as he works, folding them quickly and setting them out in perfect rows. To top it off, he's still jumping back and forth between languages.

I lean closer to him. "What are you speaking?"

"Romanian to my grandma. Mostly." He nods toward the main part of the kitchen where his grandfather has looped his arms around Shaw's grandmother and is swaying them to an old jazz song streaming out of a speaker on the counter. It's really fuckin' sweet. I can't imagine what it was like growing up with people who care for each other like that.

"German to my aunt and uncles," Shaw continues. "English to you. And my parents and Raleigh."

"How do you keep it all straight?"

"I just do." He laughs, looking around. "This is how it always is."

"I like it."

"Yeah? You like not understanding what we're saying? All cramped in a hot kitchen together?"

"I do." My tortellini pops out of my fingers before it's pressed. "I like everyone talking. My house was pretty fuckin' silent growing up." I pick up the little package of pasta and try again. "Everyone was thinking a bunch of different thoughts, but no one talked except for my father."

"Sounds uncomfortable." Shaw folds another tortellini without looking down. "It never gets quiet here. Sometimes it's the opposite—so much talking that my head hurts—but I think I'll take that over silence any day."

"Me too." I fumble and drop my tortellini again. Shaw smiles down at my bumbling fingers. The last one is squished on one side, and the filling is popping out. Well, mine are pretty much all like that.

"Be delicate." He leans close to my ear, his breath warming my neck. "Pretend it's my sack, *coaie*. Not too rough."

I laugh, softening my fingers to do what he says. And fuckin' loving the way he doesn't fully move away, his thigh pressed against mine, our elbows knocking.

I do a pretty good job on the next one, inspired by his confidence, and set it carefully on my cookie sheet. When I look up, Shaw's dad is watching from across the table.

He's not watching strangely. Or meanly. Or anything except curious. His head is tilted, eyes that greenish brown, just like Shaw's. His hands are paused over the pasta sheet he's rolling out.

I think about everything that Shaw has told me about him. About losing a home and struggling and working to get back things that I've taken for granted all my life.

I can't see that in the faces of his family—like I can't see it in Shaw's face—but I can feel it hovering in this apartment.

There's so much warmth, his family all crowded together and chatting over each other. The way they work together in this tiny kitchen on something as simple as tortellini with the kind of grace that my family has never possessed.

No, that's wrong.

My sis and mom and me—we possess that.

But there's one person who always gets in the way.

I blow out a breath. I should have called my mother earlier. I've texted her every day, but I'd been so focused on getting to Chicago that I didn't yet today.

"Eden?" Shaw nudges my knee with his.

"I need to go make a call," I say. "Can you take over?"

He laughs. "Not sure you're doing all that much."

I frown at my six misshapen tortellini. Then at his perfect ones, running in two lines down his baking sheet. There must be at least twenty-four of them. All identical.

"Point taken," I admit with a laugh.

He winks at me. "I like yours. They have personality."

"Yeah, sure. Personality."

But I'm smiling down at my six misshapen tortellini.

I like them too.

Shaw slides out of his chair so I can squeeze out after him. His hand settles on my lower back as I pass, his fingers tugging the top hem of my jeans.

Heat wells up to my cheeks.

Fuck, I'm blushing. I drop my head to let my hair fall forward as I step out into the brown-carpeted hallway. I take a deep breath and then pull out my phone.

Mom answers on the first ring. "Merry Christmas, Eden. I'm so glad you called."

"Thanks, Mom. Merry Christmas to you too." Relief hits me at the relaxed sound of her voice. "Everything good there?" It's her first Christmas alone.

"Mostly." A timer goes off in the background. "I'm

making a bit of Christmas Eve dinner, then I'm going to curl up with a book. I'm, ah, reading a hockey love story."

I laugh. "Really?"

"About two men."

I blink. "You're reading gay romance?"

"My first." There's a smile in her voice, and shit, I did not expect that. I've been surprised by how hard she's trying, and I itch at the nape of my neck, that heat from Shaw still lingering.

"I'm so excited about the Kindle you got me," she continues. "You didn't have to do that, hon."

"Yours had a crack."

"I'd learned to read around it. But thank you."

"No problem." I step farther down the hall, toward a door at the end that must lead out to the fire escape. "So, you're good?"

"Mostly," she says. "I miss you and Lacey being here. But also it's nice not to have to worry about anything else." There's a catch in her words, and I remember our father getting on her for everything—a slightly burnt roll, a dry piece of meat, the microwave fan being too loud. A constant barrage of how everyone around him was always failing.

Although I'm hard pressed to remember him stepping into the kitchen and offering to help. Definitely not like everyone squished together at the kitchen table, all folding tortellini.

"It's the first time in years that I've felt peaceful," she says.

"I'm happy for you." I blow out a breath, my shoulders loosening. I didn't realize how worried I was about her.

"If you want to call him," she continues, "he'll have his phone. He went to Eagle Lake with his friend Carl. The reception's pretty bad there, but of course you should call him if you want to."

I frown. "I don't need to call him."

As I say the words, I realize how deeply true they are.

"I understand," she says. "You're visiting your friend Shaw?"

"Uh, yeah."

"Maybe this summer he can come down here."

"Are you sure that would be okay?" I scrub a hand over the back of my neck, my hair tickling my knuckles.

"Of course," she says. "Do you think I should get to know him?"

I smile at the question. I guess she's noticed the undertones when I've mentioned him. Admittedly, I probably don't have much ability to play it cool when I talk about Shaw.

"Yeah, maybe," I say.

Would he want to? Will we already be heading our separate ways before summer?

But I can't help picturing Shaw in the Delta. Pink athletic slides on his feet as we traverse the creek. There's an ancient bald cypress not far from the house that he'd probably like— so different from the lodgepole pines back in Colorado. Something tells me he'd jump into it all. Cotton fields stretched out under a cloud-laden blue sky and weather-worn sheds and, honestly, as much as I've got conflicted feelings about where I grew up, there's not another place on earth quite like it.

Shaw's about the exact opposite of the Delta, but I think my mom and sis would probably love him. It's pretty easy to.

I ask about Lacey, and we talk for a few more minutes. When I'm tucking my phone in my pocket, I turn to find Shaw standing outside his door.

"Is your mom okay?" He lets the door click closed and walks down the hall toward me.

"She sounds relaxed," I say as he stops before me.

"That's good." His hands are deep in his pockets, stretching the slick fabric of his athletic pants. His pecs are outlined under a light blue t-shirt that's tight enough I can see the buds of his nipples. Not that I'm noticing.

Especially not noticing the way his shirt hugs across his stomach, letting me watch every breath he takes. I drag my gaze back to his face.

He bounces on his toes. "It's cool you being here, isn't it?"

My smile expands. "Yeah, it really is."

His eyes flick to my mouth, and my lips automatically part, my tongue swiping over the bottom one. But I stand my ground.

I don't know what's cool here. With his family.

Or with us. But fuck, I want to kiss him. Back him against the wall and feel the hard hit of his chest against mine.

I always want to kiss him. No matter where we are or what we're doing, and I can't see that ever changing.

He takes another half step forward. My body jumps into high alert at his nearness, stomach tightening, breath shallowing. I watch him, taking in every beautiful detail as he rises onto his toes and tips forward. A flicker of a smile crosses his lips before they press against mine, his tongue caressing into my mouth. Our breaths fall into sync.

We don't grab at each other, don't force for more. His hands stay in his pockets, mine are at my sides. It's an unhurried kiss, sensual and lingering. Eyes closed and hearts thumping and a softness that's so sublime I barely have words to describe it.

Sweetness lingers between us. Friendship and understanding. The steady comfort of being right next to each other.

I have so *much* with Shaw.

The strength of our friendship never leaves. Even when I'm watching him fist his dick or drop to his knees. It's always right here. Like this framework that supports everything we do. Every moment between us.

It's unreal.

More than I'd ever thought I'd have.

And I'm not sure if it's something I can walk away from.

But what if he could? What if he's not feeling this in the same way that I am?

I don't question if Shaw cares for me.

I'm *positive* he cares.

What I don't know is if he cares for me the same way I do for him.

When he tips back onto his heels, he smiles at me, and that little smile loosens the tightness that's been growing in my chest. The hallway lights make everything a bit sallow and yellowish, but somehow he still looks as gorgeous and vibrant as ever.

"That was a nice kiss," I say.

He waggles his brows. "Do you like nice?"

"I do like nice." I raise a brow. "Do you?"

"For sure." His smile widens and his gaze slides down me —from Adam's apple to stomach, from dick to thighs—and then back up. "I also like dirty."

I drag in a sharp inhale at the way he's looking at me. Cupping his hips, I drag him closer so I can whisper in his ear. "Are you thinking about something specific?"

"Might be." He slips two fingers in the top of my waistband, tickling along my happy trail. "Having trouble concentrating."

I slide my hands around to his ass. "Want some help? Or is that not appropriate for Christmas Eve dinner?"

His fingers slip lower. "*Yes*. Right freaking now. Dick wiggles, *coaie*. I kept thinking about pulling over the van and climbing in the back. I would have asked, but I . . ."

I lean back, brows knitting. "But what?"

His eyes move around my face. "I didn't want you to think that I'm only missing you because of the hot sex."

I laugh. But my smile fades when I realize he's serious.

"Shaw, you invited me to a holiday with your entire

family, where we're making tortellini in a crowded kitchen. You picked me up at the airport—with a *sign*—and the first thing you asked me about when we got in your father's work van was if I had a nice fuckin' flight and what the snack was. We've been best friends for two and a half *years*—no sex involved. I have never *once* thought you're only thinking about the hot sex."

"You sure? Because—"

I kiss him, pressing him back hard with my chest, his heart kicking when I grip his jaw. He likes this little edge of roughness. He's never asked for it, but I can feel it in the way he responds. In the way his breath shallows as I tighten my fingers and turn his head to the side so I can speak close to his ear.

"I like the way you want me," I whisper, my eyes tracking over the slope of his smooth jawline before rising to meet his. What I said is so fuckin' true. No one has ever made me feel wanted before. No one has ever consistently chased away those negative voices like he does. "Want to slip away for a few minutes?"

"Oh, hell yeah." He nods toward the fire escape. "Let's do the hot sex."

I laugh. "It has to be freezing out there."

"Probably." He tilts his head, eyes lit with excitement.

I fist the front of his shirt, tugging him with me backward down the hall. We push out the door, my lips covering his as his shoulders hit the brick wall. His hand slides under my shirt, palming my abs.

Snow bites the nape of my neck, the wind whipping through my hair. I fit my knee between his legs, keeping him pinned as I hunch to taste his throat, his ear, his lips again. I release him to kiss lower, over his tight t-shirt, biting lightly through the fabric until my knees hit the metal fire escape. His fingers fist in my hair, wet snow soaking into my jeans. I drag down his pants, taking his boxer briefs down at the same time. I groan as he springs out.

Every part of Shaw is beautiful. I suck him down, warming his shaft in my mouth, slicking him with my saliva. His head falls back as I roll my tongue around his head, letting my saliva pool and getting him even wetter so that he can push in and out of my mouth with ease.

"Fuck, you're hot, Eden." His fingers tangle in my hair. "I can never get enough."

The wind whips between the slats in the metal stairs, and he's shivering as he fucks into my mouth, sliding so deep that it cuts my breath. We're exposed to the world on the edge of a building, snow swirling so thickly that it's impossible to see beyond the railing. He moans, shallowing his strokes as his lips open, pre-cum coating my tongue. He releases my hair to catch the brim of his hat, buffeted by the wind.

I shiver hard, but I'm transfixed by him. The clench of his jaw as he gets closer, the way he tugs on my hair. This burning heat ignites deep inside.

I could tell him that I love him.

Right here and now. Mumble it around his cock. Or pull off and say it, on my knees, looking up at him.

And I would mean it. I would mean it more than I possibly know. I don't think I understand how deeply I want him. I think I've only gotten a glimpse.

It'll take years for me to really understand.

Do we have that?

"About to come," he whispers, barely louder than the wind. I grab his ass, pulling him deeper. His dick spasms against the back of my tongue, spilling his release down my throat, warm and tangy, masculine and thick. He groans as I engulf him, my throat contracting around his head.

As soon as he empties in me, he pulls me up, his lips on mine. I slip his hat off his head to stash it safely in my back pocket.

He breaks from me, brows rising. "You?"

"I'll wait." I run my nose along his jaw, then down the side of his neck. My shoulders shake from the cold as I inhale him, but it's hard to smell him over the wet scent of the storm.

"You sure?" He squeezes my ass.

I kiss back to his ear. "I want to fuck you later. So hard that all you can do is whimper."

He smiles. I can't see it, but I can feel the loosening of his jaw as I trail my nose across it, and then he clicks his tongue. "You better. I got tested. Negative."

I still, my nose under his ear. "Me too. Also negative."

"Now I'm gonna have a hard time thinking of anything besides you filling me with a giant, hot load of cum." His palms slide up under my shirt, his fingers ice cold. "Maybe we should do it now. You can plow me against the railing, twelve stories up in a snowstorm. Whatcha think?"

I drag my nose down the slope of his neck and then back up, tasting along his jaw with open-mouthed kisses, feeling the vibration of his moan, the rasp of his stubble, before hunching down to suck his Adam's apple, feeling his swallow against my lips. Then back to his ear. "Or maybe you can fuck me."

He leans back, his eyes fixing on mine. But he doesn't say anything.

I watch him, anxiety prickling. I rarely see Shaw hold back his words. I'd expected him to say something dirty. Something about driving his dick into me. Or maybe something playful. He's been all in on everything we've done.

Does he not want to?

"Shaw?" I ask gruffly. There's a voice in the back of my head that pops up with "maybe you're not good enough". But I don't fuckin' listen to it. I want to listen to him instead.

"It's completely fine if you don't want to," I continue.

"The last thing I want is to do something that either of us isn't into."

"It's not that." His fingers dig into my sides, as if he's anchoring himself to me. "Trust me, I want to."

I study him. "Alright."

A shiver racks through his body. "Shit, we should probably get in for dinner. My dick's about to freeze off."

"Well, we can't have that." I step back, taking in his wind-pinkened cheeks and the way his clothes are plastered to him.

I want to talk to him about it. But I'm not sure that on the side of a building in a snowstorm while we're at his parents' house for Christmas Eve dinner is a good time.

"Come on." He gives me a quick kiss and then twists toward the door and tugs on the handle.

"Shit." He pulls harder. "It locked behind us."

"Fuck, seriously?"

"We're stuck." He pounds on the door.

I run a cold hand over the arc of my neck, snow clustering on my eyelashes and dripping from the ends of my hair.

He finally steps back. "I don't think they can hear us."

"Fuck." I look down between the slats. I can barely see the ground below. "Can we call?"

I slip out my phone and hand it to him. He dials, and it rings for a few long minutes, but then he shakes his head and hands it back to me. "We should just go down. Someone will hear the intercom from the front for sure."

"Guess that's our best bet, then." I grip onto the railing, which moves slightly, but feels generally solid. "Think it's doable?"

He waggles his brows. "For us, anything is doable."

Fuck, yeah. He's got that right.

We make our way down. Shaw slips once, and my heart jumps into my throat, but he reaches back to grab me, and sure as fuck, I'm there. We finally get to the ladder that slides to the ground, and he goes down with it. Once he's on the ground, he smiles up at me, and my chest damn near buckles.

I don't know that I had fantasies growing up. I was way too confused about what I wanted and what everyone else around me was saying I should want. But I have them now.

They're him.

Looking up at me from the bottom of a fire escape ladder, shivering, his cheeks pink, his eyes bright, snow gathering in the streetlights beyond.

I'd rather be here with him than anywhere else in the entire fuckin' world.

Right here.

With him.

Stuck outside in the snow.

I pick him.

Over and over and over. Even if it's not the same for him. Even if he never picks me back. Even if all these feelings are too damn big.

"I pick you," I lean over to look at him.

He blinks up at me. "Pick me for what?"

"For anything."

"I pick you too." He laughs, squinting as snowflakes batter his face and clutch onto his backward ballcap. "But get your cute ass down here. I'm ready to go in."

I turn to go down the stairs.

He said the words back.

He always says them.

But I don't know if he means what I mean.

I stop at the bottom. He shoves his hands deep into his pockets, shrugging his shoulders up near his ears.

"I fuckin' mean that, Shaw." I say. "I pick you."

Over everything.

Maybe over an NHL dream.

He grips my shirt, yanking me in for a kiss. But my teeth are chattering so hard that I can't even try to fit my mouth

290

against his, so we laugh and then trudge around the building and into the front courtyard. Inside the first set of glass doors, he jabs a button by the speaker.

"Mom," Shaw says into the speaker. "Can you buzz us in?"

"*Shaw*?" she asks, confusion thick in her voice. "What happened? Are you okay?"

"Yeah." He smiles over at me. "We're perfect."

Words that I will forever remember:

1. "I think you should trust yourself, Burkie."
2. "I kinda don't want it to stop."
3. "I'm quiet, because I wanted to."
4. "We would have been there for you in a heartbeat."
5. "I don't think it's actually about the bed."
6. "I'm with Burkie. All the way."
7. "I'm happy."
8. "I just want to be us."
9. "I want people to know that I miss you. That you're important to me."

CHAPTER TWENTY-EIGHT

Shaw

He picks me.

Burkie sits next to me, eating his tortellini. The scruff along his jaw is thicker than normal, and all I want to do is slide my cheek against his. Or feel it on my palms. On my thighs. Lightly grazing over my sack. Pretty much everywhere.

Do I want to fuck him?

Hell, yes.

I really, honestly don't know what held me back from jumping all over him immediately on the fire escape. But there's this chilly tightness across the back of my shoulders that I can't ignore.

My dick clearly wants it. Even sitting here now at the dinner table, *thinking* about everything we could do. Full-on fantasies running through my mind to the point where I'm fully hard and cramped in my pants. My balls are tight and my ass is clenching.

I spear a green bean and stare at it before putting my fork back down on my plate.

Burkie's been quiet during dinner, a wrinkle appearing between his brows every so often. Like he's thinking about how I just fucking *rejected* him out there on the fire escape.

I can't even wrap my head around that thought. I never want him to feel that way. And I'm pretty damn sure this issue is about me, not him.

I scoot my chair an inch closer to him and then squeeze his thigh, my thumb rolling over his knee. I don't like that we've got our own chairs. I want to be all up on his.

"Want to," I whisper. I'm not sure if anyone else can hear or not. But I'm not sure I care if they do. "Be all over you."

I *do*. Absolutely.

I'm just . . . My shoulders are still tight.

But they release a little when he glances over at me, those dark brown eyes taking me in. I just . . . breathe out.

It's all going to be okay.

But is it?

I chew on my bottom lip and try to reinsert myself back into the dinner conversation.

My dad's waving around a fork laden with tortellini and listing out all the roadside attractions between Chicago and IFU, including the landlocked lighthouse in the middle of Nebraska and also the world's largest time capsule, set to be opened a few years from now.

I join in here and there, trying to leave space for Burkie to talk too, which can be challenging when everyone's speaking all over the top of each other.

But when Dad talks about the world's largest collection of marbles, Burkie's brows go up.

"No shit?" Burkie straightens.

"None at all," my dad confirms, deadpan. "More marbles than you've ever seen in your life."

"I don't doubt that." Burkie laughs, looking genuinely happy about that fact. I have no idea why marbles caught his attention so clearly, but he's smiling so cutely and joyfully, and I squeeze his thigh again, loving the way his muscles flex against my fingertips.

I lean closer to his ear. "Wait until you hear about the giant head of Abraham Lincoln."

My father narrows his eyes on me. "We almost got the cops called on us, thanks to Shaw."

Burkie twists to look at me. "At Lincoln's head?"

I wink at him. "How can you see a giant head and *not* want to climb it?"

Burkie laughs. Jeez, he's cute. I have to tear my eyes off his pinkened cheeks when Dad points a fork at me.

"You didn't have to talk your mother and brother into doing it with you," Dad gripes, but there's humor tugging at his lips.

I roll my eyes, grinning widely. The truth is, it's not all that interesting of a story, but it's one of those stories that comes up every holiday, and it's part of being *home*. I've heard all these stories before. I've heard all the comments that everyone will make. And I'll hear them again next year.

But Burkie hasn't heard them. And that makes it all new.

"They're making up stories." I shift so close to Burkie that my chest hits his shoulder. "It was my mom's idea."

"Sure it was," my father shoots back at me.

I laugh. "It was! Mom?"

"Shaw." Mom shakes her head teasingly as she stands. "Help with the plates?"

"You know it." I slide out, and Burkie starts to get up, but I put a hand on his shoulder and lean close to his ear. "I've got this. Stay and listen to my dad's stories. He's having fun telling you."

"I'm having fun too," he whispers back. And, shit, I get this wash of relief. I want him to get along with my family. I should have asked him to come home with me before. He could have been here every Christmas since I've known him.

How would things have been different if we'd hooked up

months ago? All those nights in his bed. What if I had rolled over and kissed him?

I should have.

I snag his plate and clank a few dishes on top, then head into the kitchen behind my mom. I set the dishes next to the sink as she flips on some music, the low tones of soft jazz filling the small kitchen.

"Eden's sweet," she says, giving me a look as she tugs her thick curls back into a hair tie.

I nod. "Yep."

"Is he your boyfriend?"

"No," I say softly.

She keeps looking at me with her brows up. Using that Voodoo-Mom magic.

"We haven't talked about it," I finally say, bouncing on my toes and glancing into the dining area.

I don't know why my shoulders are getting tight again. I mean, I dig the idea of calling Burkie my boyfriend. And I think he might like it too.

So what's my issue?

Mom smiles. "I've been wondering ever since you mentioned he was coming. I wanted to ask, but your father said to wait and see." She laughs. "But now I think we all see."

"Aww, Mom. Is it that obvious?"

"Yep." She turns to the sink. "And you're well aware I follow your Instagram too."

I nudge her aside to grab the top plate and rinse it off. "Is it that obvious on Insta?"

I've posted pictures of Burkie and me together, of course. But I also post pictures with Leslie and Vain and Dare. And I haven't posted that picture from the airport yet. I want to talk to Burkie about it first.

Mom takes the rinsed plate from me. "It's in your expression. Like the swing."

"The swing?"

Her eyes get a far-away mom-look. "Do you remember the dino-swing?"

"I'm sensing a 'when Shaw was little' story coming on."

"Guilty." She bends to stack the plate in the dishwasher. "You probably don't remember this, but when you were four and your brother was just born, there was a park by the house we lived in. There wasn't much, but there was this dinosaur swing. It was a normal swing, except it was shaped like a T-Rex with a saddle on its back. You *loved* that swing. Every time you saw it, your little four-year-old face would glow with pure, unreserved excitement."

"Awesome?" I say, not sure where she's going with the four-year-old story. "Sounds like a kickass swing. I'd probably still swing on it, assuming I could fit now."

She laughs and takes the next plate from me. "You would. And it's also the look you have around Eden."

"Like he's a T-Rex swing with a saddle? That sounds kinda kinky."

She rolls her eyes at me. "I was more referring to the pure, unreserved excitement part." She tilts her head, her smile becoming soft. "The joy you have around him. He's good for you. I saw it before when we visited last year, and I see it now. And . . ." She twists her lips, considering me for a moment.

"Just say it."

She nods, straightening. "It's hard to lose things when you're a kid. It can scare you. Make you worry about losing things in the future."

My forehead lines. "Yeah, okay. But I'm not following."

"You and Raleigh lost a lot when you were little." She pauses. "I bet it can be hard to open yourself up to losing like that again."

I flip off the water. "I think I'm pretty well adjusted, Mom.

I mean, yeah, it sucked, but things are good now. I'm good now."

"I know you are." She squeezes my forearm, her fingers warm from the plates. "I don't doubt you, Shaw. I'm saying that fear can keep us from doing a lot, sometimes when we don't even realize that's the reason."

"And the fact that he's a guy?" I ask.

She takes another plate. It's Burkie's plate. I remember because he didn't eat any of his green beans, and for some reason, that makes me smile.

"Well, you have to ask yourself if that matters to you," Mom says. "But if you're asking about us, it's none of our business what his gender is. I like Eden. He's good to you, and he makes you happy. What more could a mom ask for?"

My chest tightens. I've always felt accepted by my parents, so I didn't doubt that bringing Burkie here would be an issue, but there's still something that loosens with her words.

"I don't know," I say. "What more could a son ask for in a mom?"

She pats me on the forearm. "I love you too, sweetie. It's always so good to have you home."

"It's good to be here." I take a breath. "And there's a chance I might be heading to AHL next year."

Her eyes widen. "Really?"

"I know I'd be leaving IFU a year early, but I think this is what I want."

Even if there's not a spot in California, there will likely be one somewhere. It's time for me to get moving toward the next step in my life. Maybe somewhere closer to Montreal. New York isn't far. Or there are teams in Canada.

Regardless, another year on the Wolfpack without Burkie doesn't feel right. There will probably be some balking back at IFU when I tell everyone.

But it's my decision.

Mom sets Burkie's plate in the dishwasher. "That's one of those good surprises. What about Eden?"

"He, uh . . ." I shrug a shoulder, trying to keep my voice casual. "I bet he'll get an offer from the Canadiens."

She scans my face—no doubt reading me more clearly than I can read myself.

I dry my hands off on the dish towel, my heel bouncing.

"Do you know much about his family?" she asks.

"I think that's confusing for him right now. His parents are splitting up."

"That must be hard for him."

"Yeah, it is. I know he worries about his mom and sis. But he thinks it's for the best."

Mom starts to say something, but then she pauses. Whatever she reads on my face makes her twist to look around me.

"Eden?" she calls out toward the table. "Can you bring in some plates?"

Burkie perks up, standing immediately and gathering a stack of plates. "Yes, ma'am."

Mom smiles. "It's cute when he calls me ma'am."

"He's cute all the time." I watch him gather plates, being careful not to clink them together too hard.

Burkie brings them in and sets them on the counter. "I'll get more."

"Actually, I wanted to ask you something." Mom steps in front of him. "Do you have your phone?"

"Uh, yes." He glances between us, that crease in the middle of his brow appearing. "Do you need something?"

She dries her wet hands on her jeans. "I thought I might give you our number here. You know, if you're ever on a layover. Just in case."

The line between Burkie's brows deepens. "Just in case?"

Mom wraps her arm around me, locking me to her side in

a half hug. She's so tiny between us, but her arms are strong —they always have been.

"It's so good to have you boys around the apartment," she says, focused on Burkie. "I miss Shaw when he's gone, and I know you'll both be traveling a lot over the next few years. I'm sure you'll be through Chicago now and then, and you don't have to, but you can always stop by. We'd love to see you."

A beat of time passes. Mom's jazz music plays, and the conversation from the dining table winds back to us. My dad laughs, happy and easy. Raleigh asks when we're going to have pie.

A small smile tips Burkie's lips while he looks down at my mom. "I'd like that."

It feels right having him here.

It feels right having him *everywhere*.

He's the person I want to be around more than anyone else. That never stops being true.

And maybe I have been holding back with him. Knowing what's going to happen—a few months from now. Maybe I am scared.

Maybe I'm fucking petrified.

Does he feel that?

Mom points a finger at him. "Maybe we'll even root for you when you're here against the Hawks."

He laughs, holding up his hands. "I definitely don't expect that."

"Well, we'll see. You're on our favorites list anyway." My mom's arm squeezes around my waist, but I'm staring across at Burkie.

And trying to figure out what's in my head. Maybe I've been ignoring the complicated parts.

Maybe that's not fair to either of us.

CHAPTER TWENTY-NINE

Shaw

"There's not much furniture." I unlock the apartment that my dad said we could use for the week. "I dragged a few things up from storage but didn't have time to do much."

"I'm sure it's great," Burkie says as I switch the light on, balancing the small stack of leftovers I'd packed for us.

It's a small studio apartment. There's a corner kitchen and a balcony that looks over Churchshire park. But it's been freshly rehabbed with pale beige walls and parquet flooring. I also snagged a folding table and chairs from the basement storage and borrowed a couple of kitchen items, but otherwise, the place is the definition of sparse.

I carry the leftovers into the kitchen area. "Sorry, just sleeping bags." I nod to the little corner where I'd put them and the foam mattresses. "Much crappier sleeping arrangements than you'd have back at IFU with your big fluffy pillow."

He sets his duffle bag by the wall and folds his coat over the top. "I wouldn't say that."

"Yeah, but you wouldn't have to sleep on the floor." I

open the fridge door. "I probably should've figured out how to get us something nicer."

He laughs. "I don't give one single shit about sleeping on the floor."

I stack the leftovers in, taking time to make sure they won't topple. My fingers are a little fidgety, popping off the lid accidentally. My chest is tight too.

I keep staring at those leftovers, like they'll suddenly explain everything going on in my head. I mean, I'm not sure what not ignoring the complicated parts entails.

I've never been here before. Not with anyone. And I—

"Shaw?" Burkie's low, husky voice raises goosebumps up the back of my neck.

I straighten and close the fridge door. I've seriously been standing in front of the cold draft for so long that I've got some minor ball shrinkage.

I pivot to look at him and then stop dead, my thoughts scattering like leaves.

All week, I've had that voice in my ear at night on the phone. With his soft drawl and the way he always cuts off some of his words. And now he's standing on the far side of the ledge that separates the kitchen from the main room.

He's just standing there like normal. Like I've seen my best friend stand a million times. But, jeez, he *strikes* me as he sets his forearms on the ledge, his brown eyes stacked full of thoughts. The scruff along his jaw is so damn kissable. And his lips. And just . . . him.

The way he looks at me.

The way I look at him.

I feel like I'm standing at the edge of this precipice, staring at what Burkie and I could be. And it's *big*. Like really freaking huge.

So, yeah, it's making my heart beat double-time. Because life has taught me that just about *everything* can be taken away. A brother's health. A home. A scholarship.

A best friend.

Nothing is certain.

I drag in a slow breath, trying to stop the steamroll of thoughts. We're here now. And I plan to pour myself into this week like nobody's business. Because I don't know if this will happen again. A solid seven days with no focus other than being us.

How many people ever get time like this with someone they—

Shit.

I mean, wow.

Did I almost have that thought?

I did.

I'm falling for him. And I'm not going to run from it. I'm not going to shove it off as 'just fun' or keep calling it simple.

There's no one else I'd rather do this with.

I'm glad it's him.

"You okay?" Burkie's forehead lines as he looks me up and down. "Something wrong?"

"Nah, I'm *good.*" So damn good. I step around the ledge, taking in the rest of him. His shirt is tight across his muscular pecs, falling looser around his abs. His jeans fit the same— tighter around his powerful thighs and then easier over his knees and down to his ankles.

I don't even try to pretend like I'm not checking him out.

"Just like having you here," I say. I really, *really* do. I've been thinking about him non-stop since he left for Montreal.

Possibly a little obsessively.

"I like being here." He nods toward my t-shirt. "Can I see the tattoo?"

My lips rise. I thought maybe he saw it on the fire escape, but I suppose he was busy with other things. I pull up the bottom hem of my t-shirt slowly, tilting my head and watching him as he takes me in. His lips part as soon as my shirt is halfway up, that glint of his tongue deep in his mouth making me smile.

My stomach flexes when he steps forward and brushes his fingers along my side, touching a few inches above the ink.

"It's an exact copy of the patch." His thumb rolls over my obliques and then down to my hip, his callouses scraping in a way that's already spiking heat low in my gut. "Identical."

"We kinda came up with it together." My voice gravels at how he's touching me, stroking his thumb back and forth, soothing me. "Wanted to keep it forever."

"Like a memento?"

"A permanent one," I say. "Of something that means a hell of a lot."

Not just the patch, but everything from IFU. Especially because I do think I'm leaving after this year. And for me, my memories of the Wolfpack revolve around him. If I think back to anything important over the last two and a half years, Burkie is right there, strong and steady and *there*.

I pick you.

His thumb tracks once more over my side, an inch outside of the tattoo, before his hand falls.

I lower my shirt. "I got you something."

His brows rise. "You did?"

I cross over to my duffle and crouch to pull out the crumpled, wrapped package. There's this gift and another too—a smaller one in a velvet pouch. I slip the second gift into my back pocket because I'm not sure it's the right time for that one.

I head back to him, a twist of nerves crawling between my shoulders as I hold the squashed, bright red package out. "Hope you like it."

"I'll like it." He takes it from me. There's not a speck of doubt in his voice. "And I got you something too. I wasn't sure if we were giving gifts, but . . ." He licks his lips. "Of course I got you something."

I laugh. "I was nervous about it too. Still am. Open it."

"Alright." He flips it over and slides his index finger under the tape, unsticking it gently. He pulls off the paper and unfolds the gift, a smile crossing his face. "It's a beanie."

"Where you're going, they call it a toque."

He laughs. "They do."

"I know you like to wear one when you jog in the mornings." I point to it. "It's got Bluetooth. So now I can call you and bug you while you're running. Or you can listen to music."

"It's perfect." He flips it over and stills when he sees the Habs logo.

"It's not a big gift," I say with a shrug, worried about the line forming down his forehead. I thought he'd be pretty ecstatic to see that logo. The excitement in his voice for the last week has been unmistakable. Every time he talks about it, there's awe hovering under the words.

I know he wants an offer. No matter what else is going on. He's worked for this his whole life.

"I love it." He tugs the beanie on, his hair sticking cutely out the sides, and my chest releases when he smiles, his whole face warming. "Thank you." He steps closer to me, dropping the wrapping paper. Grabbing my neck, he pulls me in for a kiss.

All the space between us is gone in an instant.

I freaking love kissing Burkie. The softness of his lips, the sweep of his tongue against mine as he backs me up against the ledge. Can't believe I used to avoid kissing.

But then, I'd never kissed a Burkie before.

I slide my hands underneath his shirt, palming his abs. "Got something else for you too."

Something I wasn't fully sure about giving him.

But, fuck it.

He leans his forehead against mine. "You didn't have to."

"Wanted to." I slide my hand lower, fitting it between us to cup his zipper. "Drop your pants."

He laughs. "Getting right to it?"

"Well, it's necessary for the gift."

"Sounds like a good gift."

He steps back to drop his jeans, then he folds them in his careful way before turning away to set them on top of his duffle, his muscles flexing, all that hockey power in his glutes and thighs.

He reaches back to grab his shirt under the neckline and tugs it over his head. The toque pulls halfway off, but he resettles it as he turns back to look at me, his boxer briefs tight against his semi-erect cock.

So damn hot.

And exactly what I want at the moment. If I wait much longer, he'll be too hard.

Curiosity lights his eyes as he steps back over to me. I suck in an eager breath and slide my fingers along the top of his boxer briefs, then yank him another inch closer. I tug the briefs down until his cock half springs out.

I'm tempted to drop to my knees, but instead I pull out the velvet pouch.

I opened his present earlier.

Cleaned it. Debated if he'd like it.

Shit, I'm so nervous.

He watches me fumble with the pouch. "What's the—"

I slip out the cockring, and his eyes widen.

"Whatcha think?" I ask, trying not to bounce on my toes.

"Uh." He blinks down at it. "Not sure yet. Put it on."

"Yeah?" I slip the black silicone ring over the head of his cock—not far down, an inch below the flare of his head. It's not tight at all yet, just lightly circling him. His breath catches, his cock twitching.

And, holy shit, I can't stop staring.

It's even hotter looking than I thought it would be. The

sight of that black band decorating his shaft is so damn alluring that my stomach flutters.

"This okay?" I ask.

He swallows thickly. "Fuck, yeah, that's okay."

"We should probably lube it." I lick my lips, not wanting to take my eyes off how sexy it looks, and we still haven't positioned it at the base of his cock. "Make sure it'll come off later. We don't want you stuck."

"No, we don't." He laughs. "Do it."

My eyes rise to meet his dark brown ones. "There's a packet of lube in my pocket."

He fishes in my pocket to grab the lube packet and then tears the corner off with his teeth. I watch, mesmerized, as he lubes around the base of his cock then up his shaft to just under the ring, his fingers moving with efficient confidence, that sexy vein starting to stand out. And, jeez, that's hot too.

I want to run my hands all over him, but I stay there, just grasping the ring, my fingers trembling a little.

"Alright," he says as he tosses the lube packet aside.

I slide the ring down, my eyes bugging out as it glides lower, tighter toward his thick base, his hair brushing my fingers. He trimmed a little down there, but I'm so glad he left a decent amount of hair for me. And, fuck, it's so *hot*. My mind goes on repeat again, not able to think of anything else.

I pause at the base of his cock. "Balls in or out?"

He frowns slightly. "No idea."

"Maybe balls out for the first time?" I settle the ring at the base of his shaft. "Too much?"

"Not too much." His mouth opens as I fist him and stroke the full length of him. He thickens in my hand, a bead of pre-cum welling up.

"Fuck," he mumbles, his head tipping back, stomach flexing. "You always feel so good. Don't know how you do it."

"Easy with you." I roll my thumb over his slit, gasping at the slickness of his pre-cum as I smear it around his head. His eyes hood, his cock twitching in my hand. He arches back, his entire rugged, hockey-honed body flexing. Hair curls out from under his toque, his jaw tensing as he groans.

I never get tired of watching him, and it brings me back to that first time I saw him come, so powerful it sucked the air out of the room.

He still sucks all the air out of the room.

I scrunch down to lick along his sternum, his smattering of hair dragging on my tongue.

"Shaw." His eyes haze as I look at him, his mouth opening and closing. "Why does that feel so fuckin' good? I'm getting really *hard*. Jesus."

I smirk at him. "Wonder what'll happen when I do this." I drop to my knees and take his cockhead into my mouth, sucking and licking around his crown.

His head lolls back, his abs constricting so hard they tremble. "Fuck*me*."

"Too much?"

"No." He reaches down and clasps my cheek. "I mean it. *Fuck* me, Shaw."

I inhale sharply. That pressure lights across my chest.

"I want to." I want to do this with him. "I'm just . . ." I lick my lips. "I'm a little nervous. Remember back when we first kissed? When I asked you to go first? I'm feeling like that again."

His thumb tracks along the side of my face, a light, soft caress. "Like what exactly?"

I sort through the avalanche of thoughts in my head. The parquet floor is hard against my knees, a draft whispering in under the sliding glass door to the balcony. It chilled me last night, and the only thing I could think while snuggled into the sleeping bags was that it'd be better if Burkie was there, cuddled next to me. His big hand cupping me, his gravelly drawl close to my ear.

I couldn't wait to see him today.

For the last two years, I've lit up every time I've seen him. Not just a little excitement—I feel it right down to my toes. This pure, unreserved thrill that he's there. That he's close to me.

But there's still some nerves right now. And I feel like I want to talk about it.

"I'm feeling a little anxious," I admit, completely dialed in on his expression even though he's all thick cock and rigid muscles and pure sex-distraction right in front of me. "About what's gonna happen next."

Anxious might be an understatement, but he seems to get my meaning as his brows rise.

"You mean in the next five minutes?" he asks. "Or a bigger 'what's next?'"

"Both." I tip into his hand cupping my jaw, soaking up every bit of his touch. "I guess I want you to know that it's not just an experiment. Or just messing around. It means something."

His Adam's apple bobs, his fingers stilling against my jaw. "It's meant something for a while now."

Shit, a tremble starts low in my throat. I swallow it back.

"Yeah," I say. "It has. And I want to do this. I just needed you to know that it feels kinda big."

His chest expands with a deep breath.

I pick you.

Again and again. And again.

I stand to kiss him. Gripping his neck, I pull him flush against me. His arms squeeze me so tight I can hardly breathe, the contact between us head-to-toe.

All the tension seems to vibrate out of me as we meld into each other, opening to each other, mouth on mouth, hands exploring as we stumble toward the sleeping bags, both of us tugging up my t-shirt, and I kick everything off somewhere, tossing off my hat. We crawl down on the little nest I'd made for us in the corner.

He settles on his back, and I prop over the top of him. My heart gives a solid kick as his hands smooth up my arms and flatten on my shoulders.

I dip to kiss along his jaw, rasping my lips over his stubble before nibbling along the curve of his pec to his tight nipple that I suck into my mouth.

He groans as I tease him with my tongue across his nipples and navel and abs, then down to where he's so freaking hard in that tantalizing black band, so beautiful nestled at the base of his shaft.

I drag my tongue along the top edge.

He shudders. "Holy *fuck*."

I draw my tongue along the ring again and then lightly clamp my teeth on it, giving the faintest tug.

He emits a guttural groan, clasping my shoulder hard as a blush runs up his neck. "More, Shaw. *Fuck*. What are you doing down there?"

I let go with my teeth and tongue around the band, one hand moving up to cup his balls, massaging them gently before returning to sucking over the ring.

"*Yes*." He shudders again, his shoulder arching back. "Fuck, your tongue feels so good."

I keep tonguing around the ring, my own balls throbbing, then lightly bite and tug on the silicone again.

He garbles out words, pre-cum glistening across his upper abs, his body writhing, muscles all flexed, his mouth opening and closing. I have never seen him like this before, and I don't stop, licking and nibbling—pausing only to grab some lube and then squeeze it out, eagerness vibrating in my fingers as I circle the tip of my finger around his hole. He brings his legs farther up.

"Shaw." His moans ripple through the small apartment as I push my slicked finger into him, opening him slowly.

"You're so damn hot." I crook my finger to stroke his prostate, and he bears down on me.

"*There.*" He grips the top of my shoulder hard, his roughness creating a thrum deep in my pelvis. "Feels so fuckin' good. I want your cock."

I moan at the sheer sexiness of his words and squeeze my eyes shut. There's still a tightness in my chest, but I want this too.

When I open my eyes and look down at where my finger's inside of him, my dick throbs. The pure need to be in him strikes me so hard that my head spins, and I have to take a calming breath as I work a second finger in.

He moves with me, grinding down, his pupils wide and lips parted. He's still gripping me roughly, his fingers digging into me. I can hardly think. I just want to be inside him.

He groans, his thighs shaking. "*Please.*"

"Hold on." I grab the lube packet and slick myself, my fingers shaking so hard that I'm a freaking mess. Adrenaline spikes. My nerve endings feel raw. "You ready?"

"*Yes.*" He widens his thighs on either side of me. "Now."

My heart clenches as I position myself at his entrance.

I pause.

Fuck.

I completely forgot.

"Do you want me to wear a condom?" I ask.

"No," he breathes out.

I debate. We talked about barebacking, of course. But maybe we should have discussed it again before we got to—

"*Just us.*" His gaze fixes on mine, pupils wide and mouth slack, but I can see his thoughts. Strong and steady and sure.

I nod.

Nothing between us.

It feels right. Burkie and me. Here, now. Together.

I fit the head of my cock against him and slowly, with a needy throb through my entire body, push in. My mouth falls open as his tightness squeezes my crown. Tears spring to the corners of my eyes.

"It's too good," I grit out. My ass cheeks clench, my toes curl. The pressure is unbelievable. And only my head is inside of him.

He palms at my ribs, like he's trying to pull me closer.

Our eyes meet.

Breaths shallow.

Heat swells in my throat. Being inside him is so fucking *emotional*. Like we're both exactly where we should be. And, shit, I have to hold back some kind of a sob. It's relief and satisfaction and hot-edged need all wrapped together.

It's so *much*.

"You good?" he asks.

I nod, struggling to talk, breathing through flaring nostrils, my knees digging hard into the slippery fabric of the sleeping bags.

He grasps at my sides. "Need you to wiggle your dick."

I rasp out a surprised laugh and lean closer to kiss him, fitting between his thighs and moaning as I press into him, my eyes rolling, my legs shaking.

"Oh fuck." He arches underneath me. "There. *Fuuuck.* That's . . ." His fingers gouge into me, his head tipping back. He's shaking almost as hard as I am, a deep blush racing across his chest.

His thighs widen out to either side as I bury myself to the hilt.

Holy hell.

He looks so masculine on my dick—his jaw clenching, pecs hard, knees kicked up, his cock thick between us, beautiful in the ring and leaking over his stomach. He's perfect.

"Want to . . ." I gasp, not sure how to finish that sentence. I'm shaking so hard that I can barely hold myself over the top of him. " . . . fuck you hard."

"*Yes.*" He arches underneath me. "Fuckin' *do* it."

Tears leak over the corners of my eyes as I shift my ass back and then thrust into him. I moan at the perfect pressure, already two seconds away from busting my nut, but somehow I hold on, hovering on the edge as I pull almost all the way out and press in deep. I hit a spot that makes him writhe and pant out fractured words, his hands gripping me hard enough to leave fingerprints. We both start to move, desperation and need tangling together, our rhythm feeling like this innate pulse resonating between us.

Something so far beyond what I ever thought sex could be.

Hell, I *thought* I knew what sex was.

I didn't.

It's the entire world folded down to him. It's grasping at each other with an unceasing need to be closer. To touch. To feel the heat of his skin and taste the salt of his sweat. To reach for this *thing* we have—the one I can't name—that draws us together, that makes my heart pound and tears leak from the corners of my eyes.

And when he whispers my name in a ragged plea, it sends me off the edge.

I break apart. Break down. Shatter. I don't even know. I'm fucking crying. And thrusting so deep that he braces his palms back against the wall, both of us panting, sweat-slicked and shaking and moaning.

"Come," he groans, and I don't know if he's talking about me or him, but it seems like a good idea all around. The head of his cock deepens in color, his thighs tensing and knees coming up. His hands come off the wall to grab at my shoulders.

My thoughts fragment.

I let go, my release shooting deep into him. It wells around my shaft as I keep thrusting, slicking us even more, hot and liquid on my balls and wetting my thighs.

"Need to feel it too." The raw words hardly come out of my throat, sputtering out with the last of my release. "Need to feel your cum in me. Eden . . . you gotta . . ." I pull out of him and grab another packet of lube. I reach a shaking finger to ready myself. "Need you to fuck me."

He shoves me down to my hands and knees, moving behind me and driving away my fingers before replacing them with his own. He stretches me quickly, our urgency ratcheting up.

"Take me," I beg. I want him to pound me. To fucking *own* me. "Don't care if I'm ready."

"I won't hurt you," he says strongly.

I close my eyes as he works me then lubes his cock. When he finally grabs my hips and presses in, I whimper. His cock is so huge and hard that it stretches every corner of me.

He drives deep, and my eyes roll back.

"Harder," I pant. "*Fuck* me, Eden."

I want all of him.

All his power and strength. Every bit that he uses when he slams full throttle into the boards. I want that.

A growl rises in his chest. It's hard and possessive. I *want* to be possessed by him.

It's a heart-pulsing desire that I've never come close to feeling before, and it only grows as his chest hits my back, his weight shoving me down into the sleeping bags.

"I can feel your cum in me," he says, close to my ear, and I about lose it for a second time right there.

He's big and muscular on top of me, all of his body over mine. His arm snakes underneath me, and he braces us together, angling his hips so that he hits that sweet spot every freaking time.

I'm gone—shaking and gasping. Panting and begging. Beyond anything and everything.

He covers me. Holds me. Hugs me. Fucks me. Buries his cock between my spread legs and makes me whimper.

And at the same time, makes me feel so fucking secure.

Like he won't ever let go. He won't disappear.

He hugs me tighter, nearly crushing my ribs, rocking

deeper, more desperate. I mewl into the sleeping bag, my mouth falling open as he groans my name, an orgasm wrecking through him.

I feel it all.

His cock twitching deep inside me as his weight slackens, the heat of his release, slick and damp, the pounding of his heart against my back. The embrace of his arm underneath my chest. His warm breath on my neck.

He doesn't move.

I don't want him to move.

I reach a hand back, palming the top of his shoulder. "Stay."

He squeezes me tighter in response. I want to say something else, but I can't sort out the right words, so I clutch him to me. Keeping him with me in any way that I can.

CHAPTER THIRTY

Shaw

"Merry Christmas, babe," Burkie whispers into my ear. We're snuggled under a sleeping bag with a hushed morning light seeping in through the glass balcony door.

I quirk a lip. "You just called me *babe*."

"Uh, yeah." He stiffens.

"I like it." Especially in that soft drawl. I snuggle back against him, feeling his chest expand with a sharp breath when my ass nuzzles against his morning chub. "*Miroşi bine.* You smell so damn good." A bit sweaty from being warm in the sleeping bag, which makes it even better.

"Do you want to get up?" he asks. His thumb rolls over my sack. He's cupping me, massaging lightly. Not in a sexual way. Just in this soul-deep, comforting way.

"Nope." I snake a hand out into the cooler air to grab my phone and check the time. We're heading over to SHC with my family to help serve Christmas brunch, then coming back to help cook, but that's not for a few hours. I flip open the camera and hold it above us, snapping a picture of us snuggled together under the sleeping bags.

"Damn, we're cute," I say as we stare at the picture. "But we should talk about Insta."

"Alright." He trails the tip of his nose into the side of my neck, lighting goosebumps. "What about?"

I clear my throat. "There's been a suggestion that it might be obvious we're snapping bed frames and giving each other cockrings in non-platonic ways."

"Can you give a cockring in a platonic way?" He laughs, his breath tickling. "Maybe that should be our next offering for the team. Wolfpack cockrings."

"Holy shit. Can you imagine SCU's faces when we show *those* off?"

"It would give our team rivalry a whole new slant." His smile presses into my neck as our laughter fades. "Have you posted that much of us lately?"

"Not more than usual. Nothing more than what I would have posted with any of our roommates. But people will put two and two together if I post pics of us here in Chicago." I thumb back to the picture of us in the airport, and it makes me smile.

His breath heats my ear. "I like being on your Instagram."

"I like you there too." I wiggle my ass back. "Like you all sorts of places."

He groans as his hips press forward, his cock nuzzling between my cheeks. "What if you post whatever you want? And we let them think whatever they want?"

I flip back to the photo I just took. We look so content, our hair mussed, our eyes sleepy, a satiated *Burkie-is-cupping-my-junk* smile on my face.

We look *happy*.

I want to share that.

"It's more up to you." He squeezes my junk carefully. "It's your Instagram."

"It's both of our futures on the Wolfpack." I pause. "And maybe the NHL."

318

It's gotta be hard being out in the NHL. Even if you do find a team that's cool, that doesn't stop the digs that you'd get on the ice from other players. Or from fans. Or from who-the-fuck-ever feeling like they have a right to comment on your life.

Ever since I posted the pic of my tattoo, I've seen a hell of a lot that I didn't know was out there, and it's not always easy to delete and block in real life. There could be consequences for both of our careers.

There's also the issue of us being teammates.

He kisses my neck. "I said that I would risk it all. I'm done hiding."

I twist to see his face. His dark eyes are serious, his jaw strong. He knows all the same things I do about the NHL. And he's saying that, *knowing* there might be some hard times because of what we do right now.

"Jeez, I missed you," I say. "Like a whole freaking lot. And when I was lying there in your bed—by my lonely-ass self—I thought about how I want people to know that I miss you. That you're important to me."

His eyes rove around my face. "I want them to know too."

I pull up Insta. There's a flood of comments and messages to respond to, but I bypass them all and load the picture, changing a few coloring options, but not that much needs to be altered. We look pretty damn perfect just as we are.

I pause, a little flutter in my stomach. This is a big step.

There's no going back.

But I don't want to go back.

I take one last glance at Burkie.

"Done hiding." He nuzzles into my neck, tracing up to my ear with the tip of his nose. "Feels good."

I hit post then toss my phone aside. The comments will come rolling in, but I'll deal with it later. This is a moment just for us. "I guess it'll be an interesting couple of days when we get back to IFU."

"Suppose so." He nips at my ear. "You didn't open your gift last night."

"Shit, I forgot about it with the way you were plowing me like a feral beast."

He laughs. "Me too." He rolls away, pushes to his feet, and crosses to his duffle. When he gets there, he bends over, and I stare blatantly at his bare ass and the swing of his hefty balls as he digs in the inside pocket. He returns with a flattish rectangular package and crawls back in under the sleeping bags. "Hope you like it."

"Of course I'll like it." I tear off the paper to find a photo frame and envelope. I set the envelope aside and concentrate on the photo, my throat tightening so fast that I don't have time to take a steadying breath.

It's a picture of Raleigh, Mom, Dad, and me. One that I sent to Burkie when I was at the hospital with them. All of us with tremendous smiles. It was a good moment.

"You said you wanted a picture," Burkie says. "If that's not a good one, then I can—"

"It's perfect." My eyes heat a little. "You remembered that?"

Of course he did.

He nods toward the envelope. "There's something else."

I carefully set the frame aside and tear open the envelope, scanning the two tickets inside.

"For real?" I sit up. "These are Blackhawks tickets. Right above center ice."

"Timing worked out, so I thought we could go. Maybe grab a bite to eat after. Or drinks or something."

Shit, I have so many emotions again. I swear, they don't stop with Burkie. It's like he brings something out of me.

I gloss my thumb over the tickets. "Are we going on a date?"

"Yep." He pauses. "I mean, if you want it to be."

"*Yeah*, I do." I grin down at the tickets, then the frame, then back at him, then at the tickets again. My entire body feels so electric, like everything is zapping and jolting around inside of me. "Thank you. It's gonna be so cool."

It was.

Not just the game, which was a back-and-forth high-scorer where we hardly sat down. Or the dinner after at a tapas place over on Halsted I'd always wanted to try. Or helping out over at SHC.

But the whole week. A *perfect* week.

We slept in most mornings before getting in a quick run together if it wasn't too cold. Then home to shower, which was usually less quick. Then we just *did* stuff. Whatever we wanted. Like skating at Millennium Park, holding hands as we looped around the rink, kids darting all around us. We went on a night-time walk around the Butterfly Haven, the little creatures flitting all around us. We hit up Fiona's for the fried pickles and cheap beer and then headed back to play Rummy with my parents before sneaking off to stream some SportsCenter, our legs tangled as we lounged on the sleeping bags, me sorting through Insta comments that were not being shy about how they wanted more pictures of me and Burkie, and we were just . . . us.

It was so easy.

He's unlike anyone else I've ever been around.

We couldn't get enough of each other.

Like not at all.

So it's a sharp turn when it's suddenly time to catch our flight and Burkie looks over at me. He already seems so far away from me, packing his duffle a few feet away. Every second, I itch for his arms to be around me. For his fingers to thread with mine.

I can't get enough of him.

Don't want to get enough.

He sweeps a strand of hair behind his ear. "Are you ready to get back?"

"Nah, not really." I flip my hat backward, trying to sound easy, but that damn pinch in my chest starts again. "Not really at all."

"Me neither." He lays his joggers out on top of his duffle and then carefully rolls them up, which is how he packs so that he has no fold lines in his clothes. It's ridiculously cute.

"Are you nervous?" I ask him as I shove all my t-shirts into a big ball in the corner of my bag.

He scrapes his teeth over his bottom lip. "Very."

"Yeah, I am too." I itch at the side of my hat. Everyone knows now. Maybe not Coach yet, but enough of the team follows me on Insta that I'm sure it got spread around pretty quickly. "But I am jonesing to get back on the ice with you. About to jump out of my skin."

I've been thinking about it off and on all week. What's better than doing my favorite thing in the world with my favorite person?

Nothing.

"Me too." A soft smile curves his lips. "Fuck, I miss being out there with you."

On the ice together. For half a season. Assuming that everything goes normal once we get back.

Shit, what if it doesn't? What if we get kicked like Kazi?

Will Burkie regret posting on Insta?

Would he regret this week?

I swallow, staring across at him as he goes back to carefully packing his duffle, my stomach twisting into a giant knot.

No, he won't. He won't regret it.

Just like I never will.

Regardless of what happens when we get back.

Although half a season with him isn't nearly long enough.

Not even close.

And I'm realizing something. Or maybe I knew it all along, but it took this week away to fully understand it.

I want more.

CHAPTER THIRTY-ONE

Shaw

"Hey," Burkie whispers. "You okay?"

"Shit, no," I say. We're standing outside the ice rink doors, both of us laden down with our duffles and gear, my heel bouncing in my slides. And, fuck, I'm anxious. I don't think my stomach has unballed since we left Chicago.

I'm not good at confrontation. I'm not like Burkie, ready to bomb across the ice and shoulder someone into the boards.

But I need to step up to this. Because I want to be with him.

I'm lucky enough that I didn't have to be nervous about coming out to my family. This feels different.

He swings his duffle so it thunks against mine. "Do you not want to go in? I can go first."

I take a breath. "No, we both should go. And I don't want to be late. I'm feeling edgy."

He nods strongly, his brown eyes fixed on mine. "It'll be alright. We've got—"

"*Burk.*" Vain's low voice resonates behind us, and Burkie and I both turn to see him jogging across the pavement, a grin splitting his face. Somehow he swoops between Burkie and me, wrapping an arm around each of us and pulling us both into a hug. "Fuck, I'm so glad to see you guys."

"Hell, yeah." I toss on a smile, trying to quell the roll of my stomach as we step through the doors, pulled along by Vain's exuberance.

I glance at Burkie, and he meets my eyes again, his brows rising slightly.

I nod.

We need to do this.

Vain is talking a million miles a minute as we head down the hallway. He palms Burkie's shoulder as we walk, a bit of purple paint in the crevices of his fingernails.

"Tell me *everything*, bro," he says. "How was it? How was Chicago? How was Montreal? What did the *ice* smell like?"

Burkie's lips turn up. "Kinda like ice."

"But *Habs* ice," Vain insists. "You have no idea how pumped I am that we might be going together next year. I mean, fuck. It's the dream."

A little line appears on Burkie's brow. "Guess so. Honestly, it was pretty amazing. I don't know if I can fully describe it." He looks over at me, this deep, thoughtful look in his eyes. It stops me up. Makes my footsteps falter. My own thoughts spin. He loved it in Montreal. I know it.

"Well, I want details." Vain upnods at me. "Grub after practice? I gotta catch up on all your shenanigans."

"Yep," I say. Although Vain's been pretty up on our shenanigans. He commented on every single post over the last week. With the same enthusiasm that's jumping through him right now. I wink at Burkie. "You in?"

"For sure." Burkie lowers his voice. "Has, uh, anyone said anything about Shaw and me?"

"I'm sure they've talked about it." Vain steps through the locker room entryway ahead of us. "But let them talk. There's no way that—"

"Are you fucking serious?" A voice echoes off the tiles, pissed off and reverberating back at us.

I stop dead at the entrance to the locker bays. Almost the entire team is here, and the tension ratchets up about ten more notches when the guys turn and take us in.

Shit.

I swallow hard.

The only person who doesn't turn to stare at us is Dare. He stands rigidly in the middle of the team, most of who are half dressed and deadly quiet.

He takes a heavy step toward Cassidy. "Tell me you're not fucking serious."

Cassidy holds out his phone. "I'm *not* trying to start shit. But this is—"

"I don't fucking care what's on there." Dare raises his voice, his words cutting hard. He jabs a finger at the big white wall. "Doesn't this means something?"

But, shit, the big white wall isn't white anymore. I blink at the wolf's head, brilliant and bold, rainbows of color woven into its fur. It's only half painted, most of the wolf outlined in purple, but it's freaking *breathtaking*.

I blink over at Vain's purple fingers, but I don't have time to register a full thought about it before Cassidy snaps back at Dare.

"You know it does." Cassidy holds his ground, even as Dare takes another step forward. "But you're misreading shit."

Dare's jaw clenches hard. "Fuck that. I'm not—"

"Hey." Vain's sharp command fills the locker room. "What's going on?"

Dare inhales a sharp breath, his nostrils flaring. "Cassidy has things to say."

I brace myself. Just like I do in the crease. Steadying myself for whatever is going to come flying my way. For the hit that's going to land, maybe right between my pads.

"Let's hear it." Burkie drops his duffle on the floor. Tension tightens across his shoulders as he steps halfway in front of me. Right there on my right. Where he always is.

I breathe out. Steady my feet.

We've got this.

That's what he was going to say earlier when Vain cut him off.

"Cassidy's saying shit behind our backs," Dare spits out, his deep red hair shining in the lights. "And it's pissing me the fuck off."

"I'm *not* saying shit." Cassidy holds up his hands, his phone still clutched in one. Even from here, I can see what's on it.

My Insta page.

Dare bristles.

"*Alright.*" Vain steps closer to them. "Can we take the temperature down a touch?"

Dare presses his lips, still looking like he's about to launch at Cassidy.

"Dare?" Vain asks, his voice softening. "Come on, bro. Let's sort it out."

Dare hesitates like he's going to argue, but then he nods sharply and takes a few steps back, his hands jamming into his pockets.

Vain turns toward Cassidy. "Do you want to say something?"

Cassidy glances at his phone and then over at Burkie. "I think I need to talk to Coach."

Vain nods. "Let's do that now, then."

"Talk to me about what?" Coach asks as he steps past me. I'd been so distracted I hadn't seen him come in. "What the hell is going on?" His frown shifts to Dare. "I could hear you outside in the hall."

"I've got zero issues, Coach." Dare glares at Cassidy. "This is the fucker who has issues."

Cassidy shakes his head. "I don't have issues. You're misreading things. You jumped in the middle, hotheaded and pissed."

"I saw what I saw," Dare says stiffly.

Coach's eyes narrow as he steps into the middle of the room. "Someone needs to tell me what the hell is going on. Then we'll figure it out and get on the ice." He pivots to Cassidy. "Cassidy? Everyone keeps glaring at you."

Silence.

Cassidy looks from Dare to Burkie to me, then down at his phone. He shoves it in his back pocket. "Sorry, Coach. It's nothing. I made a mistake asking about it."

Well, shit, I didn't expect that to happen.

Burkie twists to look at me, his brows rising in a silent question.

I nod.

This is it. It has to be.

Right here, right now.

We've got this.

Nerves crackle down my spine as Burkie slips out his phone, unlocks it, and steps toward Coach.

"The excitement is about this. Shaw and I are . . ." He frowns. "Well, I don't know exactly what we are. But we are."

The locker room is beyond silent. My heart hammers. My heel bounces, but I stop it.

Coach takes Burkie's phone and scans it before handing it back.

"Get on the ice, puckheads." Coach turns toward the door, yelling over his shoulder as he heads out. "Ten minutes or your ass is on the bench next game."

"That's it?" O'Hern steps forward.

Coach pauses. "That's it," he says gruffly.

"But they're *together*." O'Hern's lips twist up. "You're always talking about team balance. How does this not mess with that?"

Coach nails him with a look. "Who's your roommate?"

O'Hern blinks. "Cassidy and Valdez. But that's not—"

"No." Coach stares him down. "It's not the same. But I've coached you kids for longer than some of you have been alive. I've coached roommates. I've coached lifelong friends. I've coached brothers. I've coached guys who have hated each other so intensely they could barely look at each other. And I can guarantee you I've coached guys who were hooking up or bumping uglies or whatever you kids call it these days. I just didn't know about it. I won't pretend that it can't impact things on the ice, but *all of you*"—he looks around at us pointedly—"have different relationships with each other, and it's not my business to control that. How many times do I have to tell you knuckleheads that I care about what happens on the ice before it sinks into your thick skulls?"

Silence.

We all just take it in. O'Hern licks his lips and turns his head, his jaw ticking. But it looks like he's thinking too.

Coach grunts. "Actually, Keenan and Burkehammer have been tearing it up this entire season. They've been running circles around you, O'Hern. Maybe you and Cassidy should think about following their example."

He shakes his head before steamrolling toward the door. "On the ice, puckheads. Ten minutes or you'll be doing Herbies for a solid hour."

There are groans all around on that one. Which, I realize, took the emphasis off Burkie and me.

And *holy shit*.

We came out. To our families. Friends. Teammates. The whole freaking world.

I'm staring at Burkie, my eyes welling up. My body feels light as air, like anything is possible. Like there's nothing that can hold us back now.

It's me and Burkie.

Just like it should be.

Words that I will forever remember:

1. "I think you should trust yourself, Burkie."
2. "I kinda don't want it to stop."
3. "I'm quiet, because I wanted to."
4. "We would have been there for you in a heartbeat."
5. "I don't think it's actually about the bed."
6. "I'm with Burkie. All the way."
7. "I'm happy."
8. "I just want to be us."
9. "I want people to know that I miss you. That you're important to me."
10. "It's you and me. We can do anything."

CHAPTER THIRTY-TWO

Burk

The locker room is dead silent.

I know we've only got ten minutes, but I don't give a fuck about anything else right now.

I'm staring at Shaw.

There's an energy buzzing between him and me. It's not a new energy. It's been there for as long as I can remember, but it feels different now. It feels honest.

Open.

For the first time, we're out there. For everyone to see.

Shaw's eyes are raw and watery, and I get this pang of worry.

Then he winks at me.

And, fuck . . . I'm near breathless, just looking at him.

He drops his duffle, a smile slowly lighting his face. It's a familiar smile, gorgeous and eager and a touch devious, and I feel it everywhere, zinging in my cells, making me just . . . so damn ecstatic. Like this moment—and our lives—mean something.

I mean something.

I mean something to Shaw.

Just as I am, standing here, imperfections and all.

Everyone is stock-still and watching us. There's not even a click of skates.

I take one step toward him, and then another, until my toes are three inches from his. He tilts his head, a question flashing through his eyes, and then I kiss him.

Right there in the middle of the motherfuckin' locker room.

I kiss him the way I always want—like my whole life depends on it—clasping his neck and dragging him to me. His lips are still arced in that smile, and his hat tumbles off, bumping against my knuckles as it falls. He grips onto my biceps, pulling me closer, and we stumble together.

Someone lets out a whoop. Then a *"fuck, yeah."* Someone claps. And then there's a howl, picked up, one after the other. All around us, echoing off the tile walls, low voices rising together.

I pull back to find him still grinning.

He leans closer to my ear, his jaw brushing mine. And I'm brought right back to the first time he leaned that close to me, standing outside the kitchen, and I was so confused. So fuckin' lost.

I'm not lost anymore.

"That was a good kiss," he whispers.

"Really fuckin' good."

"And that word you were looking for earlier?" He leans back to wink at me. "I think it was boyfriends."

I close my eyes. "I'm pretty sure it was too." It feels like my happiness is all around us, fuckin' everywhere. It always does around Shaw though. He brings it out of me.

He smacks my ass. "Good. Now let's get geared up."

"Sweeter words were never spoken."

———

We leave it all on the ice.

Shaw and I are perfect. We're on point. In complete, mind-melded sync.

Nothing is left to argue. And when we step into the locker room later, there's not a single peep from O'Hern.

That's fine.

He can go to his own fuckin' corner. I could confront him, but honestly, I'm not sure I give a shit. The rest of the team spoke more than clearly, and he'll either learn something or he won't.

Either way, I'm not sure there's anything I can do about it, so I stop thinking about it as we head out and toss our gear in the back of my truck.

Shaw slides in next to me, tucks his hat backward, and then pats his stomach as a growl rips out of it.

"Still up for meeting the guys?" I ask.

"Hell, yeah. Starving." He pats his stomach again. "And I'm really curious what kind of favors I can get out of you this time. I'm thinking . . . something new."

I laugh as I pull out onto Fifth, following behind Vain. "You're always thinking of something new."

"Well, *yeah*. Do you blame me?" He blinks at me. "There's like a whole world of stuff out there we haven't even gotten close to trying. And I wanna do it all, *coaie*." He pauses. "At least twice."

"Works for me." I clear my throat, trying to look calm as I drive toward Mexicali's.

A whole world of stuff. Twice.

How long would that take?

I glance over at Shaw, suddenly hyper-aware of him in my truck. Of how my back is warm against the seat. My hand is on the console, only a few inches from his thigh.

"I fuckin' love that smile," I blurt out. I tear my eyes off him to focus on Vain's dark green SUV with Wolfpack logos on the back window. "And I fuckin' love that hat too."

Shaw clicks his tongue. "That's it? A smile and a hat? Nothing about my sharp wit or impeccable tongue skills?"

"Those things too." I laugh and reach my hand over a few inches to settle it on his thigh. "Honestly, it's everything. I love it all."

Fuck, that was really close to the words lingering right on the tip of my tongue.

I pull into Mexicali's parking lot and take the first spot.

I don't know if I can say it yet.

If it would be too much?

I rub the back of my neck, glancing over at him again.

He's looking across at me, a few strands of hair sticking out from under his hat, head tilted, eyes thoughtful.

Should I say it? My throat thickens just thinking about what I want to tell him.

I lean over the console. "Shaw—"

My phone rings. I groan.

"You gonna get that?" He raises his brows when I don't move to dig it out.

"No." The ringing stops. Then starts again.

His brows rise higher.

"Fuck." I dig my phone out of my pocket.

The area code is from Montreal.

"What's up?" Shaw leans over to see the screen.

"I think it's Debra."

"Holy shit." He leans over the console. "Answer it."

"I, uh." I shake my head. "I feel like we're in the middle of something here."

"Yeah." He points to my phone. "And we can be in the middle of it again after you get off the phone. It's gonna stop ringing."

I take a breath and then answer. "Um, this is Burk."

"Hi, Burk. It's Debra." Shoes click on a hard floor in the background. "Do you have a moment?"

"Yes, ma'am." I put the phone on speaker. "How are you?"

"I'm fine. Thank you for asking. I'm calling about yesterday's game. Did you happen to see it?"

I frown. "No, not yet. I was traveling. I can watch a replay if—"

"No need." The echo of her heels stops. "Unfortunately, Bowman's out for the rest of the season due to an ACL injury. Gonzales is still out on concussion protocol. The hope is he'll return soon, and Windmacher is moving to the first line, but since he's still healing from a broken jaw, the defensive bench is looking very thin."

"That's rough." I frown, not sure why she's calling to tell me this. "I hope recovery is fast for all of them."

"We all do." She pauses. "But it's also progressed the timeline for us when it comes to you."

I swallow. What does any of this have to do with me?

"We've had some good prospects from the minor league teams," Debra continues. "But the defensive coordinators and coaches were extremely impressed with you. Toussaint recommended you strongly." Her voice becomes a touch louder. "Make no mistake about it, Burk, we want you."

Cold rushes over my shoulders.

Shaw punches me on the arm, and I blink over to see him grinning bigger than I've ever seen and looking like he's about to launch over the console at me. I fuckin' love his excitement. I always do.

But right now it seems far away. Like he's in a different truck, listening to a different phone call. I'm not there with him.

"That's great," I manage to say, but it feels like I'm out of my body. Like it's someone else talking. "I'd be over the moon to play with the Canadiens."

Would I?

I'm still staring at the man next to me.

"We're glad to hear that," Debra says, "because with the injuries on our current roster, we'd like to have you now."

"Now?" My throat closes.

What the *fuck*?

"It's exceedingly uncommon to bring someone out of the NCAA mid-season," she continues, "and I had to review the regulations to be sure of the process, but we were already on board for negotiating a contract at the end of your season." Papers rustle in the background. "I realize this might create complications for you, and we'll try to help with whatever we can. That includes making sure you can graduate and providing flight and living arrangements and . . ."

I struggle to comprehend as she lists the details, my heart thumping so loud that it's hard to hear anything else.

Debra is talking about me leaving tonight. I would be dressed for an NHL game before the end of the week.

My entire dream served on a silver platter.

Holy fuckin' shit.

I'd be leaving.

Not in a few months.

Now.

And once I step into an NHL game, there's no coming back to college hockey.

"Go," Shaw whispers. "It's the only choice."

"Are you there?" Debra asks.

"I'm sorry," I say. "I'm here."

"I realize it's probably a lot to think about," she continues. "And I don't normally like putting people on the spot with a decision this large, but we need an answer. I understand this is an unusual situation."

My hands shake. Debra keeps talking, filling me in about how Burton McClaw moved from the University of Minnesota to the Sharks mid-season last year, like she's trying to put me at ease. And I'm trying to listen, but about a thousand thoughts are rolling around in my head.

"Go." Shaw reaches over the console and squeezes my thigh. "You gotta. This might not happen again."

I can't take my eyes off him.

He's right. *This won't happen again.*

"Burk?" Debra asks.

"Yeah, I'm here," I croak out.

A call like this—it's been my dream.

What if you have two dreams?

Debra's heels click again. "I can give you about an hour if—"

"I'll come." My chest hitches as I try to speak. I'm not sure that I'm saying the right thing. I'm saying the thing I should say. But what do I actually want? "I'll be there. I, uh. Thank you. Really, this is . . ."

"I'm glad you're on board," she says. "I understand you'll likely want to go over the contract with an agent or lawyer, so I'll send it over right away."

Agent or lawyer? Well, fuck.

"And I'll work on the travel details," she says. "I'll call you back in about an hour. Will you be available then?"

"Yes, I can do that."

"Good. Talk soon." She clicks off.

I sit there, still holding the phone. Sitting in the same position, staring across at Shaw.

Did that just happen?

I think it must have because he's suddenly moving, somehow fitting himself over the console, his ass hitting the horn as he jumps on me, straddling me awkwardly. He shouts my name, and then he's peppering kisses all over my face, and he's laughing. I'm completely dumbfounded and shocked, but I tip my lips up to his, and he plants his hands on my jaw, kissing me before he leans back.

"You're going." His eyes are lit, bright as I've ever seen them, and then something else washes through them. He presses his lips slightly, but then they're arced in a smile again.

And I don't know how to read him.

But he's right . . .

"I'm going." My voice is rough, and my hands cup his hips.

I'm going.

To the motherfuckin' NHL.

Without Shaw.

CHAPTER THIRTY-THREE

Burk

I scratch at the scruff on my jaw, staring down at the duffle that I *just* unpacked.

Debra set me up on a red-eye flight out of Denver International tonight. That's a minimum two-hour drive to the airport, and I've got to take care of a million things before leaving.

I've only got a few hours left with Shaw.

That's it. I know there will be other times.

There *has* to be, right?

I watch him out of the corner of my eye. He's sorting out laundry on my bed, rolling up my joggers carefully, his hat backward, the tip of his tongue sticking out of the corner of his mouth as he concentrates. He makes a neat pile of my clothes. Because he knows I like it that way.

And, fuck. That hits me right in the gut. A solid punch.

I knew this was coming. I've known since the first time I stepped foot on campus that I'd be leaving the Wolfpack someday. I've thought about it every day since Shaw and I started hooking up.

Before then too. Because it didn't take an ass toy or Shaw's hand on his dick to make me realize what an incredible fuckin' person he is.

I've known it from the first moment I met him. The attraction part took longer, but I sure as fuck didn't need to feel that in order to see what kind of person he is.

"I think that's it," Shaw says as he reaches the bottom of the laundry basket and then dumps his clothes back inside. "Let me throw this in my room, then I'll help with whatever."

"You don't have to. I know you've got stuff to—"

He blinks at me. "I *want* to. I'll be back in a bit. Get those emails sent to your professors."

Oh, fuck. I'd forgotten. I reach for my phone. "On it."

He heads out the door, but instead of sending those emails like I should, I cross to my dresser. I flip open the little black box there and slip out a folded piece of paper. One that Shaw pulled out a couple of weeks ago. He didn't read this one, though. I clutch it in my palm before walking back over to my bed and tucking it in the outside pocket of my duffle.

This feels surreal.

I thought I'd have time to figure things out with him, a few months at least.

And now . . . do I lay it all on him? Everything I'm thinking? Everything I'm hoping for?

My jaw clenches, my duffle shifting on the bed as I sit down next to it.

I scrub my hands over my face. I don't know if it's fair to dump it all on him right before I leave.

But I've got a two-hour car ride to figure out what to say to him.

And then I'll be gone.

———

Two hours goes by in a blink.

We chat about hockey for most of the way, going over the Canadiens' upcoming games and then talking about how to hire an agent, which I need to sort out. Then we talk about when I'll come back to get my truck.

And through it all, I can hardly keep focused on the conversation.

I just keep thinking, thinking, *thinking*.

The week we were apart was hard, and it was only *one* week. What if it's longer?

What if we're in two different countries? Playing for two different franchises? What if all we have is FaceTime and Instagram DMs.

Can we survive that? Would he even want to try?

The questions don't stop.

And then I'm suddenly pulling up to the airport drop-off.

I park and turn off the ignition. The sun set while we were driving, and it's dark now, lights illuminating the drop-off area.

I run my teeth over my bottom lip.

"Are you nervous?" he asks, tilting his head. His legs spread wider, his fingers tapping on his thighs. "You look nervous."

"Yeah," I say. "I'm nervous about everything."

"You'll be great." He gives me a thin smile, one that doesn't feel like *him*. "You always are."

I swallow thickly. "Thank you."

The edge of his lip quirks into something more genuine, but then it suddenly falls, like he's had a thought, and fuck, I don't want to do this.

I do not want to get out of my truck.

Ever.

I want to stay right here. With him. Never more than a handful of inches away.

Could I give it all up for him?

Could I walk away from this? Would I regret it?

Could I take an NHL career and chuck it away without a single look back? Just so that I don't have to leave his side?

I think . . . I could.

I think I'm so fuckin' in love with him that I could.

His eyes shift around my face. "It's not going to be the same."

"No, it won't." My heart is drumming. I need to tell him.

A knock raps on the window.

"Unloading zone," a man calls. "You need to keep moving."

I scowl—my darkest, meanest hockey scowl—and the man jerks back from my truck.

Shaw's brows go up. "Clearly he doesn't know what an ooey-gooey cinnamon roll you are under that glower. But I guess we better get moving."

He pushes out of the truck and then swings open the back door to snag out my duffle.

I scrub a hand over my face and step out too, leaving the keys in the ignition for him. I walk around the truck as he sets my duffle and roller bag on the curb.

I stop by my bags.

"Shaw . . ." *Fuck.* I lick my lips.

He folds his arms across his chest. "Text me when you land."

"Alright."

"We'll still see each other."

"We will."

He smiles thinly again. "It's the NHL. Go get it."

I stiffen. "Alright."

I glance down, and then crouch in front of him to tie his errant shoelace. My fingers shake, the knot coming out unevenly. I can't let this moment go.

When I stand back up, his lips are pressed. His shoulders stiff. He steps closer and brushes a kiss against my cheek. I

343

turn into him, closing my eyes and taking his lips for a last kiss. Soft and aching.

Then another kiss.

And another because I can't fuckin' help myself.

When I finally lean back, I pull in a long breath. What do I say?

"I'll call you," I bumble out.

He swallows—*hard*. Lines dig in around his lips, his hands are gripped on my forearms and he doesn't let go, his eyes a dark green in the halo of the lights. My throat tightens.

I need to lay it out there. To my best fucking friend. To my teammate and roommate. To this man who means so much to me. Beyond what I ever realized one person could mean to another.

Of course I've seen people in love before, but I had no idea how consuming it would feel, how complete.

How intensely he makes my life better.

How desperately I want to make his life better.

How painful it is to think about losing him.

I lean forward to scrape my cheek against his, pulling in the smell of cotton and lemongrass as I linger by his ear.

The truth of what I want to say is like a rock in my chest, but it rises, firm against my Adam's apple, but then soft as it crests my lips.

"I love you." It comes out quietly, tenderly. But strong. Like the truth that it really is. "I want everything with you. A life. A home. Marriage. I'd give up Montreal in a heartbeat for that. I'd give you a home you'd never have to lose."

He stills, hands gripping my biceps tight, his heart pounding. I step back from him. His eyes are wide, taking me in, like he's seeing something he's never seen before. His lips part slowly, but he doesn't talk.

Fuck. Was that too much?

Voices echo around us.

Static comes through on the airport speakers. The man

who knocked on the window earlier steps to the car behind us.

And he still doesn't talk. I shouldn't have even hoped he would want that.

A chilly wind flits through my hair as I take another step back, out of Shaw's grasp.

I never expected him to love me back. I've wanted it. I've hoped for it.

But I've never expected it. I got into this knowing full well who Shaw is. Relishing who he is.

I won't change him. That much will always be true.

"Eden," he breathes out. He shivers when the wind hits him. He's only in a t-shirt and those thin pants with the pink stripe down the sides. The same ones he wore that morning I ran into him outside the kitchen—right after our first jack-off session.

It feels like so long ago.

I need to go. If I can't have a life with him, then I still want *something*. Friendship. Whatever he'll give. I don't want to fuck that up.

I reach into my duffle pocket, pull out the folded piece of paper, then shove it at him.

"Here," I grit out, staring at the paper because I can't stomach whatever expression is in his eyes. I don't know how I'll deal with this hurt. It's too fuckin' big.

"I, uh, need to get going." My voice cracks. "But this is for you. It's a thank you. And I'll never regret anything. No matter what happens."

He takes it, his fingers shaking, and I grab my bags, turn, and walk through the sliding doors.

I don't look back.

It would wreck me.

CHAPTER THIRTY-FOUR

Shaw

My thoughts are a riot.

My skin's hot, a contrast to the freezing wind battering against my back. Burkie's paper is clutched in my hand, the hard edges of the fold pressing into my palm. My throat is too tight to talk.

And now he's walking away from me, through the frosted doors, his wide shoulders weighed down by his duffle, rolling his Rollaboard, his coat hitched under his arm, hair curling over the back of his shirt.

Love. Home.

Marriage.

Holy shit.

It's been just over a month since I walked into his room with that toy. One month where everything has changed so dramatically that I haven't been able to keep up. Where I've tried to sort through so many new things—what it was like to be with him, to kiss, to snuggle, to flirt and DM, to be on the ice together. To fall in love with my best friend.

And now to watch him walk away from me.

It *hurts*.

This searing pain wrecks right down the center of me, tearing through my gut and fisting hard in my stomach.

I don't know that I fully understood how much I've fallen for him until right now. I've had glimpses of it. But I haven't really, *really* known.

He's the person I want to be around more than anyone else.

The person I will always pick first.

The paper trembles in my hand. It's worn, something he's folded and unfolded, again and again. I open it, scanning his neat print.

> *Words that I will forever remember:*
> *1. "I think you should trust yourself, Burkie."*

I hold in a choked sob.

There are nine more things listed underneath.

Things I've said. Things that he must have felt.

Things that mattered to him.

I refold the paper, my fingers trembling so hard that it's difficult. Seeing them all listed out like this, in his handwriting, it settles something in me.

He's not leaving. No matter how far he goes. Part of him is always right here with me, standing on my right. And part of me is always with him.

I'm moving before I realize it. Full speed, hot air blasts my face as I pass through the glass doorway. My shoes squeak on the white tile.

I don't see him. A bubble of sharp panic rises.

What if he's already gone?

But it's only been one minute. Maybe two at the most.

People are everywhere, suitcases and security and noise. The guy from the drop-off lane steps through the door and yells something at me, but I don't care. He can tow the damn truck—I'll figure it out later.

What I need is—

Burkie. He's stepping up to a ticket kiosk, scraping his hair back behind his ears.

I bellow out his name, and his head whips around.

He stops, hand raised by his ear. "Shaw?"

I bolt toward him. All out. White tile underneath us, lights far overhead, like I'm skating to him. Tracking his movements, reading his thoughts, syncing with him in the way that only he and I can.

I crash into him. He shifts his weight to hold me, his hair brushing against my jaw as I bury myself into him, squeezing my eyes shut and holding on. I'm shaking—from cold, from the weight of emotion that's locking my throat. He's saying my name, but I can barely hear it because I'm clinging so tight to him.

"I pick you." I squeeze my eyes tighter, feeling him, the change in his breath, the shift of his stance to balance us, the edge of his list folded in my palm. "I *love* you. So freaking much." My best friend. My whole damn world. Standing right here and hugging me back with all his strength. I sniffle, tears slipping out and rolling down my cheeks. "I don't know why I'm always crying around you. I'm always feeling so *much*. Like it's leaking out all over, and jeez . . ." I hiccup on my words. "I can't hold it in."

"*Don't.* Don't hold it in." His arms lock harder. "I love you back. With everything I have. Like fuckin' everything." He pulls back to look at me, and I pick my head up off his shoulder. His eyes are so serious that I shiver. "I would give up the Habs. Go anywhere you want to go. California, I don't care."

"No." I shake my head, my tears running faster. Because I hate what I'm about to say.

But I have to say it. No matter if it terrifies me. No matter if it'll be one of the hardest things I ever have to do.

His lips press. "Shaw, I—"

"You can't give it up." Heat wells in my chest. It hurts to talk. Hurts to think. "And somewhere deep down, you know that. You know what it felt like on the ice in Montreal. Neither one of us can give up on the NHL. Not yet. Not before we've even gotten there."

Our dreams *matter*.

His and mine.

We'll only get this life once.

"Do you want to give it up?" I ask. "Not what you think you should do. But what *you* want."

He closes his eyes, and when they open again, I'm leveled. They're reddened, so raw, and I can feel the rip that's tearing right through him because I feel it too.

"No," he says. "But I want you more."

I pull in a slow breath, feeling the weight of my shoes against the floor, the shift of him against me. The alignment between us, the rhythm.

The certainty.

We can do anything.

Him and me—when we're in it together, with our game faces on—we can do anything.

"I'll fight to be with you," I say. Resolve plants my heels solidly on the tile. "I'll do whatever it takes to get back on the ice together. Maybe it won't be this season. Or the next. Or the next after that. I don't know when. But we can do this. We can make it happen."

He stares at me with those soft brown eyes. "You would do that?"

"Hell, *yes*, I would." My lips tip into the barest smile. "I'm with you, Eden, all the way. Always have been. Everything's going to be okay."

I *believe* that. Because Burkie's here. Because we're in this together.

So I say it again.

"Everything's going to be okay, Eden."

He shudders out a breath, and for the first time, it's not just me with tears pooling.

We're standing in the middle of all these people, in front of the ticket kiosk, putting it all out there for each other. No holding back.

I take a shaky breath, emotion clobbering me so hard that I have to hold fast onto him to keep standing. "You and me in the NHL together, we'd be unstoppable."

His eyes flick around my face. "We'd have to be willing to go anywhere."

"I'm in." No question. No hesitation. "I pick you. I love you." My words come out in a rush, and then I smile. Because there's no way I can say that and not smile. "I'm sorry it took me three minutes to say it back. You surprised me with the marriage thing."

"Fuck, Shaw." His voice catches. "I would have waited longer." He presses his forehead against mine, closing his eyes and swallowing thickly. "And I'll keep waiting. When or if. Doesn't matter, I'll be here."

"I know," I whisper. Shit, I *know*. He'll be right here. Even when we're apart. He's not going to disappear. I grip onto him, feeling his breath warm my cold nose. "I like your list."

"It's not done yet."

"Hell, no, it's not." I smile. "We're gonna need a second sheet of paper. Maybe a whole freaking notepad."

He laughs, tipping his head back to look at me. "I'll buy two."

He just looks so *happy*.

Eden is happy.

And I can't express what that does to me. How light it makes me feel.

"I like seeing you happy," I say.

He smiles, but then it fades. "I fuckin' love you."

He says it the way he did before, soft and cut with so

much feeling, and I think he'll say it that way every single time. Like it will never be an offhand thought. It will never just be a habit or carelessly said. Like he'll always mean it.

"I love you too."

"We're going to do this?" he whispers. "You and me?"

I'm grinning so big it stretches my cheeks. Grinning and crying and holding onto him. "Yeah, we are."

He nods, that deep emotion in his eyes telling me that he's right there with me. Next to me. Ready to dig in and fight. "Let's do this."

CHAPTER THIRTY-FIVE

Six months later . . .

Eden: Defenseman for Montreal Canadiens
Shaw: Goaltender for Coachella Valley Firebirds

Burk

I'm here.

Shaw's message is tagged under a picture of him in the stands, his phone held up so I can see the ice spread out behind him, and a rush of excitement pushes through me so strongly that I can barely still my fingers enough to text back an *I love you.*

I'm due to be announced on the ice in ten minutes, but I've been worried as fuck because his flight was delayed.

He didn't know if he was going to make it in time.

It's a struggle trying to fit our schedules together between practices and away games and all the commitments that come with our jobs. We DM every day. We FaceTime whenever we can.

It's challenging to be apart.

But we make it work.

There's no other fuckin' option.

The team manager hollers for us to get a move on, so I tuck my phone into my locker and wait, stretching my calves and dragging in a breath that fills every corner of my lungs. A familiar anticipation rolls through me as the guys move around me. Everyone goes through their last-minute game rituals.

Mine is telling Shaw that I love him.

Every game.

Every *day*.

Someday, I'll get to look across at him, with his goalie mask propped up on his head as he double checks his pads, and tell him in person.

It'll happen.

"You ready?" Toussaint slaps me on the back. "We'll kick these fuckers around a bit."

I nod strongly. "We will."

First game of the Stanley Cup finals. I can't fuckin' believe it.

Toussaint steps aside, and I move one step closer to the man whose locker bay is next door.

Vain palms me heavily on the shoulder. "Shaw here?"

"Yep." I'm smiling as we step out of the dressing rooms. And when the first players are introduced, the raucousness of the crowd grows so loud that we can't hear each other.

The rumble of the stadium amplifies with each step, until it vibrates, until it's all we can hear. And fuck . . .

We're *here*.

The only thing that would make it better is if Shaw was lined up with us.

But today, I'm fighting my heart out for the Canadiens. As soon as I step onto the ice, my name booming across the stadium, I search the family section, squinting into the lights.

I raise a hand and skate to my place in line, but I'm still looking.

I can't see him with the spotlight glaring down at me, but I know he sees me. I know he's there, probably yelling at the top of his lungs, sitting with my mom and Lacey, wearing my jersey—with my name across his back. That thought makes my smile grow bigger as I stand there, my mind churning during *O Canada*.

And then it's game fuckin' on.

It's a fast-moving first period. Which is to be expected for the first game out in the finals, both teams hopped up and skating quick. I take and give a couple of hard slams into the boards, one of which knocks my helmet clear off, but I'm up and moving afterward without a thought, tearing in front of that puck to block a slap shot at goal.

I stop that one, but they snag a powerplay goal halfway through the first period, the fuckers celebrating while I glower through my face shield.

And it keeps going that way. The hits get harder, the skating gets faster. Toussaint has me get rough with an opposing D-man midway through the second, earning me a spot in the penalty box. After that, we get a bit of a burst and lots of shots on goal, but their goalie stops every single one.

We're not playing together. Shit's off and it's not a pretty sight.

Coach Hart's words to us before the third period aren't pretty either. The offense works on keeping their goalie moving for rebounds, and we work on cutting off the line their forward keeps carving in, but it's not enough.

When they go into their fuckin' dogpile to celebrate after taking the first game, I rip off my helmet, frustration burning through me.

I'm beat to shit and exhausted and fuckin' pissed off about how I played as we head toward the locker room. We toss our gloves in the bin on the way, all of us silent down the hallway that's lined on both sides by assistants and coaches and stadium personnel who are also deathly quiet as we leave behind the echoing sounds of the celebrating crowd.

"*Eden.*"

Shaw comes from out of nowhere. I don't know how he got in here—I'm pretty sure he's not supposed to be—but I step right into him, hugging him hard, my chest pads firm against him, my jersey sticking to my forearms. I know I smell like blood and frustration and hockey, but I don't fuckin' care. I grip on to him, my legs shaking from exhaustion, my world swimming as I hold on so tight that I'm probably crushing him.

He doesn't say anything. He doesn't have to. He *knows* what this feels like. And he's not about to fill me up with false hope and promises that are all bullshit. He's also not about to tell me what I could have done better because he knows that's not what I need right now.

These are the moments where I thank my fuckin' life that I have him.

The happy ones too. But these moments, when it feels like I'm slipping down that mountain of gravel, questioning myself, calling myself names, he's fuckin' *there*. Giving me a rock to stand on. Pulling me over and giving me a way out of that spiral.

He means so *much* to me.

"I love you," I whisper. "They were all over us in the third. Like a fuckin' swarm. We couldn't hold them back."

His lips brush my ear. "You held it together as best as you could. We'll watch the tapes, and we'll review what the coaches and coordinators say. We'll go over it all and get you some ice for your back too. That hit you took in the first power play has to be hurting like a bitch."

"Can't feel it." I kiss his jaw, then his lips. My hands smooth down the muscular lines of his waist to grip his ass and hitch him up around my hips. My pads are thick between us as my tongue moves against his. His back hits the wall, and I know there's a million fuckin' people in this hallway, but I don't give one single shit—I need Shaw. I don't stop kissing him until Toussaint taps my shoulder.

"Time for the wrap-up," he says in my ear.

"Fuck," I grumble, tearing myself away with a backward step. "You'll be here?" I ask Shaw.

"Right here." Shaw slaps my ass as I turn, and I smile a little, despite everything else.

Toussaint leans close on the way into the dressing room. "Don't tell my wife this, but I'm jealous. He must understand what it's like after games like this, no?"

I clear my throat, wiping under my eyes. "There's nothing like it."

We step into the tense dressing room. Most of the guys stew silently while they wait for the coaches to talk to us.

Someday it'll be Shaw walking next to me. On both the good days and the days like this.

Someday.

Someday.

It'll fuckin' happen.

CHAPTER THIRTY-SIX

Seven months later . . .

Burk: Defenseman for Montreal Canadiens
Shaw: Goaltender for Columbus Blue Jackets

Shaw

I rest my forearms on the railing, taking in the caramel sand, the setting sun, and the rolling blue waves beyond. A warm breeze raises goosebumps on my skin, so I snag off my hat and yank my t-shirt over my head and then toss them on the ledge.

This place is spectacular. And feels like a million miles away from ice-covered Ohio in January.

When Eden first DMed me the link to this beach bungalow, I didn't really look at it. I was so hyped that our bye weeks lined up this year that I didn't give a shit where we went. Could have been the Arctic Circle for all I cared, as long as we were there together.

But this? Picture perfect. A tiny island named Clua, off the coast of Mexico, with its white terracotta buildings, bustling local fruit market, and hidden beach bungalows, all ringed in by towering palms and big leaf magnolias.

I've never seen anything like it. Never been somewhere tropical.

And we'll be here for a solid week.

A *week* with him. I'm so giddy that I can hardly contain myself.

I dig out my phone and snap a photo of myself, smiling like a buffoon, on the railing with the beach beyond. I post it on Insta. No filters needed for a place this spectacular. #BurkandShaw, which usually gets a hefty response.

"Can you believe this place?" Eden's low voice rumbles from inside, and all my nerve endings jump awake.

He drops his duffle inside the front door, hitching up the sleeves of his sweater, still dressed from his flight in from Canada, and I don't even fully let him put his shit down.

I launch myself at him, and he catches me, an exhale washing through us both. We hold on.

Not letting go.

For as long as we can.

Well, until we're pulling off clothes, skin against skin, fingers digging into flesh.

We don't make it to the bed. Just right there on the floor, until we're sweat-soaked and spent. All that time apart creating this vortex that we don't try to crawl out of.

Just *him*. All around me. I need this. Touch, taste, tease. I've always needed to be physically close to him. Way back when I'd lay my head on his shoulder, listening to his breath in the solace of his room at hockey house.

Afterward, we snuggle on a lounge chair on the beach, my back to his chest, his arms tucked around me. I'm not sure how we both fit, but we're crammed together, his lips skimming against the top of my shoulder, alone on our stretch of sand—just ocean and moonlight and us.

"I think I'm going home," I say, my fingers skimming over

the hair on his forearm. "I wanted to tell you in person. My agent's been in talks with Chicago. They're looking to fill a goalie spot next season."

He sits partway up, the cushion shifting. "For real?"

"Yep." I thread my fingers through his, twisting to see his face. "But it's not the Canadiens."

"It's still fuckin' magic." He smiles. "You've wanted this."

"Wanna be with you."

His eyes soften. "The Habs are talking about trades. They're looking at maybe two offensive trades."

"For you?"

"Yeah."

I frown. "What are you thinking?"

"Obviously I'm telling my agent we'll take any offer from the Blackhawks." He pauses. "But they're rebuilding the forward line, right?"

I nod, swallowing hard. "Yeah, I doubt they'd want to trade out two offensive linemen."

"But maybe we could get closer. Redwings or hell, I can get a spot on the Hawks' farm team. Bide my time."

I raise a brow. "Redwings?"

He laughs. "Said I'd do anything."

Far-off waves beat steadily, the nighttime breeze cooling our skin. Getting back on the ice with him feels so elusive sometimes. I wish I knew when it would happen. How long we'll have to wait.

It's hard to constantly be away from him. To not have these moments.

"Hey, babe." He feathers a kiss on the shell of my ear. "We could be getting closer."

"Closer," I repeat, my words thickening. "Time is adding up."

He pulls back. "If you don't want to—"

"*I'm in*. That's not even a question." I force my shoulders to relax. "It's stressing me out to talk about it right now. I mean, have you noticed the view yet?"

He nuzzles his nose under my ear. "Barely."

That makes my smile expand. "I want this week with you. No worrying about what comes next. Maybe we can rent one of those paddleboard things? I wanna try that. Snorkeling too. There's a bar here too. The Beach Hut, I think. We could go out."

"I'm up for anything."

"Are you?" I twist to waggle my brows at him. "Because I've got a proposition."

He laughs. "I can't wait. What's it this time? Nipple clamps? Spanking paddle?"

"Neither of those things, but now I'm seriously intrigued. I'm gonna pull up some websites tonight, *coaie*. I can't even imagine how sexy your spanked red ass will be. Or mine? Hell, both. But, no, that's not exactly what I was thinking."

His eyes are bright with laughter, his smile expanding. "Then what?"

"Well, I'll tell you." I squeeze his fingers in mine, loving the way he's looking at me. This man who is everything to me. Who knows me—inside and out. Who's still my best friend. My boyfriend. My teammate, even if we're not on the ice together yet. But I want him to be one more thing.

I wasn't ready before.

I am now.

"I thought you might marry me," I say.

He flinches, his smile fading. "What?"

Shit. Did I mess up?

"Marry me?" I repeat, my nerves kicking hard. "Here. Now."

"Now?" he chokes out. His heart thrashes so hard I can feel it between my shoulder blades.

"Well, maybe tomorrow? Just you and me. In board shorts under the sun. Our toes curled in the sand. We could have a huge party back in the States later. Invite everyone and cele-brate our asses off. But just us here, now." I pause, trying to read his face. Does he not want to? "What do you think? I mean, if you need some time to think about it, then—"

"Shaw." His eyes brim with so many emotions that I can't parse them out. "I don't need time to think. I'm in."

CHAPTER THIRTY-SEVEN

One year later . . .

Burk: Defenseman for Philadelphia Flyers
Shaw: Goaltender for Chicago Blackhawks

Burk

"How do you feel about being the first married couple both playing in the NHL?" The reporter blinks at me, looking somewhat proud of herself for asking the question.

It's not the first time I've been asked.

Actually, I'm asked every single time. I don't mind. There's nothing I like talking about as much as Shaw. And besides that, I need to be vocally out. Not just for myself, but for every one of those new players coming up. To see a guy who's fully out and still making it in the NHL.

I won't lie and say it's always easy. But I think—I really fuckin' hope—that it makes a difference.

"Greatest feeling in the world," I tell her truthfully. "I couldn't be prouder of Shaw and of what he's accomplished this last year for Chicago. *Seventeen* shutouts, the highest number of shutouts by a goalie in a single season *ever*. I can't wait to see what he'll do next year."

"He's had quite a season." She tilts her head. "And your plans for next year?"

I lean back in my chair, itching at my scruff. "There's no final decision on that yet."

"But . . ." Her brows rise. "I assume you're looking for a team closer to Chicago?"

"That's a safe assumption." I glance over to see my agent, Donnelly, dressed in the full suit he always wears, frown and shake his head sharply, and I shift the conversation toward the current season. He arrived halfway through the interview, and I haven't had a chance to talk with him yet. There's one burning question I need him to answer:

Has he heard from Chicago?

I told him I'll take any deal they put on the table. I don't care if they undercut my salary by half.

I don't need money. I need Shaw. And I know that Chicago's working under a pretty severe salary cap this year. I'm terrified that will hold up a deal.

I turn back to the reporter, trying to look relaxed. Interviews are my least favorite part of this job, but the requests have been more frequent since Shaw and I posted the video of our wedding on his Instagram last year.

We drew attention. And fans.

There's a lot of support for the two of us to play together. That's why I do these interviews. With every single one, there's an opportunity to catch the right person's attention.

I'll do a million of these fuckin' interviews if it gives us an echo of a chance to get on the ice together.

After another ten minutes of questions, the reporter smiles and scans her iPad. "That's all I have for today."

I stand and shake her hand. "Thanks for having me."

There are a few more pleasantries before I head out with

Donnelly. I'm relieved when we finally step out onto the street.

"Want to grab a bite?" he asks.

"I want to hear about Chicago." The Philly evening is chilly, and I shove my hands in my pockets, rolling up my shoulders against the cold.

"We'll talk," he says. "Let's hit up the food truck that's usually over by Pattison."

I breathe out a billow of white. "You got to be fuckin' kidding me. It's freezing out here."

He nudges me with his elbow. "They've got heat lamps. Come on. Trust me."

"Fine," I grumble. Trusting him is exactly what I do. And he's been worthy of it. Staunchly there for me ever since I ran into him at a Habs fundraiser. Besides, I'll eat at the fuckin' North Pole if he tells me what's up with Chicago.

But he doesn't.

We walk a few blocks over to Pattison, talking about his kids and stopping to put in our orders before grabbing a seat at the picnic table closest to the heat lamps. It's not actually too cold, and I sit across from him as he devours a sandwich. I munch on a fruit cup, my stomach too anxious to eat much more.

"You have to fuckin' tell me, man," I finally say. "Your silence is hinting it's bad news, and I need to know. Is there *any* chance of Chicago? Any chance at all?"

He wipes his mouth and then tucks his napkin under his food basket. "I lied to you."

"What?" I was not expecting that. "What are you talking about? Thought I was supposed to trust you."

"You are. I think you'll forgive me."

I set my fruit cup down with a smack. "Donnelly? What the fuck is going on?"

He tips his chin past my shoulder, a smile growing on his face.

364

I'm tackled from behind. I let out a hard grunt as arms wrap around me, a hat tumbling off as lips smack my cheek. Fuck, his *smell*. Lemongrass and cotton and *Shaw*.

I can't fuckin' believe it, not even as he peppers my cheek with wet kisses, his flirty smile so close as I twist into him. I stumble up, grabbing for him, my heart hammering so hard it feels like it's trying to get to him. His lips are on mine, smiling as he kisses me. His hands sink into my hair.

I pull back. "*Shaw*?" Fuck, my whole world centers on the man standing in front of me. But I haven't seen him in over a month. "You're here?"

He laughs. "I'm here."

I bury my face in his shoulder, hugging him with all my strength, feeling his breath, his laugh, just . . . *him*.

It takes a few long minutes before I can think. I just hug the fuck out of my husband.

We finally sit down, and I can't stop staring at him. Just like all those years ago in my truck, I can't stop looking at this man. Can't stop smiling.

"Why are you here?" I ask him. "Is this"—I glance over at Donnelly, confused—"what you lied about?"

"It is." Donnelly digs into his jacket pocket and pulls out some folded papers. He sets them in front of me. "And I went behind your back. But I think you'll forgive me."

I blink down at the papers, and now my heart really is going to hammer its way out of my chest. It's his write-up of a contract offer. The one he gives me when we go over all the details and make our decisions. *Chicago Blackhawks* is typed across the top.

I blink at Donnelly. "This is *real*? Is this really fuckin' real?"

He nods. "I thought you might want Shaw here when you found out."

I'm shaking. I don't care what the numbers say. I don't care about anything else in this entire fuckin' world.

Shaw's eyes redden. "We did it." He swallows thickly. He reaches up and runs his thumb along my cheek. I blink and realize that he's wiping away my tears. There are so many damn emotions. So much fight to get back to where we've always belonged.

On the ice.

Him and me.

Together.

EPILOGUE

Four years later . . .

Burk: Defenseman for Chicago Blackhawks
Shaw: Goaltender for Chicago Blackhawks

Burk

The stadium thunders so loud I can hardly think.

But when I center back on that puck, held by the ref for the drop, everything quiets. I clutch the handle of my stick, my skates poised, ready for the slap in my direction.

Two minutes to go.

Game six of the Cup, and we can take it all right now. We just need this win.

We're up by one, but they're fighting back hard.

Shaw's behind me. I can feel him bolstering me, tempering my adrenaline, steadying my hand, strengthening my resolve.

Two minutes.

Two fuckin' minutes and our world might change.

For some, it might just be a trophy, but in the world of hockey, you breathe, eat, and sleep for this. Every practice, every workout, everything you've missed in order to put all your focus into this one goal.

Some guys play their entire lives and never get this chance.

I have it with my husband backing me up on the ice.

In a slow-motion second, the ref drops the puck. It's snagged by their forward, kicked back to opposing defense, and then brought around. The approach toward our net is fierce, and in a split second, their goalie is skating off the ice, leaving them with an open net and us with four fuckin' forwards to contend with.

For them, it's now or never.

They come full force, squaring us in. They pass to center, and I'm able to get an edge of the puck, shoving it back far enough that it shoots across the blue line, buying us a few seconds.

I don't know how long we have. It always feels timeless out here.

They attack with another setup, three quick passes and then a shot on goal. Shaw grabs for the puck, but it rebounds and is kicked away by our right D-man.

They re-center the puck, setting up for another attack. I shift with the passes, always conscious of where Shaw is behind me. My movements are steady, my skates sure.

Another pass to the far side of the net, and out of the corner of my eye, Shaw's body turns with it. He pivots as the puck moves to center ice.

It's going to come this way.

Three passes.

That's their setup.

Fast passes, but if I move, I can maybe snag the puck.

If I miss it, there will be nothing between the far left forward and Shaw.

I glance back. It's a split-second glance, and Shaw's eyes do nothing more than a tiny flick to mine, but I read him so clearly—as if he's talking in my head—so attuned to each other that it really is magic.

Go, Eden.

I go. Breaking position, I get a jump on the forward and clip the puck away from him to the outside. I snag it as he shoves me hard into the boards.

We scramble. Sticks digging, elbows shoving. Every second counts. Every puck touch could be the difference. It *all* matters.

I feel the weight of the puck against my blade. I push out of the tangle and fly over the blue line—sailing toward the far net.

I don't have to make it. We're up by one. I need that horn to sound.

They tear off after me, but I'm locked in—hammer down. I slap the puck toward their empty net.

It doesn't make it. *Doesn't need to.* The horn sounds, rocking through the stadium, almost drowned out by the screams. There's a crush of bodies. An instant dogpile. Helmets and sticks flying, the whole fuckin' world collides.

And *Shaw.*

He crashes into me, and I tumble down on the ice.

We won.

Holymotherfuck, *we won.*

Shaw laughs as my helmet falls back, then he kisses me, splayed out on top of me on the ice, somewhere by the blue line, the screams roaring so loud it blots out every other sound. *He's kissing me.* Heavy in with all his pads. His name is on my lips, and I've only got two thoughts in my head.

One is Shaw, of course.

And the other is this: Sometimes, you just have to dream really fuckin' big. And then hold on for the ride.

BONUS EPILOGUE

Eight years later . . .

Shaw

Eden leans in close to my ear. A few cheers from the seats behind us make it hard to hear his low voice in the arena. Luckily, it's not as big as the United Center, but the sound still echoes off the walls.

"Did you hear that the coach isn't coming back next year?" he asks, not taking his eyes off the game.

I smile. On the ice below, the puck changes hands. The leftwing misses a pass, and then everyone jumbles after it. The first D-man slips down onto his butt, his lip pushing out like he might cry. But he decides to scramble up instead. Although he forgets his stick and has to go back for it, which makes sense because he's five years old.

Eden cups his hands around his mouth. "Good job, Parker. Get it! That's it! You're doing so good, buddy!"

Parker grins up at us and waves, his glove huge on his hand.

The opposing team snags the puck, and Eden leans back

in his seat. A thick scruff covers his jaw—almost a beard—and he's wearing an old IFU tee today, tight across his pecs and biceps, loose around his waist. It brings me back.

"So that means Parker's team will need a new coach next year," he says, tracking the play. "I was thinking that maybe . . ." He drags his teeth over his bottom lip, twisting toward me. His eyes flash around my face the way they do when he's not sure what I'll say.

I already know what I'll say. I've halfway expected this ever since I heard about the opening.

"Maybe I'd take the job," he finishes. A dart of worry tightens his jaw.

My smile widens. "Hell, yeah. You'd be perfect."

His brows go up. "You sure? I mean, that's a pretty big change for us."

I turn back to the game, looking across at one particular player. Who is currently in left D and staring off into space like he's not even aware there's a game going on. I nudge Eden. "Look at him."

His laugh is warm. "He's so unlike us."

"I know, right?"

Parker looks up at the lights, seemingly oblivious, but I know a lot is going on in his head. That's how he is. I wonder what he sees up there—probably electric light fairies or unicorns racing across the rafters. He's so damn creative, full of so many stories. Things that come from nowhere.

Parker came out of nowhere too. At least, we didn't expect him. But when Eden's youngest cousin was looking to put an unexpected pregnancy up for adoption, it felt like something clicked. It's hard though, with our schedules. My brother lives a few blocks away and helps during away games, but with an eighty-two game season—

"We're gone so often," Eden says, picking right up on my thoughts. "Do you think he misses us?"

"I'm sure he does."

He nods, lips pressing. "Donnelly came to me about a new contract, but it would only be two years, considering my age."

I laugh. "Yeah, thirty-three is pretty old," I tease him. "Retirement home next week, *coaie*."

"You're only a year away." He reaches for my hand. His knuckles brush over mine as he threads our fingers together, our rings clicking. "I could play those two years, easily, but then Parker will be seven already."

I smile. "I know."

He gives me a determined look. "And we'll be there, at every game. In the stands for you."

"I know that too." I've got two more years in my contract. I want to play them. We've got a good chance at the playoffs next season—young players who are coming on strong—and every year I'm in the crease, I feel faster, more experienced. More settled.

It's weird to think of myself as settled, but I am. For years now.

He rolls his thumb over the top of mine. "We worked so hard to get on the same fuckin' team, and I—"

"Eden." I tip closer to him. "We're always on the same team."

We've played together for twelve years. Nine-hundred and eighty-four games, with only a few where one of us was out from injuries. Two Stanley Cups. So many practices, nights on the road, moments that we've had. We did everything that we set out to do.

And now life is transitioning to something else. Being dads. Maybe putting in that deck we've been talking about. Maybe a dog. A big, happy black lab or a lazy mastiff. Sunday mornings sleeping in, luggage that only gets packed for vacations and weekend hockey games, where the left D-man stares up at the lights and picks a wedgie out of his bum.

I could get into that. A home that's always there. That never disappears.

I clear my throat. "I'd like to formally put in my application."

His brows go up.

"You'll need an assistant coach," I explain. "Maybe someone with goalkeeper knowledge. I'm not available full-time yet, but I will be in about two years."

He blinks. "Shaw—"

"I don't want to miss it either." I glance down at Parker. "Not a single thing."

He leans across the armrest, his lips brushing mine. He slips his tongue softly across my bottom lip and then smiles as he leans back. "I love you."

Fuck, the way he says that. *Every* time.

I squeeze his fingers. "Still picking you."

Below us, the play continues on the far side. The clock is counting down. The other team is up by two, but no one keeps score. It's nice. I've kept score most of my life.

Maybe it's time to do something else.

"Should I tell him to pay attention?" Eden's focused on Parker, and I hear the hesitation in his voice. I know where it comes from—worry that he'll be like his father, brutal and hard, but there's not a chance on this earth that he will ever be like that. He's not that man. Not even close.

It's obvious as I watch him look across at our son, love so brightly clear in his eyes.

"Nah. There's less than a minute left on the clock." I smile at him, feeling the warmth he gives me all the way down to my toes. "Let him dream."

THE END

THANK YOU!

Thank you so much for taking this journey with Shaw and Burk. I can't express how much I appreciate you reading.

For updates on future books:

Facebook Readers Group: Loren's Starlights
www.facebook.com/groups/lorenstarlights

Newsletter
www.lorenleighbooks.com/lorens-vips

ABOUT LET'S DO THIS

It started as a novella. A quick little breath of fresh air based on a meme that I saw in a Facebook group. I only planned to write Shaw's POV, but then he was standing in the hallway, his hand poised over Burk's door handle, his part felt like a fraction of the story.

In the long run, this book feels so much like Burk's story to me, and so his voice had to be in it.

I loved working on it. Every minute. These two made me so happy, and I hope they made you happy too.

ABOUT LOREN

Loren Leigh writes contemporary m/m romance, spanning from college romance to romantic suspense, with characters who jump off the page and chemistry that's burning hot.

Her characters want nothing more than to fall in love —*wholeheartedly, deeply and wildly*—and they're ready to take you on the journey with them.

For updates, sneak peeks and freebies, sign up for her newsletter here:

www.lorenleighbooks.com/lorens-vips

Printed in Great Britain
by Amazon

46773920R00220